Killing Cousins:

"Thoroughly entertaining, especially in its depiction of a closed New England society…A smoothly told tale"

—Doug Greene, *Virginia-Pilot*

"Charming venue…A prime example of the bygone, ever-so-civilized mystery."

—*Kirkus Reviews*

"For devout mystery fans the unusual detective will be appealingly different."

—*Santa Cruz Sentinel*

"A murder mystery for classical mystery lovers whose investigative intuitions demand a challenge. Well written, with clues falling just often enough…This is no run-of-the-mill whodunit."

—*South Band Tribune*

"A plot that takes the reader on a fast chase…Readers who like…mysteries with several murders, a well-hidden killer and detectives who use brains…will love this one."

—*Abilene Reporter-News*

"Stratton's first Mort Sinclair novel is impressive and very satisfying."

—*Smyth County News*

"Will hold the reader's attention long past bedtime…More than mere reading pleasure."

—*Angleton Times*

"Loaded with characters, but the book is not hard to follow…since all the clues are provided you may be able to solve this superbly written mystery."

—*Washington Record-Herald*

Plymouth Colony: Its History & People 1620–1691

"A surprising overview, political, sexual and social, documented by primary sources."

—*Boston Globe*

"Lets us see [the people] as human beings...Invaluable...Fascinating reading."

—*Los Angeles Times*

"An absorbing and vivid account of period and people...a remarkable story."

—Barbara Tuchman, best-selling historian/writer

"Full of interesting information and also very readable—an uncommon combination."

—Dr. Richard Ehrlich, Plimoth Plantation

"Deserves the widest possible distribution...many of the sketches are better than anything else in print...[The] essays are especially useful...for their comments on legality and on sex and morality (on the latter Mr. Stratton pulls no punches)."

—*The American Genealogist*

"The work is one of great scholarship, and genealogists and professional historians with an interest in the period will find it of immense value."

—*Genealogist's Magazine* (London)

Applied Genealogy

"Have you ever wanted to curl up before a roaring fire with a genealogy book. THIS is such a book. Eminently readable with a chatty, almost gossipy style."

—*Root Cellar*, Sacramento Genealogical Society

FIT FOR FATE

FIT FOR FATE

A TALE OF BYZANTINE INTRIGUE
IN MODERN ATHENS

Eugene Aubrey Stratton

iUniverse, Inc.
New York Lincoln Shanghai

FIT FOR FATE
A TALE OF BYZANTINE INTRIGUE IN MODERN ATHENS

iUniverse, Inc.

For information address:
iUniverse, Inc.
2021 Pine Lake Road, Suite 100
Lincoln, NE 68512
www.iuniverse.com

ISBN: 0-595-28754-9 (pbk)
ISBN: 0-595-65850-4 (cloth)

Printed in the United States of America

For Peter and Jax Lovesey

Wonderful writers and friends indeed

and for

Lieutenant General George and Julia Vagenas

Who so enriched my Athenian years

For those whom God to ruin has design'd,

He fits for fate and first destroys the mind.

John Dryden

Einai i moira tous.

(It is their fate.)

Said by a Greek official to the author

Fate is always happening.

Anita Loos

Cast Of Characters

ANTONIDIS, Antoni: fifty-seven years old; former Minister of Public Security & present Minister of Scientific Development; brother-in-law of the Greek Prime Minister; friend of Spyro Roussos.

ATHERTON, Edward (Ned): fifty-five years old; Marilyn Pickering's uncle; American Ambassador to Greece. Louise ATHERTON, fifty-four years old, his wife.

JENSEN, Robert (Bob): thirty-six years old; security officer at the American Embassy in Athens.

KAROLOU, Eleni: thirty-seven years old; superintendent in the Greek Police Department of Special Investigations (DSI); member of Spyro Roussos's Special Team.

MANIATIS, Panagiotis (Pano): fifty-one years old; chief superintendent in DSI; member of Spyro Roussos's Special Team.

PAPAMAVROGIANNOPOULOS, Georgio (Yorgo): thirty years old; former army officer now an executive of a Greek insurance company.

PAPAZOGLOU, Nina: thirty-two years old; daughter of Antoni Antonidis; owns a Greek import-export company; has a husband and a business manager.

PETROPOULOS, Achilles: fifty-six years old; new Minister of Public Security over all Greek police and security agencies; antagonistic toward Spyro Roussos.

PICKERING, Marilyn: twenty-three years old; niece of the American Ambassador to Greece, who invites her to take a vacation there. At home lives with parents.

RENFREW, Victoria: thirty-five years old; American prima donna with the Athens Opera; in love and living with Spyro Roussos; divorced from wife-beating husband.

ROUSSOS, Dimitrio (Dimitri): thirty years old; superintendent in DSI; son of Spyro Roussos and a member of his Special Team.

ROUSSOS, Spyridon (Spyro): age fifty-two years old; police director; head of DSI; lives with Victoria Renfrew; separated from unfaithful psychotic wife.

SAVVAS, Nikolaos (Nick): thirty-three years old; confidence man preying on international companies in Athens.

SOMMERS, Jake: twenty-eight years old; partner in Washington, DC law firm; in love with Marilyn Pickering.

THANOS, Jason: forty-one years old; police underdirector and new deputy to Spyro Roussos in DSI; protégé of Achilles Petropoulos.

VLAHOS, Ioanni: fifty-four years old; superintendent in DSI; looking forward to retirement.

XYNOS, Pavlo: twenty-nine years old; former university student who stalks Victoria Renfrew; murdered a professor and became a trained terrorist and assassin.

ZAVALAS, Omiros: seventy-three years old; retired Greek general; back in Athens from self exile in Paris; formerly active in anti-government conspiracies.

Note

The characters and the plot of this book are fictitious. The setting is real, except that a few places intimately connected to the plot are also fictitious; for example, the peninsula of Kavouri is real, but the summer house on it of Police Director Roussos is as imaginary as he himself is.

I have used some Greek language in the story, but almost always immediately followed by the English translation the first time used. The transliteration is usually modern Greek. A few names and other words from classical Greece were left the way they are ordinarily known; for example, readers will recognize Piraeus, but they might not recognize its modern transliteration as Pireefs.

I lived in Greece seven years, studied the language before going there, worked in downtown Athens, and lived in the close-in suburb of Psychiko. I love Greece and the Greeks.

Zito Ellas! Long live Greece!

CHAPTER 1

▼

On a late June Monday morning in Athens under a bright sapphirine sky, a man in a smartly pressed police officer's dark gray uniform turned from Kanari Street into Merlin Street and made his way toward an ornate patinaed marble-clad building that was obviously a survivor from some other era. On each shoulder strap he wore a wreath and three pips denoting his rank of police director. A street vendor carrying a huge wooden tray of sesame-seed-covered thin bread-stuffs, and advertising his product in a loud singsong voice yelling "Koulouria, hot, delicious kou-LOU-ri-a," reminded the police director that he was hungry. He had shortchanged himself at breakfast that morning, as he almost always did when Victoria was on tour, and now the compelling smell of these tasty stretched-out donuts captivated his nostrils and tugged at his stomach.

But no, the minister's secretary had said, "Immediately," and the police director did not want his first private meeting with the new minister to turn into sour wine. He quickly walked past the koulouria peddler and climbed the imposing marble steps of the Ministry of Public Security building. The steps led to large open brass double doors flanked by acanthus-leaf-topped Corinthian columns. He glanced at his shoes and, finding them still shiny, he briskly strode inside, where a uniformed guard saluted him. Returning the salute, the police officer continued his way toward a black-specked, gold-filigreed pair of birdcage-like elevators, also survivors of times past. He entered and closed the doors of one of the wire-walled cages, pushed the button, and started the slow ascent to the top floor.

Police Director Spyro Roussos was a man of stature. Had someone asked the guard for his height, the reply would probably have overestimated his 178 centimeters, or five feet ten inches, by a significant measure. He had a ramrod straight back, an aquiline nose, deep penetrating brown eyes, and a dark brown moustache neatly clipped in brush-like military style. He appeared to be somewhere in his mid-forties, but again the truth surpassed the figure by a fair number of years. Perhaps a little too severe looking to be considered handsome, he seemed above all to be formidable, the kind of man that no one would cross lightly.

Roussos had never enjoyed his occasional visits to the vast chamber that was the office of the Minister of Public Security, not even that time several years ago when he had been awarded the medal of the Order of Saint George, First Class. The office with its gigantic dimensions, huge Ionic columns reaching to a five-meter-high ceiling, and highly polished white Pentelic marble floor, was clearly designed to impress. And impress it did, although to Roussos the impression was one of pretence and arrogance.

Still, he had never thought of his visits in the past as onerous. Today threatened to be different. There was something distasteful about this new Christian Socialist minister.

After three years out of power, the Christian Socialists had won the recent election and formed a new government. During those three years, Roussos had had no strong complaint against the then incumbent Radical Republican Party and the RRP Minister of Public Security. However, in his heart Roussos felt that the now victorious CSP was more understanding toward his office, and he was silently glad for their return to power. He had always worked well with the former CSP Minister of Public Security, Antoni Antonidis. It was therefore a shock to him when Antonidis was given the Ministry of Scientific Development. The new Minister of Public Security was Achilles Petropoulos, a man who could not—Roussos tried to convince himself—be as bad as his reputation.

Roussos wondered if this would be a get-acquainted meeting with the new minister, who was his superior's superior's superior, or if there was more serious business to be discussed. Ordinarily the minister would not be giving a private interview to one of his rank, but Roussos was not just another police director. The implicit power of the Department of Sensitive Investigations was out of proportion to Roussos's rank, so much so that even his superiors might fear him. Government policy held the DSI chief's rank down, and that was not by oversight.

As busy as he had been, Roussos at once dropped what he had been doing to quickly prepare for his meeting with the minister. It was just a short distance from his own building to the Ministry of Public Security. In fact, it had taken him no more than seven minutes to make the trip, and now he patiently waited to be called. He hadn't anticipated any delay; otherwise he would have brought with him some reports to read so as to make good use of his time until the minister was free. However, as the minutes dragged on and on, he began to wonder if he misunderstood. No, the secretary told him, there was no mistake. The minister knew he was there and would see him shortly.

It was almost noon when he was ushered into the great man's office. Achilles Petropoulos sat behind an intricately carved walnut desk almost the size of a streetcar. He smiled a disarming greeting to the man he had kept waiting for the best part of an hour. Either of Petropoulos's two immediate predecessors, regardless of party, would have been more punctual. These ministers knew their own worth, and each would have wanted to demonstrate his freedom of apprehension toward a powerful subordinate by personally going to the outer office and escorting him in without unusual delay. Only a novice would want to make the point that he was powerful enough to keep a man like Roussos waiting a long time.

The new minister's smile was a barely suppressed grin as he watched Roussos walk the long approach across the soccer-field-sized floor. As Roussos proceeded along the Persian-carpeted aisle, his eyes took in a trio of large-screen television sets in a darkened nook on one side, and the opulence of a new rosewood conference table with matching chairs, overstuffed leather lounge chairs, and wall tapestries on the other. Getting closer, he noted the minister's yellowing teeth and the extraordinarily long fingernail on his left little finger. This was a man who, similar to an oriental despot of old, felt a need to demonstrate that he had risen to high position and didn't have to work with his hands. Behind the minister's smile-grin, Roussos saw arrogance, pettiness, and a need to establish authority by humbling others.

In such a long rectangular room, the cater-cornered placement of the minister's desk in the far left corner seemed jarring. The normal need for balance emphasized the emptiness of the other corner, which held not even a plant. Roussos wondered why the new minister had so grotesquely re-arranged the office. It was disconcerting. Could that be the reason, to throw visitors off balance? It was as if he were saying, "That bare corner is your territory, and the rest is mine." There were large windows on both the side and front walls, and the office's location on the top floor, higher than the surrounding buildings, gave magnificent views from its windows. There could be seen Syntagma Square, the Parliament Building, the National Gardens, and at a southwesterly distance the Acropolis.

There were two chairs in front of the minister's desk, but he did not invite Roussos to sit. Previous ministers sometimes did and sometimes did not ask him to have a seat, depending on the nature and the expected duration of the meeting. Roussos hoped that in this instance it meant a short meeting.

He tried to keep an open mind about Petropoulos, but he had the burden of knowing something about the man. It was not only what others whispered in coffee-shop gossip, but also the frequency with which the name popped up in the reports that were ultimately placed in the top-secret files maintained by Roussos's department.

The brief summary that had refreshed Roussos's memory hinted more than confirmed that Petropoulos was a cowardly, graft-taking, bullying, two-faced, hypocritical opportunist. However, he was also a spellbinding orator able to arouse crowds to a feverish state of agitation. Not a polished, intellectual speaker, he was more a demagogic haranguer who could activate a mob by the sheer raw-guts emotion in his voice and body motions. His influence with the masses carried over to gain him a large enough following in parliament so that the new prime minister had had to offer him an important cabinet position. It was even whispered by some that he was a sure bet to become a future prime minister himself. Somehow, though, Roussos did not think Petropoulos would last long. Or was that wishful thinking?

In the meantime Roussos would deal with him honestly, as he had dealt with the succession of public security ministers in the past. He would obey orders; give the man sincere counsel, and try his best to protect him from his own mistakes, mistakes that Roussos knew would be inevitable. He could even hope that Petropoulos would grow with time in office.

"I have several matters to discuss with you," said Petropoulos. "First, I must congratulate you on your arrest last night of that confidence man who has been swindling international companies."

"Ah, the Greek-American, Nick Savvas. Thank you, sir." *A decent start*, thought Roussos. His eyes took in the cleanliness of the minister's desk. Other than two telephones and a pen set with a miniature calendar, there was but a single piece of paper on the desktop. A computer, printer, and third telephone were on a credenza behind him.

Petropoulos looked down on his paper as if searching for a clue. Then abruptly he said, "However, I don't think you should be working in the streets on individual cases. You are much too high-ranking and valuable for that. I might say that the prime minister agrees with me."

"I don't do that often, sir. But I like to keep up with what my people face. Every now and then I get involved directly with a case to keep myself current."

"A waste of assets. I might tell you that the prime minister is thinking of promoting you to police brigadier or even giving you a double promotion to police major general." The minister leaned back with satisfaction showing in his face as his small round eyes focused deeply to note the response. He now held the paper from the desk in the thick fingers of both hands. As he glanced at it again he studiously ran his tongue across his upper lip, making a snorting noise as he did so. A slaver of saliva oozed from the left corner of his mouth, and Petropoulos casually wiped it away with the sleeve of his jacket.

"*Kyrie Ypourge*," Roussos started, Mr. Minister. "May I ask, would a higher rank require that I leave the Department of Sensitive Investigations?"

Petropoulos took his eyes off the paper long enough to look up and say, "I should think you could answer that question for yourself. Of course it would. The head of DSI can't have more than the rank of a police director." He laughed nervously and said, "With a promotion you might aspire, for example, to be in charge of one of the inspectorates outside Athens." His eyes seemed to be focusing on Roussos's uniform, not his face.

The police director had known what the answer would be, but he needed time to think. He had spent years in building up DSI and gaining for it the respect that it deserved. He had weaned it away from being a personal political instrument for every new administration and had hammered it into a non-political entity of complete reliability. With someone like Petropoulos as Minister of Public Security, Roussos could see how easy it might be for DSI to revert to what it had been before.

"With all respect, sir, I would prefer to decline any promotion and remain as I am."

"Nonsense! If the prime minister wants to promote you, he will. But we'll leave that aside for now. Getting back to your arrest of that infamous international swindler, it was good work, but I want you to let the man go. You don't have enough evidence to convict him, and if you even try, it will make us all look foolish."

"Let him go?"

"That's what I said, *Kyrie Astynomike Diefthynti*." Mr. Police Director, he said with emphasis on each syllable. "Let him go. Now, next, have you heard of a man named Pavlo Xynos?"

Was the minister playing games? Either that or Petropoulos hadn't done his homework for their first meeting as Roussos had. If Petropoulos had properly prepared himself, he would have known that the name Pavlo Xynos had special meaning for Roussos.

He answered, "Certainly. Every police officer has, and I especially have good reason to know of him. He's a former university student who was found guilty of murdering a professor. He escaped from Averof Prison and was later known to be in a Near Eastern country where he reportedly was being trained as a terrorist and assassin."

"He's back in Greece and will probably be operating out of Athens."

"I didn't know," said Roussos. *My God*, he thought, as the image of Victoria instantly came to mind. "How did you learn this?"

"I'll send you a copy of the liaison report from the Americans. Xynos's primary mission apparently is to assassinate a cabinet officer. Do you realize what that means? Even I could be his target." Petropoulos uttered his words with a shrill laugh, as if to show disdain for the idea. "But no, we understand he is after the Minister of Scientific Development, Antoni Antonidis."

"We in DSI will do everything we can to apprehend him."

"You should consider this your highest priority case. Don't hesitate to kill if necessary."

Please don't teach me my job, thought Roussos.

As if reading from his paper, Petropoulos lowered his eyes and said, "Antoni Antonidis has been especially friendly with the Americans. Perhaps more importantly, he is the leading candidate to succeed our seventy-seven-year-old prime minister. It's interesting that, according to liaison sources, Xynos was specifically ordered to assassinate Antonidis instead of the prime minister. We also understand, however, that Xynos has some kind of grudge of his own against Antonidis."

Petropoulos squinted his eyes and looked at Roussos searchingly, then added, "Of course, I, in my modest way, ha, ha, might also be considered a potential successor to the prime minister, but that doesn't concern us at this time."

"I know Xynos made a threat…"

"Antonidis was the Minister of Public Security at the time Xynos was tried and convicted."

"But it was my department that caught him. We too have been getting reports on him every now and then, but I guess the Americans must have someone close to him. Anyway, I should think he would target me if anyone."

"Don't overrate your importance, my dear Mr. Police Director. Xynos is employed by a terrorist organization, and assassinating Antonidis would yield them much more international publicity. You are merely an expendable faceless police officer."

A hundred thoughts had entered Roussos's brain since the name Xynos came up, and he tried not too successfully to sort them out. Xynos was more than the murderer of a professor. Thief, blackmailer, stalker, he was a demented misanthrope who should have been exposed on some mountain at birth. Roussos thought the man was certifiably insane, although the court that sent him to prison had rejected that as a defense. And it was a fact that he had yelled a threat to Antonidis right after his conviction.

The minister continued. "I have more. Has your department learned yet that General Zavalas has returned from voluntary exile in Paris?" The sarcasm in his voice was an implied accusation that Roussos's office didn't seem capable of keeping track of important matters.

"I saw the Passport Control notice yesterday."

"Oh, you did? Well, there are no charges against him, so he's free to come and go as he pleases. We don't know what he's up to, but he's not the kind to keep out of trouble. He's told people that he's writing his political memoirs. But we also hear that he has some letters sent him by Minister Antonidis many years ago when my colleague was politically naïve. Forget that—I didn't mean to say it. Anyway, it doesn't help the situation that Antonidis is the brother-in-law of the prime minister, and those letters could be embarrassing to the administration."

"How does this concern my department?" Roussos was determined that his department was not going to get back in the political trickery business again, and he was not going to take action against Zavalas unless there were indications he was clearly breaking the law.

The minister stood up and pointed a finger at his visitor. "Roussos, I want you to get those letters. They were dated in the early 1970s and in them Antonidis promised to betray his political party in exchange for preferment in the dictatorship of the colonels. But the poor man should not have to suffer now for a stupid mistake made when he was young."

"You know I insist that my department operate legally."

Still standing, the minister's face reddened. "Legally or illegally, I don't give a damn how you get them. Just get them."

"You'll give me a written order to that effect?"

"Don't play stupid with me, Mr. Police Director. This matter of General Zavalas is extremely sensitive, and it's important that we don't clutter up the files with written orders, ass-covering memoranda, or other superfluous documents. I've given you an order. I don't care how you carry it out."

Roussos took the last remarks to mean that the meeting was over. As he started to turn to leave, he heard the minister speak again, this time in a calmer voice. Petropoulos re-took his seat and told Roussos, "We'll drop the matter of Zavalas for the moment. Before you leave, I should tell you that we have filled your deputy's position. I talked to the Chief of All Greek Police, Police Lieutenant General Dimos, this morning, and he is in agreement."

To himself Roussos thought, *Dimos is ready to retire and could care less. But this is the first time they've filled any major position in my department without at least consulting me first.* To the minister, he said, "May I ask who my new deputy is?" trying not to sound too sarcastic.

"Of course. We just promoted Chief Superintendent Jason Thanos of Homicide to the rank of police underdirector, and he'll report to you in two weeks."

Jason Thanos! thought Roussos with despair. *Everything this minister is reputed to be, Thanos is known to be: cowardly, two-faced, hypocritical, and opportunistic. And sadistic besides. Well, there'll be none of that in my department, no rope coils, bastinado, or electric shock torture.*

But he knew there would almost certainly be a lot of double-dealing and he would not be able to stop Thanos from reporting to Petropoulos behind his back. Petropoulos was putting his own creature in as deputy, probably with the idea of replacing Roussos as soon as it could be arranged.

Roussos suddenly realized that Petropoulos was speaking to him again. "You have a son, Dimitri, working for you." Half statement, half question.

"Yes," Roussos slowly drawled out. He had special dispensation to have his own son working out of his immediate office, and this was well known throughout the ministry. Was Petropoulos threatening to withdraw that dispensation?

"He is doing all right?"

"Yes, perfectly all right."

"Good. That is all. You may leave."

As he left the minister's office, Roussos continued thinking about these new developments and about the changes wrought by the advent of a new administration. Even more, though, he thought of the effect the news about Xynos would have on Victoria, and he recalled the words from the Bible, "Alas, that which I greatly feared has come upon me."

CHAPTER 2

▼

Other than both being presents for Marilyn Pickering's twenty-third birthday, there was no connection between the offer of a two-carat diamond ring and the invitation to spend a month in Athens. Marilyn was not surprised by the first, but the other was unexpected.

The marquise-mounted diamond coruscated in the dimly lit dining room of Georgetown's Chez Jean Luc Restaurant as Jake Sommers opened the velvet-lined box and positioned the gem in front of Marilyn's eyes. How those eyes blinked and danced, complementing fully the brilliance of the jewel.

"There's a price attached to it, you know," he said with a smile of eagerness.

In response, her honey-brown eyes blinked once, twice, three times, she then let her nose twitch in a playful gesture. They were both aware that she knew the price.

Jake said, "One little word: Yes!"

She said nothing, but he saw the answer in her face. Closing the box with ill-disguised hurt, he put it back in his pocket. From the other pocket he took out a smaller box, opened it, and placed it in her hand.

"Oh, it's a pearl. My birthstone. But I couldn't accept this either."

"It's only a modest birthday present and it didn't cost much. Think of it as a consolation prize, only I'm the one needing consolation. It'll be desolation if you refuse it."

She smiled and tried the pearl ring on the fingers of her right hand, finding that it fit the ring finger perfectly. "It looks expensive."

"Do you want to see the receipt? It's a cultured pearl, and it cost less than our opera tickets."

"Then I'll accept with many thanks, Jake. It was kind of you not to be presumptive about the diamond." She leaned over and kissed him on the cheek.

The smell of food rapidly coming toward their table, a veal cutlet for him and an *omelette aux fines herbes* for her, stopped Marilyn from saying more.

He said, "So much for third time being a charm."

"Don't, Jake, please don't spoil the evening."

"You know I'd do anything for you. I love you, Marilyn."

"I'm fond of you, Jake, but I don't know if I love you, and I'm not ready to get married yet."

"You're sure there's no one else?"

She laughed. "Only Billy Bob; Tom, Dick and Harry; and Robson Green."

Both knew they had to start eating if they were to make the Washington Opera on time. There was no opportunity for dessert, and it took a miserably long ten minutes for the valet to get Jake's car, but somehow they reached the opera just before the doors closed. They hurried to Jake's box seats and made themselves comfortable just as Placido Domingo reached the podium to thundering applause. This was the first time either of them had seen Domingo conducting.

The production was one of Marilyn's favorites, Puccini's *La Bohème*. The soprano singing the part of Mimi, Marilyn thought, was rather good, although she had never heard of her. Victoria Renfrew, she must remember that name. She glanced every now and then at Jake, whose interest in opera at best was slight. Tonight he seemed to be in deep thought and wasn't even pretending to pay attention. She wished he hadn't put her in a position to ruin the evening for him.

As they got in his car after the opera, Jake said, "Do I take you home or would you care to stop by my apartment?"

"What would we do at your apartment?"

He scowled as he looked at her. "If you don't want to, say so."

Marilyn put her hand on his right arm and stroked it. "I was just playing, Jake. Of course, we'll go to your apartment. We'll kiss and make up." She laughed again. "I'll go to bed with you, but I won't marry you, at least not tonight."

*   *   *   *

One thing about Jake, Marilyn thought to herself as she dressed and got ready for him to take her home, he was a good lover. But she just didn't feel in love with him. Whatever love was supposed to be. She didn't think she had ever been in love. All she knew was that she was supposed to feel something that unmistakably told her it was love, and not just momentary infatuation. Or was she just too hard to please?

Once home, she went to bed and immediately fell asleep. The birds were twittering noisily when she awoke on Saturday morning and joined her parents for breakfast.

Her father nodded a "Good morning" to her and continued to read the *Washington Post*.

"Did Jake propose again last night, dear?" asked her mother. "I do wish you'd say yes. He seems just right for you, works for one of the best law firms in Washington, and is already a partner at an early age. What more could you want?"

"Yes, he proposed again." Marilyn said nothing about the ring. Music from *La Bohème*, "Musetta's Waltz Song," was still swirling around in her head. How sad that Mimi had to die in the end. If she had had proper nutrition she probably wouldn't have gotten tuberculosis in the first place.

"But I don't know if I love him," Marilyn said. She was enchanted by opera in its many component parts, music, lyrics, story, costumes, and set, but she didn't like sad endings. Yet so many operas ended just that way. Why, she wondered, did the heroine have to die so young? Violetta in Verdi's *La Traviata* also died of tuberculosis. Tosca had to commit suicide. Desdemona was murdered by Othello. Norma sacrificed herself along with her lover. Rigoletto was responsible for the killing of his own daughter by mistake. Aida was buried alive in a tomb. All so sad.

"How long will it be before you find out?" her mother asked in a sweetly deceptive tone.

"Perhaps never. Perhaps I'll become a nun. Or a lesbian or something." But opera music was so beautiful. Was there something in the sadness that enhanced the glory of the music and poignancy of the story? Did the sadness in so many operas just mirror the sadness of life?

Her mother continued talking, but Marilyn's mind had wandered far away. She wondered, was sadness a necessary concomitant of ecstasy? That was what she wanted, ecstatic love offered by a dashing hero on a white horse who would give her adventure, thrills, danger. Yet if she did find it, would it lead to eventual pain? Would she be better off settling for a safe marriage with someone like Jake, never experiencing true love, but avoiding a passion that could become painful?

Putting his paper on the table, her father said, "Oh, by the way, the ambassador called last night just after you left to wish you a happy birthday."

"Uncle Ned?"

"How many ambassadors do you know? He's going to call again this morning. I expected him before now since it's seven hours earlier in Greece, but I guess he has other things to do as well. Were you planning to go out this morning?"

"Since it's Saturday, I had a vague idea I might go shopping, but that can wait. It will be nice to talk to Uncle Ned."

They continued eating breakfast with each now reading some section of the newspaper until the phone rang. Marilyn said she'd get it since it might be Uncle Ned.

It was. For a birthday present he invited her to come stay with him and his wife in Athens for a month. He'd pay the round-trip airfare, and she'd have no expenses for board and room. She had never been to Greece, and he was sure she'd love it.

She would, she knew she would. "Uncle Ned, you called at just the right time. How can I ever thank you?"

After hanging up, she told her parents, "Just what I need, a chance to get away and do some thinking."

*   *   *   *

A week later Marilyn was ready to go. It was easy to get a month off since she was working without pay for a charity organization.

Jake called and wanted to take her out to dinner on Saturday night before she left. "I've got a wonderful surprise for you."

"Not the diamond ring again?"

"No, not the ring."

"Only on condition that there's no talk of marriage."

"I promise. And you'll like my surprise."

Knowing how much Marilyn liked East Indian food with its many vegetarian dishes, Jake made reservations at the Taj Mahal in Alexandria. He stopped at the Marriott Hotel on the way, and there Marilyn met his "surprise."

It turned out to be a beautiful, slender woman about a dozen years older and some two inches shorter than Marilyn. She had titian hair, large brilliant violet-blue eyes, high cheekbones, full vermilion lips, and ecru skin as smooth as cream. She was lovely, and Marilyn had a dim notion that she had seen her before. She didn't think Jake was trying to make her jealous, and anyway she instantly liked the woman.

Jake made the introductions and seated them in his BMW, the two women together in back. And she really was a surprise—opera soprano Victoria Renfrew!

Jake explained. He was on retainer for Victoria's American agent, and when Victoria needed a lawyer to help with the sale of some real estate she had inherited from her father, the agent recommended Jake. Marilyn was impressed.

They crossed the Fourteenth Street Bridge and took the George Washington Memorial Parkway to Alexandria, turning right on King Street. An excited Marilyn continued talking during the entire drive and then inside the restaurant.

"But we saw you," she told Victoria, "in *La Bohème* only last week. I always use the aria *Mi Chiamano Mimi* as an indication of how much I like the singer, and you were just wonderful." She chattered on. "When someone first starts singing 'They Call Me Mimi,' I'm aware that it's a pleasant tune sung by a poor girl in ill health. But suddenly the music changes, and, if the soprano is really good, the beauty intensifies beyond belief, almost beyond bearing. It makes tears come to my eyes."

"I know the feeling," said Victoria. "I have a video of Renata Tebaldi in that role, and I feel the same way when I hear her sing that aria."

"I have her on video, too, and you sing just like she does."

"No, no, please. You apparently don't read my critics. They are more apt to compare me to Maria Callas, not for her greatness, but for our mutual failure to be able to hit the high range consistently. Tebaldi was a better singer than actress. Like Callas I'm more known for my acting and bel canto parts."

"I love bel canto."

"I give up," said Jake. "What's bel canto?"

Marilyn said, "It's a sort of deliberate warbling of tone—isn't that right, Victoria?"

Victoria laughed. "Well, something like that. I think of it from the technical point of view. It's a matter of breathing in a way to intensify or diminish each note as you sing. Not so much increasing or decreasing the volume, but more varying the power of a note so as to give it a greater range of expression. From the listener's viewpoint, I guess it could sound like a form of vibrating the notes."

Marilyn said to Jake, "Not all operas are sung bel canto, but those written by Rossini, Bellini, and Donizetti are among the best examples."

They ate their meal family style with ten dishes in the center of the table to choose from. Marilyn observed that the slender Victoria showed no fear of gaining weight as she liberally helped herself to portions of chicken tikka, lamb tandoori, vegetable biryani, alou gobi, palak paneer, and navratan korma, besides the raita, various types of breads, and a generous assortment of condiments. And Marilyn had plenty to choose from since everything except the chicken and lamb dishes was vegetarian.

"Victoria," said Jake with a little-hidden desire to start a new subject, "you don't act much like a prima donna. I don't mean in your singing, but in not being so temperamental in all the other things that you do."

"Lack of success has a wonderful way of keeping one humble, although I've been known to smash a vase of flowers or two if something goes wrong in rehearsals." She was smiling as she answered, but it was a bittersweet smile.

"But you're certainly successful. Even though you're not, er, well, very big in body—I think of opera singers as being really big, I mean big. You look as light as a feather."

She had a way of laughing with her lips not fully open that made her look almost shy. "I've been compared with Lily Pons because of my size. I only wish I had her success, too. You say I'm successful, but only to a degree. I guess it's just human to want something more."

"And what do you want more?" asked Marilyn. "Love?"

"No, I already have my love. I'm fortunate in that respect." After a moment she added, "But you see I'm not a regular singer at one of the really famous opera houses, such as the New York Metropolitan or Milan's La Scala. I sing mainly with the Greek National Opera in Athens. Since I'm not fully booked up years in advance, I'm often able to accept a role on short notice, which makes me popular with the artistic directors whose star for a coming performance can't make it because of illness, temperament, or some other reason. I sang at the Washington Opera just recently only because the scheduled star, Celeste Vitali, backed out a month ago."

"Why, then," asked Marilyn, "are you with such a little known opera company?"

"Because they regularly give me leading parts. You saw me at the Washington Opera singing Mimi, but that was a fluke because of the short notice. Usually when I get an offer to sing outside Athens, it's a second soprano role, such as Musetta. I'm glad to get the chance, but in Athens I'm almost always given the lead roles, the Mimi roles. All my life my ambition has been to sing the big roles in the best opera houses, but, as they say,"—she smiled again and spread out her arms in a fatalistic gesture—"if wishes were horses, beggars would ride."

Marilyn had a habit of dividing people into actives and passives, and she decided that Victoria was more of the passive type. Very likeable, but more willing to let things just happen to her, not a catalyst.

"Don't let me give you the impression," Victoria continued, "that the Athens National Opera is second rate. It's like hotels. The Athens Opera is first class, but there are a few at the top that are deluxe."

Marilyn said, "You're an American, aren't you?"

"Born and bred in the U. S. of A. But I couldn't make it as a steady prima donna here, at least not in the opera houses I wanted, like the Met. When I was in Athens on tour once, the National Opera offered me a contract with options for year after year. You better believe me, I took it, but I had other reasons, too. I needed to get away, far away."

"So now you live in Greece?"

"When I'm not on tour elsewhere."

"Where? In Athens?"

"Yes, Athens. I have a co-op apartment in the heart of the city."

"Do you live with your family? Are you married?"

Victoria didn't seem to mind the personal questions. With a hint of amused tolerance on her face, she said, "It depends on what you call family. I'm divorced and I live with my companion—my lover if you will—who's a Greek police officer.

Marilyn said, "Did you know, I'm going to Greece tomorrow?"

Jake interjected, "She's staying in Athens for a month with her uncle, who's the American ambassador to Greece."

Victoria said, "Is he? I've met the American Ambassador, Edward Atherton. My policeman companion, Spyro Roussos, has taken me to several American Embassy receptions. And I, too, am going to Greece tomorrow. We'll probably travel on the same plane, Olympic Airlines?"

"Yes, that's terrific. And we'll probably see each other in Athens. I'll certainly be going to the opera there."

"I'm singing *Tosca* at the Athens Opera in two weeks."

"Oh, I hope I can get a ticket."

"You shouldn't have any trouble, especially for the higher priced seats. In fact, if you want, I can send you two complimentary tickets. I'll send them to the Embassy for you."

Marilyn thanked her, and Victoria reminded Jake that she had to be getting back. Jake drove her to her hotel first, then continued onward with Marilyn.

He said, "Well, you certainly hit it off with her."

"Jake, it was so sweet of you to arrange for the two of us to meet. Just imagine, I already have a friend in Athens, and such an important one. I think you're wonderful."

"It was worth it if it makes you think I'm wonderful. Now do you see what you'll be getting if you marry me."

"You promised no mention of marriage."

"Sorry, I thought I had a good excuse in this case."

Marilyn laughed. "Okay, this time you certainly had a good excuse, and I'll have to forgive you. Anyway, I'll promise you this. I'll be away for a month, and while I'm gone, I'll make up my mind."

"Sudden death? I'm afraid."

"If you put it that way. But I know I've got to make up my mind, and I will."

Jake said, "When you get back I'll have to tell you about some of my other impressive clients. You'll like them. Think of me as you stroll the Acropolis or admire those guards parading around in their fancy skirts."

"Evzones," she said. "It's a traditional costume going back to the Middle Ages." She was silent for a minute, then said, "Don't turn here to my home. I think it would be nice to go to your place first."

*   *   *   *

The next day Marilyn's mother drove her to Dulles International Airport, where they said their good-byes. Marilyn engaged a skycap to help with her luggage and looked for the Olympic Airways ticket counter.

"I see you made it in good time," said a woman's voice from behind her.

She turned to see Victoria Renfrew. Marilyn said, "I was hoping I'd see you here. Are you all checked in? What's your seat number? I'll see if I can get one beside you."

Victoria still had her ticket in her hand, and she looked for the number.

"Oh," said Marilyn, "that says first class. I guess there's no chance of sitting beside you."

"I'm sorry, but I usually travel first class. I might as well since it's all for business and tax deductible."

Victoria was dressed in a smart business suit that looked as if it were an original Paris creation designed just for her, and she was made up so glamorously that she resembled a movie star. Seeing Marilyn appraise her outfit with raised eyebrows, she said, "I'm meeting a reporter and a photographer for an interview in five minutes."

After Victoria departed, Marilyn mused that she wasn't at all what she expected an opera star to be, but then Victoria was the first professional singer that she had met. *The poor woman has apparently had some disappointments,* thought Marilyn. *Another case of sadness,* she mused. A feeling of unhappiness momentarily came over her, but she didn't like to feel this way, so she quickly turned her mind to more pleasant thoughts.

* * * * *

Two suntanned men in well-pressed business suits stood outside the roped area in front of the Olympic Airways counter.

"That is the one, the one with reddish hair," the huskier of the two said to his companion. After taking another furtive glance at Marilyn, he turned to stand with his back to her."

"She is beautiful, Jimmy," said the other. "Look how her facial features are almost classical."

"Don't let her see you. And try not to attract the attention of the security police. We don't want to be taken for terrorists." Jimmy took a flight schedule from an inner jacket pocket and pretended to be studying it. "Yes, she is indeed as lovely as her photograph. I'm glad we didn't have any trouble recognizing her."

The two men looked to be somewhere either side of thirty. They stood outside the queue lines where the passengers checked in with their tickets. As Marilyn passed close to them inside the ropes of the queue, they again averted their faces.

The men looked similar, with the difference that one of them, Yorgo, was quite thin, while the other man, Jimmy, although he had a trim figure, also had wide shoulders, making him look physically powerful. Both could be called attractive, and both could be said to know it—they had that cocksure look in their eyes and a chin that jutted upwards in an assertion of masculine self-confidence.

As if their movements had been choreographed in advance, they separated without another word. Yorgo joined Marilyn's queue, and Jimmy walked around the corner out of sight from the airline counters to stand with his back against the wall.

Coming up immediately behind Marilyn, Yorgo heard the ticket agent saying, "You already have 26A reserved, that's a window seat."

"Will it be crowded today?" Marilyn asked.

"There'll be some empty seats, but not too many."

She left the counter and looked around to see if she could spot Victoria again.

Yorgo exchanged a few words with the ticket agent, handed him his ticket, and waited to get it back. He carried a boarding tote bag with him, but had no luggage to check. He then departed taking the opposite direction from Marilyn. Reaching his companion, he turned his back to him, but stood close enough so they could have a guarded conversation.

"Were you successful?" asked Jimmy.

"It went well," said Yorgo. "I'm in 26B. Where will you be sitting?"

"I'm in 33G. That's on the other side of the middle section, far away from you."

Yorgo smiled, "Well, I don't think I'll need any help." There was an uncomfortable moment of silence, then Yorgo suddenly turned to look at his companion. "Jimmy, what's wrong? Why are you looking so strangely?"

Jimmy, appearing undecided, answered, "I just thought of something, and I'll have to leave. I can take another flight later."

"But your ticket? The money? And when we get to Athens?"

"The others will meet you in Athens. And the money can't be helped. Look, Yorgo, I'll take another flight later and see you in Greece as soon as I can." He started running toward the nearest exit.

"Hurry, Jimmy, we need you."

CHAPTER 3

▼

It was long past quitting time. Police Director Roussos sat back in his office chair and checked his watch. It was the same time as the clock on the wall. Both watch and clock were only three minutes later than the last time he looked. He had at least an hour and a half to sit and wait. Better to do it in his office than at the airport. At least he could get some work done.

He picked up a random pile of papers from his desk, unenthusiastically slid the top one to the bottom, and took a half-hearted glance at the next document. Shaking his head, he tossed the papers back to where they came from.

He looked at the large photograph on the wall in front of him, the most prominent of all the pictures in his office. His grandfather, also Spyro Roussos, wearing the uniform of a Gendarmerie major, looked severe, although the police director remembered him as a kind man. There was no longer a Gendarmerie in Greece. That service had been merged with the Cities Police to form the single-service Greek Police. Having two national police forces that the king could play off against each other might have been a useful scheme at one time, at least for the king, but Greece no longer had a king. Konstantino II was living in Italy or Portugal or somewhere else in exile.

There was a knock on the door and Pano entered. "I hope I am not disturbing you."

"No, no, Pano, my dear friend, I'm just spinning cobwebs."

"Anxious to pick up Victoria, huh?"

He smiled. "You know me well."

Roussos and Chief Superintendent Pano Maniatis indeed knew each other well. They had served together for years, and Pano was his unofficial lieutenant and confidant in DSI.

With the familiarity he allowed himself only when he knew he was alone with his chief and the occasion was informal, the stocky chief superintendent with the dolphin smile sat in one of the chairs facing Roussos's desk and slouched with his legs resting on another chair. He said, "You and Victoria are like one of my cousins and her husband. They dote on each other and resent every hour they have to be apart."

"Is this the one on Chios?"

"Yes, he is a fisherman and has to be away at sea a lot, but they both hate it."

"Sometimes I wonder if I should have been a fisherman." He closed his eyes and thought about some of things he used to do before he met Victoria, fishing, sailing, hunting for boar in northern Greece—when he had the time.

Pano reached to pull a third chair close to him for an arm rest. "You wouldn't like it. There aren't any good fish left. Like on land, there are only sharks these days." He ran his fingers through his tousled graying hair and asked cautiously, "Have you heard any more from the new minister?"

"Not a word." Roussos opened his eyes and yawned. "I'm waiting for the next blow."

"Yesterday I saw my cousin who works in the Ministry of Public Security. He says that Petropoulos isn't in his office very much, and when he's there he confers with cronies and doesn't talk to anyone else. Then he issues new directives, all the time new directives. About keeping shoes shined, wearing neckties, and of course the women have to wear suitable dresses. Our new minister is very concerned about the women in his ministry. He is always ogling them and making them feel self-conscious. Like my grandfather, who was always lifting skirts in the village."

"Oh, yes, your grandfather."

"The men hated him, but the women liked him, even though he was always bumping against them to feel them. But he gave them some attention and talked politely to them. They liked that."

"I remember your telling me about your grandfather."

"Would you like me to get you some coffee? Nescafé? Anything?"

"*Tipote.*" Nothing. "Well, perhaps a glass of water."

Pano left and Roussos stared at the picture of his own grandfather. He was proud of the senior Spyro Roussos. A good man. A brave man. He remembered hearing about that time during the Communist War in 1949 when his grandfather was in charge of a Gendarmerie station in the southern part of the Peloponnisos. One night his men had surrounded a house where there were a dozen or so Communist guerrillas. They had captured Major Roussos's brother, Gendarmerie Captain Byron Roussos, and were holding him as a hostage, threatening to kill him if the Gendarmerie did not let them have free passage to escape. And Major Roussos knew that another larger Communist force was gathering behind him. He couldn't wait for reinforcements.

Pano returned with the water for the police director and a small cup of Turkish coffee for himself. Using the fourth chair as a table for his coffee, he resumed his sprawled out position and continued. "Did I ever tell you about the time my grandfather was discovered in his neighbor's house with the neighbor's wife. He quickly threw on one of the wife's biggest dresses—she was a big woman, and…"

Roussos had his eyes closed again. He vaguely recalled hearing the story, or a similar one, before. He smiled so as to appear to be listening, and Pano went on.

But the police director's mind was again on his own grandfather. Major Roussos had several of his men loudly sing a popular song, *Garyfallo S'Afti*, Carnation Behind Her Ear. It was a joke between him and his brother, who liked the song so much that he always went around singing it at the top of his voice. Major Roussos got so he couldn't stand it, and he was always ordering Byron to shut up.

He hoped Byron would get the message now and look out for him. He told his men he was going behind the house to see if he could enter and find his brother. At any rate, in exactly thirty minutes his men were to charge the house. On being questioned by one of them, he replied, "Under any circumstances whatsoever. Forget about me and come in firing."

In the darkness he skirted the house and checked out the door and windows in the rear, working slowly so as not to act rashly. Eventually he found he could open a bulkhead door to the cellar, and cautiously he entered. A small bare light bulb let him make out the contents of the room. His brother was there, tied and suspended from a wooden cross beam supporting the floor above. Time was flying, but he had brought with him an extra gun, just in case. He untied his brother and furiously rubbed his hands. "Can you hold a gun now?" he asked.

"I think so, Spyro. Thanks. I knew you'd be coming when I heard the singing."

Then his men charged, and loud shots and shouts of confusion echoed from the floor above. Spyro and Byron heard a door at the top of the steps creak open and loud footsteps coming down. There were two of them, and Spyro shot the first while his brother killed the one behind. Then it was over. Only three guerrillas remained alive, but the attacking force had not lost a single gendarme. Major Roussos was a hero and was decorated by King Paul himself.

Pano was saying, "But then my grandmother found out about it and she locked him out of the house." There was a moment of silence before Pano said, "Spyro, are you asleep?"

"No, no," said the police director, opening his eyes. "So your grandmother finally found out about his misdeeds, the old goat."

"No, that was my father. I finished with my grandfather long ago. My father was still young and was already picking up the ways of his father. But he was forced to marry my mother, and then he settled down." Pano rose from his chair, stretched, and said, "I guess I'd better make my rounds." Taking his empty cup and his superior's glass, he left the office.

At least, the police director thought, that was one son who took after his father. His own father had been different, and he was not proud of him.

Major Spyro Roussos had but one son, Leandro, who became a chief inspector in the Personal Protection Service of the Cities Police. Leandro was well thought of and had had some commendations, but something in him changed at the time of the Colonels' Revolt.

When the tanks came rolling down the main streets of Athens on that grim morning in April 1967, most police officers did nothing. They knew they couldn't fight the army, and many of them had varying degrees of sympathy with the colonels anyway, but they remained passive and waited to be told what to do by the winners. Leandro Roussos was in charge of a protective squad at the Parliament Building. When a large group of parliamentarians opposed to the revolt tried to make their individual escapes, Leandro rounded them up and turned them over to the army.

The colonels rewarded him by promoting him to chief superintendent and making him the head of a punitive group that was expert in giving heavy doses of castor oil to dissidents, beating them with heavy sticks on their bare soles, and threatening them with mock executions. "Greece was sick," said the new ruler, Colonel Papadopoulos, "and needed strong medicine." Chief Superintendent Leandro Roussos was one of the most conspicuous ones supplying some of that strong medicine.

After the downfall of the colonels and restoration of democracy in 1973, many officers in the army and police were forgiven in a general amnesty, but a few were held for trial. Leandro was not tried in court, but he was booted out from the Cities Police in disgrace. He lived the remainder of his short life in Corfu taking care of the farm that his wife had inherited.

By this time the younger Spyro Roussos was a student at Athens University, and he strongly felt the shame his father had brought on the family name. Like his grandfather, he was neither a leftist nor a rightist, and didn't involve himself in politics. After he graduated he himself joined the Cities Police, having a secret need to do whatever he could to compensate for his father's disgrace. He was already making rapid advancement in his career when the Gendarmerie and the Cities Police were combined into an overall Greek Police in 1984.

He looked at the clock again. It was close enough to the time to start out for the airport. As he left his office, he took another look at the photograph of his grandfather on the wall. There was no reminder in his office of his father.

CHAPTER 4

▼

As Marilyn entered the plane, she noticed Victoria sitting in an aisle seat in the first class section. The man in the window seat seemed to be talking continuously to her. Marilyn waved as she started to pass. Victoria took her hand to pull her close and whisper in her ear, "How I wish you were sitting beside me. I've run into a b-o-r-e." And then aloud she said, "Do let's keep in touch in Athens."

In the next compartment Marilyn looked for her window seat and quickly found it. An elderly woman had taken the aisle seat, and in the middle was a rather nice looking young man with light olive complexion and charcoal eyes. Marilyn made a rough guess that he might be a Mediterranean type, probably Greek since they were flying to Athens. His look toward her was one of friendliness and consideration.

Their flight taxied down the runway, waited for clearance, and took off. Marilyn always felt relief when a plane was at last airborne. Accepting the black plastic headset from a flight attendant, she plugged it into its socket and reviewed the music menu found in the airline's magazine. She clicked to "Opera" and was transported to the world of Mozart, Verdi, and Richard Strauss. As she listened, she felt complete relaxation for the first time in days. The rhythmic soft thumping of the plane's vibrations added to the illusion of weightlessness and timelessness.

Sometime later her reveries were broken by a flight attendant backing down the aisle with a trolley of drinks. "Would you care for anything?"

Taking off the headset, Marilyn said, "Some wine, please. Red."

"I'll have red wine, too," said the man sitting next to her. As if the serving of drinks had sounded a signal, he now started a conversation with her. She felt even more relaxed with the wine and was glad that this pleasant man had taken the initiative in talking.

"You are staying in Athens?" he asked.

"Yes, I have relatives there."

"You do not look Greek. Perhaps one of your relatives is working for a foreign company?"

Her natural instinct was to be warm toward him, but with all the terrorism and crime stories in newspapers and on television, she was becoming increasingly wary of conversations with strangers. Still, they were on an airplane surrounded by hundreds of other people, and she knew her uncle was having somebody from the embassy meet her, so she should be safe. She guessed there was no reason for any reluctance to identify herself.

"My uncle is the American ambassador. He's sending someone to meet me."

"Oh, you are a very important person then."

Marilyn blushed. "Not really. Do you live in Athens?"

"I do now. I had been living in Kifisia, one of the northern suburbs, but recently I bought a flat in the center of Athens."

His English was just lightly accented, although it sounded a bit more British than American. She said, "Then you must know Athens well."

"I should. I was born there and have lived there all my life, except for my service in the army."

"The Greek army?"

He laughed. "Oh, yes, the Greek army. I was a career officer, a *lohagos*—you call it captain—but I was required to take a medical discharge after some heart problems. Now I am working in my father's company. He owns the largest insurance company in Greece."

The aroma wafting from the front of the plane told Marilyn that the attendants were serving meals. She wondered if the food would be Greek or American. She had not thought to ask in advance for a vegetarian meal and was afraid of what she might get.

When a tray was served to the woman in the aisle seat, Marilyn could see that the meal was some kind of chicken dish with a baked potato. There were also some carrots, a salad, a roll with butter, and a dessert that looked like Shredded Wheat swimming in syrup, something almost certain to be vegetarian. She could ignore the chicken and still have sufficient food.

Her companion was just picking at his food, eating far less than she was. He saw her looking and explained, "I am just not hungry. I'm anxious to get back to my home." Then he said, "Excuse me, I should introduce myself. I am Georgio Papamavrogiannopoulos."

She gulped on hearing the name.

"You can call me Yorgo—that is the nickname for Georgio, or George."

She said, "I'm Marilyn, Marilyn Pickering. Yes, I think I'd prefer to call you Yorgo rather than, well, than your last name, Papamavro…. I forget. It's rather long, isn't it?"

"I am apologetic for a name that is long even for us Greeks," he said with a smile.

They talked a bit more and then she returned to her food. She delicately poked at and finally tasted her dessert, and it was delicious. Yorgo called it *kataifi*, pronouncing the first "i" separately and giving it the accent. Marilyn intended to pay close attention to Greek words and their pronunciation. The syrup was much like that of *baklava*, which she was used to having in a Greek restaurant back home.

After the attendant had cleared away the trays, Marilyn decided to walk the aisles a bit to exercise her legs. Unused to being cooped up for so long with so little leg room, she walked up one aisle and down another. As she approached the first class cabin, she saw Victoria coming her way.

The soprano said, "I was going to the W.C. when I saw you and decided to see how you're coming along. I hope it's not too uncomfortable for you."

"I'm making do. But how about you? Is your seatmate still talking without letup?"

"I hate to be rude to anyone, but I put my earphones on and started reading, and then he hushed up."

"He was probably overwhelmed by your beauty and just talking nervously. You must have a lot of admirers."

"You probably have a lot of your own. I like fans, but I decidedly do not like aggressive romantic admirers. I'm very much in love with the man I live with?"

"Will you marry him?"

"Long story. I'll tell you about it some day. I could also tell you about a certain horrifying stalker who made my life hell. Thank God that's over now. Another story I'll save for later. Anyway, how is your seatmate?"

"The man beside me is pleasant enough. Have you noticed him? That nice looking thin man in the middle seat back there?"

"Oh, yes, he looks nice from here. I hope he's not talking too much."

"Just the right amount. He tells me he was in the Greek army and got a medical discharge. Now he works for his father's insurance company, which is the largest in Greece."

They continued talking for another few minutes and then parted. Marilyn walked some more until her legs felt sufficiently exercised, then returned to her seat. She sat in silence while letting the various thoughts passing through her mind compete with each other for her sustained attention.

Victoria's comment about an admirer who frightened her so much made Marilyn think of how nice Jake was. Good old Jake, always there when she wanted him and never making himself obnoxious. She supposed that she was ungracious not to appreciate him more. She could do a lot worse. Well, that was the aim of this trip, wasn't it, to decide if she should marry him?

Gradually her thoughts focused on the handsome man beside her. Well-mannered and cultured, he had a certain attractive air of mystery about him. She fantasized that perhaps she would come across him again in Athens. He might even offer to show her some of the sights. It would be nice to have a male escort who really knew the city.

It occurred to her that being in Athens for a month might be an opportunity for a little last-time fling before settling down with Jake. The trouble with that idea was that she didn't think she'd care for a last-time fling with the particular man sitting beside her. Yorgo would be fine for escorting her around the city, but she didn't think she'd want to have an affair with him. He was nice, yet something about him made him just not her type.

But then, having a brief affair wasn't exactly the same as marrying a man, was it? Thanks probably to the importunacy of her mother, Marilyn tended to speculate about every presentable single man she met as a potential husband—she assumed that Yorgo's lack of a wedding band indicated he was single. Would she want to go through life with this or that man? What were his strengths and what were his drawbacks? They all had drawbacks. Yorgo, although he was somewhat handsome, didn't impress her as either good lover or good husband material.

"You seem distracted," said Yorgo. "Your mind must be miles away."

"I was thinking about many things," she said as her face reddened. "Such as my boyfriend back home. And about the man who's meeting me at the Athens Airport. And about my friend who's an opera singer."

*   *   *   *

In the first class section, Victoria had not put on her earphones again and her loquacious seatmate was ready for another try. "It's nice going first class," he said. "I suppose you go first class all the time, but it's the first time for me. I got an upgrade. You want me to tell you how I did it?"

She wished he could take a hint, but she wasn't sure how strong to make it. Perhaps the kindest thing would be to give him a frozen look. She did just that, and he stopped, gave her an offended look in return, and turned away.

Now, what had she been thinking about? Oh, yes, Marilyn. She seemed like a nice girl, intelligent and pleasant, but not too experienced. She and Jake made a nice couple. They'd probably marry. It would be a nice stable marriage for Marilyn, and Victoria couldn't imagine Jake beating her or otherwise being mean to her. It was so easy to make a mistake on a first marriage, as Victoria well knew.

Thinking of Spyro crowded out her other thoughts. He'd be meeting her at Ellinikon Airport. It had almost been unbearable. It would be so nice to be together with him again. She hoped he'd have some free time and not be working night and day. After her tour, they'd need a long while together. Next week she'd be starting rehearsals for *Tosca*. Between Spyro's work and her career, they seemed to have so little time together.

Her career. What career? Victoria who? Although Marilyn had seen her in *La Bohème* the week before they met, it had been apparent that she had never heard of her before that. She got the big roles at the Greek National Opera because they ordinarily couldn't afford the fees commanded by the great international stars, yet people told her she was just as good as some of the best. Were they just flattering her? She didn't think so. She had always wanted to be a prima donna. All her teachers told her she was going to reach the top. Her peers always seemed to envy her for her voice and presence. What had happened to derail her?

Of course, she knew the answer. It had to be that crucial period in her marriage that had stopped her career. She had lost momentum, couldn't practice properly, and failed miserably in the roles that came her way just at the time when her career should have been developing. How could she sing her best when the thought was always in the back of her mind that after the performance she would be going home to a monster? Why had she wasted so much time before she came to her senses and left him? Even after she freed herself of him, she found herself cursed with a reputation. Victoria Renfrew, she's good, but you never know when she'll let you down.

True, but that wasn't all. She wanted to be honest with herself. She wasn't a pusher. In her younger years she had been a nice, sweet, non-assertive, shy child. When she grew up, she still found herself a nice, sweet, non-assertive, shy adult. She had always been indecisive, seldom took initiative, and never dared do anything bold.

Thank God Spyro came into her life. If he had been her business manager rather than her lover, she might have had another chance to reach the top. If, if, if!

On the other hand, wasn't he in a way holding her back?

She wished she hadn't thought of that. She should wash her thoughts out with soap and water.

She really meant she was so content with Spyro that at times she seemed to lose some of her artistic aspirations. In Washington she had had five minutes alone with Placido Domingo, five valuable minutes during which she could have told him how much she would have liked more roles with the Washington Opera—after all, hadn't she done well with the lead in *La Bohème*? But instead they just made small talk. She had missed opportunities, too, when she once subbed with the San Francisco Opera and on another occasion with the Chicago Opera. She had never sung at the Met or La Scala, but no doubt she would have been just as passive at those two. Spyro's work was in Athens and there he had to stay. As long as he wanted her, she would stay, too.

She shouldn't complain. Counting several opportunities abroad, she usually sang in some fifteen operas a year, and sometimes she'd give as many as six performances of a single opera. It wasn't too demanding; she enjoyed it; and her total income was enough so she could always add to her savings. But, oh, God, before she got too old, how she would pray for a breakthrough.

The plane had descended into the Athens corridor and was hitting a few air bumps as it lowered its landing gear. Then the Boeing 747 was screeching on the ground, and before Victoria realized it she was inside the airport and making her way toward the immigration and customs clearances.

Seeing Marilyn again, she joined her in line. Marilyn had been with her seatmate, the one called Yorgo, but Yorgo, walking away, was saying that as a Greek national he had to enter a separate line.

"My friend will be outside waiting for me," said Victoria to Marilyn. "Can we give you a ride to the American Embassy?"

"No, thanks. My uncle is sending someone to meet me, a man named Bob Jensen. I don't know what he looks like, but my uncle probably gave him my photo."

*   *   *   *

At that moment Bob Jensen was speeding down Vouliagmenis Avenue in a car he borrowed from the embassy's pool. His own Volvo had been disabled on Syngrou Avenue with two flat tires. He called the embassy and they sent a pool car to him, but he had lost a valuable forty-five minutes and was kicking himself for it.

He was now only some fifteen minutes away from Ellinikon Airport. If the ambassador's niece's flight were still on time, as the airline had said when he called some two hours ago, he'd be late, but not by too much. With the help of delays for immigration and customs and retrieving her baggage, he might just make it. He floored the accelerator in an effort to cut the fifteen minutes down to ten.

Suddenly he had to jump on the brake and come to an abrupt halt. A truck had swung around and was sitting crossways to block traffic in both directions. Jensen started honking his horn, then put the car in reverse to avoid the blockade by turning into a side street. Only now he couldn't even do that because a smaller truck had stopped so closely behind him that he couldn't back up any more. He rushed out of his car determined to see if he could get the driver of the truck in front to move, or failing that to persuade the driver behind him to back up a bit.

As he began walking to the first truck, he became aware that someone was standing behind him. Before he could turn to look, he felt a horrible pain in his head and he sank to the ground.

*   *   *   *

At the airport Marilyn's passport had been stamped and her luggage cleared. She walked outside customs to the main waiting area to confront what appeared to be orchestrated confusion. There were perhaps several hundred people waiting for the travelers to come out, but not waiting peacefully. Everyone seemed to be yelling and jumping around. The voices so melded into one loud cacophony that she wondered how anyone could hear anyone else.

She had had the vague thought that all she had to do was appear and her uncle's man would pop up in front of her. There were a number of people holding up signs with just a name on them, "Mr. Simons" or "Gladys Schmitt" or "Carlo Moresini," but nothing for a "Marilyn Pickering." After waiting a while, she went outside, where perhaps she might recognize an American Embassy car.

As she waited by the curb, car after car stopped to pick up passengers, but nothing seemed intended for her. She was about to go back in the airport, when from behind she heard a vaguely familiar voice.

Yorgo said, "You are looking as if you are lost."

"I can't find the man who was supposed to pick me up."

"You must have been waiting a half hour now. Perhaps something happened to him."

"I guess the best thing for me is to call the American Embassy."

"Let me get the embassy for you." He took a cellular telephone from his pocket. "Do you have the number?"

"Somewhere in my luggage."

"I'll call the operator to get it." He talked into the telephone speaking Greek, and after a minute said in English, "Hello, is this the American Embassy? Yes, thank you. Yes, I'll wait." A bit later he spoke again. "I have the niece of the American ambassador with me and no one is here at the airport to meet her. Oh, accident? I see. Yes, I guess that would be best for her. Certainly the quickest."

Ending the call, he said to Marilyn, "I talked to the ambassador's personal secretary. The ambassador is away from the embassy, and the secretary explained that his aide just telephoned and said he was in a car accident. The secretary said the best thing now would be to take a taxi to the embassy."

Marilyn looked confused. "Do Greek taxi drivers understand English?"

"Look," said Yorgo, "I live not far from the embassy. Would you mind if I shared a taxi with you?"

Her face lit up. "Oh, no, I'd be grateful. That would be wonderful."

He hailed a taxi and they loaded the luggage in the trunk.

It was after the taxi had started off that Marilyn began wondering if something was wrong. Yorgo was staring at her in a strange way. He seemed to have a possessive look in his eyes, as if she belonged to him. Was it a lovesick look or something more menacing? She had read newspaper stories about how violently romantic Greek men could be. Apparently it was common practice to kidnap the women they loved and force them to elope. Of course, she knew that these stories were about a statistically insignificant number of cases, but she began wondering if she might not be joining the statistically insignificant.

Shortly after they left the airport, the taxi stopped to pick up another person waiting at a bus stop. A large man with a determined look on his face got in beside the driver, turned to look at Yorgo and Marilyn, nodded in perhaps a routine greeting, and faced the front again as the car sped off.

"It is common in Greece for a taxi to pick up several passengers going in the same direction," said Yorgo.

Marilyn gave him an insecure smile. They drove through dark streets for a long time, and from what she could see through the window, they were successively getting into less dense areas. Then they drove through a brightly lit place, only to have it succeeded by a dark highway. She could hear the sea on her right, which was strange because she had studied a map of Athens and knew that there were two ways to get from the airport to the main part of the city, one was with the sea on the left, and the other immediately cut inland and didn't follow the sea at all.

"Is this the way to Athens?" she asked.

"We are taking a shortcut," said Yorgo.

Marilyn grew more and more nervous. Now she was certain something was wrong. The new passenger in front was conversing in a low tone with the driver, and it appeared that they knew each other. Occasionally they laughed and sometimes Yorgo joined in. Marilyn now realized that all three knew each other.

"Where are you taking me? This is not the way to Athens."

Yorgo's voice became so fierce that it jarred her. "Be quiet. You will be all right if you are quiet. Don't cause trouble or you will suffer."

She didn't need further confirmation. They were kidnapping her. She wanted to scream, but who would hear her. After Yorgo's last remark, she hesitated to speak again. Why had she accepted his offer? She had been warned about strangers. What was happening to her?

After what seemed to be a long time, the car made a sharp right turn and entered a small, dimly lit harbor. In the moonlight she could make out a number of boats at their moorings. She didn't care about his warnings. She was going to speak up anyway. "Where are we? What are you going to do with me?"

Yorgo said, "We will continue the rest of the way by boat. No one wishes to hurt you, Marilyn, if you will cooperate. You must understand that you are our prisoner now, and you must obey orders." He showed her his fist. "Whatever you do, don't scream or cause trouble. I don't want to hurt you, but I will if I have to."

She pulled at her mind to make it act in a helpful way. Don't struggle, don't scream, she told herself. She knew her best chance was to remain rational. She must not panic. She must conserve her strength. She had to learn as much as possible about her captors and her location, and above all she must remain alert to possibilities of escape.

Leading her roughly by the arm, Yorgo took her to a small cabin cruiser and said, "Go aboard."

She stopped moving and turned to face him. "I'm not afraid of you, you know."

"Good. As long as you obey orders, there is no need to be afraid."

"Suppose I don't want to go aboard this boat?"

His look turned ferocious. "Understand, the others are not as well disposed toward you as I am. You don't realize what a dangerous position you're in."

"I'm not moving."

Without further warning, he slapped her hard across the mouth. She involuntarily moved backward and raised her hand to her stinging face. She felt blood and thought her lips were swollen, probably cut.

Lifting her up, Yorgo carried her aboard the cruiser and set her down on deck.

She said, "Am I allowed to know why you're doing this to me?"

"No! And that was just a tap. One more word and I'll beat you senseless."

CHAPTER 5

▼

Police Director Spyro Roussos and Victoria Renfrew sat on their balcony high above Kolonaki Square holding hands and disinterestedly watching the busy street scene below. After getting her home from the airport, Roussos had prepared dinner while she unpacked, took a shower, and put on a comfortable shift.

She had been married early in life when everything looked as if the world was her bowl of cherries. It didn't take long to realize that her husband was an alcoholic, a womanizer, and a man who tried to make up for his incompetencies by abusing his wife. She didn't want to admit that her marriage was a failure, but when he threatened to kill her, she made up her mind fast.

After her divorce, she got an offer to become a member of the Greek National Opera, which decided her on taking up residence in Greece, where she made a successful effort to learn the language quickly. She was almost certain that her ex-husband wouldn't come after her there. And then she and Spyro found each other, and each knew the peace of responded love.

Spyro looked at her, lovingly squeezed her hand a little, and smiled an inward smile as he soaked up the pleasure of having her home again. How had he become so dependent on her?

He, too, contrary to Greek custom, had been married young. His wife had been unfaithful to him, but before he could seek a divorce, her mental instability degenerated into a form of insanity. Some concept of honor made him decide that he couldn't divorce her under those circumstances. He gave his wife back the house and income that she had brought into the marriage as her *proika*, her dowry. There she stayed under the care of an unmarried sister.

Roussos kept for himself only a small beach house he had inherited from an uncle located at exclusive Kavouri, a peninsula resembling a crab located on the Saronic coast fairly close to Athens. Although it was far from being luxurious, not matching at all the newer construction at Kavouri, the beach house was for several years his primary year-round official address; later he used it as a vacation home. The value of this house and its constantly appreciating land was also all he had of substantial value to leave as an inheritance for his son, Dimitri.

His real home now was with Victoria in the Kolonaki apartment she owned. Since she furnished the quarters, he paid for all their other living expenses from his relatively modest salary. Even high-ranking police directors did not earn much in Greece, and all he had to supplement his salary was the income from a few inherited investments.

There were, of course, opportunities for making extra money, big money, but not for him. There had been that wealthy Greek-American who told him he was setting up a bank account for him in Switzerland, no obligation attached, with an initial deposit of $100,000.

"Thanks," said Roussos, not even bothering to be offended since such offerings were commonplace. "But I do not need or want the money. Give it to some more worthy cause." There was no sense in reporting the attempted bribe since nothing would come of it at law. One man's word against another's, and even the way it was broached could make it sound ambiguous. Other bribes were proffered, not so large, but substantial. Eventually word got around that Roussos was an honest man. Some people wondered if he were not an honest fool.

The one luxury Roussos had allowed himself in the days following his separation from his wife and before he met Victoria was to make certain that Dimitri lacked nothing. Roussos had spent much of his money on the best schools for his son. When Dimitri entered the military academy, Roussos had the opportunity of saving a little money again. But after the son's graduation, the father insisted on supplementing Dimitri's meager starting salary as a military officer and helped him buy a co-op apartment in a high-cost area of Athens. He tried to help him out financially later when his son took a salary setback by resigning from the army and emulating his father to become a policeman, but Dimitri refused to accept any more of his charity. It was questionable whether the police director was more proud of his son or Dimitri more proud of his father.

Spyro Roussos's life had been mostly work. His recreation was reading and listening to operas. He had owned a sailboat that he seldom had time to use, and occasionally he had been able to go hunting with friends, but for the most part he was wedded to his work. His friends and relatives worried about him. Having time to pursue only a few interests in his personal life and being alone so much when not at work were not good for him. And then Victoria came into his life.

He knew of her before he met her. Sitting by himself on occasional visits to the opera, he watched her on stage and liked her voice and her person. He never imagined he would one day be living with her. Then she complained to the police about a stalker, and because she was a foreigner of some fame, the case came under the jurisdiction of the Department of Sensitive Investigations, but as one of their more routine matters. Nonetheless, Roussos decided to assign this one to himself.

He introduced himself to Victoria backstage. They quickly determined that her Greek was better than his very slight English, and so they spoke in Greek. She recognized that she was talking to a high-ranking officer and was impressed. She explained that a man had tried to force himself on her. He looked and spoke Greek, wore a thin moustache, was young, maybe twenty-two, had hazel eyes and fair hair with a distinct widow's peak, and was perhaps six feet one inch tall. Roussos quickly calculated and said, "About 185 centimeters, rather tall. About how much does he weigh?"

She was not good at estimating in metric, so she said, "About 200 pounds."

"Hmm, perhaps 90 or 91 kilograms. When and where did he accost you?"

"The first time was about a month ago outside the theater as I left by the stage door after a performance. I thought someone was following me and turned around. He stopped and said, "I just wanted to look at you. You are very beautiful."

"In Greek?"

"Yes. I thought he was just another flattering fan. I thanked him and continued on my way. He skipped up to my side—I mean he was literally skipping like a child—and gave me a very peculiar smile. He said something like, 'I love opera and you *are* opera, and that's why I've fallen in love with you.'"

"So he was an opera fan?"

"That's what he said. But I was a little concerned. I was going to walk home since Akademias Avenue is not many blocks from where I live on Kanari. But because of him I went to the front of the theater and took a taxi home. He was standing at the curb staring at me when the taxi drove off. I didn't think any more of it until one evening I left my apartment planning to walk to the theater when I saw him again, just staring at me. He walked behind me and told me again he loved me. I told him to go away and leave me alone. He said I should treat him nicer because he was a peaceful man unless someone insulted him and then he could become very angry. I quickly changed my mind about walking and took a taxi again. That night when the opera was over and we were taking our bows, I saw him in the audience, down front, staring a hole through me."

"Did you see him when you left the opera house?"

"Not this time, but after the next performance I saw him outside the theater."

"He was waiting for you at the stage door that night?"

"In back a little away from the stage door. He said nothing and kept his distance, but he followed me to the front and stayed there until I caught a taxi again. Then one afternoon when I was shopping at Diamantis Department Store, there he was standing in front of me. I told him that if he didn't leave me alone, I would go to the police. He turned and left. But the next day, yesterday, as I was about to leave my apartment, he was standing outside the door waiting for me. I don't know how he even got in the building, but sometimes people unlocking the front door are careless about who comes in behind them. I tried to close my door, but he was too quick for me, and he pushed it aside and rushed in. He seemed almost hysterical when he told me again that he loved me and must have me. He was sputtering, slobbering, drooling I guess. He said he knew I would probably destroy him, but he felt like a moth attracted to a flame and couldn't help himself. He grabbed me and put his arms around me and...." She started sobbing.

"I know this is difficult, but you must tell me all the facts."

"I'm sorry. He reminded me of my husband, I mean my ex-husband, who beat me and threatened to kill me. It was like *déjà vu*. I was terrified and screamed as loud as I could. The door was still open and a neighbor was passing by. That's when this man ran out. But I decided I had better call the police this time."

Roussos, already strongly attracted to the woman because of her voice and looks, was much touched by her story. Quivering as she was, she made him think of a lost kitten out in the cold. He wanted to put his arms about her, stroke her shoulders, and give her comfort, but he wondered what was coming over him. He had never felt that way about a complainant before. What was he doing at his age to think of this younger woman in such a romantic way? She must have been almost fifteen years his junior. Marriages between young women and older men were not uncommon in Greece, but somehow he felt too old for this beautiful, successful opera star, and too tied to his work. The only reason he had any right even to talk to her was that she had already been greatly discomforted by one unwelcome suitor. He asked her a few more questions and gave her his office and home telephone numbers in case she needed him. The last thing he did was to tell her of his plan for police coverage after her next performance.

The next night Roussos was at Victoria's performance in *Madama Butterfly*. How true to the part she was. Her singing reached into his breast to grab his heart and not let go. He couldn't take much more, and several times he thought about getting up and leaving. Why was he being so ridiculous? Above all, how could he blame this unwanted stalker for being enthralled by the singer as much as he himself was? Ah, but he did not reach to touch, did not threaten, did not frighten, no, there was a great difference. Even when he was standing in front of her, Roussos was admiring her at a great distance.

When the opera was over, Roussos left as the cast was taking its curtain calls. He hurried to the rear of the theater. Having deliberately dressed in dark clothes, he quietly slid against the unlit wall of an adjoining building until he reached the rear corner, which gave him a good view of the stage door. After a minute he noted with satisfaction that he was not alone. Across from the stage door, standing behind a parked car that served as cover, there was a man who could fit the description of Victoria Renfrew's unwanted suitor.

Others came out of the stage door and walked away. The stalker remained motionless, as did Roussos himself. Two women passed closed to him, and he was apprehensive lest they give an alarm on seeing him, but they were too absorbed in their conversation. Still more men and women, some carrying musical instruments, came out and walked away. Then Victoria appeared. She stood in the light made possible by the open door for just a second, but it seemed minutes to Roussos, and probably to the other man, too.

By prearrangement, Victoria walked toward Roussos and then past him out toward the street. The stalker disappeared around the car and then as a shadow silently hastened to approach Victoria from the rear. Just as he was passing Roussos, the police director's hands shot out and grabbed him by his coat collar, spinning him around and against the wall, which he hit with a loud thud. Although it had knocked the breath out of him, the man could still fight back, and he rushed at Roussos with lowered head and battering fists. The man was several inches taller than Roussos, outweighed him by perhaps twenty or more pounds, and was years younger.

But the police director had the advantage of experience. He knew how to fight with a view toward overcoming his opponent in the least amount of time possible. His knee came up like a sledgehammer against the man's crotch. He grabbed the man's right hand and spun him around again. Twisting his hand behind his back and with the aid of his knee in the small of the back, he threw him to the ground on his stomach, leapt upon his back, and quickly had him in handcuffs. He then blew a whistle, and three of his men came running.

Victoria, too, had stopped and turned around to watch her defender overcome her enemy. She rushed to Roussos and threw her arms around his neck, gasping to him that she hoped he wasn't hurt. No, he was fine. It was the other man who needed attention.

From that man's facial expression and crouched way of walking, it was plain who got the worse of the brief scuffle. As the stalker was being led to a police car, he turned to Victoria and snarled, "I'll get you, you whore. I'll make you pay for this, you ungrateful slut. You aren't clean enough to wipe my ass."

Victoria, visibly shaken, accompanied Roussos and his prisoner to a nearby police station, where the man was identified, signed in, and put in a cell. "Pavlo Xynos is his name," said Roussos, "according to the identification in his wallet. Have you heard that name before?"

"No, never. But that's the man, the one who's been frightening me for a month. Now I can sleep more easily. Thank you so very much, Mr. Police Director."

Roussos was gratified. He drove her to her apartment building. While still in the car, she reached in her pocketbook for her keys. Looking at Roussos, she said, "You were so brave. But why did you fight him all by yourself? Why didn't you let your men do it?"

He replied to her in a low voice and with downcast eyes, "Perhaps I wanted to impress you."

She turned her face away, opened the car door, and said, "Thank you for the ride, and thank you for everything." He watched while she unlocked the outer door to let herself in.

Two days later he telephoned to ask her to lunch, explaining that he would like to keep her informed on the latest developments. They both knew that this was something normally done in an office, but they pretended that lunch between a policeman and a stalker's victim was the most normal thing in the world. At lunch he told her that she should be prepared to testify soon at Xynos's trial.

"Must I?"

"Either that, or they'll have to let him go. Only you can convict him."

She testified at the trial, and Xynos was found guilty of harassment and assault and sentenced to a year in prison, but he had to serve only three months, and was put on probation for the remaining nine months. After the trial Victoria clutched Roussos's arm and said that she wanted to talk to him. They went to a coffee shop and sat at an outside table.

"What happens when he has finished his term?" she asked.

"Nothing, I hope. He's a student at the university and will probably just continue his studies. You have the advantage that while he's on probation, he will have to keep away from you or complete the remaining nine months of his sentence."

"Will that hold him back?"

"We'll have to see. But if you need me for anything whatsoever, please call me. Remember, my office is only two blocks away. I'll be there if you need me. If I have to confront Xynos again, he won't get off so easily next time."

His office was only two blocks away, but his home in Kavouri where he stayed at night was far from his office. He invited Victoria to his beach house once on a Sunday. It was a modest place with two bedrooms and a combined living-dining room, plus kitchen and bath. However, it had an unobstructed view of the sea from its house-wide veranda, which the police director had furnished with an outdoor table and two comfortable chairs. They sat out on the veranda drinking the pine-flavored white wine called *retsina* and eating shrimp with chunks of Greek bread. In the distance they could see ships and boats of all sizes plying between Cape Sounion and Piraeus.

They talked of many things. He told her of his separation from his wife. "I stopped the divorce because I thought it might seem too vindictive. She had never loved me and she betrayed me with other men, but I couldn't be mean to her when she was down. She has moments of lucidity, and I'm told that whenever my name comes up, she curses me. But since I thought I would never marry again, I wasn't so concerned about a divorce."

Victoria told him of her ordeal leading to her own divorce. "He used to stay out getting drunk, then come home and pick a fight with me. He got pleasure out of slapping me around. Sometimes he would take off his belt and threaten to use it on me. Later he did—I still have marks on my waist. Once he put a knife against my throat and threatened to kill me. He finally stomped out of the house and didn't come back that night. The next morning I took my personal possessions and left the house forever. I started divorce proceedings immediately. Some mutual friends told me that he was searching for me, but he didn't contest the divorce and I never saw him again. Still, I tremble every time I think of him. I never used to have fear like this."

"He can't touch you here."

"Probably not, but look what I have instead: a madman has attached himself to me now. I like a simple life and can't understand why it has become so complicated for me."

"Perhaps," he said, "you are too beautiful. You arouse men to their worse instincts."

She laughed. "Should I get plastic surgery to become less beautiful?"

He drove her back to her apartment and saw her to the door, and for the first time, they kissed.

*   *   *   *

After Xynos had spent three months in jail, he was released and went back to his classes at the university. Less than a month after that, he murdered a professor and became a fugitive. Roussos assigned a plainclothes officer to keep a discreet eye on Victoria at her apartment and at the opera house.

But Xynos had become cleverer in the meantime. He still stalked her and evaded the police at the same time. No longer would he wait for her after a performance at the opera, but sometimes he would arrange to see her en route to the theater, making sure that she also got a glimpse of him. He had also taken to disguising himself. Once coming home Victoria saw a bearded man sitting at the coffee shop across the square from her apartment house; she was certain it was Pavlo Xynos only because the wind took off the hat he was wearing and displayed his hairline with its unique widow's peak.

By the time she crossed the street to get the attention of the plainclothesman, the bearded man had disappeared.

The worse time was when she returned from a performance one night to find him sitting in her living room. He had climbed the fire escape and pried open a back window. He had a knife in his hand and told her not to scream.

She was almost too paralyzed to scream. His knife seemed just like the one her ex-husband used to carry. She gazed at him without blinking, immobilized except for her trembling. The muscles in her throat tightened. It was as if she were staring at a cobra and dared not move for fear she would provoke it to strike.

"I am not going to hurt you," he said, "if you will be reasonable. My only sin is that I love you. Do not fear me. Show me compassion and I will be your slave." His face was contorted into a weird grin so that he resembled a child making faces while playing. Standing, he closed his knife, put it in his pocket, and took a step toward her.

Her heart was pounding as if it were being hit by a hammer from within. The closer he came, the more she was certain she was going to die. "No, don't touch me!"

He took another step.

Her voice was hoarse as she said, "I haven't done anything to you. Please leave me alone."

He stopped his approach, his eyes widened, and he replied, "I have killed a man for you. I would do anything for you."

"If you mean it, just go away. That's all I want you to do for me." She was amazed at herself for even being able to get the words out. Now she felt she was able to move, and she took a step backwards.

"Yes, I will go now, as you say. I will do as you ask. If only you will kiss me first, one little kiss, not even passionate if you don't feel that way yet, just friendly. Show me you don't hate me by giving me one little friendly kiss." He closed the distance between them with two forward paces.

She couldn't. She couldn't. It was her husband all over again advancing on her. Oddly enough, she believed that he really would go if she allowed him that kiss, but it was impossible for her to even think of kissing him. He was anathema. He became the amalgamation of every fear she'd ever had. It was as if electric charges were emanating from his body to repulse her from him. She could feel herself being pushed further back by the evil aura of the magnetic force that veiled him.

He continued forward as she retreated. Just as he reached her with arms out-stretched for an embrace, she spit in his face. The effect was astounding. From pleading, beseeching, praying, his face first turned to featureless stone. Then Victoria saw in slow motion the mouth twisting into a grimace of rage, the eyes burning with a penetrating hatred, the nostrils flaring, the muscles of the chin and neck tightening, his teeth now showing like fangs, and his hand reaching for his knife and clicking it open again. He raised his hand with the knife and slashed it toward her. At the last possible moment he turned the fist that held the knife so that his wrist careened off her face, the blade not touching her. But the blow produced an agonizing hurt and she saw blood dripping from her face onto her blouse. She staggered back until she was supported by the wall. A framed picture dropped to the floor and the glass broke.

He approached her again staring at the blood on her chin, and suddenly he dropped the knife. His face underwent another metamorphosis to display a shocked little boy look. His mouth opened widely in surprise.

"I am sorry. I did not mean…. I would not hurt you. Please, you must forgive me. I will go now. I will leave you alone. For now." He picked up his knife, closed it, and returned it to his pocket. Backing away toward the kitchen, his face still displaying shock, he looked as if he might cry. She heard him open a window as he yelled to her, "I will come back for you, my darling." And he was gone.

Victoria's nightmare was over for the moment, and she quickly caught control of herself. Rushing to the front of the apartment, she opened a window looking out on the street. There was a car parked on the square with a man leaning on it from the sidewalk. She yelled to him, "*Itan edo. Efyge ap' to parathyro piso apo to ktirio.*" He was here. He got away using the window behind the building.

It was enough to put the plainclothesman in action. He ran toward the alley beside the building, and then Victoria couldn't see him any more.

She collapsed on a sofa, rested a moment, then telephoned Spyro Roussos at his beach house. Speeding to her as he did, he still needed more than an hour before he could join her. Again she collapsed, this time in his arms. Roussos tried to do the double duty of comforting her while making contact with his men via his cell phone.

"They are following him up toward Mount Lykavittos," he told her. He put both arms around her and held her tightly. She entwined her arms about him and took comfort from the support of his strong chest.

After a moment, Roussos continued. "He made a mistake in going uphill. They will surely catch him. There are at least a dozen men after him now." He led her to the sofa and had her sit down. "You need something to drink." He remembered where she kept a few bottles, and he poured out two small glasses of Metaxas seven-star brandy. She drank hers in two swallows.

"You must get some sleep," he said. "I'll stay here on the sofa until he's caught. If I have to leave, I'll let you know."

Pavlo Xynos was caught that night. He was tried first for the crime of murder. His plea was not guilty by reason of both self-defense and insanity. His excuse was that he had tried to talk to his professor about his obsession with Victoria, hoping to get understanding and encouragement. When the professor told him he must leave her alone and never see her again, they first argued and then fought. During the fight Xynos took out his knife and killed the man. It was justifiable homicide, he yelled to the courtroom, because he could not help himself. He was sentenced to twenty years in prison. As the guards led him away, he yelled a death threat to the then Minister of Public Security, Antoni Antonidis, and turned to smile leeringly at Victoria, "As for you, know that I will come back for the kiss you owe me."

Victoria did not want to face what she thought would be more public embarrassment if she testified against Xynos for assaulting her. She persuaded the public prosecutor to drop the charge, feeling that the twenty-year sentence was sufficient. Police Director Roussos, using his influence with Minister Antonidis, had been able to keep Victoria's name hardly mentioned in the newspapers.

Peace was not yet to be hers. Within six months Xynos had escaped from prison. Roussos told Victoria to prepare to leave the country until Xynos was caught. The man was too wily for the police to be able to guarantee her safety. Then the police learned that Xynos had fled the country, and Roussos informed Victoria.

"You should be safe now. We heard that he is in a Near Eastern country and is in training as a terrorist. Now he will have police forces all over the world looking for him. I doubt that he will come back to Greece."

So he told her, but in his heart Roussos feared that Xynos would return. He prayed that he was wrong.

It was not long after the trial that Spyro Roussos moved in with Victoria Renfrew. They owed that much to Pavlo Xynos that he had brought them together. For that they were glad.

*   *   *   *

All these happenings seemed so far away as Roussos and Victoria sipped wine and ate pistachio nuts on their balcony above Kolonaki Square. The evening was warm, but there was enough breeze coming down from Mount Lykavittos to make them feel comfortable. The city lights displayed the amazing extent of Athens as a sight of perpetual beauty and helped to relax them that much more.

He let her catch him up on all she had done during her American trip, the success of the performances she gave, the newspaper reviews, the people she met, and how much she had missed him. Then he told her of all that had happened of interest in Athens while she was gone. This led to the experience he had had with Minister Achilles Petropoulos.

"That was a horrible way to treat you," she said. "And imposing this minion of his on you as your deputy, how could he do it?"

"Ministers have great discretionary power as long as they are in office. Of course they come and go. This one is too much a megalomaniac to last long. But while he's in office…"

He then went on to tell her about the specific assignments Petropoulos had given him, the Greek-American swindler Nick Savvas, and General Zavalas's returning from exile. He saved for last the one that he knew would affect her directly and perhaps crush her. For that one he just didn't know how to begin, and he remained silent for a long time, holding his glass up to the light and contemplating the wine inside.

"When you do that, *agapi mou*," my love, Victoria said, "I know you're deeply troubled. Whatever it is, we can discuss it, can't we?"

He smiled at her. "You're right, of course. There is one more item, *carissima*, and truthfully I've been afraid to tell you."

"What, Spyro? Why afraid?"

"I don't know how to express it, but here it is. Pavlo Xynos has returned and is in hiding somewhere in Athens."

She felt as if all the air had been sucked out of her. Clutching her hand to her chest, she screamed, "Oh, no! It can't be. But you said…. Omigod!" She let her head sink to her bosom and began trembling all over.

"I know I said it would be doubtful that he would come back, but I was wrong. However, we have the largest manhunt out for him that I've seen in many years. And now I'm justified in having continuous coverage on you by a trained team. There will be at least three men guarding you day and night."

She had moved to snuggle up to him and place her head against his shoulder. Raising herself to kiss him, she said, "I love you, Spyro, you know I do. But we must be honest. He *will* find a way to get at me, won't he?"

CHAPTER 6

▼

Bob Jensen walked into Ambassador Edward Atherton's office on Monday morning fully expecting to get his ass chewed out. His expectation was not disappointed.

On the walnut-paneled wall behind Atherton, flanked by American flags were two large framed and inscribed photographs: one of the president of the United States on a visitor's left and the other of the secretary of state on the right. A persimmon leather sofa flanked by lamp tables and six matching overstuffed chairs rested majestically across the room from his desk, all making that part of the room look more like a gentlemen's club than an office. On the wall above the sofa was an oil painting of an oblique aerial view of Washington, D.C. centering on the triangle formed by the White House, the Washington Monument, and the Lincoln Memorial.

"You weasel, you halfwit, you nincompoop," began Ned Atherton, "where do you keep your brains anyway? Where is my niece, you asshole?"

"I don't know, sir. Like I told you last night, I had the airport security people searching hours for her, and they were convinced she was not in the airport. All I can say for sure is that she's missing."

A secretary brought in two cups of coffee. The ambassador looked at her, then said, "I only need one. Take the other back."

The secretary reached for one cup and saucer, but Atherton waved her away. "No, let him have some coffee. I'm pissed off but not petty."

He took a sip of coffee and continued. "I wasn't tremendously upset when you phoned last night, Jensen, because this is just the kind of foolhardy stunt that Marilyn would pull."

"You weren't, sir?" Jensen asked in a somewhat incredulous voice. "Oh, sorry for the interruption."

The ambassador glared at him for a few moments, then continued. "She's got a history for going places without telling people. But even she must have realized that she can't behave in a foreign country the same as in the States. And especially in these troubled times. So I've been doing some checking myself."

"I'm sure you've been very thorough, sir."

"You are, are you? Well, I'm not. But I did call her mother, and her mother tells me that she drove Marilyn to the airport and she had to be on that plane. It was non-stop and she was on the manifest, so she had to have arrived in Athens yesterday."

"That's what the airport police told me." Jensen was almost certain that before the interview was over, he'd be sent back to the States in disgrace. It wasn't the first time that he had fouled up with the ambassador. He looked at his coffee, not really wanting to start drinking from it, but reluctant to leave it untouched. Finally he took a sip, clutching the handle tightly so as not to spill any.

"How many ways can you foul up?"

Jensen paused as if he were thinking, but before he could answer, the ambassador spoke again. "Let me count the ways. You get two flat tires on the embassy car that's assigned to you. We give you another one, and you say you got high-jacked, but that's not proven. The police find you lying drunk in the road beside your car…"

"Not drunk, sir. They said I reeked of wine. That wine was poured on me. I didn't have anything to drink at all yesterday, at least until I got home late last night." He had needed a triple Scotch and soda after he phoned the ambassador.

"That's your story. You get to the airport late looking like a tramp, and you lose my niece. What can you say for yourself?"

"She may be kidnapped, sir."

"Oh, great, she's not missing, she's kidnapped. How soon before we get a ransom note?"

"You must believe me. The first car may or may not have had real flat tires. I mean legitimate flat tires, you know, caused accidentally, not on purpose. But much more likely they had deliberately been made flat just to delay me. Certainly with the second car, I was set up. I was trapped by trucks from behind and in front, and when I went out to do something about it, I was hit on the head and knocked out. Someone poured wine on me and that's how the police found me. When I showed them my identification, they helped me get to the airport, but it was too late. Your niece was gone."

"She could have been disgusted with you for not showing up and taken an airport limo or taxi to the city center."

"I have the airport police working on that. But doesn't it seem more likely that I was stopped from getting to the airport on time for a reason? And the only reason I can think of is that someone wanted to kidnap her. More than someone, there must have been a gang. You say she's intelligent. When I didn't show up, wouldn't she have had the sense to telephone the embassy if she could?"

"In any case, what do you suggest we do about it?"

"I plan to contact the Greek Department of Sensitive Investigations this morning and ask for their help."

"They catch spies, international crooks, and plotting politicians, don't they? What do they have to do with a kidnapped American girl?"

"They also have responsibility for any serious matter involving a foreigner."

"DSI, that's Roussos. I understand he's competent and honest. How are your relations with him?"

"Er, fair, sir. As you say, he's both good and able."

"Only fair, huh? Okay, what did you do to make your relations anything less than excellent, superb, or outstanding? Let it out."

"Well, there was a little mishap the last time I saw him. You remember the Nick Savvas case? Well, you know how you always get a little cup of Turkish coffee when you enter a Greek office for liaison…."

"Greek coffee, Jensen. We're in Greece and even I've been here long enough to learn the Greeks don't like to call things Turkish. They don't even have Turkish delight candy any more; now it's Greek delight."

"Yes, sir, sorry, sir. Well to make a long story short, I spilled some Greek coffee on his desk and it wet some papers and some went into his lap, and he got up and yelled and swore."

"Should I send someone else? Is that what you're suggesting?"

"No, sir, I'll go. I've got to make my amends with him sometime."

"Yes, but where my niece is concerned?"

"No one at the embassy's had as much experience in dealing with the Greek police as I have, and if your niece really has been kidnapped, you'll need someone with a lot of experience dealing with Roussos. He's well, you know, enigmatic. You have to know how to read him."

"And you do, huh?"

"Well, I know how to take it when he calls me a *gamoto kerata*; that is, whether he means it or is just excited over the circumstances, such as when I spilled the Turkish—I mean Greek—coffee all over him."

"So it's all over him now, is it? And what's a *gamoto kera*-something anyway?"

"A fucking bastard, sir."

"You certainly are. Jensen, you're the biggest fuck-up in this embassy. But you're also the best investigator that we've got—other than those spooks down the hall whose name we don't mention. I might have to get them in on this yet, but I hope not because this kind of thing is not exactly their line of business. In the meantime you get over to DSI and start some action on finding my niece no matter where she is. Understand?"

Closing the door of the ambassador's office behind him, Jensen wiped his brow, then walked nonchalantly past the secretary, giving her one of his best smiles.

"How'd it go?" she said.

"Piece of cake. He loves my ass."

*   *   *   *

Police Director Roussos considered his own office spacious, even though it was only one-tenth the size of the minister's office. From his one large window he could look out on Kanari Street, and see buildings that were not far from the apartment he shared with Victoria. Aside from his own desk and chair and the four guest chairs that were arranged around the desk to face him, the only other furnishings were a bookcase, a confidential file cabinet, and a small computer table with computer, printer, and lamp.

On the wall behind him were photographs of the President of the Greek Republic in the center with the prime minister on the right and an empty place where the photograph of the most recent past Minister of Public Security had been; Roussos was a little late in getting a photograph of the new minister. On the opposite wall there was a large photograph of his grandfather surrounded by smaller portraits that Greek and foreign officials had autographed for him and a number of framed letters of commendation. On his desk where he could always look to see it was a small photograph of Victoria in the role of *The Merry Widow*. Inasmuch as his son Dimitri worked for him, he did not think it proper to display a photograph of him.

His secretary sat outside in an office that also served as a waiting room for visitors. There had been a conference room across the hall, but Roussos had had it converted to accommodate six more desks for staff personnel to alleviate some of the overcrowding. Under his direction the DSI had grown greatly in size, yet there was still far more demand for their services than could be filled. It was an illustration of the old adage that a job well done created a demand to have more jobs done.

In addition to the various branches, sections, and staffs handling the routine work of the department, Roussos had a select team of three investigators working on those matters where he personally took charge. This personal team was called the *Eidikos Monas*, Special Unit, and it had wide latitude in carrying out its assignments. It could also draw on the other DSI groups whenever the three unit members felt they needed assistance.

Ten days following his interview with Minister Petropoulos, Roussos held a meeting with his Special Unit sitting in front of his desk. In one of the chairs sat the senior member, *Astynomos A'*, Chief Superintendent, Pano Maniatis, who had been with Roussos for years and was of unquestioned loyalty. Maniatis was an old-line police officer, not a deep thinker, but one who led by experience, and he had experienced everything.

In the center was *Astynomos B'*, Superintendent, Eleni Karolou. A university graduate, Karolou was highly trained in finance and technology, and she was most successful in resolving various types of "new crime," such as those involving computers. She was also very good at developing personal relationships with people.

The third member of the unit was *Astynomos B'*, Superintendent, Dimitri Roussos, whose position as the chief's son was perhaps the most difficult one in DSI. Because he thought so highly of his son, Roussos insisted on greater effort from him than from any other officer. Dimitri spoke several languages fluently, including English, and when still in the army he had served in the Greek military attaché's office in London and had attended a training course in the United States. His language ability and his pleasant personality resulted in his being frequently used for liaison with foreigners. He was also one of the most handsome men in all Athens.

Today the police director had called a meeting to hear progress reports on a number of assignments, including the three special ones he had been given by Minister Achilles Petropoulos. As senior officer, Chief Superintendent Pano Maniatis spoke first.

"Regarding the fugitive Pavlo Xynos, *tipote*." Nothing. "*Nichts. Nada. Rien. Nyet.* Absolutely nothing, Chief, and I must ask, how reliable do you think that report from the Americans is? We can find no trace at all of Xynos's being in Greece."

Roussos said, "It is to be expected that the most important criminal of all will be the hardest to find. The fact that he is a fugitive in itself is good cause for him to stay in hiding. We cannot expect to find him at a sidewalk coffee shop."

"Except," said Superintendent Eleni Karolou, "that he was good at disguises even before he got his terrorist training." There was usually a cheerful lilt in her voice, even when she was serious. "Can't we expect him to be a master of disguises now? I could make a mistake, but he might be sitting out at a sidewalk coffee shop at this moment, perhaps one within walking distance from here."

"You're seldom mistaken, Eleni," said Roussos, "but it had better not be any of the ones around Kolonaki Square. Pano, you still have three well-trained men keeping their eyes on Victoria Renfrew with relief teams for continuous coverage? Victoria is the magnet that will draw Xynos, but we must make sure that she is well protected."

"I have two men in front and one in the rear of her apartment building. Whenever she goes to the theater or shopping, one of my men will go with her. When she comes back, they will check out the inside of your—er, her—apartment thoroughly before she enters." A smile appeared on his dolphin-like lips. "You remember, just as before when we had only one guard?" He hesitated, then added, "And he came in the apartment when you were taking a bath?"

Roussos ignored the last remark. "Good, Pano. You know the golden word of police work: persistence. And you have five men assigned to protect Minister Antoni Antonidis?"

"Yes, sir, five men, three by day and two at night. In the case of Miss Renfrew, I have assumed that you will be her security in the late night and early morning."

"Your assumptions are usually right, Pano. All right, next, Eleni"

"I have formed an acquaintance with an attractive young woman named Marika who works for General Zavalas as a cook and maid. So far I have asked for nothing, but I try to elicit information from her. She has mixed views on the general. On the one hand, he is easy-going. He treats her kindly and does not insult her as so many employers routinely do. Neither does he attempt to use her as a concubine. On the other hand, he is tight with his money, and he has her render a strict accounting for everything she buys for him. She has no opportunity for making the extra money that so many servants rely on. The general even checks the amount of ground coffee each day to make sure that she does not steal any to sell."

"Interesting," said Roussos. "He did not have a reputation for being a miser before. This could mean he is very short of money. We might later put this potential opening to good use. What do you plan for your next step with this maid?"

"I will try to convince her to let me in the apartment so I can make a clandestine search. I think I can also have her give me advance information on his movements and contacts. One good thing, he does not seem to be very security conscious."

"That might mean he has nothing to hide. This is still a very nebulous case, and I almost have to apologize for assigning it to you, Eleni. It seems it might be more political than criminal. I don't like the looks of it. Nor do I like entering his apartment, but as long as the maid lets you in and we don't have to break in, I guess it will be all right. Let me get back to you, but I want to check with Dimitri now."

Turning to his son, the police director asked, "Now for our international swindler. What have you found out, Dimitri?"

"Since we've had to release him, I assume Savvas will resort to his old tricks. He hides his true interests under an avalanche of contacts. He visits perhaps a dozen businessmen everyday. We'll continue as before with those of his contacts we think we can trust. Several businessmen have already informed us that Savvas tells them he represents an American or British or other foreign company, tailoring his story to meet their needs. He claims that he can save them a lot of money on exported goods by having the end part of the manufacturing process done in the foreign country. No one that we know of has made a deal with him yet, and he has not yet asked for any money."

"About what percentage of these businessmen do you think we can trust to be completely honest with us?"

"Completely honest? Probably about a quarter of them. Relatively honest, perhaps 90 per cent. I have a list of about 20 people he has talked to since we released him."

"Twenty? *Po, po, po!*" Well, well, well! "He's been busy, this little man."

"I don't see how we can do anything until he obtains money from a victim and has actually committed a swindle. With the attitude of the new minister, we'll have to have a tight case against Savvas."

"You're right, of course. We need a break there. Some businessman, informant or not, will hand over money to Xynos and we'll catch him in the act. So far, though, it looks as if I'll have very little to tell the minister on any of these cases. All we can do is to keep after…"

He was interrupted by the telephone. Knowing that his secretary would not have put the call through unless it was important, Roussos picked up the receiver.

When he finished speaking to the caller, the police director turned to his assistants and said it would be necessary to continue the meeting later in the morning. Robert Jensen from the American Embassy was on his way over to discuss an urgent matter concerning the niece of the American ambassador.

"Is it one of these awkward, embarrassing matters," said Maniatis, "where the niece has come to Greece and got herself in some kind of *endiaferousa katastasi?*" Interesting situation (pregnant).

"I don't know yet."

Maniatis said, "Did I ever tell you about my great uncle's daughter who eloped with her boyfriend? He had his evil way with her and then abandoned her."

"I imagine your uncle was relieved when she came back," said Eleni Karolou, speaking with a note of suspicion in her voice.

"Oh, no," said Maniatis, giving emphasis to the negative by clicking his tongue against the roof of his mouth. "He felt disgraced because she was no longer a virgin. And later her brother killed her with a knife for bringing dishonor to the family."

"I thought so!" said Eleni, the look on her face turning to anger and disgust. "Tell me what happened to her brother."

"The court found him not guilty because it happened in hot blood."

"And how long was this after the fact?" said Eleni.

A shrug of the shoulders. "Oh, three, maybe four months."

Eleni's facial muscles strained with rage and her usually pleasant voice lowered an octave. "I tell you," she said to Roussos, "Greece is going to have to change. We cannot have these barbaric customs any more."

"Eleni, my dear," said Maniatis laughing, "you're going to make some man a wonderful husband one of these days."

"The day I get married you can have your bloodthirsty nephew slit my throat."

"Attention," said Roussos, "the American will be here any minute. All of you go."

*   *   *   *

As Jensen entered the office, Roussos buzzed for the man who fetched the coffee. He spoke to Jensen in Greek. "How will you have...? Ah, yes, I remember now. Plain, no sugar at all. Yes, I remember very well the last time you were here."

"Well, you don't have to get coffee just for me. Actually, I can't say that I like your kind of…. I mean, I've already had enough coffee this morning."

"Look the *kafetzis* is here already," said Roussos. Turning to the coffee man, who had just entered, he said, "*Ena scheto kai ena variglyko.*" One plain and one heavily sugared.

Jensen, who knew no liaison meeting could proceed without a cup of strong syrupy Greek coffee in its mini-demitasse cup, shrugged his shoulders. "Well, perhaps I could have one more." Knowing that his reputation for dropping everything he touched was well justified, Jensen ordered himself to be extremely careful with the coffee when it arrived. He explained to Roussos that his purpose was to seek help because the ambassador's niece was missing. "I have verified that she got on an Olympic plane in Washington and that it was non-stop, so she had to get off at Ellinikon."

"What other investigation have you made?"

"No other, except that I asked the airport police last night to see if they could find her. The passport control and immigration forms had already been sent downtown. Perhaps you could get them. I also checked with the American Embassy staff to see if she had made any effort to contact the embassy."

"Very well. We consider this most important, and I will put some of my best people on it. We'll check with all the hospitals and police stations. We'll question every taxi, limousine, and bus driver who was at the airport last night. Of course, we'll talk to immigration and customs officials and Olympic personnel. If she landed at Ellinikon, there will be some official trace of her. Ah, here comes the *kafetzis.*"

The coffee man returned, this time gently swinging his coffee-laden tray from three rigid metal rods attached to a handle that he held with one hand. Jensen was used to seeing this tripod-like arrangement, which was in effect a stabilizer that kept the tray steady and the coffee from spilling.

Jensen accepted the cup of coffee and placed it in front of him on the edge of the police director's desk. Taking an envelope from his inner jacket pocket, he gave Roussos a photograph and a written description of Marilyn Pickering.

Roussos said, "She is attractive. Was she traveling alone?"

"Yes. She was coming to visit the ambassador for a month. She doesn't speak Greek and she has never been here before. In fact, she's had very little experience in traveling outside the United States."

"This is a delicate question, but it is necessary to know. Is she given to…what we might call wild adventures? Has she ever disappeared before? Do you know what type of person she is?"

"The ambassador assured me she is a quiet woman," Jensen lied, "and when I talked to her mother this morning on the phone, I was told that she was as good as engaged in the United States and will probably get married not long after her return."

"Well, there is little at present to help us decide if she is lost, has amnesia, took some other plane out after she arrived in Greece, or was the victim of foul play. You know that here in Athens we are always alert to terrorist activities, so we will not treat this matter lightly. Please tell your ambassador that we will do all possible."

"Please contact me the minute you learn anything."

"Of course. Ah, but you have not had any of your coffee. Well, leave it there. I hope to telephone you soon."

As Jensen closed the door behind him, pleased with himself that he had not spilled the coffee, Roussos reached to bring the still-filled cup away from the perilous edge of the desk, but stumbled, and dropped it on the floor. The cup broke and the coffee splattered all over the rug. Jensen was fortunate that he did not see the latest impression he had made on his important liaison contact.

✳   ✳   ✳   ✳

When his three assistants returned, Roussos explained to them that they had a new top priority. He gave them details on the missing American woman, then said, "I will handle this myself with assistance from Dimitri."

They discussed other cases, then came back to the original three.

Eleni Karolou said, "I don't understand about these papers that General Zavalas is said to have. Are we supposed to get them without permission from the general?"

"I don't understand either," said Roussos with a wry smile. "You have an onerous task, Eleni, but do the best you can. At this time don't do anything that might require a court order. Have you found out who will be the publisher of his book?"

"I haven't confirmed yet that he is even writing a book. My contact hasn't mentioned it. I should think that he'd be in his study writing all day, but according to the maid he spends most of his days in the coffee shops talking to old friends from the time of the colonels' dictatorship."

The outer door suddenly opened with a loud metallic noise, and Jason Thanos rushed into the room, the shoulder straps of his tunic displaying a wreath and two pips as evidence of his recent promotion. "I am reporting for duty, Police

Director Roussos." His disheveled hair hung from his forehead to partly hide his eyes. A long, dour face, though still retaining some of the good looks that he must have had in his youth, held dark brown recessed eyes and a scraggy moustache, giving him the appearance of a cadaver in a pathologist's laboratory.

"I wasn't expecting you until next week."

"I always like to give something extra." He looked around at the officers sitting in front of Roussos. "Let me see, who have we here? Maniatis I know."

"How are you, Jason," said Pano. "Congratulations on your promotion. I haven't seen you since my cousin's funeral."

"Ah, yes, your poor unfortunate cousin. Wasn't it his girlfriend's husband who killed him? I grieve with you." With a nonchalant motion he offered his hand to Pano while his eyes continued to stare at the others. "Ah, the beautiful Eleni Karolou, and now a superintendent. We must celebrate your promotion. We have something in common, don't we, my dear Eleni, aside from promotions—we both like pretty girls."

He offered his hand, which Eleni just barely touched with hers before withdrawing it as if she had been holding a scorpion. She said, "Perhaps the difference is that pretty girls like me in return."

Ignoring the remark, Thanos said, "Now who is this handsome Adonis? Can it be the army officer who changed teams to fight alongside his father?"

The thirty-year-old Dimitri, who was already sitting at attention, straightened up even more. His lips tightened and his hands held the seat of his chair, as if he were trying to hold himself down.

Thanos continued. "Ah, yes, of course, young Roussos. I guess I need say no more." He did not offer his hand to Dimitri, but merely waved at him.

"How interesting," he went on. "We are all in uniform, rare for DSI—is it not?—and between us we represent so many ranks." Maniatis as a chief superintendent wore a wreath and one pip, while the lesser superintendents, Eleni and Dimitri, each had three pips and no wreath. "Only the single pip of a plain inspector and the two pips of a chief inspector are missing. Ah, but young Roussos has moved up quickly. I'd watch out, Eleni, he might exchange two of his pips for a wreath before you do."

Dimitri's grimace told how much restraint he was forcing on himself.

Having dramatically reminded the others of his own newly acquired rank and of the subordinate positions of all but the police director himself, Thanos strode over to the empty chair and sat. "Now what were we discussing?"

"I had not expected to have you present for this discussion, *Kyrie Astynomike Ypodiefthynti*," said Roussos in an even tone, "but now that you're here, please be gracious enough to take a seat," thus reminding all present that Thanos had rudely presumed to sit down without first having been invited. "Eleni, you will forget any assignments we discussed earlier. Now that the police underdirector is here, I must reconsider assignments. Mr. Thanos, you are perhaps aware of the three cases Minister Petropoulos assigned me ten days ago?"

"I am indeed," said Thanos with the sober aspect of a man who knows he has done his duty.

"Then, since you did not hear of them from me, you must have talked to the minister before coming here. No matter. I will fill you in." Roussos proceeded to review all the cases for Thanos, except that he did not mention the matter of the American ambassador's missing niece. "I am personally assigning you, Mr. Police Underdirector, to handle the delicate matter of General Zavalas and those sup- posedly damaging letters. If you need one or two police constables to assist you, you can get them from Alfa Team. You are specifically ordered not to take any action that we cannot justify under our charter. Do you understand? And if you are not acquainted yet with the legal limitations on our operating authority, I suggest—no, order—you to read the appropriate general rules before you do any- thing else."

Thanos looked perplexed. Waving his hands in the air excitedly, he said, "But Mr. Police Director, Minister Petropoulos has strong feelings about senior offic- ers getting involved in detail work. We are supposed to direct the work of others, not stick our own oars in, so to speak."

"Mr. Police Underdirector, I am perfectly aware of the minister's views. But I am your superior officer. If you feel you cannot obey me, you have my permis- sion to go over my head to my immediate superior, Chief of Athens Police Major General Fotidis, or to his superior, the supreme Chief of All Greek Police Lieu- tenant General Dimos, or even to the minister himself. Is that your wish?"

Thanos face reddened. "No, no, I have no desire to go over your head." He had gone too far and he knew it. All the higher people, even the minister, in any dispute between Roussos and Thanos would have been obliged to side with Roussos, and Thanos could face possible demotion and transfer to some dull pro- vincial place. "I just thought you would want me to spend my time becoming acquainted with all the outstanding cases so that I would be in a position to take over from you." His face seemed to grow redder and he quickly added, "I mean, if necessary, sir. I mean, such as if you might be ill, sir."

"I understand your good intentions, Thanos. Now here is the information I have collected so far on Zavalas, including the pertinent papers that the minister sent over. Superintendent Karolou can also tell you what she has learned so far.

Take the file now and study it in your office, which, in case you don't know, is on the second floor. That will be all."

Thanos stood with his head considerably lower than when he entered, and he took the file with obvious reluctance. Straightening up, he saluted and left.

After he had closed the door, Roussos turned to his aides and spoke in a sharp voice, "Get rid of those grins, all three of you. Jason Thanos is your superior officer and you will treat him with respect."

Maniatis was the only one who dared to speak after that. "With due respect, I was not exactly snickering, sir. I was rejoicing that you now have a capable deputy to take some of the burdens off your shoulders."

"Very well, Pano. I rejoice at your rejoicing. Now, Eleni, since Thanos is taking over your case, your new assignment will be to take over the Nick Savvas case from Dimitri. Dimitri, I want you to take full charge of the case involving the disappearance of the American ambassador's niece. That way I will not have to offend the minister and get directly involved."

To Maniatis he said, "I'm not sure how the ambassador's case might necessitate some later re-ordering of these assignments, but tracking down Xynos is of paramount importance, taking equal priority with finding the American ambassador's niece. You know Xynos has threatened—no, sworn—to assassinate Minister of Scientific Development Antoni Antonidis. You must prevent this at any cost. In addition to the men protecting Antonidis at his residence and office, have surveillance men from Vita Team keep their eyes on Antonidis. Xynos eventually will be following him, too. I don't want to tell you your business, but if I were doing it, I would have a loose team following Antonidis and a crack team following the loose one at a distance. We could then hope that Xynos would place himself between our two teams. And, of course, don't forget Xynos's fanatic interest in Victoria Renfrew."

Finally to Dimitri he said, "Here is the photograph of the missing woman, and here is her description. Get to work on it immediately."

*   *   *   *

The Special Unit had no sooner left than the secretary announced that Minister of Scientific Development Antonidis was in the outer office and wished to see the police director.

"It's so good to see you, my old friend," said Antonidis as he swept into the office, extending his right hand for a handshake and his left arm to place around Roussos's shoulder so he could pat him on the back. It was half a politician's greeting and half a sincere expression of appreciation for a high-ranking officer with whom the minister had always had good relations.

"It is a delight to see you, *Kyrie Ypourge*," Mr. Minister. "I'm pleased to find you back in government, but only wish it were in your old post."

"So do I. But it's difficult for the prime minister. He must please so many people, and Petropoulos is especially a problem because he has a large following in parliament. And how is your soprano friend, the delightful Miss Victoria? I saw her a month or two ago at the National Opera as Rosalinde in *Die Fledermaus*. Ah, she gave a superb rendition of *Die Klänge meiner Heimat*. I have never heard it sung better."

"Coffee, *ouzo*, perhaps a little sherry?"

"Just a little cold water would do nicely at this moment. I had a late breakfast with that sinfully rich ship owner, Barvaros. I apologize for calling on you without an appointment, but I was just at my daughter's. She lives nearby, and as I left I realized I should see you."

The secretary brought in a pitcher of ice water, and Roussos filled two large glasses. The minister looked good, he thought. A little loss of weight had been ideal for him, although his roundish face was as cherubic as ever.

"And now," said Roussos, "I guess to business. First, I want you to know that we are on top of the situation. I have given the assignment to my most senior chief superintendent, Pano Maniatis. You might remember him, the one with all those relatives."

The minister looked a bit put out. "Yes," he said, letting the word slowly issue from his mouth, "I recall him."

"You seem disappointed. I assure you for all his sometimes seeming to be old-fashioned, Maniatis is a very clever, competent police officer with many successes in his record."

"You seem to know all about it, Spyro. But I just learned myself from my daughter. You really are on top of things. Did she call you?"

"Your daughter? How did she know?"

"Are we talking about the same thing?" said Antonidis, sitting up straight.

"I am talking about the report of a plot against your life that the Americans gave to Minister Petropoulos."

"Uh, that. That is nothing."

"But I thought…well, suppose I sit back and let you talk."

Antonidis said, "Petropoulos told me all about that stupid threat. I have a copy of the report, and I've even discussed it with my American liaison contact. If we spent all our time barricading ourselves every time some such report comes in, we'd never get any real work done."

"I take a threatened assassination as something serious, Mr. Minister, especially from this man Xynos. He is extremely dangerous."

"Well, rest assured that I'd not going to take any foolish chances, and I have no objection if you want to assign a policeman to give me discreet protection. Mind you, I said *discreet*. But that is not why I'm here to see you."

Roussos leaned forward across his desk in a dutifully attentive pose.

"You know that my daughter is the managing director of a large export-import firm?"

"Yes, I have met her, and I know of her firm."

"Well, she just told me of some dealings she is having with an American businessman who represents a bottling company in the United States. This American has suggested that he could save her a tremendous amount of money if she ships Greek wine to the United States in large containers instead of bottles. All the bottling can be done at the destination, and the savings in freight expenses would be substantial. Or so she assures me."

"I have heard of such things, but I know nothing about how much money can be saved."

"Nor do I. But I'm inclined to believe that it's not as much as she seems to think. After all, labor is higher in the United States, so the greater costs of bottling would seem to offset the transportation savings. When I told her this, she threw up her hands as if she were exasperated at my lack of comprehension. Then she said she was not capable of explaining all the important details, but she will invite both me and the American—who incidentally was born in Greece—to dinner Saturday so I can talk to him myself."

"That seems reasonable," said Roussos, beginning to feel uncomfortable.

"I met this American recently at a reception, and he seems respectable and knowledgeable, but I thought I'd check with you. Perhaps you have something in your files on him."

"It could be," Roussos said, his face blank with caution. "What is his name?"

"Savvas, Nick Savvas. Could you make a check on him?"

"For you, anything, my dear minister. Let me write down that name, Nick Savvas."

"I don't really think there should be anything wrong with him. But I'd feel more comfortable—if you know what I mean."

"Of course. Of course. Oh, er, you won't be seeing him again before your daughter's dinner party?"

"No, not before Saturday."

"Excellent. Just promise me one thing, sir. It's important. Promise me this. If he makes any attempt to contact you before then, please let me know." Roussos hesitated, then spoke in a more emphatic voice. "By all the saints! I apologize for playing games with you. Savvas is a con man. He's on our watch list. I arrested him about ten days ago, but Petropoulos ordered me to let him go for lack of evidence. I don't know what to tell you at this moment, but this is serious."

"I can see that now. If you feel so strongly about it, I'll do as you say. You've never given me wrong advice. I have to leave now, Spyro, but thanks for not playing games with me. I wouldn't have liked it once I found out."

Long after Antonidis left, Roussos sat at his desk in deep thought. He hadn't believed that Savvas was so stupid as to play his con game on a minister of government. And the same minister who was the object of Pavlo Xynos's assassination plot. Coincidence? Could be, but only time would tell.

✳   ✳   ✳   ✳

Roussos got through two more appointments, then heard the secretary's tap again on the door. He yelled, "*Ela.*" Come in.

She no sooner opened the door than a cyclone rushed past her and stood in front of Roussos. "I...I don't know what...." the secretary tried to explain.

"Get back to your desk," Minister Achilles Petropoulos ordered, "and don't let anyone else in while I'm here. You do know who I am, don't you?"

She nodded meekly and left.

"Have a seat, Mr. Minister," said Roussos, thinking that this was his day for ministers.

Petropoulos sat in a formally upright position. "I just had a telephone call from the American ambassador. Haven't you heard about his niece?"

"Yes, I've written the name down, Marilyn Pickering. I had a visit earlier from a security official of the American Embassy."

"Oh, you did, huh? Well, at least you're dealing on the right level. You're expected to confine yourself to embassy subordinates and keep away from the ambassadors."

"Of course. I have no desire to play a political role. I have been having liaison with various American Embassy subordinates for years. The only time I see the ambassador is at a large annual reception, and then just to shake hands."

"Get Thanos in here so I can talk to you both at the same time."

When Thanos arrived, he remained standing until the minister said, "For God's sake, sit down, man. Of course, you know all about the American ambassador's niece."

"Of course."

"Why haven't you done anything about it?"

"I have been obeying the orders of Police Director Roussos. He assigned me to work on the matter of General Zavalas."

Petropoulos glared at Roussos.

Roussos glared at Thanos. "You mean to say you knew of the disappearance of the American ambassador's niece and didn't say a word to me?"

Thanos shrugged his shoulders. "You were busy discussing other cases. I was working on what you assigned me. I assumed you knew."

"And how did you happen to find out about this niece?"

Thanos gulped and looked as if he were seasick. "Well, er, I heard it somewhere."

"Where?" said Roussos.

"Er, sir, I forget."

"What? You, an experienced police officer, learn about an important matter like this that could have tremendous political, as well as criminal, implications, and don't even mention it to me, your immediate superior? Then you say you can't remember where you heard it? That's absurd. That's grossly incompetent. And I suspect it might be insubordinate. Now I'm giving you a direct order to tell me where you heard it."

Thanos glanced at the minister, wrung his hands, and tried to speak, but no words came out.

The minister yelled, "For Christ's sake, Roussos, stop torturing him. I told him. I telephoned him immediately after the ambassador called me."

"What? You deal with my subordinates and leave me in the cold?"

"I telephoned him mainly to learn how he was getting along in his new position, and while I had him on the phone, it was natural to tell him the news I'd just heard."

Roussos turned to Thanos and yelled, "You understand this and don't ever forget it. Anytime you hear of something from Minister Petropoulos or any other minister or any other high-ranking government official, you tell me immediately. Officers of your rank do not deal with ministers, understand? Now get out. I'll call you if I want you."

Petropoulos stood up. "I called him in, and he'll stay until I dismiss him."

"So you wish to overrule me in my dealings with my own subordinates, Mr. Minister. All right, stay, Thanos. You are making new rules, Mr. Minister, but be careful what you do. You are making an issue over my relations with my new deputy, a deputy who was imposed on me without my consent. You are making it very difficult for me to allow Thanos to remain in DSI."

Thanos, still sitting, was visibly getting more uncomfortable and increasingly nervous. He wiped his brow with the sleeve of his tunic and started to rise to his feet, then sat down again. He lowered his head, but glanced with his eyes upward to peek covertly and see the looks on the faces of the two men who were having a dispute over him.

"You had better leave, Thanos," said Petropoulos. "Go, and leave us alone."

When a cringing Thanos had gone, the minister said, "You have won this one, Mr. Police Director. But don't push me too hard. I can make issues, too, and I think you know where you would stand in any political showdown between us."

"I think we both know by now where we stand, Mr. Minister."

Petropoulos took out a handkerchief and wiped his brow as Thanos had done. "Yes," he said, "of course. We were getting too heated." His voice was much calmer, but his eyes looked deadly. "All right. There is not much more. You apparently have all the details you need on this missing niece. So there is no need for me to be wasting my time here. But be warned. Keep me fully informed of developments."

As he started to go out the door, he turned back and said, "I don't want any more trouble with you, Roussos. Just know your place and keep it. And frankly I'm surprised that you haven't something to report on this American girl's case already." He started to leave again, then stopped with another thought. "And I'm warning you on Thanos. Don't take your frustrations out on him. He's a fine officer and he has a brilliant career ahead of him."

"I won't unless I have to. But I suggest you deal with this office through me and not through my subordinates."

Without another word, Petropoulos left.

CHAPTER 7

▼

Rosy-fingered dawn revealed a wine-dark sea as Marilyn Pickering woke up and looked about her. She had slept well, so well that she suspected she might have been drugged. Sitting up in the cot where she found herself, she noticed the sea outside, but her window was not a porthole. It was barred and seemed to be in a house. The thumping of the boat's engine was gone, and there was no motion under her. She had no recollection of being taken off the boat, yet she apparently was on land now. Sitting on a lumpy mattress on a small cot with two moth-eaten blankets at her feet, she felt uncomfortable and very moist. As she rolled over to one side to check, she discovered that she had wet the bed.

She jumped out quickly, pulled her clammy slacks and panties loose from sticking to her skin, and took them off. But she wasn't going to stay naked in this mysterious place, so she shook out her clothes as if that would help dry them, then put them on again. She stood for a long while in discomfort and despair. She walked to the small window, looked out, and saw that she was one story above ground level. From left to right, the range of her vision went from surrounding rocky hills down to a small sand and shingle beach with the sea in front and then to more rocks on her right.

She trembled as fear began to seize her body. Why had this happened to her? She also became aware of a great sensation of hunger; she hadn't eaten since dinner yesterday. How long ago, perhaps three-quarters of a day? And her dirtiness! She felt filthy and was disgusted at the way she must look.

Turning to take in her cell-like room, she noticed that there was a door opposite the window, four otherwise bare walls, and nothing more. She cautiously tried the door, but it was locked. The floor was bare and seemed to be made of concrete. She tried to think things out logically.

She had been kidnapped. Why? Possibly because her uncle was the ambassador. Would they be holding her for ransom money, or was there a political reason behind it? Could she be in the hands of terrorists?

Yorgo had seemed nice when they were on the plane. What a horrible judge of character she was. Even now, though, it was difficult to think of him as a criminal. He didn't at all seem the killer type. But he was definitely a part of a gang that seemed desperate. That was it. Yorgo seemed to be acting out of desperation. Something was making him act differently from his true nature. Such as when he hit her. She felt her jaw and it was still sore.

Counting the men who were in the car and the boat, she had seen six men in addition to Yorgo. They, too, for the most part did not seem like criminals. Marilyn couldn't quite explain to herself what she thought they might be. They were in a way like dedicated businessmen. Of course she knew that crime was big business these days.

Could she either escape from them or get a message to her uncle and the police? Certainly by now the police would have been alerted and were looking for her. A new thought came to her. Was it in the kidnappers' interest to keep her alive or sooner or later kill her? Some noises coming from below reassured her that she had not been abandoned to starve to death. In that case, why hadn't they fed her? Perhaps it was early in the morning. Perhaps they didn't know she was awake yet.

She walked to the door and knocked on it, softly at first, then louder. They had to have heard that. She heard footsteps outside her door. Slowly the door opened and a face cautiously peered in. It was Yorgo. As he opened the door fully, four other men came in behind him and stared at her. What were they going to do with her?

Yorgo said in a severe tone, "What do you want? You must keep quiet."

The other men started speaking excitedly in a foreign language that was probably Greek. Marilyn was sure she hadn't seen any of them before, so that meant her captors now numbered at least eleven, including those who manned the boat. Didn't that seem too many to be a gang of kidnappers? Actually, though, what did she really know about kidnappers? Again she wondered, terrorists, assassins?

"I'm hungry," she said, trying not to cry or scream. "I haven't had anything to eat since we were on the plane. Are you trying to starve me to death?"

"I'll bring you some food," said Yorgo. "In the meantime, keep quiet."

"Can I have my suitcases, too? And is there a toilet? I'm filthy and I need to wash up and go to the bathroom. And I wet my bed last night, probably because I was drugged. Do I have to sleep in it again?" Her slacks and panties were in the process of drying on her. How she wished she could change them.

Yorgo spoke to the others. There was much discussion and gesturing between them. One of them whispered something and laughed, and the others joined in, but it seemed a nervous laughter. Finally Yorgo turned again to her and said, "We'll see. I'll come back soon."

She had the impression they were all confused and perhaps even embarrassed.

They backed out and Yorgo closed the door. She heard a click and knew it was being locked. Food! Yes, she needed food more than a bathroom now, but how long could she hold off? She needed to think clearly. It was possible, she thought, that they really didn't know what to do with her. It was as if they had never held a prisoner before. Could this be all new to them?

Some twenty minutes later Yorgo unlocked the door and came in with a tray. She looked eagerly at it. There were no dishes, just food resting on some blank paper looking like cheap, manila paper towels. He put the tray down on her bed, and she saw that it contained a large part of a loaf looking like brownish French bread, about an ounce of something looking like hard cheese, some purple olives, an orange, a part of a watermelon, and a large bottle of what was probably mineral water. No meat, good. She didn't dare show herself to be too fussy as a vegetarian. She saw him watching her as she ate.

He spoke again while she greedily opened and drank from the bottle and followed it up with some bread and cheese.

"Marilyn, you do not have to believe it, but I am your friend. The others are curious about you, but they are nervous also, so please don't do anything to irritate them. We do not have much food here, but we will share with you what we have. Finish your food and then I will come back again and we will talk some more. As for your wet bed, turn the mattress over. That's all we can do for you."

Sitting on a corner of the hard mattress, she looked up at him with food still in her mouth and nodded and tried to smile. He started walking away. Choking down a mouthful, she said, "Thank you." He left and locked the door.

She ate every bit of the food and drank every drop of the mineral water. Then she put the tray on the floor by the door and rested. After some minutes she got up and looked out the window. It was a clear day, and far away she could see two ships on the horizon. Immediately below her window were two of her captors smoking cigarettes and talking to each other. She wondered if she could open the window and eavesdrop, but realized she wouldn't be able to understand the language anyway. However, later she would try the window just to test it.

She felt much better with the food in her stomach, but now she needed to go to the bathroom or she'd have an accident. Should she knock loudly on the door again? Yorgo had warned her not to irritate the others.

Suddenly the door opened. Yorgo entered and said, "I'll take you to the toilet. I will stand outside, but please be quick. There is no lock on the inside. Are you acquainted with a Turkish toilet?"

She shook her head.

He led her out of the room and down a flight of stairs. The ground floor seemed mainly to be one large room, plus a hall, kitchen, and toilet. They had to pass through the large room, where five men sprawled out on wooden chairs with cushions while they talked, gestured, and smoked. She noticed little things such as ashes falling to the floor as they put emphasis on their words to each other with cigarette-laden fingers. The high ceiling of the room was partially covered with swirls of cigarette smoke.

One of them was playing with amber-colored beads, each the size of a large peanut. She recognized them as Greek worry beads; her uncle had sent her a string of them once. Her captor held the string of beads in one hand while seemingly counting them with his other. The men stared at her as she passed through the gauntlet. One of them gave her a cautious but friendly smile, and she smiled back, grateful for any show of friendliness even though she was frightened beyond her ability to think.

In the toilet room there was a small porcelain lavatory attached to the wall with a shelf above it. There was no mirror. Beyond the sink was a hole in the concrete floor with two large foot-sized impressions formed in the concrete facing away from the hole. Above was a chain. Yorgo explained that it was both toilet and shower. A piece of canvas attached to an overhead wire could be extended across the little room to divide it in two halves. He told her, "You can go to the toilet in that hole. It is for everything. If you want to take a shower, you can put your clothes on this side and close the curtain so the water will not splash on them. If you have a bowel movement, you will want some of the paper that is on that shelf," he said, pointing toward the lavatory. "Flush the paper down the hole, but do not use too much and block it. If you block it, we will not let you use it again."

She looked at the paper and saw that it was a very thin and smaller version of the manila towels, and she wondered how it would be possible to block anything with such tiny sheets. Overcoming her initial shock, Marilyn quickly commanded herself to adjust to reality. It was all so primitive, but she had had the experience of an Outward Bound training course in Maine, and she felt that there would be enough facilities to serve her most pressing needs.

"My suitcase and clean clothes?" she said. "I need my toothbrush and toothpaste and comb and other things from my suitcase and handbag."

Yorgo looked puzzled. He was in thought for a minute then said, "Do what you have to do urgently and close the curtain. I will come back on this side and bring you some of your things."

He disappeared. She stripped off all her clothes, leaving them on the sink. She approached the primitive shower/toilet, closing as tightly as she could the canvas curtain behind her. She was able to make do. Half of her mind protested indignantly, while the other half told her she had to adjust to the circumstances if she was to survive. Again she thought of the survival course in Maine she had taken during a college summer vacation, and she was now so thankful that her father had insisted she take it. Above all, she was determined to survive.

She used the hole as a toilet, then stood under the primitive showerhead and pulled the chain. The water was dreadfully cold. She let the chain go, thankful that she had some control. Reaching for the chain again, she slowly pulled it once more and commanded herself to brace for the cold water. She suddenly realized that it was not just cold, but salty, too. Salt water?

But then she had had to use salt water in Maine, and she knew she could do it again. There was no soap and she had to rub herself vigorously with her hands to try to get clean. Perhaps the salt even helped. When she finished, she felt much better. As she was about to move the curtain aside, she heard the door open, and she stood still.

Yorgo hollered out to her, "I've put some things on top of the dry part of the clothes you put on the sink. It's the best I can do. We have decided you cannot have your suitcases or handbag, but I took out what I thought would be enough for a change of clothing and freshening up."

The door closed, and she waited a minute before peeking through the curtain. The room was empty. She checked the items that Yorgo had brought her. There were clean panties and bra, slacks and blouse, her toothbrush, a tube of her special whitening brand of toothpaste, and a comb. He had also brought her a rather ragged towel, which otherwise looked clean and dry. All the bare essentials, she thought, and she had to laugh to herself as she thought how appropriate the word "bare" was at the moment. She dried her body quickly and put on her underwear and outer clothing.

She brushed her teeth after gingerly testing the water from the single faucet of the lavatory to see if it was salt, too. It was sweet water. When she finished dressing and combing her hair, she felt like a human being again. She washed her dirty panties and bra the best she could with water from the sink. As she was considering how she could wash her used slacks and blouse, too, there was a knock on the door.

Yorgo entered with a cloth bag from one of her suitcases and said she could keep her things in it. "If we are still here, I'll see if I can get some soap for you by the end of the week."

"The end of the week? But I'll want to take a shower every day."

As if he couldn't help himself, he burst out in sudden laughter. "Look, Marilyn, if you can convince my friends to carry enough sea water to the roof everyday, it's all right with me, but I don't think they'll like it. It's not far to walk to the sea, but carrying water from it over and over again is not the kind of work these men were trained to do, and they don't much care for it."

She wanted to ask, *What were you trained for?* but held her silence.

His face changed to take on a more somber look. "This is important. Some of them have already complained that they heard you using too much of the water from the sink. That is even worse because that comes from our supply of drinking water, and we have damned little. You must not make them dislike you."

She understood from his tone and his pained look that she had better pay attention, and she remembered using the sink water to wash her bra and panties, too. "How long are we going to stay here?" she asked.

"I don't know. We are waiting for someone, and he will tell us."

"Am I in any danger?" She felt that Yorgo was sufficiently well disposed toward her so she could ask that question.

His voice snapped. "Of course you're in danger. We are all in grave danger. This is not a child's game we are playing." In a softer tone, he said, "You must take all your cues from me."

"She said, 'Yes, Yorgo, I will.'" She hesitated to ask another question, but finally decided there was really a need for it. "Will I be allowed to get any exercise? May I go out to walk or anything?" She hated being so dependent on his good will.

"I will ask what they think. Now I must take you to your room." At her doorway, he took a paperback book from his pocket and gave it to her. "This might help pass away the boredom."

She took it and said thanks. It was in English, a Hemingway novel, *The Sun Also Rises*.

After he locked her in, she turned the mattress over and upside down, then sat on her cot and opened the book. Hemingway—she hadn't read him since high school.

She had liked him as a writer, but felt his novels were more like lengthy short stories. Still, it was nice of Yorgo to give her the book. What kind of a man was he really? Putting the book on the floor, she lay back on the cot and gave freedom to her thoughts, most of which were repetitious. Basically she wondered: Where was she? Why? When if ever would she be free?

Yorgo was a puzzle. She knew there was a tendency in kidnappings for the kidnapped to be so grateful for little favors that there was a danger of falling in love with the kidnapper. She did not want that to happen, and she didn't think it would. Yorgo had been mean to her. He had hit her, sworn at her, refused her simple amenities. She had to watch every word with him. And he apparently was acting the part of the good guy. What might the bad guys be like?

They had taken her watch so she had no idea of how much time had passed. Picking up the book again, she started to read. At first it was interesting getting back in the story. Marilyn liked the character of Lady Brett. Brett was in love with Jake Barnes, but couldn't marry him because he had become impotent from a war wound. So Brett became engaged to the Englishman, Mike Campbell. But then she had a brief affair with Robert Cohn, a rich expatriate American who was on the fringe of the group. And after Robert she went immediately into another affair with a twenty-year-old bullfighter, Pedro Romero. How did she meet so many men? Marilyn supposed it was body language or something.

Jake Barnes was the protagonist of the story. He reminded her of her own Jake, whom she refused to marry. Jake Sommers was sort of impotent, but that wasn't the right word. She could testify that he wasn't impotent, but it was just his personality that was bland. He was too much a faultless good guy, that was his fault. He was too…too…unexciting, too undangerous. In the story even the simple Robert Cohn symbolized an element of daring for Brett, and certainly the bullfighter represented an elegant aura of danger.

Yet for all that, wouldn't the real adventure for Brett have been if she had married her Jake anyway in spite of his disability? He was still the one she was in love with. But then—no sex. At least not in the customary sense. But Marilyn's Jake was good in bed. Why did she need a more exciting personality in the first place? Look where her quest for excitement had got her. Kidnapped, maltreated, perhaps even under threat of death. She tried to direct her thoughts elsewhere.

She considered Yorgo again. Could he be thought of as exciting in his way? Perhaps. He had a certain amount of continental charm about him. But he was not really the type of man who appealed to her. In a way he was like her own Jake, but with bad characteristics. She couldn't imagine Jake Sommers ever hitting her under any circumstances.

She closed the book and put it on the floor. It was interesting getting back to it for a while, but the interest wore thin. She got to her feet and went over to look out the window. There were no ships anywhere on the sea within her vision. Four of her captors were on the hard part of the beach kicking a soccer ball around. From where she stood, they looked like children. It was after lunchtime, late afternoon she knew even without her watch. Were they going to feed her, or was it to be like the shower, once a week? She felt like pounding on the door and demanding some food, but knew that wouldn't do.

She wished she had some other book. Suppose downstairs they had a library and she could choose any book she wanted. What would she select? Something long, she guessed. Something that could keep her mind occupied even though she had read it before. The Victorian novelist Anthony Trollope would be just the thing. But which of his many novels would she pick? Perhaps *Can You Forgive Her?*—one of her favorites.

In this book she found the character of Alice Vavasor interesting, someone torn between a decent but bland John Grey as a suitor and her indecent but exciting cousin George Vavasor. First Alice chose George but got burned, so then she chose John, then went back to George, and at last married John and lived happily ever after. Hmm, there was Jake Sommers again, decent but bland, bland but decent. What was it in *Can You Forgive Her?* that George had told Alice on that balcony in Switzerland? Something like "You can never go back to water after tasting brandy." But Alice had finally found the brandy too intoxicating, too hangover producing.

Marilyn lay on the cot and gazed at the ceiling. What were they going to do with her? What did they want her for? Finally she got up, went to the door, and knocked loudly. The man who answered was one she hadn't seen before. She again wondered how many there were? She told him she had to go to the bathroom.

"No English," he said. "*Sprechen sie Deutsch? Parlate Italiano?*"

She recognized the languages, but couldn't speak them. However, the Italian was a little close to Spanish, which she had studied. "*Yo tengo que orinar. Necesito W.C.*" "W.C.," she knew, was almost as universal as "okay."

His eyes opened widely. "*Ah, thelete to W.C. Okay.*" He led her downstairs to the toilet, waited for her, and brought her up again.

"Lunch?" she said. "Food? *Comida? Comer?*" She gestured with her hand as if she were using a spoon to place something in her mouth.

"*Ah, fayito! Okhi.* No chow. Later." He held up two fingers. "*Solamente due tempe.*"

She guessed that meant she could expect only two meals a day. Her first thought was one of fairness. Did that rule apply to them, too? But she didn't really care how many meals they had. She was just hungry. Before leaving the States, she had wanted to lose five pounds; well, now she had the feeling that she would be losing more than that. She turned away from the doorway and heard the door lock behind her.

Back to reading her book. She was at the part where Robert Cohn, fascinated by Lady Brett, was sending his mistress, Frances, away, when Marilyn heard a noise outside in the bay. Looking out the window, she saw a cabin cruiser arrive. Three men in a dinghy went out to meet the boat and climb aboard. Three other men loaded the dinghy with packages and something that looked like a water container. When the dinghy returned to the beach with the three new men, others shook hands with them and helped them carry the supplies into the house.

A short while later, Marilyn heard the door unlock, and Yorgo came in. He said, "You told Hari you were hungry?"

She nodded her head.

"I told you not to irritate people."

"How did that irritate him?"

"Do you think any of us want to be reminded that we're not treating you very decently? There is only a little food here. We had stored more, but some vandals on the island had broken in before we arrived and stole our supplies. We've all been hungry." But a faint smile came over his face. "However, a boat just arrived with new supplies, and we'll be all right for a while. But we still have to ration food and drink, especially the water. Here, I brought you an orange."

He tossed the fruit to her, and she eagerly caught it. She wanted to tear into it and start consuming the sections, but she waited to see if he was going to say anything more. He started to leave, so she quickly implored him, "Did you ask about my being allowed outside to get exercise?"

"You may walk outside a bit, but only if I go with you."

"Will you?"

"I'll be back for you in a half hour."

When he returned he led her downstairs, past the big room where the men had gathered, and out the door. Once outside, he gave her two large cookies and said, "Since we all had a little to eat, I thought we would share with you."

"That was kind of you."

As she took the cookies, he reached for her other hand and held it tightly.

She tried to pull it away, but his grip was too strong.

"Why are you hurting me?"

"I'm not trying to hurt," he said, loosening his grip somewhat, "but one of the conditions of your being outside is that I must hold onto you are all times." He stopped walking and turned to face her. "The others are drinking wine to conserve water. It is difficult to bring in enough water with our boat. If you don't conserve the fresh water, you may have to brush your teeth with the sea water."

"Why? You seemed to have everything planned carefully. Has something gone wrong with your plans?"

He turned sharply to her. "Marilyn, I like you, but you must be careful about what you say. We are waiting for someone, and he is late. As a result my people are getting nervous. They are drinking too much, and any wrong word could get them mad."

"Who are you waiting for?"

"You will meet him soon. He is my friend Jimmy. He must have been held up in the United States. Everything is more difficult until he arrives."

She quickly ate her two cookies and bent down to wash the crumbs from her hands in the water. Seeing what she was doing, he released her hand, but quickly reached for it again when she got up. Her shoes were getting wet in the surf, but she didn't care. She took them off and threw them in the direction of the house. She wore no stockings, and it was a delight to let her feet play with the warm fringes of the tide while her toes dug into the sand.

It was a pleasant day, partially overcast, but bright. In fact she had never seen such a bright sky before. It dazzled her eyes, but if she lowered them, they were caught by the effulgence of the sparkling bluish crystal sea, and she still had to squint. She turned to look back at the house, nestled between the rocky hills, and it was as if she were seeing the scene through a gossamer film that greatly intensified the range of colors, something unreal and dreamy.

She had been told that Greece was deceiving, and now she understood why. Standing in the light and warmth of a brilliant sky, and comforted by the anodyne of a murmuring sea, she could almost believe she was happy. She blinked and thought how ironic her situation. Hungry, uncomfortable, dirty, deprived of all comforts normally taken for granted, fearful for the future, possibly facing death, she could yet be almost deceived that she was on an exotic, joyful vacation.

She almost felt like stripping down to her bra and panties and taking a swim, but she doubted they would allow her to do any swimming for fear that she might be capable of escaping and swimming all the way back to the United States. Besides, although she wasn't too modest, it might give her captors the wrong idea. She had the impression that they were the kind of men who divided women into two classes. They would respect her body as long as they thought she was lady-like, but if they thought of her as a loose woman, all restraint might be gone.

Hand in hand, she and Yorgo walked up and down the beach for an hour or more, sometimes serenely quiet, sometimes talking. Yorgo was so strange. Sometimes they could be talking like equals, while at other times he asserted his position as strict captor. She tried to find out more about him and the others, and he didn't seem to mind talking a little about the situation, but every now and then she would ask the wrong question and he would get cross.

The more they talked, the more she became convinced that her captors were not professional kidnappers. But using all her imagination she still couldn't figure out just what they were after. Professionals or not, they had in fact kidnapped her, and that was a crime in any country. Their goal had to be something with a great deal of meaning for them, and she was beginning to think that it wasn't money.

Suddenly Yorgo snapped at her. "You have kept me out too long. We must turn around and go back." He seemed nervous and worried, perhaps almost frightened. She started back as he commanded, but she wasn't moving fast enough for him and he started pulling her by the arm. The spell was broken. Now she knew that her illusion of comfort was like spotting a mirage in the desert. Deceptive. Unkind. Unfair. There was no longer any feeling that she might find any ray of happiness amid the bleakness of her reality.

CHAPTER 8

▼

Like most working Greeks, Spyro Roussos was accustomed to going home for lunch, followed by a long siesta. After the heat of the day had diminished, he would come back to the office around six o'clock for the second part of his split shift and work until nine, or at times much later. Although in a position where he could set his own work schedule, he almost always worked more hours than any of his staff.

Today he walked the short distance to Victoria's apartment, nodding every now and then to acknowledge a greeting from someone who recognized him. Politicians, movie stars, bureaucrats, foreign diplomats, the international set, they all recognized Roussos, even though he wasn't acquainted with half of them.

Victoria knew better than to plan lunch for a given time each day since his regular schedule could vary a lot. At least several days each week he couldn't get away on time, and would come home anywhere from fifteen minutes to hours late, and of course sometimes he would either skip lunch entirely or just eat a quick bite at his desk. Today Roussos left the office late, but that was better than not at all.

Victoria had made a *sofrito*, a form of stew popular in Roussos's native Corfu, made from slices of beef simmered long in a vinegar and garlic sauce. Spyro had told her that in Corfu it was made with rabbit. It went well with huge hunks of Greek bread. A bottle of Aris beer complemented the meal, and some cheese for dessert put a fine finish on it.

They ate on the balcony as they often did during summer and watched the activity in Kolonaki Square. It was a leisurely meal with plenty of time for talk. Victoria had an offer to sing the part of Adalgisa in the opera *Norma* in six months' time with the Santa Fe, New Mexico, Opera. She turned it down because of her commitment to sing the title role in *Lucia di Lammermoor* with the Greek National Opera.

Spyro smiled and asked, "Suppose they had offered you the part of Norma instead of the second soprano part, and with the Metropolitan in New York instead of the Santa Fe, would that have enticed you away from your commitment?"

"You know the answer to that, *caro*. Didn't I say no to the Baltimore Opera under similar circumstances when they offered me the role of Rosina in *The Barber of Seville*?"

"Now let's be fair, *agapi mou* and compare oranges with oranges. I asked you about a lead role with one of the world's two best-known opera houses."

"You always do this to me. Well, I guess one doesn't turn down roles with the Metropolitan or La Scala under any circumstances." She took on a pensive look. "Yet I think I might have declined even those prestigious houses if I couldn't get out of any obligation I might have here in a friendly way. I wouldn't want to jeopardize my relationship with the Greek National Opera." She paused, turned her head to one side, then said, "Hmm, you did say the Met or La Scala, didn't you? It would be a hard decision."

"Are you saying yes or no to my original question?"

"Well," she said, with a moue of a pout, "I guess I'm saying it depends. I'd accept if I could without jeopardizing my career here in Athens, but I wouldn't let anything interfere with my staying in Athens with you. You know that, Spyro."

They kissed lightly and continued eating, and there was silence for a while. Victoria cleared away the dishes, and Roussos put his feet up on a chair and stretched out. As he frequently did, he puzzled over the dilemma of his position and his department. Having power far beyond his rank forced him to introspection. Had he wished to take advantage of all the de facto power his office gave him, he could have made himself an *éminence grise* to the prime minister to control the entire machinery of government. But he was not the type.

He admitted to himself that he was tempted at times to go beyond the loose restrictions that parliament had felt necessary to impose on his jurisdiction, but he virtually always rose above the needs of the moment to preserve his faith in democratic institutions. And he felt strongly that DSI was a necessary, but necessarily limited, arm of government.

Some of his de facto power came from the general knowledge that DSI maintained dossiers on people under investigation. Information was gathered in his files from confidential informants, routine police reports, tax and customs information, and even medical information, all kinds of data. This was the nature of investigating known and suspected criminals. However, thanks to the cross-referencing power of the computer, information in any given dossier could be retrieved during an investigation using any other dossier, sometimes impliedly incriminating information on, say, government officials or important businessmen and other community leaders. Sometimes such information was not so much incriminating as potentially embarrassing, indicating extramarital affairs, business secrets, or sensitive political arrangements.

As a rule, Roussos did not act on this type of by-product information unless he felt there was some real threat to national security. But others who had had his position before him had abused their custody of classified information, or gone on fishing expeditions, and given DSI a bad reputation, a reputation that took Roussos years to change. And that was before the department had grown so large and efficiently computerized. The potential for misuse of DSI information and for causing real harm to innocent people was huge.

The dilemma of Spyro Roussos was caused by the question of who would eventually replace him? Would his replacement have as much respect for honest use of the files? Sometimes this question bothered him so much that he thought he might recommend the dissolution of his department when he left, with the various functions being divided and placed in other government agencies. But he knew that the effectiveness of DSI's mission was in the centralization of its files.

He justified the system by his knowledge of how much good was being done, how many evil-doers had been convicted and imprisoned, how many plots against the government had been detected and thwarted, and how many innocent people had been exonerated or delivered from financial loss or erroneous prosecution. It was the age-old question of the good Roman emperor versus the succession issue, and experience had shown that so many times the good ones had been succeeded by depraved men.

At times he longed to retire and have more hours each day for Victoria; after all, with their age difference, how much more time would they have together? He knew that if he asked for retirement, the prime minister would promote him first so he would have an adequate pension; the pay increase to police brigadier was high. However, at this moment there was the problem that Minister Petropoulos was preparing Thanos to assume his position, a man who wouldn't hesitate to corrupt the charter of DSI to keep his protector in office and to empower himself as the commander of a modern-day praetorian guard.

How Roussos wished he could groom his son Dimitri to take over. But even if he could ensure such a thing, he wouldn't because it would be nepotism, and he would be acting in the very way he so much deplored. There seemed to be no solution. Even if he recommended breaking up his department, would the prime minister support him? Not if Petropoulos had anything to say about it.

"You look so deep in thought and unhappy," said Victoria, coming out on the balcony again. "Is it the office? Or what? You were unusually late today, and I didn't even ask what you were so worried about. Anything particularly bothersome?"

"Just the usual, only more of it."

"Shouldn't we take our nap now if you plan to return to the office on time?"

He took his feet down from his chair, rose, and embraced her. "Do we have any iced tea made? I've too many things on my mind to be able to get much sleep. You take a nap. I'd only stay awake in bed."

"Oh, no, not if you're staying out here. I don't have much to do until *Tosca* goes into real production. The rehearsal this morning was short, really just blocking, so I don't really need a nap. I'll get you some iced tea. I worry about you."

"Don't worry, please. I've got to think things out. So many delicate matters have come up recently."

"Why don't you tell me about them? Talking them out is sometimes better than thinking them out."

He let his lips form a wry smile. "Knowing you, I wouldn't be surprised if you came up with a solution to at least one of my problems."

"I probably will. I'll get the tea." She returned and sat cross-legged on the wicker love seat at the back of the balcony. Now she was ready to give him her full attention, and the sympathetic, loving way she looked at him gave him all the encouragement he needed.

He had previously told her about his meeting with Minister Achilles Petropoulos more than a week ago. He repeated in some detail the problems arising from the matter of the international swindler, Nick Savvas, and the unexpected return from voluntary exile of General Zavalas. He also referred briefly to the return of Pavlo Xynos, but tried to avoid exacerbating the alarming effect on Victoria.

"I had the honor"—at this he made a face as if he smelled rotten eggs—"of having Minister Petropoulos himself visit me. I'm not being paranoid. He wants to get me out and replace me with his toady Thanos, and he doesn't care if he has to tear down my entire reputation in order to do it. Thanos, incidentally, is so eager that he showed up early for his new job as my deputy. He tried to take over a meeting I was having with Pano, Eleni, and Dimitri. I stopped him cold, but I know he complained to Petropoulos because later Petropoulos warned me not to pick on him."

"Can Petropoulos sign a directive and force you out?"

"I don't think it would be politically expedient for him to do that. Even if the prime minister tried to retire me without my consent, there would be a big backlash from all the main political parties. Even the extremists on both sides might object because they'd be afraid of who would follow me—better the devil they know."

"So I don't see the problem."

"The problem is that Petropoulos will just wait until I make some mistake and then use it to crucify me. If I won't retire or accept a promotion to some other office, Petropoulos's easiest way of getting rid of me would be to use something to ruin me. Look what they just served on my plate. Being responsible for an international swindler can make me very unpopular with the big companies. General Zavalas may be plotting a coup. Pavlo Xynos might be able to assassinate Minister Antonidis, and that will make me look careless even though Antonidis won't take the threat seriously enough to protect himself. Then I have this matter of the missing niece of the American ambassador."

Victoria put her feet down and sat up straight. "Niece of the American ambassador? You haven't told me about that."

"It just came up this morning. A security officer from the American Embassy visited me and said the niece arrived in Athens yesterday and disappeared. I have Dimitri working on the case. We don't know if she wanted to disappear, or just got lost, or was kidnapped, or what happened to her."

"Marilyn Pickering?"

A surprised Roussos turned anxiously to stare at Victoria and demand, "Yes, where did you hear her name?"

Excitedly jumping up from the love seat as if she couldn't contain herself, Victoria said, "I know her. I met her in Washington, and she was on my flight yesterday."

Roussos mentally slapped himself for failing to connect Victoria's flight with Marilyn Pickering's. He said, "You were sitting with her?"

"No, I was in first class and she was in economy. But we got together and talked during the flight, and I saw her leave the plane."

"You did?" said Roussos, catching her excitement. He took a pad of paper and a pen from his pocket. "Let's start from the beginning. This might be just what we need."

The smile on his face brightened as she talked. "Good, you saw the man she was sitting with. Could you identify him from photos?"

"Perhaps, but I'm not sure. He was an attractive, thin man of about thirty years. Marilyn said his father owned the largest insurance company in Greece—that should help. And she said he had a long Greek name starting with Papamavro-something."

"You're certain about the name?"

"I'm certain that's the partial name she told me, but she's not well acquainted with Greek names and I don't know how correct she might be."

"It's worth trying. While I go back to my office, you look in the telephone directory under all the names beginning with Papamavro-something. Now you say she seemed very friendly with him?"

"I'd say friendlier than you usually get with a stranger sitting beside you in an airplane. Of course, I don't know her that well, and this may all lead to nothing."

"At the very least we should be able to find this man and learn something about the state of her mind. Perhaps she gave him some clue as to what she intended to do once they landed. On the other hand, he could be the one responsible for her disappearance."

*   *   *   *

Roussos was surprised to find both Dimitri and Eleni at the office early, and a few minutes later Pano Maniatis came in."

"Why are you sacrificing your siestas?" he asked them.

"I guess I had nothing better to do," said Eleni.

"I wasn't very tired," said Dimitri.

Pano said, "We have so much to do that I couldn't keep away."

"It seems that Pano is the only honest one among you," said Roussos. "But I'm glad to see you all so enthusiastic, and I'm especially glad to see you here now. I just got the first real lead on the disappearing niece."

He related to them what he had learned from Victoria. "Pano, you should be able to find out who owns the largest insurance company in Greece. Eleni, I want you to check with the airlines and see if the manifest for that flight had any name on it sounding like Papamavro-something. Dimitri, I want you to check car registrations for all cars belonging to anyone with a long Papamavro-something name. There can't be too many of them—it's not that common, like Papadopoulos, for example."

Victoria phoned. "It almost has to be Papamavrogiannopoulos, and there are only two in the directory. Nestor and Georgio. And Georgio could be the Yorgo that Marilyn mentioned to me."

Roussos reached back into his memory and recalled that there was a Nestor Papamavrogiannopoulos who owned an insurance company, but he hadn't known that it was the largest in Greece. A quick file check showed that Nestor Papamavrogiannopoulos had a son named Georgio who worked for his company.

Pano returned and said, "No one by that name in the largest insurance company, but the third largest is owned by a Nestor Papamavrogiannopoulos, and his son, Georgio, is the manager of the Athens office."

Eleni came in and reported, "The manifest is garbled, but you could make something very similar to Georgio Papamavrogiannopoulos on it."

Dimitri's information from car registrations again confirmed the name. Now the question was to find the man.

Two hours later they started to make progress. Eleni, posing as a friend of Yorgo's, phoned Nestor Papamavrogiannopoulos's house, but succeeded only in learning that Nestor was in the hospital with a broken leg. The maid answering the phone said she had no idea of where Yorgo was. He lived in his own apartment in the Kolonaki area, and the maid didn't even know if he had returned from his trip to America.

Pano contacted the concierge of Yorgo's apartment building and was told the same thing: he was unaware that Yorgo had come back from his American trip.

Finally Dimitri reached a reliable contact who had business relations with Yorgo. The man knew nothing about Yorgo's present whereabouts, but he said Yorgo might have taken a holiday and be staying at the family's vacation villa on the island of Skyros.

Pano phoned the police outpost at Skyros village and learned that the Papamavrogiannopoulos vacation house was at the extreme other end of the island in an isolated area. Three hours later the policeman called back and reported that he had driven as close to the house as he dared and then continued on foot. He saw lights inside the villa. Further, he had questioned some reliable fishermen who lived not far from the Papamavrogiannopoulos house, and they said there were a number of men in the house and one woman who seemed to be a foreigner.

"How could they tell?"

The Skyros policeman in charge said, "They carry binoculars in their boat, and they were curious about the activity at the house. She did not look Greek. She was walking on the beach with one of the men."

Roussos and his Special Unit studied a large-scale topographical map of the island, which was about 160 kilometers northeast of Athens. "Apparently," he said, "the house is in or close to this cove. The house is sheltered on three sides by low hills, so we could place a strong paramilitary force behind the hills and then stage a surprise attack in the middle of the night."

The police director phoned the police paramilitary command, asking them to make available to him a platoon of specially trained men plus two helicopters. The duty officer said he would contact the police brigadier in charge and call him back.

"Are you going to do this tonight?" said Dimitri.

"Certainly. We're only guessing that the girl is there, but if she is, she must be in constant danger. A delay could be fatal to her."

"How about Police Underdirector Thanos," asked Eleni. "Are you going to use, or at least inform, him?"

"The devil I will! He would only contact the newspapers and tell them about the brilliant plan that he personally is going to put into action. And a leak could alert the kidnappers."

The phone rang. The head of the police paramilitary command said that he would need permission from Minister of Public Security Petropoulos before he could provide the men and equipment.

"What?" yelled Roussos. "You have standing orders to make whatever I need available to me. And you've never had to go higher up in the past." He kept getting more excited as he talked.

The others in his office knew from his words and rapidly changing facial expressions that all was not going well. Finally he hung up the phone in utter disgust.

"Petropoulos has given special orders that we have to go through him to get what used to be routinely available to us."

"What are you going to do?" asked Dimitri.

"I have no choice. Eleni, get Petropoulos on the phone for me."

Eleni made several telephone calls, then told Roussos, "He's not in his office and not at home, and no one seems to know where he is."

Roussos said, "Isn't he supposed to let one of the officers at the ministry know his whereabouts at all times?"

Pano said, "I have a cousin in his office. Do you want me to see if he might know what Petropoulos does when he doesn't sign out?"

Roussos brushed his hand over his forehead. "Yes, Pano, I guess you might as well. Without his permission, our hands are tied."

Now it was Pano's turn at the telephone. It took him two calls to reach his cousin. Pano talked, then hung up and turned to Roussos. "My cousin says that Petropoulos is very mysterious, unlike any other minister the people at the ministry have ever known. When he is unavailable like this, he is absolutely unavailable. The chances are that he probably will not even be at home tonight. One subordinate at the ministry thinks that he has satyriasis and spends a lot of time in whorehouses. They say the women in the ministry are all afraid of him and whenever they are in an elevator with him, they turn their backs to the walls and cover their private parts with their arms and hands. They also say that some of the women employees in the Parliament Building have told confidantes that he raped them, but they were too afraid of him to complain officially. Anyway, there will be no way to contact him until he gets into his office late tomorrow morning."

"The devil take him! All right. We'll get his permission tomorrow and make our plans accordingly. We'll schedule it for tomorrow night, and the extra time will give us a chance to plan it better. Now that we've verified the girl is most likely at the Skyros house, we must act soon."

*   *   *   *

The next morning Roussos had the Special Unit assembled again in his office. "Have you called the minister yet, Mr. Police Director?" said Pano Maniatis.

"Not yet. I'm thinking now I'll hold off until this afternoon."

"Isn't that taking a chance he might disappear again?"

"His private secretary tells me he plans to be in the office until four o'clock, and then he will leave to accompany the prime minister to an important political debate in parliament."

"But I don't understand…."

"You will, Pano, you will."

At that moment the door opened and Jason Thanos walked in. "I understand you were working late last night, Mr. Police Director. Was it on something important?"

"I consider everything I do important, Mr. Police Underdirector."

"Is it something I should know?"

"It does not concern the case I assigned you. How are you coming along on the matter of General Zavalas?"

"I have Chief Inspector Larhis working on it. I will let you know when I have something."

"I'm sure you will. It occurred to me this morning that we are sort of stumbling around on the Zavalas case."

"But you don't mean me. I was just assigned that case yesterday, and already I have someone looking into it. You can't call that stumbling."

"When I gave you the assignment, I had in mind that you would look into it directly and not just reassign it to a subordinate officer. You have no authority to be making such an assignment in the first place. I have to approve all assignments of police inspector and higher."

Thanos curled his lips in a serpentine smile. "I did not want to bother you with a small matter like this. The minister tells me that I am too high-ranking to be walking the streets like some shiny-ass tyro police officer."

"Oh, the minister? You talked to him again after he left my office yesterday?"

His face getting red, Thanos said, "I saw him leaving the building and he asked me about the case I was working on."

Roussos sat straight in his chair and looked his deputy in the eye. "Understand this, Thanos. Any person working in this department gets his assignments from me, not from the minister. If you find this arrangement not to your liking, you can always ask for a transfer."

"Yes, sir," said Thanos, a trace of an arrogant smile still on his lips.

"We will talk more about that later. Anyway, when I said stumbling around, I meant that we're not being thorough. Zavalas spent seven years in Paris. What does that mean to you?"

Thanos laughed. "That he knows how to pick a good place for self-imposed exile."

"No. It means that he had seven years of making contact with Greeks and others in Paris. It means that he had seven years of planning what he was going to do when he returned to Greece. It also means that French security would not have ignored him as notorious as he is."

"So…? Ah, you want me to phone French security."

"No, Jason. I am assigning you to go to Paris immediately, no later than three o'clock this afternoon, to work directly with the French to see if you can find out what Zavalas was doing all the time he was there."

"Paris?" His face lit up. "But this afternoon—how can I get ready? The time is short."

"Do you want the assignment?"

"Yes, of course."

"Then be on a plane no later than three o'clock this afternoon."

"Yes, sir."

"And pay attention to this, Mr. Thanos. I order you not to contact the minister or tell him anything about this if he should—shall we say, by chance?—contact you. Understood?"

"Yes, sir."

When Thanos left the office, Dimitri and Eleni looked at the police director with puzzled faces, but Pano smiled broadly. Tapping his finger against his temple, Pano said, "You are *poniros* like a fox, sir. I see what you're doing."

Although *poniros* meant sly or cunning, it could also have a connotation of wicked, and Roussos said with a laugh, "Pano, you're incorrigible. The fact is that I am merely giving an important assignment to one of my subordinates, and on a matter like this, speed is important."

Eleni said, "Ah, so the police underdirector will not be available to insist on accompanying us on any raid tonight. But will he obey you and not tell the minister?"

"I think," said Roussos, "that we already have enough people so we will not miss him on our raid. And I doubt that he will want to put such a lush assignment as Paris in jeopardy by deliberately disobeying me. You can all leave now. Take your lunch and siesta early, but do take them, I insist. You will need your food and rest. Come back at three-thirty and I will call the minister. Oh, one more thing, Dimitri, call the American Embassy and talk to this Robert Jensen. Tell him there is an important new development in the matter of the ambassador's niece, and I will give him the details if he can be at my office promptly at three-thirty this afternoon."

*   *   *   *

Victoria brought Roussos some lunch from home, which he ate at his desk as he made notes on the logistics of the night's planned activity.

Promptly at three-thirty, Bob Jensen presented himself at DSI headquarters and was shown into the police director's office. He said, "The ambassador is excited and gratified. Just to get some action on the matter is encouraging."

"I hope you will not be disappointed, *Kyrie* Jensen. You will excuse me for not offering you coffee."

Jensen's facial expression was neutral. "That's all right. I can do without."

"This is a genuine lead." Roussos proceeded to tell him all that he had discovered so far.

There was a knock on the door, and Dimitri, Eleni, and Pano came in. "You know my assistants, *Kyrie* Jensen? They are working with me on this. Now what we don't know for certain is that the woman observed at the Skyros villa was actually *Despoinis* Pickering, but we must act as if she was. We will use scouts to crawl to the sides of the two-story house, break every window, and throw tear gas canisters in every room, up and down. At the same time other men will enter with massive fire power."

"But suppose the kidnappers still get a chance to kill her?"

"We have to take calculated risks. I will not be using amateurs. My men will be some of the best trained and most experienced paramilitary policemen in all Greece."

"What's the alternative?"

"There's been no demand for ransom, nor any other communication from these people, even though they've had her for some two days now. I think it's significant that she's the niece of the American ambassador, and I think it's a political matter. They are desperate men, and when it comes to keeping things secret, Greece is like a sieve. They may very well decide to dispose of her as the main witness against them. Her life is in grave danger no matter what decision we make."

"I need to call the ambassador."

"Use my phone," said Roussos, stepping around his desk and standing in a corner with his three aides.

Jensen made his call. "All right," he said, "the ambassador is willing to take the chance. However, I want to go with you."

Roussos looked shocked. "Go with us? Of course not. You're an inexperienced civilian. We can't take a chance with you. It's not allowed."

"I insist that I go with you."

"I am sorry, no," said Roussos, looking at his watch. "Now I must make a telephone call. Please wait with me. I want you present."

He telephoned Minister Petropoulos and explained the new developments. At first Petropoulos was delighted.

Roussos mentioned that he would need his approval to get necessary men and equipment from the paramilitary unit.

Petropoulos said, "What does Police Underdirector Thanos think about your plan of attack? Will he lead the raid?"

"The police underdirector is not available. He's on assignment in Paris."

"What! Roussos, you mean you sent your deputy to Paris at a time like this?"

"We're always working on important cases, sir. There's no good time to be unavailable. And he's working on the Zavalas case, which you consider so important."

"I see what you're doing, Roussos. All right, I'll play the way you play. Call off the raid until you can get Thanos back. I will not authorize any use of paramilitary forces until Thanos can go with them. Is that understood?"

"Sir, I have the American ambassador's security representative with me and he has already cleared the raid with the ambassador. They understand, as we do, that this matter has become time crucial. You know how this kind of thing gets leaked out, and that will only make the kidnappers more nervous and desperate."

"You have someone from the American Embassy with you?"

"Yes, would you like to talk to him and tell him that you can't authorize the use of paramilitary troops? If we have to go to Skyros without a paramilitary force, it will be that much more dangerous for the American woman."

"Roussos! Roussos! Go to the devil! All right, you'll have your damned authorization in five minutes, but you'll hear a lot more about this later. Let me talk to the American."

"At this moment, sir, I'm only concerned with the safety of the ambassador's niece. Here's the American representative, Robert Jensen. He speaks fluent Greek." He handed the phone to Jensen.

Covering up the mouthpiece with his hand, Jensen smiled and said, "Do I go with you tonight?"

Roussos suddenly realized that he had been outfoxed in his own maneuver. "What! Oh, all right. Yes, yes, anything, just let him know that your embassy approves."

Jensen talked a few minutes to the minister and hung up. "Minister Petropoulos just wanted to verify that the embassy understood the risks, and he said he had full confidence in your executing his plan."

"I'm sure he has. Dimitri, I want you to stay here as my main contact with headquarters in case there is any need for a change in plans. Don't look at me that way. We can't all be heroes at the action. Also get a proper uniform without insignia of rank for Mr. Jensen so he won't get shot by mistake. Pano, get a large car to take the rest of us to the police airbase. Eleni, get a paramedic to meet us at the airbase. We'll get this resolved by tonight or...or I might not be around much longer."

CHAPTER 9

▼

Victoria put the telephone down, a little rueful that Spyro was not coming home that night. He didn't have to explain what he was doing. She was certain it had something to do with following through on the information she had given him about Marilyn Pickering. He would tell her about it later as they sat on the balcony and drank some wine together.

Not having practiced her daily singing, she went to the piano and rehearsed for her part in *Tosca*. She had great respect for the ambiguous role of Tosca, for which her dramatic voice as a spinto soprano fitted her well, but Puccini's opera also involved some high notes that could be treacherous. Two hours later she felt she had practiced enough. She had a light dinner of a cucumber, tomato, and feta cheese salad and a sliced chicken breast sandwich. She wouldn't have wine, not without Spyro.

She had grown so dependent on just his presence. When he was there she soaked him up as a piece of dry bread would soak up water. She had become so in tune with him that his presence or absence had become the same for her as being alive or dead. How ironic, she thought, that her meeting Spyro had resulted from the ordeal of being terrorized by Pavlo Xynos.

Her thoughts turned to Marilyn again. She hoped she was all right and would soon be found. If anyone could find her, Victoria knew Spyro was the one. She seemed like such a nice girl, a little confused about life, perhaps, but she was still young and would learn. She was a pleasant young woman.

When all this was over, she and Spyro would have to invite Marilyn to come to dinner some night. She wondered if there were anyone else, some young bachelor, she might also invite. It must be horrible to get your first impression of

Greece by getting lost, or worse, kidnapped. Victoria would have to do her part to see that Marilyn got a more favorable view of Greece.

She undressed, washed, and put on a light négligé and wraparound robe. The sun having gone down and some of the heat of the day along with it, she went to the living room and pulled up the heavy wooden slats of the *rolladen* outside the window, which she now opened. A gentle breeze entered the room, making her feel comfortable. She sat in a Venetian version of a *Louis Quinze* chair that she had bought at the Athens flea market and had restored. Soft music played in the background as she sipped a cool orange soda. She thought of how pleasant her apartment was, so secure from the cares of the world, a castle of content.

Suddenly she heard a noise behind her. Turning her head she saw the one person in the world of whom she was most terrified: Pavlo Xynos!

She had almost forgotten how evil looking his leering grin was. He was standing in the arch between the hallway and living room, only a sofa between them. He put the forefinger of his right hand up to his lips and silently ordered her to be quiet. In his left hand he held a knife.

The tiny fuzz hairs on her body straightened as if electrically charged. The muscles in her throat tightened. She could hardly breathe. She trembled. She could feel the beat of her heart wild and erratic as if being played by a drunken drummer. As Xynos approached her from around the sofa, she felt that she would die.

"I won't hurt you," he said, with his grin that seemed etched on steel. "I had to see you again as I promised."

She summoned enough strength to say, "How did you get in?"

"You mean past your guard? I saw him but he didn't see me. I was invisible."

"Get out! Please. Go away. Leave me alone."

You are so beautiful," he said with slobbering lips. "I just want to look at you and worship your beauty."

As she stared mesmerized at his face, she saw the drops of saliva oozing from the corners of his mouth. He reminded her of a mad dog she had seen when she was a child.

He folded his knife and put it in a pocket.

"How did you get in?"

"Without a key? It was easy. I've been trained. I can do many more things now than before when I was a nobody. Now people pay attention to me. You have not forgotten that you owe me a kiss?"

Her body involuntarily jerked. Seized with fear, all she could do was say over and over, "Please go away. Please leave me alone."

"You must be kind to me. I won't even ask you to love me now. Just don't hate me? We will start with a kiss."

"I can't stand the sight of you. Why do you want to frighten me?"

"I love you, Victoria. I killed a man for you. And soon I will kill another, this time the man who was responsible for bringing me to trial."

Thinking that he meant Roussos, she said, "No, you can't do that. He was only doing his job."

"Antonidis, his job? His job was to condemn me for accidentally killing a professor who insulted me? I will kill Antonidis and satisfy my employers at the same time. Then I will come back for you, my lovely one."

"Does that mean you will go now?"

"After you give me the kiss you owe me." He took another step toward her.

"Never!" She shuttered with icy cold all over.

"I will go now only if you kiss me first. Just one little kiss. Not even a passionate kiss, just one little friendly one. Please, my Victoria."

As he took each step toward her, she walked backward until she felt herself up against a wall. Now he placed himself so closely in front of her that they were almost touching. He grabbed her around the waist and brought her body even closer into a tight embrace.

She felt like screaming or fainting. She wondered what he would do if she spit in his face again. But she was too afraid to try it a second time.

Suddenly there was a loud knock on the door, and Xynos jerked his head around to confront whoever was there. The knocking was repeated more loudly than before.

"*Despoinis Victoria. Einai i astynomia. O Pavlos Xynos einai sto ktirio.*" Miss Victoria. It is the police. Pavlo Xynos is in the building.

Victoria took a step toward the door. Xynos barred her and in a whispery voice told her to be still. "Don't move until I am gone." He ran to the kitchen and disappeared from sight. Victoria began moving again and, seeing it now safe, opened the door.

A man she recognized as one of the undercover policemen guarding her came in and apologized. "I am sorry to disturb you, Miss Renfrew, but I think Xynos is somewhere in the building. I have called for help."

She started to say something, then collapsed in his arms. Quickly regaining consciousness, she rose to see that the undercover man had been joined by another plainclothesman and a uniformed policeman.

"He was here," she said in faint words. "He was here. How could he get in?"

The plainclothesman who had just come in and who seemed to be the senior officer, ordered the other two to search the apartment. He then introduced himself as *Ypastynomos B*, Inspector, Roditis, and explained that the policeman on guard had noticed the usual tenants coming in and out during the day. One of them was the man who lived in Apartment 2-Delta. About ten minutes later, however, the same man who lived in 2-Delta entered the building again without having left. Apparently there were two men, one disguised as the legitimate resident.

The uniformed policeman appeared in the kitchen doorway. "*Den einai edo, omos to parathyro stin kouzina einai anoikto.*" He is not here, but the kitchen window is open.

Xynos had again made his escape through the window, which opened on a fire escape.

"Get after him," yelled the inspector. "Sotiri," he called to the policeman who had been stationed in the alley.

They heard many footsteps below, then silence followed by loud swearing. One of the guards shouted up to the inspector. "Sotiri is dead. Xynos must have knifed him and escaped."

At this moment, Victoria collapsed again in the inspector's arms.

*   *   *   *

It was late afternoon, and Marilyn and Yorgo were walking along the small beach. Bare rock hills gently descended from opposite directions to almost touch each other, but they left enough of an opening to form a sandy beach. Behind the two strollers the large gray-green dinghy in much need of paint rested on its side against the solid rock. In front of them at the other end of the beach was a net where her captors frequently played volleyball. To their left perched on a rocky plateau was the kidnappers' villa with its 360-degree view.

The men inside the house were mostly newcomers to Marilyn. The ones who had taken her to this villa had been replaced by other men as the cabin cruiser came and went, and only Yorgo remained of her original captors. Marilyn had the impression that these men had families and regular jobs so they couldn't afford to remain away from home too long. She was aware, as they must have been, that she was getting in a position to identify more and more of them.

Yorgo had said he was not married, and being virtually self-employed plus having fluent English must have made him the natural choice for her main contact. She could see that he was getting worried like so many of the others, and once when she asked him about it, he mentioned again the non-appearance of his friend Jimmy.

She had tried to elicit more information from Yorgo, but although he was talkative on some matters, he became a clam on others, and sometimes turned quite angry at her questions. She knew she was taking a chance every time she asked a new one, but she could feel that his growing discouragement was making him weak and vulnerable and even careless. She had learned for certain that these men were somehow interested in her uncle, not her for her own sake. Nor did they seem to be holding her for a ransom. She felt she was more a hostage, but couldn't guess for what.

Something else that impressed her was the apparent character and background of her keepers. They all seemed well educated, clean-cut, usually polite, and not at all like criminals. To while away the time, they read books in English and other foreign languages, listened to symphonic and light classical music on a CD player, and spoke to each other in Greek in a manner that appeared to her to be aristocratic, a sort of *noblesse oblige* manner. Although some of the men seemed to be more deferential toward a number of the others, no one appeared to be in charge. In the morning before it got too hot, they practiced at soccer and volleyball at the net end of the beach. In the afternoon they frequently went swimming, and Marilyn noted that they wore swimming trunks—modesty in the presence of their unwilling guest?

She was not allowed outside without an escort, but Yorgo was apparently the only one willing to be with her. The others seemed formally polite toward their prisoner, but kept her at a distance. It was as if they didn't want to get too involved on a personal basis. They had resolved the issue of escorting her to the toilet by giving her a chamber pot, and she was allowed one visit to the bathroom each morning to empty the pot and give herself a light washing. Again, it was Yorgo who escorted her downstairs for her daily ablutions and back up again.

Marilyn suspected that Yorgo was giving her extra food whenever he could, perhaps from his own share of the rations. At times he would go out of his way to make sure she was as comfortable as could be under the circumstances. Yet at other times he would refuse to talk at all to her, and they could walk up and down the beach for an hour or two without his saying more than a few necessary words. She didn't know what to make of him. He seemed to have two relationships with her, captor and bashful beau. He seemed to want more out of her than he was willing to ask for or she would be willing to give.

This afternoon the weather was pleasant and the sea calm. Marilyn knelt to pick up a variegated seashell with her free hand. Yorgo was holding her other hand, as he had explained was necessary in order for her to be allowed outside. She couldn't understand the reasoning behind this restriction; after all, where could she run to? He was usually gentle with her, but once when a low-flying airplane seemed to be coming toward them, he pulled her down roughly into a crevice in the rocks so they would be difficult to distinguish from the air. The plane veered off without coming any closer, but Marilyn had scraped her knees badly.

They ambled over to the volleyball net, stood there a minute or two, turned, and slowly made their way back. She knew well the route between the net and the dinghy, having now walked it at least a hundred times. There was not much to do. Occasionally Yorgo would briefly release her hand so he could pick up a large stone and like a discus thrower vigorously hurl it out across the water, trying each time to make it skim further. Sometimes they would leave their shoes by the rocks and wade barefoot in the surf.

He asked her if she knew much English poetry, and she said a little, both English and American. He said he'd be pleased if she'd recite some for him. Of the Americans he especially liked Robert Frost. For British poems there was one by Henley that appealed to him with the line "captain of my fate." After Marilyn repeated the little that she could remember of this poem, he completed it for her and then said that someday he planned to translate it into Greek.

They started walking back to the villa. He was looking down at the sand and kicking stones out of the way. Suddenly he said, "I like you very much."

For a moment she was stunned and didn't know what to reply. She wanted to say, "If you like me so much, why are you holding me a prisoner?" She didn't want to offend him, but she was not going to tell him that she liked him, too, in the sense that he undoubtedly meant. What could she say, "I like you as a kidnapper, but only in a sisterly way?

He had stopped walking and turned to look at her, his own face searching for a response.

Marilyn silently returned his stare, then said softly, "Help me to get free, Yorgo."

"I can't." He seemed to be pleading with her to understand. "It's impossible for me."

"Why?"

"Because my cause is greater than any personal interest I have."

"What is your cause?"

"I can't tell you."

"Well, I'm glad that you like me, and I thank you for any kindness you may have shown me above and beyond those of the normal kidnapper to the normal victim."

"You're being sarcastic."

"Call it what you will. I'm tired of the way I've been treated, or mistreated, and I want to be free. You can say you like me all you want, but that doesn't seem to help me very much."

He spoke again. "The others are getting nervous because Jimmy is so late."

"And you're not?"

"Oh, yes, I, too. Perhaps I am more nervous than the rest. I seem to have most of the responsibility for the thankless job of taking care of you. If Jimmy does not come soon, we are all in trouble. Perhaps even you."

"I know so little about your situation that I don't understand what you mean."

"It means that some of my companions want to abandon this place and the whole idea of keeping you as a hostage. It was a foolish idea in the first place. We're not going to influence the American government."

Her face lit up as she clutched at hope. "That sounds as if I might be free soon."

"Perhaps. If I were in charge I might set you free. But some of my associates feel that you have become more a danger than asset to them. You can recognize and identify them to the authorities."

Her body jolted and her hand tightened in his. Still shuddering, she realized that he had come close to saying what she had been fearing. They wanted to kill her. Part of her wanted to crumple up in despair, but another part prodded her to fight as much as possible for her life. She said, "Does that mean what I think it does?"

"Yes."

"But you wouldn't let them do that to me, would you, Yorgo?"

"We go by majority vote. There is too much at stake to consider the interests of any individual."

"What's at stake? What's so damned important for you to put me in this position?"

"I cannot tell you. But we do not intend to do evil to the world. If we sometimes have to take drastic steps, it is because our cause is so important. We don't expect the American government to help us, just not interfere with what we're doing. We need them to stay neutral. It was stupid to think that an ambassador's niece was going to influence American foreign policy."

She would have liked to have pursued his interest in the American govern-ment, but the danger to her life was a more immediate problem. She spoke in an angry voice full of disdain. "So the bottom line is that you wouldn't lift a finger to stop them from killing me?"

He let his head fall as if he no longer had the strength to hold it upright. Holding her hand more tightly, he said, "We must return." He increased his pace as he led her back up the path.

Entering the villa, they passed in front of his lounging companions. Hereto-fore they had at least seemed outwardly courteous toward her, but now she noticed that two of them were scowling as they looked at her. Locking her in her room, Yorgo said, "I'll bring you some dinner soon."

Marilyn looked around at the four bare walls, the small window, and the nar-row cot with its two frayed blankets. As dismal as her surroundings were, they represented life. They were still here. She could perceive them. As long as she could sense something, anything, a prison cell or what, she was alive. She was too young to die.

Going to the window she could see various ships in the distance. The sky was darkening, and some of the vessels already had lights on. She could still make out the shapes sailing far away, but in another half hour she would be able to see only the lights. Where was she? How long would she go on living? When would they be coming for her?

Yorgo brought her dinner: a piece of fried fish, a hunk of bread, some purple Greek olives, a slice of watermelon, and a large glass of water. She knew the men were drinking wine, but she was glad for the water and she drank it greedily. This was the first time they had given her meat or fish. She wondered if there was any significance to it, like the last meal before an execution. She ate everything, including, with great reluctance and feeling like a cannibal, the fish. She wanted to throw up, but with great effort she kept the food down. For her part, she was going to do everything possible to survive.

She lay on her cot staring at the ceiling. Not especially tired, she knew she wouldn't sleep yet, but there was nothing to do. Even if she had had some light in the room, she would not have felt like reading the book Yorgo had given her. There was nothing to do but wait. It was the waiting itself that was killing her. Why didn't they get it over with? She began gently sobbing and, without realiz-ing it, dozed off.

Sometime later she heard the door softly open. "Who is it?" she said, while asking herself, *Is this it? Has my time come?*

She heard Yorgo's voice and relaxed a little. It was almost a certainty in her mind that Yorgo would not be in on the final kill, neither as killer nor observer.

His whispered voice tried to reassure her. "Shhh. It is I, Yorgo. I can't sleep because of you. I want to be with you. I want to sleep with you." The voice in the doorway was so pleading.

She heard him advance into the room and quietly close the door. She breathed a deep sigh. Her time had not come yet. She couldn't imagine that he would knowingly have sex with her just before the executioner played out his role. The fact that Yorgo was here pleading with her for sex meant that she was safe for a little longer. Could she turn that to her advantage?

She dissembled to stall for time. "I don't know what you mean?"

"I want to join you in bed and make love to you. I've fallen in love with you, Marilyn, and I want us to know each other sexually."

"No, I can't do that." She knew that he could force himself on her and she would have no choice, but if he were giving her a choice, she'd make him negotiate for her consent. Of course, if he did use force, she might scream and wake the others. In that case, would he get in trouble, or would they just watch and applaud? In any event, her position would be no better.

"Please, Marilyn. I don't want to wake the others. Please let me make love to you."

"And then what would you do? Scorn me because of your old-fashioned morals?"

"No, no, I'd love you all the more. I'd become more attached to you."

"If you really loved me, you'd help me escape."

"No, please don't ask that. I can't do that."

"No, it would conflict with your sense of honor to help me get away from being killed by your companions because of some quest you have. The honorable thing to do would be to make love to me first, then stand by while your companions slit my throat."

He remained silent and motionless for what seemed to be a long time. "Please believe me, I've been your counsel in discussions we've had about what to do next. I've defended you to the point where I'm almost an outcast. I've done everything possible to save you."

"But have you succeeded? Even from the way you talk now, it seems as if I have been condemned to death. Don't ask me for sex, Yorgo, not unless you're prepared to help me escape after. We could leave together in the middle of the night. We could take the dinghy and go around the coast of this island; surely there must be other people on it, some kind of village or other. And your companions couldn't pursue us because there is only one boat. You'd know where to go. You could save me and at the same time get yourself out of this stupid mission that seems to motivate you. Save me, Yorgo. Do you want to see me murdered?"

She realized that he could lie to her, promise her anything and then laugh after, but he didn't seem to be the type. He had a strange code of honor, which she couldn't quite fathom, but she didn't think he would lie to her under circumstances such as these.

"I cannot betray my friends, Marilyn. We took an oath. I can only promise that I will speak to them again, even more strongly than earlier, before they make any final decision. And that's the truth, there is no final decision yet."

"But a final decision is understood, isn't it?"

Again silence. Then she heard the soft sweep of the door being opened and closed, and the metallic click of her being locked in again. She was alone now. She began wondering if she should have acted any differently. Was there anything else that she could have said—or done—to have improved her situation?

She knew it was late, but had no idea of the time. Was it closer to midnight or dawn? Looking between the bars of the window, she saw fewer lights now, and they seemed further in the distance. Yet because of the bright moonlight, she could still make out the outlines of some of the nearer ships. She didn't think she could go back to sleep again, so she waited by the window for a long time.

How long she didn't know. She was sure the minutes had passed into hours. She was tired, spent by her thoughts and fears. She had gone over her life in her mind and had dwelled on those times when she knew she had made mistakes. Perhaps the biggest mistake of all was in her treatment of Jake. She should have accepted his offer of marriage, even though she knew now that she could never love him. But when she was gone, she knew that he would be the first person to mourn her.

Still looking out the window, she wondered what was happening on the beach. There was no artificial illumination, but in the cloud-veiled moonlight she could make out shapes, almost human shapes. Yes, they were humans, and they were along the side of the dinghy. Now she realized there was an even larger craft partly in the water and partly on shore, and not too far away there was a still larger boat. Were they more of the kidnappers coming back? At this hour? But neither of the two new boats, large and small, seemed to be the usual cabin cruiser.

Why were their shapes keeping so close to the cover of the rocks instead of coming directly to the villa? The sand was light so that the dark shapes would have been given away had they not moved quickly toward the rocks, where they appeared only as shadows. Only their movements betrayed them. They darted in and out among the rocks, and frequently disappeared for a few moments. Now she could see them advancing from the edge of the hilltop toward the house, looking like a single file of ants on the trail of food.

Staring mesmerized in her sleep-deprived frame of mind, stupefied even, Marilyn needed a little time to realize that these shadows were her rescuers. Greek police coming to free her. There could be a battle, but the newcomers had the benefit of surprise. Possibly some of the kidnappers would be killed. Even Yorgo. She hoped Yorgo wouldn't get hurt. But she was going to be free. She wasn't going to die after all.

Unless? Anyone could get killed in a situation like this. In battle no one was safe, not even Marilyn herself. She could be killed by the very people who had been sent to help her. Also, once the attack began, the kidnappers would realize that she was the main witness against them. Some of them possibly—no, probably—would rush to eliminate her.

The figures were getting closer. Now her thoughts were with them. Suppose the kidnappers had posted sentries. Suppose they opened fire on the handful of men from the boat and killed some, perhaps all. Perhaps the rescue attempt would be a failure.

How many were there of the rescuers? As they approached the house, they started spreading to the left and right so as to surround their target. She thought there might be a dozen, perhaps more. They probably outnumbered the kidnappers two to one. So they should indeed prevail if there were no alarm.

Now in the moonlight she could also see eyes showing from the slits in the masks that the rescuers seemed to be wearing. At least she thought she could see them. The men were almost immediately below her, now motionlessly clinging to the walls. She knew she was imagining some things, but really seeing others. This was all so make-believe. She began praying for the attacking force. She hoped they could maintain the element of surprise. She could almost tap on the window to let them know where she was, but she dared not for fear that she would give them away. They knew what they were doing. She couldn't say the same for herself.

They must have the house surrounded now. And still no alarm. Good. It was going to start almost any second. She hoped that she would survive the attack. She wished she were among them, advancing with an automatic attack gun to fight her kidnappers. She wished she could so direct the attack that it would come out exactly the way she wanted.

But if she could see the threat to the kidnappers, why couldn't they see it, too? Why didn't they have someone looking out? Had they made themselves too drunk to assign a lookout? By the clear light of the moon she could see that the attackers were starting to move again.

Suddenly it happened. A gigantic explosion from the front of the house lit up the entire sky, illuminating the clouds as if beginning a huge celebration. Another explosion from the rear. More fireworks seemingly from all over. An explosion to the side, almost beneath her, let her see illuminated debris flying past her window. She felt the force of that one, but thought she was not hurt. Then the automatic guns began firing as if on cue. Large bursts, short bursts, and continuing bursts were followed by a brief silence that seemed to last for minutes but was probably no more than a few seconds. Then gunfire from every part of the house. Marilyn felt as if the roof was about to blow off.

With a bang her door burst open. A blinding light flashed on her face. Men grabbed her and led her away. In her blindness she couldn't tell if these were the good men or the bad ones. Her rescuers or her killers? They led her downstairs. In actuality they pushed her down the stairs so that she could hardly maintain her balance. Only the tight grip on her shoulder by the man immediately behind her kept her from tumbling. They were pushing her too much. Was there any need for this if the battle was over?

The lights were on in the large room downstairs, and even in the hallway she could see who had possession of her. They were men dressed in black from head to foot. Only slits for eyes, nose, and mouth defied the blackness of their forms. Their uniforms were black sweaters, black pants, and black boots. They were wearing black balaclavas over their heads, and they had belts with pistols, grenades, and ammunition clips, all black. The automatic weapons in their hands resembled Uzis that she had seen back home. These men were her rescuers. But couldn't they treat her less roughly?

They pushed and pulled her hurriedly to the middle of the big room, where the kidnappers used to congregate. It was like a slaughterhouse. She recognized her former captors more from their clothes than anything else. Some of them seemed to be torn to shreds with blood oozing from dozens—hundreds?—of holes in their bodies. She counted quickly. Six. There were six dead bodies on the floor.

And yet. And yet there was one standing, blood slithering down his arm, wounded but alive. Yorgo! She couldn't help but yell out, "Don't hurt him. He has been kind to me. He can't harm you now."

A black-clad man approached her. The others stopped and watched him. He seemed to be in charge, and she knew he was the man to whom she should make her appeal. But raising his arm, this man, the leader, slammed the back of his hand across her face. The unexpected blow spun her around. She struggled not to fall. When she recovered she was in almost the same position as before the blow, having been turned in a complete circle. She could tell from the taste of blood that at a minimum her lip was cut.

The man pointed to Yorgo and barked out some orders which sounded like gibberish to her. Two men pulled Yorgo to the wall where he could face her and look into her eyes. What she saw there was hopelessness. But he tried to smile.

He only managed to say, "I'm sorry, Marilyn," before the leader aimed his weapon and pulled the trigger. The gun hardly moved as the man held it down, using his strength to keep it from rising as a myriad of 9mm. Parabellum bullets concentrated on just one part of Yorgo's belly. Or what had been his belly. That belly was now completely ripped out.

The leader turned toward Marilyn and drew a pistol from its holster, raising the butt end high. Down it came on her head, and she lost consciousness.

CHAPTER 10

▼

The island of Skyros, in the Aegean Sea about 100 miles northeast of Athens, resembles a poorly drawn kidney roughly twenty miles long and eight miles across at its widest point. The village of Skyros in the northeast of the island is inland from the coast. As in olden times when it was settled with a view of protection from primitive pirates, it is still located behind a coastal ridge. It is especially noted for the midget-size furniture the villagers make and also for the nude statue of British poet Rupert Brooke, who died on Skyros of blood poisoning during the First World War.

The Papamavrogiannopoulos villa was in an isolated southwestern part of the island. Roussos had ordered the policeman in the small outpost in the village to reconnoiter the area around the villa, but above all not to be seen while doing so. This policeman took a jeep and a pair of high power binoculars to the point where the mountainous territory descended to meet the sea; there he could perch himself behind rock cover and spy on the villa. He did not take a radio with him because the budget for the police in rural areas was too small to afford state-of-the-art equipment, and the radios they had were primitive hand-me-downs. The policeman was able to observe that the villa was occupied by a good number of men, and on one occasion he saw a man and woman taking a walk on the beach. The man looked like a Greek, but the woman seemed to be northern European.

Roussos sent a small team from the much bigger island of Evvoia to reinforce the lone observer, and these police officers took turns so as to keep the watch going every hour of the day and night. Again, their orders were first to use extreme discretion and second to observe as much as possible without taking any action. Nonetheless, they were able to confirm that the woman on the beach strongly resembled the woman in the photograph of Marilyn.

The action would come from the crack teams Roussos brought from the mainland in two helicopters. They flew over Evvoia to the island of Skopelos and then circled to approach Skyros from the north so they would not be noticed by anyone in the villa. Landing about two-and-a-half hours before dawn behind the highest point of the island, an 850-foot peak, they divided into two forces and continued by foot. But by the time the two teams met again where their original scout had been situated, the action was over.

$$\ast \qquad \ast \qquad \ast \qquad \ast$$

Accompanied by Pano, Eleni, and Bob Jensen, Roussos walked toward the police scout to get briefed on the current situation. That policeman in turn excitedly ran toward Roussos with his arms flailing the air, so the police director knew instantly something was wrong.

Struggling to regain coherent speech, the policeman made his report. At 2:40 a.m. he had heard explosions and much gunfire coming from the villa, and the sky was lit up with flames. The villa was on fire. Because of the way the villa was oriented, he did not see any individuals, but shortly after the noise ceased, he saw a boat heading out from the villa's bay to a larger ship in the distance. Mindful of his orders, he waited a while, then cautiously approached the villa. The flames had died down because there was little wood for them to feed on, the villa being made mainly of stone and concrete. Looking in, he could see men lying on the concrete floor. He went in to see if any were still alive. It looked very doubtful, but he dragged each body outside. There were seven in all, all riddled with bullets and assuredly dead. Answering a question from Bob Jensen, he said no, he had not seen any woman in the house, but he had not gone upstairs in the still smoking building.

The group rushed down to the villa, where Roussos and his men examined the stretched out bodies. Jensen ran inside and climbed the stone steps to the second floor. It was still full of smoke and he knew he was in danger of asphyxiation. Covering his nose with a handkerchief, he darted in and out of the several rooms, finally convinced that Marilyn Pickering was not in any of them.

"May he go to the devil," shouted Roussos to the air.

"You mean Little Achilles?" asked Pano.

"You know damned well who I mean. We should have been here one day earlier and this never would have happened."

Jensen came out of the house, his eyes full of tears from the smoke. "There is no one upstairs."

Roussos had sent some of his own men in, and they reported the same for both floors. Marilyn Pickering, if she had ever been there in the first place, was certainly not there now.

"I don't believe this," said Jensen. "I don't dare report this to the ambassador."

Suddenly the situation changed. One of the policemen accompanied by a civilian dressed in village attire approached Roussos and said, "This man is a fisherman from the other side of that ridge. He found a foreign woman with bare feet limping down the road. She is now in his house with his wife and she seems in a daze."

There could be little doubt that it was Marilyn Pickering. She was resting in a sitting position on a narrow cot with her back against the wall and her feet soaking in a bucket of water. She looked tired, yet she seemed grateful to be able to rest and relax, much as a soldier might lean back with comfort against a tree at the end of a fourteen-mile march.

Roussos started eagerly to question her, but his few words of broken English were of no help. Nor could any of his inner team converse with her. Pano tried, but his English was as scant as Roussos's; Eleni didn't even try.

"Where is Dimitri when I need him?" Roussos yelled to no one in particular.

Pano said, "You ordered him to stay behind."

Jensen said, "Aren't you glad now that you brought me along?"

Roussos scowled, but nodded his head affirmatively. "Ask her what happened. Ask her who the dead men were. And ask who killed them."

"If you don't mind, shouldn't we have your paramedic examine her first?"

He said it in Greek, but Marilyn smiled appreciatively as if she could sense what he meant. "Do you speak English?"

"I'm from the American Embassy. Bob Jensen. I was supposed to meet you at the airport, but I got waylaid."

On hearing his words, she eagerly moved forward and tried to rise from the cot, forgetting that her feet were still in the bucket so she almost fell over. She sat again and smiled at Jensen. "What a relief? You mean it's over? I'm with friends? I can't tell you what I've been through. Who are all these other people?"

"Let's take it gradually," said Jensen. "Are you physically hurt?"

"I don't think so, except for sore feet and an aching head."

"We have a paramedic here. We'll all leave while he examines you. And then if you're up to it, we'd like to ask a few questions."

The paramedic opened his bag and took out a stethoscope. Jensen suggested that the rest of them should leave the house, which they did.

Outside Roussos said, "She seemed clear-minded. Do you think she's all right?"

"Your paramedic should tell us. In any event, we should get her back to Athens as soon as possible and take her to a hospital for a complete examination."

"Of course," said Roussos. "But if the paramedic says it's all right, I would like to ask a few questions. We must find out what happened and what is behind this."

Fifteen minutes later the paramedic said she seemed to be in good condition and was able to talk with a clear mind. Roussos and Jensen proceeded inside again.

Jensen said, "Do you feel ready to answer some questions now?"

"I don't mind. Let's both ask each other questions. Where am I? How soon can I see my uncle? And now I'm hungry again. My mind is clear—it's just that it was so horrible. And poor Yorgo." She said the last three words mournfully. "I rejected him and he only had a few hours to live. It was all so horrible."

The fisherman brought in some bread and cheese for her together with a little wine.

She ate while still talking, and gradually she was able to sketch in the entire picture of what had happened to her from the time she left the airport until she regained consciousness outside the house and started walking. "It's funny," she said. "They hit me with a gun butt before there was any fire, and I fell to the floor inside the house. But when I awoke, I was a good distance away from the house. They must have carried me out."

"In other words," said Jensen, "apparently they didn't want you to die. Interesting." He turned from Marilyn to explain everything to Roussos.

Roussos was impatient yet sympathetic. There was so much he needed to know, but he took his cues from Jensen and tried not to ply too hard with his questions. The advent of the killers in black commando costume for the moment mystified him. He could cope with the kidnappers and had a tentative idea who they might be. He had had one of his men photograph the seven dead men, and he didn't think it would be too difficult to identify them when they got back to Athens. But who were these men who had killed them so viciously and why? They were not a part of any Greek government organization that he had ever heard of.

Jensen suggested that Marilyn was worn out and they had better stop the questions. She had given them the highlights, but she wasn't in any condition to be drilled over and over on the small, but important, details. They should get her back to Athens and have her checked by doctors.

"Yes, of course," said Roussos. "But do mention this to her that I'm a good friend of Victoria Renfrew, and Victoria will be delighted when I tell her tonight that she's safe."

Marilyn said, "Oh, yes. Are you her fiancé then?"

Jensen translated.

Roussos's face reddened. "Ah, well, let's just say that we're very good friends."

They flew her to Athens and took her immediately to Evangelismos Hospital on Vasilissis Sofias, just a short distance from the American Embassy. Knowing that his people would be having the annual Fourth of July reception, Jensen decided to walk to the embassy and tactfully get the ambassador away from his guests. Ned Atherton, who had been informed earlier by radio of Marilyn's status, was eagerly waiting for word of her arrival. He and Jensen drove back to the hospital, arriving less than half an hour after Marilyn first appeared there.

After another hour, two doctors who had checked Marilyn thoroughly were able to say they could find nothing wrong with her internally or externally, except that she had a lump on the back of her head that would take days to go down. They gave her some strong analgesics. Although her head might be sore and her feet bruised, she seemed otherwise all right and could be released.

Atherton and Jensen took her to the ambassador's residence in the chauffeured embassy Cadillac. Before they left, Roussos asked if Marilyn could appear at his office tomorrow morning to answer some more questions.

Jensen called the ambassador aside and said, "Roussos has been extremely helpful, sir. We would never have found her without him."

"Oh! I had the impression from Minister Petropoulos that his office had done all the work of discovery and Roussos was merely performing a rather low-level task under orders."

"Don't you believe it, sir. It was all Roussos from beginning to end. He discovered where she was being held and he planned all the details for her rescue. His lieutenants tell me that all Petropoulos did was to delay the operation twenty-four hours, even taking the chance that it might have been fatal for your niece. That's why I think we should be as considerate as possible with Roussos."

"Okay, but you accompany her and don't let them put her through any third-degree."

Marilyn's meeting with the police director had to be postponed for a day. Her head and feet still hurt, and her uncle insisted she remain one more day in bed, where he and his wife did all possible to pamper her. By that evening she was feeling much better and actually looking forward to her interview with the police. It sounded exciting. And she was also eager to learn more about both her kidnappers and the commandos in black sweaters who had butchered them.

*   *   *   *

On Friday morning Bob Jensen telephoned DSI to re-schedule the postponed appointment for Marilyn with Roussos. The police director was working on a tight schedule. He wanted very much to interview her, but the only time he could fit her in was at eleven o'clock. In the meantime, he was catching up on the progress being made on other current cases.

Police Underdirector Jason Thanos was still in Paris. He telephoned and said he needed a couple of days more there. Roussos quickly balanced the expense to DSI of the extra time against the desirability of having Thanos out of sight for two more days. He decided it was a cheap price to pay. After all, the bulk of the cost was for the air fare and that wouldn't change. Approved.

After some prodding from Roussos, Thanos made a quick report over the telephone. He had visited the French police, but all they would say was that General Zavalas had not engaged in any suspicious anti-French activities. For the most part Zavalas associated with former Greek army officers who had fled Greece after the overthrow of the revolutionary Colonel's Regime in 1973. These men were mostly too old to get in trouble.

Zavalas himself was one of the younger ones in that revolution, and had survived the purge in Greece because he was unimportant at the time. Remaining in the army, he rose to major general, then was tried for participating in a conspiracy to restore the Colonels' Regime. However, the case against him could not be proven, and he was found not guilty. Nonetheless he went into voluntary exile, and only recently returned to Greece.

"He is too clever for the French," Thanos told Roussos. "He obviously is still conspiring to overthrow the government, else why would he come back?"

"You say obviously. What indications do you have?"

"Well, the very fact that he returned to Athens. He has a reputation for being a trouble-maker."

"Hmm. Guilt by reputation. Well, you keep after any incriminating information. Somehow we'll get along without you."

Thanos said, "Incidentally, I understand that you had an abortive raid against the kidnappers of the American ambassador's niece. I'm glad I wasn't involved in that. It doesn't look good on one's record."

"Oh, so you'd agree that I did you a favor by sending you to Paris?"

Roussos thought he heard a "tee-hee" on the other end of the phone, and he could imagine the wide smirk on Thanos's face. "I'd say you did me a double favor, sir."

Next, Chief Superintendent Pano Maniatis reported on Pavlo Xynos. "Still nothing, sorry, Spyro." They were alone and both felt relaxed. "No sign of Xynos anywhere. I used the two surveillance teams as you suggested, and I think we can safely say that Xynos has not been following Minister Antonidis. We have also been keeping a sharp eye out for any sign of him near your apartment in Kolonaki or around the opera house, and nothing there either. Of course, we've checked out relatives and student acquaintances, but he's smart and I think he's deliberately kept away from them."

Roussos said, "His terrorist employers will have a certain amount of patience with him, but if he has been assigned to assassinate Minister Antonidis, he cannot afford to waste too much time. Other than sending his photograph and description to all police units, the only thing we can do is to keep watch on both Antonidis and Victoria Renfrew. Xynos's fanatic interest in those two people will have to bring him out of hiding."

After Pano left, Superintendent Eleni Karolou was scheduled to see Roussos at her own request.

"It's about the Zavalas case," she told him.

He ordered coffee for the two of them and said, "Thanos is in charge of that case now, if there is in fact a case. I have no idea why we're investigating him, except for those letters that Petropoulos seems so anxious to get."

"I was glad you took me off the case, but it seems I'm not really off. Do you remember that I was developing Zavalas's maid, Marika, as an informant? I told her she'd have to work with Thanos now, and she absolutely refused. She will only work with me. In fact, sir, I suppose I had better tell you. She says she's in love with me."

"Hmm. Did you do anything to encourage that?"

Eleni focused her eyes downward. "I…, well, yes, I admit, well, I had an affair with her?"

"Affair? You mean sexual?"

"You and I haven't discussed it in so many words, but you know I have sapphist inclinations, and Marika does, too."

"We had no need to discuss it. What you do in your free time is your business. But now you have an informant problem."

"Well, that's it, sir. I think it best that I continue on this case. Oh, I know I could see Marika on the side and avoid any further inquiries on the matter, but if the case is to continue, I can be far more effective than Thanos—meaning no disrespect to him, of course."

"Of course. You must always be respectful of your superior officers. Well, what do you suggest as far as the Zavalas case is concerned?"

"I've met him, you know. I was visiting Marika, and Zavalas unexpectedly came home. Showing good presence of mind, she introduced me to him as her aunt. And you'll never guess what—he came on to me. He likes me."

"I can see where that could be awkward, especially given your sexual preferences."

"Oh, no, sir. I told you I was a sapphist, but not exclusively. Sex is sex with me. If you don't mind my telling you so, I have affairs with both men and women. Of course, I draw the line at superior officers—that's why I felt it necessary to reject Pano's advances once." She was blushing deeply now.

"I see. But again, what are you suggesting?"

"Marika is very observant. She tells me that Zavalas has a heavy safe in his study. She says that because of my interest, she watched him open it once and remembered the combination. Later she opened it herself. It contained some money, bank accounts, a will, and other formal papers, nothing else, not even his passport. But he also keeps a locked box under his bed, and he keeps the key on his person all the time. Now, since we're looking for some letters, I could give in to his entreaties, and perhaps Marika could drug a drink for him. When I have him in bed sleeping, I could…"

"I think we'd better stop there, Eleni. I don't want to hear the details. But I understand what you're saying, and I can appreciate the sacrifice you're offering to make. If I'm not mistaken, Zavalas is in his early seventies."

"It wouldn't be a sacrifice," she said with a smile. "I've had men his age before and some of them have performed rather well. He appears to be quite virile. It could be an interesting experience."

"Eleni, Eleni, we're getting into uncharted territory. I don't want to know about your sex life, and I can't ask you to get in bed with anyone. However, I keep Thanos on the case only so that it will not look to Minister Petropoulos as if we are dropping our investigation of Zavalas, but I don't expect much out of Thanos. His successes are based more on arresting some innocent beggar off the streets, beating the shit out of him, and getting him to confess to something he didn't commit. Now, our *modus operandi* allows us to investigate a case from more than one angle, and we don't have to have the right hand keep the left hand informed. Since you've, er, developed an, er, extraordinary source, I'll let you continue."

"My objective would be the so-called incriminating letters of Minister Antonidis. If they exist, they're probably in that locked box."

"I understood that was what you were saying. I won't inquire into your methodology. And you're right, Minister Antonidis has always strongly supported DSI in the past. Perhaps we owe him our support now, in addition to trying to protect him from assassination. *Entaxi.*" All right. "Use your own discretion to continue, and if you can get any letters without embarrassing our department, I want to see them first."

"Thank you, chief. I knew you'd approve."

"Keep in mind foremost what I said about not embarrassing our department."

Eleni left and Roussos looked at his watch. It was ten minutes past eleven, and he was late for his appointment with Bob Jensen and Marilyn Pickering.

*   *   *   *

Jensen was not waiting in Roussos's outer office, although Marilyn Pickering was. They had arrived around quarter of eleven, and almost immediately the receptionist received a telephone call for Jensen. The ambassador wanted him and Marilyn to come back to the embassy.

Atherton said, "We'll leave Marilyn at the embassy, then you and I will go to the airport. The Secretary of State has an unexpected layover at Ellinikon for four hours. He wants to discuss installation security, so I'll need you. You and I are to pick him up and bring him and an adviser to the Embassy. We'll also have lunch with the Greek Foreign Minister and one of his aides, so there'll be six of us. Then you and I can drive the Secretary back to the airport. Don't foul up this one. And hurry, we have no time to lose."

As Jensen was fond of saying, things just happened to him. In this case it was Marilyn who made it happen. She refused to go back with him.

She said, "We've already postponed this meeting long enough. I've been looking forward to it. Besides, the police director is a special friend of Victoria Renfrew, and she's a special friend of mine."

"Come on. There's no time to waste. Your uncle is waiting."

"I'm not going and you can't make me. I'm keeping our appointment."

"Your uncle won't like this."

"It's all his fault for always postponing the appointment. Don't you have to hurry? You don't want to keep my uncle and the Secretary of State waiting."

"*Chingado*," said Jensen under his breath, resorting to the street language of his last assignment.

"I understand Spanish and I don't think that was a nice thing to say."

"Come on, Marilyn, please. Look, Victoria's in an opera next week, and if you'll come with me now, I'll promise to take you."

"Victoria's sending me tickets anyway."

"Oh, great!"

The telephone rang again for him. It was the ambassador's secretary checking to see if he had started out. She said, "The ambassador's outside the embassy expecting you to arrive any minute now."

Putting down the phone, he yelled at Marilyn, "You can't do this to me."

She replied, "Then you've got nothing to worry about, have you?"

"To hell with it," he yelled as he stormed out of the office, leaving Marilyn by herself with a satisfied expression on her face while she patiently waited to be called by the police director.

After a short while, Eleni Karolou came out of Roussos's office, and the receptionist ushered Marilyn in.

Roussos was as disappointed as Jensen with the change in events. "Delight," he said. "Big joy, but English no good."

Pano Maniatis appeared in the outer office before the door was closed, and Roussos called for him.

"Interpret for us, Pano. Tell *Despoinis* Pickering that I am delighted to see her, but I expected Mr. Jensen, too, as an interpreter."

A shocked Pano started to comply. "Director great pleased Mr. Jensen not..., not you, but here." He smiled, hoping he got the right thought across.

A puzzled Marilyn threw out her arms in a gesture of hopelessness that was more clearly understood by them than their words had been by her.

"She doesn't understand anything you're saying," said Roussos. "Why can't you do a simple little thing like speaking English?"

Pano, now desperate, spoke to her again. "*Parlez vous français?*"

Roussos wondered why he hadn't thought of that himself, since he spoke a decent French. But it was to no avail. Marilyn shook her head; she didn't know French. "*Español?*" she asked with hope in her voice.

Exasperated, Roussos said to Pano, "*Fyge, Pano, fyge!*" Go, Pano, go! "*Thelo Dimitri amesos.*" I want Dimitri immediately.

Pano left, and Roussos made a few gestures to indicate that all would be resolved in a minute and please sit down. "*Kafé?*"

She nodded her head. "*S'il vous plâit*," she said, thinking that the display of the little French she knew would please him.

Since she had just told him that she didn't speak French, he felt more confused than ever, but he called for the *kafetzis* and ordered a *varyglyko* for himself and a c*afé au lait* for his visitor.

As she waited, she looked at Roussos and thought to herself that he was rather good looking—for an older man. Although she knew he was not showing himself at his best, she could sense behind the bluster and confusion that here was a strong man who could make a powerful impression anywhere. He obviously had made a good impression on Victoria, and Marilyn was happy for her.

Time passed and the coffee was served. Roussos had a noon appointment and hoped the interview would be over by that time, but feared not at this rate. Marilyn sipped her French coffee and said in English to the police director, "It's very good. Is it Turkish?"

Roussos smiled and said, "Is French and…."

The door opened. Dimitri entered wearing his uniform, and Marilyn almost dropped her cup. He was a Greek god, handsome, tall, strong, bronzed, and kind looking. She had never seen anyone like him. *Be still, my heart*, she told herself. It was only with great effort that she restrained herself from falling in love with him instantly.

CHAPTER 11

▼

Police Director Spyro Roussos introduced Superintendent Dimitri Roussos to Marilyn.

She looked at them both with inquisitive eyes.

Dimitri said, "Yes, we have the same last name because he is my father."

The police director said in English with halting words and hesitant smile, "Yes, Dimitri bad fortune be child of mine."

"Son, sir."

"Son okay. No favor. He work hard." He explained to Dimitri in Greek what he expected of him as an interpreter.

Dimitri, who had learned the proper role of an interpreter during his army career, knew how to make himself as invisible a part of the proceedings as possible. He looked straight between the two of them and was prepared to give a word-for-word account of what each said without adding any expression of his own.

Marilyn was glad that Dimitri was not looking directly at her. In his role as interpreter, he made her feel as if she were alone with the police director and speaking to him in mutually fluent English. But every now and then she stole a glance at Dimitri and thought he had the most wonderful profile she had ever seen.

Roussos asked her to go over again the highlights of her story from the time she met Yorgo on the plane until the police found her in the fisherman's hut.

When she finished, he asked, "Do you think there was any possibility of the killers in black sweaters knowing the kidnappers personally? Is there any possibility that the kidnappers knew their killers?"

"Six of them were already dead when the commandos brought me downstairs, and they killed the seventh, Yorgo, in cold blood immediately when I entered the room. All he had time to say was, 'I'm sorry, Marilyn.'" As she re-lived the events in her mind, she broke into tears and slumped forward.

Roussos waited until she had dried her eyes and sat up straight to show herself ready for more questions. He said, "Doesn't it seem strange that the kidnappers had not set out sentries?"

"I wouldn't know. Maybe they did. Maybe one of the seven men had been acting as a sentry. But Yorgo told me he thought they were drinking too much wine and not at their best. Oh, I just don't know." She didn't want to think about it any more, but she had insisted on being questioned at this time.

"When you last saw the kidnappers alive, did they seemed relaxed? Or did they seem under pressure?"

"It depends. They were relaxed in an alcoholic sense. I told you Yorgo said they were getting nervous because their leader, Jimmy, was late, and they were drinking too much wine. They were getting worried about what to do with me. I think they were planning to kill me. But if you mean they were expecting some kind of attack, I don't think so. I think they were always aware that the police might come, but they seemed to feel they would be gone before you arrived."

"Is there any chance that the commandos in black could have been a competing offshoot of the group that included the kidnappers?"

"No. Oh, I guess I can't say that. I don't really know."

"But you instinctively said no. You must have had some reason. Something you had seen or heard that made you feel there was a significant difference between the two groups." Although he was speaking in Greek, he talked slowly. He didn't want to seem to be cross-examining her.

"Well, only that the killers were so organized—so ready for their dirty work, while the kidnappers were so casual. As if kidnapping were not their everyday business."

"But killing was the everyday business of the ones dressed in black?"

"Oh, yes. They seemed to be professional killers all right. As I said, in the beginning I saw their forms moving outside the house, and they moved like clockwork. Very professional, well-trained, merciless. Human life meant nothing to them."

"And the kidnappers?"

"Even though Yorgo said they might kill me, I felt that they were a kinder type. Dedicated to their business, whatever it was. But more like gentlemen amateurs."

"What do you think was their business?"

"Well, more and more I got the impression they wanted to use me as a hostage for some reason in dealings with my uncle. I don't mean for money. I think they wanted something else out of him." Recalling what Yorgo said about it being stupid to expect the American government to give in to them, she tried to repeat his words verbatim.

"So they were using you as a hostage for future dealings with your uncle. Do you have any idea of what they might have wanted from the American government?"

"None."

"And this Yorgo was ambiguous toward you?"

"Oh, yes. I think he really liked me." She did not want to mention how he importuned her for sex. "But he was dedicated to his cause. They all seemed absolutely dedicated to some unknown cause."

"Thank you, Miss Pickering. You have been most helpful, and I appreciate it. I hope you won't mind if we call on you again if we think of something else where you might help us. You make a good witness."

"Thank you, sir." She smiled, now comfortable in the knowledge that the interrogation was over. Bob Jensen and her uncle didn't have anything to worry about after all. "You have been so sweet about this, just charming. I can recognize a great policeman when I see him." She waited, then prodded, "Go ahead, Dimitri, tell him what I said."

The police director beamed as he heard her words coming from Dimitri. He looked almost embarrassed, but pleasantly so. With a half-suppressed smile, he waved her off, "No, no, no. Very kind."

"Oh, but you are the kind one. You've been so considerate of my feelings, you know, in view of what has happened to me. Would you mind if I asked a question or two? You know, just to satisfy my curiosity."

Roussos's smile lessened a bit, but he indicated with an upward motion of his open palm for her to continue.

"That is so decent of you. Do you yourself have any idea of who these groups might be? Or why one of them kidnapped me? Or why the other one massacred the first?"

Dimitri interpreted.

The director said, "None at this time, but we are investigating."

"Have you been able to identify the dead men?"

"Not yet. Well, Yorgo we know was an insurance company executive. We don't have much to go on with the others, but we are working on it."

"Yes, of course. Well, thank you."

Roussos looked at his watch and indicated to his son that he should take Marilyn to the outer office.

Escorting her through the outer office to the door of the corridor, Dimitri asked her, "May I offer to take you to lunch?"

She thought quickly. Both her uncle and Bob Jensen would be tied up with the Secretary of State. She had no plans for lunch at all, nor any plans for the rest of the afternoon. And Dimitri was so good-looking....

"I'd love to," she said. "Let me call the embassy to leave a message for my uncle."

"Tell him that I'll drive you back to your embassy."

Dimitri took her to Dionysos, a restaurant across Dion Areopagitou Street from the Acropolis known both for its fine food and its magnificent view. He said a few words to the headwaiter, and they were led to an outdoor table on a terrace. There in front of Marilyn's eyes at last was the Parthenon. It seemed like a dream. Below the Parthenon in their direct view was the Herodos Attikos Theater, worn down by time but still used for outdoor stage presentations.

"We have performances in the theater just as in olden times," said Dimitri. "There are drama and comedies, and music, including classical, operatic, ballet, and popular." As he smiled his teeth displayed brilliant white enamel. His eyes played with hers.

"Now, today?"

"Yes, today, well, tonight. I think there's a ballet from Russia performing tonight."

"But they do have ancient Greek plays? I would love to see some Greek plays."

"I think there are both a comedy and a tragedy at some theaters in town. I would be happy to take you tonight. You may select whichever pleases you, Aristophanes or Euripides."

"Oh, no, not tonight, I can't." Briefly she toyed with acceptance, but she knew her aunt was preparing a special dinner for her, and she had better stay home.

She asked, "You said opera, and I guess you are acquainted with Victoria Renfrew."

"Through my father, yes. They are good friends."

"Does she sing at the Herodos Attikos Theater?"

"During the summer festival, of course. I think, however, that there is a conflict in scheduling. Her coming performance in Tosca should have been at the outdoor theater, but instead will be at the opera house in the center. She will undoubtedly sing here later in the summer.

Only the heavy traffic with its smells and noises interfered with the beauty of the moment. They were given menus and Marilyn said, "You order for me. Something Greek, but not too daring. No octopus today, I think."

"Do you like veal? Veal is always good to order in Greece. We don't have much beef because we lack grazing facilities. So we have veal."

"Oh, I wasn't thinking. I can't. I'm a lacto-ovo-vegetarian."

"Hmm, vegetarian I know, but lacto and ovo?"

"I'll eat milk, cheese, and egg dishes. A pure vegan won't eat even those."

"They must live by bread alone."

She laughed. "You can guess I eat an awful lot of omelets when I'm out."

"How about shell fish?"

"No, I'm sorry. It's a nuisance, I know. After someone's eaten out with me once, they seldom invite me again."

"No apologies allowed here." He smiled. "How about a truffle omelet?"

"You mean with real "truffle" truffles, not the candy?"

"Of course, real truffles. Imported from France, fresh from Provence."

"It sounds like just the thing."

"And for a starter, we can have grapevine leaves stuffed with rice, pine nuts, and raisins served with an egg-lemon sauce. They're called *dolmades* or *dolmadakia*, and I should warn you that the entrée version is made with meat, but the appetizers are not."

"I'll try it, even though an omelet and an egg sauce might be a bit much for my cholesterol."

"For dessert we might have *galaktobouriko*, but I don't want to overfeed you."

"Why? Do I look fat?"

"No, but we will want to take a walk after. You couldn't have had time yet to visit the Parthenon. We'll go there after lunch, but we'll have to climb a bit."

"It doesn't look too far or too steep. But I must be careful because my feet still hurt a little from that horrible walk on Skyros."

"I don't think it will be bad for your feet. You will have a full stomach, especially if we order dessert, so we'll proceed slowly. Would you care for some wine?"

"I don't think so. Just water, please."

"We have delicious water in Greece," he said with pride. "When you are in a Greek house and they offer you water, accept it, because they want to show you how fine our water is."

Marilyn found something almost childlike in him, especially in the delight he took in ordering for her. They ate their meal and she even had room for the dessert, a delicious custard in sheets of pastry, like a double portion of baklava with crème pâtisserie instead of honey and nuts. Forget about the cholesterol today, she told herself.

Dimitri tapped a spoon against his glass to get the attention of the waiter. "*Garsoni, to logariasmo.*"

Marilyn guessed he was asking for the check. She observed that both the headwaiter and the table waiter treated Dimitri with the utmost of respect. Was he known here, or was it just because he was a police officer?

The street they had to cross was busy with traffic, but Dimitri, in uniform, merely held up his hands and the cars quickly came to a stop.

"You act so...so authoritatively," Marilyn said with admiration in her voice.

He laughed. "Inside I was trembling. These drivers are unpredictable, and we've lost more than one police officer in the traffic."

The Acropolis was all that Marilyn imagined and more. In its ruined condition it left much to the imagination, and she wondered if the Parthenon in its pristine condition could have been any more breathtaking than it appeared now. They walked up the path where millions of feet had trod, then continued with the steps through the propylaia, or foregates.

As she limped up the path, Dimitri offered her first his arm to hold on, then as they walked over more broken ground, he put his arm around her waist to steady her. His support let her take some of the weight off her feet, and she found it comforting. She thought that even if her feet weren't sore, it would be nice to walk with him like this.

Dimitri explained everything as they walked along. To their right was the small temple of Niki Aptera, the wingless goddess, Victory. Then at the top of an inclined rise, could be seen the temple of Athena Parthenos—Athena the Virgin—itself, so situated that visitors had to lift their heads in respect as they gazed upon it.

Marilyn shivered from just the thought of being where she was. The Parthenon's patinaed columns seemed to beckon her, bidding her to come closer. The fact that it was surrounded by scaffolding could not camouflage its magnificence.

"We can't go inside now," said Dimitri. "The destruction that began centuries ago with the pounding of Venetian cannon has been continued, first by many years of neglect and now by pollution. It is being strengthened, but I do not know when we will be allowed to enter it again."

They circumnavigated the Parthenon, and Marilyn peered through the spaces between columns so she could see the inside from as many angles as possible.

"There was in olden times a large statue of Athena inside, bedecked in plates of gold and ivory. The temple is the glory of our city and nation. Someday perhaps we shall rise to the position our heritage requires."

They were at the front of the Parthenon again, and Dimitri pointed to the top of the temple. "That is where the so-called Elgin marbles belong. They were stolen from us and are now in the British Museum in London."

"I thought the British paid for them," said Marilyn.

He frowned. "It is a long story. They paid the Turks. We Greeks had nothing to say about it."

Marilyn gathered that it was best for her to keep away from the subject. She knew the Greeks were a proud people, and she did not want to step on Dimitri's feelings. They continued walking, and Dimitri pointed out other structures to her, each time with a few words of explanation, showing that he knew the area well. He could have been a tour guide. Behind the Parthenon they walked past a small, squat workshop to a low wall where they could see all Athens laid out before them.

"Look there," he said, "that mount in the center of modern Athens is Lykavittos, much taller than the Acropolis, and we can take a cable car to the top, where there is a church, a restaurant, and a belvedere with the best view in all Athens."

Lykavittos with its circlet of green trees had a tonsured look. Marilyn thought that a fortress on top of it would have been impregnable.

Now Dimitri became enthusiastic again. "I shall take you there sometime. Would you like to go?"

"Oh, yes, I would. I'd be delighted. It is so beautiful here, Dimitri. Thank you. Here we are on the Acropolis, the glory of Athens, and to think, Athens was the glorious capital of the ancient Greek Empire."

"Oh, no. Athens had a maritime hegemony over many of the other Greek states at various times, but you couldn't call it the capital of the Greek Empire. Ancient Greece was divided into many city-states, and no one ever controlled them all until King Phillip of Macedonia conquered them. However, his capital was at Pella, and the dominance of the Macedonians was short-lived. We Greeks are proud of our ancient heritage, but we do not look upon the past glory of ancient Greece the same as Hellenophile foreigners do. They look to Athens for the grandeur. What concerns us much more is the glory of the Byzantine Empire. The real capital of the Greek world was Constantinople."

"You mean Istanbul."

He laughed, but she could tell it was a serious laugh.

"Yes, but Istanbul is merely a name from Greek words that the Turks adopted from the Greeks and gradually applied to Constantinople. Istanbul comes from '*eis tin poli*,' meaning 'to or in the city." Constantinople was simply known as 'the city,' as if it were the most prominent city in the world, which it was."

"But it is Turkish now."

"For the time being, they hold it." He stood rigidly straight and took a deep breath of satisfaction as if in heavy thought. "Yes, they have it for the time being."

"You mean it will become Greek again?"

His face took on a stargazing look. "Yes, it will become Greek again."

"But wouldn't that mean a war?"

"Yes." It was said matter-of-factly. "Yes, it is true, and many of us will die. But it is our fate." The last words were pronounced emphatically, and he repeated them in Greek, "*Einai i moira mas.*"

As Dimitri drove her to the Embassy, Marilyn glanced at her bronzed companion and was thankful to him for a wonderful lunch and afternoon. So far her visit to Greece had turned out to be amazing. First the bad, the kidnapping, and then the good, a companion beyond her wildest dreams. Already she adored Dimitri. He had said he'd like to take her to other places. She hoped he wouldn't forget. If he did, she decided, she'd prompt him.

*   *   *   *

That evening Marilyn's uncle and aunt invited Bob Jensen to have dinner with them. It was more the aunt's doing than that of the uncle, who was still enraged over how Bob had let their niece slip loose of him at Roussos's office. In deference to Marilyn's special diet, Aunt Louise prepared a meatless lasagna, and they drank California wine.

After dinner, the aunt suggested that Bob and Marilyn might like to go out on the veranda, where there was a pleasant breeze and a good view looking south to the center of Athens. When the ambassador started to protest, his wife hushed him and later explained, "You have some degree of control over Bob Jensen, don't you? Then you couldn't ask for a better companion for her, could you?"

Bob and Marilyn took their wine and sat in comfortable outdoor chairs. The night was relatively clear, and a good number of stars could be seen. The weather was perfect, neither too hot nor too cold. Somewhere from within the house, soft music wafted through the open windows. The clean, fresh smell of pine was all about them.

Marilyn repeated Dimitri's words to Bob. "'It is our fate,' he said. He's very nice, but I thought that was a rather strange thing to say."

Bob repeated, "'It is our fate.' In Greek the words are *Einai i moira mas.* Those words have been repeated by Greeks probably ever since the beginning of civilization. I suggested to a Greek statesman once that in view of the strife on Cyprus between the Turkish minority and the Greek majority, Greece and Turkey should exchange populations between Istanbul and Cyprus. He looked horrified and told me emphatically that the Greeks in Istanbul could never leave that city. I told him it was better than having the Greek population that is still in Istanbul remain there and perhaps get massacred, as the Turks massacred the Greeks in Izmir in 1922. He looked at me as if I were a dolt and said, 'They have to stay there even if they die for it. It is their fate.'"

Marilyn said, "I had the impression when I was discussing these things with Dimitri that he was looking at me as if I were a dolt."

Bob said, "There are many Greeks who believe that Constantinople will become the capital of a Greater Greece."

"But Constantinople was the eastern capital of the Roman world. When did the Greeks ever have it?"

"It just gradually became Hellenized. Greek culture and the Greek language gradually conquered the Romans, especially after the fall of Rome itself. And in a sense even today the Greeks consider themselves the inheritors of the Roman world. In fact, in Greece the popular word for "Greek" is '*Romaios.*'"

"How strange. But can the Greeks really re-capture Istanbul from the Turks?"

"Who knows? It is a fact that those fierce Turks would not give up their city without a fight. The Turks have larger and stronger military forces. Even an attempt could ignite World War III. I don't think the Greeks, if they were the aggressors, would get much support from the rest of the world. However, they are a patient people, and your friend Dimitri Roussos did not necessarily mean now, in our time. They can wait another hundred years, even more. But the idea of re-establishing Constantinople and restoring the Byzantine Empire will never die among the Greeks."

He went in to refill their glasses with Chardonnay, and then continued talking on the topic. It was clear to Marilyn that Bob Jensen was an enthusiastic student of Greek history and politics. Although her uncle had spoken of him in rather a disparaging way, she gleaned that he had hidden appreciation for his aide's knowledge and usefulness.

Bob said, "Most parts of Greece were occupied by the Turks for well over five centuries. The main part of Greece—*Sterea Hellas*, Solid Greece, they call it—

including Athens, freed itself with foreign aid in the 1820s. In 1881 much of north central Greece was taken back from the Turks; in 1913 much of the rest of northern Greece and the island of Crete were recovered; and as recently as 1923 Thrace, that part of Greece closest to Istanbul, was won back. The Greeks even got back the Dodecanese Islands in 1948, although that was from Italy, not directly from Turkey. But as you can see, the Greeks have made tremendous progress in recovering the lands they lost in medieval times."

He was about to say more when Marilyn interrupted. "That's a part of my education that has been neglected. But do you think Dimitri is conscious of these events of the past?"

"The way you describe him, yes, decidedly. But there are more serious matters than that one to concern us in the embassy at the moment. Your uncle wonders if the kidnappers who took you to Skyros, and the commandos who killed them, might be involved in some kind of plot to stir up international mischief for Greece."

"Mischief is an understatement," said Marilyn. "When I was talking to Police Director Roussos today, he seemed very much interested in both groups, and I got the impression it was as much for their own sake as for the kidnapping and massacre. Remember only seven of the kidnappers were killed, but I must have seen some twenty or so during the few days I was on Skyros. So they are very much alive as an organization, and of course the commandos didn't lose any men at all." She stopped, listened, then said, "Is that Greek music they're playing inside?"

"It's Greek popular music. Unique and catchy, isn't it? It blends Western popular music, especially European and Latin American, with overtones from the Near East. It's really beautiful, and I'm surprised it hasn't captured the rest of the world yet. Americans loved the few pieces of it we heard in movies such as *Zorba the Greek* and *Never on Sunday*."

"I'm sorry. What were you about to say before I interrupted?"

"Forget it. I was just wondering if those two gangs on Skyros gave you any possible clue to their identity."

"Director Roussos covered that ground thoroughly. I've searched my mind again, but I just can't think of anything I haven't already told both of you." She took out her compact and re-touched her lipstick. Then, "Bob," she said, stretching out the single syllable.

"Yes?"

"Getting back to Dimitri and Istanbul, or Constantinople, or Byzantium— whatever they call it—I just can't imagine the Greeks' expecting to get the city back. It sounds like just a lot of talk, wishful thinking."

He poured another glass of wine for himself. Marilyn declined having her glass topped up.

"Well," he said, "let me give you an example. Do you have any idea who the head of the Greek Orthodox Church is?"

"This is going to be a lesson, isn't it? Well, I've never heard of them having a pope, but maybe they have something the equivalent. Something like an archbishop or higher?"

"Where do you think this archbishop or higher might be located?"

"Here in Athens, of course."

Bob lifted his eyes and clicked his tongue against his hard palate in the emphatic Greek gesture of the negative – "*Okhi!*" he uttered, No! "There's a metropolitan in Athens; he's higher than an archbishop. But the highest official in the Greek Orthodox Church is the patriarch. And the patriarch lives and functions not in Athens, but in Istanbul. Does that help you understand anything."

"You mean the highest official in the Greek Church lives in a foreign country?"

"It's not foreign to the Greeks. But yes, the seat of the patriarch of the Greek Orthodox Church is still in Constantinople as it always has been."

"Then Dimitri really has something to go on."

"Never underestimate a Greek. They've been survivors for a long time."

They sat in silence for a few more minutes, then Bob said, "My invitation to show you around Athens still holds." He smiled and continued, "I'd be willing to take you to the opera even if it's with your tickets."

"We might do that," said Marilyn, wondering if Dimitri liked opera. "I'll let you know."

CHAPTER 12

▼

Saturday morning Spyro Roussos was at his desk as usual. Pano and Eleni sat in front of him, the two of them quietly joking around with each other while Roussos read some papers. They stopped the instant they saw him look up.

"The minister is late, but that's the privilege of ministers. Let's hope he can follow instructions better tonight. Why don't we go over the plan one more time."

Eleni raised a hand and said, "Suppose he makes a play for me?"

"He won't. He knows you're a police superintendent and he would be taking a horrible risk."

"I've had men take that risk before. Haven't I, Pano?"

Pano scowled. "Don't talk to me in riddles, dear Eleni."

"You'd prefer me to be more explicit?"

"I think we are wasting the police director's time."

"Sorry. Anyway, Chief, suppose Antonidis shows an interest in me?"

"Let me put it this way, my dear Eleni," said Roussos. "If you have a short-term goal of replacing me in my job, you may go ahead and accept if you choose. But if you want to keep our present relationship, I'd suggest you politely decline. I know Antonidis, and he would never pursue a woman against her wishes."

"Be assured, sir, I will absolutely decline. That is, if anything like that takes place in the first place."

"Good. All right. He will pick you up here at six-thirty. It's only a short walk to his daughter's place. She will be with her husband and her business manager. So it will be a nice little dinner party for six. Nick Savvas should arrive more or less on time at seven. He should not be surprised or suspicious to see Minister Antonidis accompanied by such a lovely escort."

Pano said, "Suppose Savvas makes a play for Eleni?"

Roussos squinted his eyes and replied, "He won't. When he leaves the Papazoglou apartment, he should be under arrest anyway."

"Am I to go in there at a certain time, or wait until they come out of the room?" asked Eleni.

"I think it better to wait, so you can be certain that it is done. He should have the cash on him, and Mrs. Papazoglou will have her copy of the contract. Then you arrest him, being careful to comply with all the legal necessities."

Pano said, "How will I know when to go up from the lobby?"

"At first I thought of having you enter at a certain time, but perhaps it would be better to have the minister call you on your cell phone. You should go in the apartment shortly after the principals go in the study, but stay in the kitchen until needed just in case they have to leave the study for any reason before the deal is completed."

"Understood."

"You will be there merely to back up Eleni. She will make the arrest, and you will have a police car ready to bring the three of you here."

Eleni said, "Suppose Savvas puts up a resistance?"

"That's why Pano is backing you up, Eleni. However, knowing you, I doubt that you will need any help, and I doubt that Savvas will resist anyway. So we're clear on all the details?"

At that moment the door opened and Minister Antonidis entered, making apologies for being late. Roussos asked Eleni to repeat all the details to the minister.

After she did so, she asked Roussos, "Should we have a dry run? Neither Pano nor I have ever been in that apartment before."

Roussos looked to the minister, who said, "I have the time to take them over now, if you wish. Let me call my daughter first."

The call was made and the three of them left. Alone, Roussos wondered if he had left any room for a slip-up. He was still suspicious because Minister Petropoulos had ordered him to release Savvas the last time Roussos made an arrest. His police experience had taught him to think in terms of normalities, and it was not normal for a minister to take the side of a crook.

He also wondered if the American Embassy would enter the case after the arrest because Savvas had become an American citizen. Roussos had always been aware of the need to maintain good relations with the American Embassy, and he thought that he got along as well as could be expected with his chief contact there, Bob Jensen. Other than being clumsy, Jensen seemed like a decent, reasonable, and likeable chap. Would Jensen be more inclined to take his side if he notified him in advance? He decided against it, and anyway, even if he couldn't keep Savvas in prison, as a worse case he could at least have him expelled from the country. Roussos was not vindictive. His object was more to stop crime than to fill the jails with criminals. Savvas was an interesting man, very clever and very personable. Roussos reflected to himself that Savvas probably could have been highly successful in business without being a crook.

His mind turned to Victoria. She was at a rehearsal for *Tosca*, with only ten days until opening night. This would probably be her most important performance of the season because *Tosca* was so popular. All the Athenian top brass would want to see it, and on opening night there could even be representatives from foreign opera houses. Hmm, the more Roussos thought of it, the more concerned he became.

Supposing, just supposing, some important opera house, such as La Scala, offered her a regular contract. He couldn't stand in her way, but he was afraid that the kind of separation that foreign residence would require might gradually be fatal to their relationship. He did not fool himself. He knew that love had to be constantly reinforced, and that proximity was one of its most important ingredients. And there was the age difference. Nor could he offer her marriage, although at times he wondered about the possibility of getting a divorce from his wife. Anyway, he might not even have a job if Minister Petropoulos succeeded in getting what he wanted.

And then there was Pavlo Xynos. Would Victoria be safer if she lived in Milan or New York, or would Xynos find a way of haunting her in one of those cities as well? In any event, he had to do something to find Xynos. There would be no peace for Victoria as long as that lunatic was loose.

He decided to go to the rehearsal. The families of the cast and the opera staff were always welcome at such times because seeing a live audience, even if only a few people in number, was helpful to the performers. At the theater, Roussos automatically assessed the audience at somewhere between sixty and eighty people. He waited in the rear for a while before walking down the aisle, then took a seat in the middle of a row about halfway down. Victoria would be sure to see him. She had said that whenever he came, she wanted him in some prominent place so that she could know he was there and take confidence from the fact. She was not in sight, but then he wouldn't expect her to be.

When the action continued, he realized that Act Three was starting, where Cavaradossi is imprisoned in the Castel Sant'Angelo and would soon start singing the masterpiece *E lucevan le stelle*. Although this, plus Victoria's solo, *Vissi d'Arte*, in the second act, were the favorites of most opera lovers, Roussos's personal favorite was the end of Act One when the *Te Deum* was played, and he was sorry he had missed it.

The tenor finished his aria, and at this moment Tosca was supposed to enter. No one appeared. Several people yelled out for Tosca, and the opera director went to look for her. After a few minutes he returned to the stage and told everyone that Victoria Renfrew was suddenly not feeling well, so they would break for lunch now.

A worried Roussos rushed backstage to Victoria's dressing room. He knocked on the door, but entered without waiting for an answer. Victoria was on a divan with her head and hands on the arm piece. He knelt and asked if she was all right.

"Yes," she said with sobs. "I think maybe now." She turned to look up at Roussos and put her arms around his shoulders. "I didn't want to interrupt the rehearsal, but I couldn't go on."

"What happened?"

"Pavlo Xynos. I saw him everywhere."

Roussos straightened up. "Xynos, he was here?"

"No, no, I don't think so. It was an illusion. I think I must have been hallucinating. I was singing *Vissi d'arte* when I thought I saw him in the audience on the left side in a row about halfway up. I couldn't believe it, but when I looked again he was gone. I finished my aria and continued with my role. Then I saw Xynos again, this time on the right side toward the rear. Then he was gone again. I continued with my role of killing Scarpia and saw Xynos again in the middle rear, then suddenly he was in the middle front. He couldn't have moved that fast." She was gently, softly crying, and her body was shaking.

"So he wasn't really there. As you say, it was an illusion."

"I struggled through the second act, but I just couldn't return for the third. I don't know why my mind played tricks on me. Oh, Spyro, what am I going to do?" She slowly got control over her trembling and looked up at him again.

"Do you want to stop for the day? I can tell the director for you, and I'll take you home."

"No, I think I'll be all right. He said he was going to stop for lunch. I think I'll be able to continue after lunch, but I won't eat. I'll just stay here and rest, and you'll be with me. You won't leave me, will you, Spyro? And you'll stay for the rehearsal?"

"Yes, I won't leave you. I'll stay. I will probably have to go to the office tonight, but we can discuss that later. Perhaps you might feel better going with me. But I won't leave you alone at the theater."

He stroked her forehead and she gradually maneuvered her body to a comfortable position on the divan and fell asleep. In the afternoon he resumed his seat in the center of the theater, and Victoria continued with her performance. The director wanted to re-do several parts, and it was four o'clock before they finished, but they finished without further mishap. Roussos took Victoria home, made them a light dinner, and sat quietly on the balcony with her.

He knew there would be a telephone call for him shortly and he would have to leave. He was ambivalent about her accompanying him to his office, but he didn't want to leave her alone. He finally decided, if she agreed, to take her with him and leave her in his office while he talked with the prisoner he was expecting.

*   *   *   *

Eleni Karolou, who was seeing Nick Savvas for the first time, realized why he had gone into the confidence racket. The man had so much confidence in himself that it was contagious. After a few minutes of talking to him, people found themselves believing in him. He was the kind of man, Eleni thought, who could convince you of his absolute honesty right after you caught him picking someone's pocket.

Savvas arrived punctually at seven at Nina Papazoglou's apartment dressed in a tuxedo, as the other three men present were dressed. He was thin and of average height, and he had the kind of face that would have got him the part of Jesus Christ in a modern DeMille-like epic. His handshake was firm, his eyes steady and penetrating, and his smile ingratiating. Eleni felt that she wanted to do something nice for him, but she didn't lose sight of what she knew she really had to do. Perhaps when he was in jail she could visit him and let him know that she was merely doing her job, no hard feelings. She knew the Greek courts; he wouldn't get too many years.

The hostess served pre-dinner drinks, and they all engaged in routine small talk. On being questioned by Savvas, Eleni admitted that she was new in the group also, having previously known only Minister Antonidis. She reached over to play her part as the minister's mistress and put her hand between Antonidis's arm and chest. She felt Antonidis adjust himself to her grip, and she had to tell herself not to overdo it. She in turn asked Savvas how long he had been in Athens, what made him decide to go to America and become a citizen, and which country did he prefer to be in?

Savvas responded with a modest smile, "Whichever country I happen to be in at the moment. I love America. I love my native Greece. And I love all people everywhere."

That's a lot of love, thought Eleni.

Nina announced that dinner was ready, and they sat down to a meal featuring roast lamb. Nina had an excellent cook, and all the food was delicious. Savvas asked, "May I go in the kitchen and personally compliment your superb chef?"

Nina, flattered, agreed. Eleni was glad that Pano was not yet in the kitchen. In a couple of minutes Savvas was back again. After dinner, Nina apologized to her father, her husband, and Eleni, saying that she and her business manager had a little business to conduct with Savvas. Could the three of them be excused to go in the study? They wouldn't be long. Why didn't the others have a second cup of coffee or an after-dinner drink while they waited?

Nina's father and husband weren't quite sure what to talk about, so they made more small talk. Eleni could appreciate their feeling that it might not be wise to discuss what was going to happen before it happened, as if the wall to the study might have ears. She knew she herself was getting a little nervous when she realized that she was frequently looking at her watch. She had thought that it would be over in perhaps twenty or thirty minutes, and only ten had yet passed.

She nodded to the minister, who picked up the telephone, and softly told Pano that now was the time. The husband walked over to the door, quietly opened it, admitted Pano, and showed him to the kitchen. It was not too soon, for a minute later the door to the study opened and the three business people emerged. Nina led the way, and Eleni sensed an inner trembling in her. The business manager was second, and he too looked nervous. Savvas came out with a pleasant smile on his face, a smile that denoted general satisfaction without cockiness.

Eleni looked to Nina. Almost imperceptibly Nina nodded. Eleni stood up, took her police credentials from her handbag, and said, "Nick Savvas, I'm Police Superintendent Karolou and I'm arresting you for fraud and misrepresentation."

Pano came out of the kitchen and also flashed his credentials at Savvas. He stood at Savvas's side as Eleni put handcuffs on him. Pano patted him down and removed the money and the contract from his pockets.

Savvas did not resist. Nor did he even look surprised. His face still held a confident look, and he said, "I think this is a mistake. I am a businessman and I have not committed any crime. May I call my lawyer?"

Eleni said, "After we get to headquarters."

Savvas said, "I really must protest. But I will gladly accompany you to your station, where we can perhaps get this misunderstanding sorted out."

Eleni felt sorry for him. His face was all bravado, but he must have known inside that he would most likely be going to prison for some years. They had caught him with the goods. They knew he had no connection at all with the American company he claimed he represented, and the prosecution would have witnesses in court to prove it. Nick Savvas would not be swindling any more companies for a long time to come.

CHAPTER 13

▼

Sunday morning Roussos and Victoria drove to his beach house in Kavouri. Nick Savvas had been formally charged and put in a cell the night before. The calendar was getting a little cleaner with the rescue of Marilyn Pickering and now the arrest of Savvas. There was still the matter of Pavlo Xynos, the most important case of all for Roussos personally. However, he knew the two gangs, kidnappers and commandos, were potentially the greater danger to state security, and he planned to have a meeting during the coming week with other government security agencies to discuss DSI's future course of action in this case.

Roussos felt he could afford to take off a Sunday. There was not much requiring his immediate action in the outstanding cases. In addition to the others, there was still Zavalas, but there was something funny about that one. At any rate, Eleni had taken it upon herself to resolve the matter and Roussos had complete confidence in her. The other multitude of DSI cases still open was being handled efficiently by his regular staff. It was Victoria's condition that worried him the most.

Crab-shaped Kavouri was a small peninsula off the main road from Glyfada to Sounion. It was next door to a popular large beach at Vouliagmeni. There were a number of fine small beaches on all sides of the Crab, and there were many expensive new hotels and houses studded throughout. Some of the older houses, such as Roussos's, were still small summer places that would eventually disappear as the value of the land continued to skyrocket. Besides the hotels, there were an increasing number of stylish restaurants encroaching on the small grocery store and taverna that had been there for decades.

Roussos house was not right on the beach; rather it was higher up and looked over a clearing between two other beach habitations. It had a path down to the beach on which he had a right of way whenever he wanted to go swimming. He had once belonged to a Kavouri polar bear club, where to maintain membership it was necessary to take a dip in the sea without fail every day, summer and winter, but he had given that up when he moved in with Victoria.

Roussos had brought some needed provisions with him, and he put these away while Victoria made them a cup of coffee. She served the coffee with croissants on the veranda, and in front of them they enjoyed the anodyne of the ever-changing sea. Victoria thought it would be nice to have music, and she started playing some CDs. In addition to opera and other classical music, she enjoyed Greek popular songs, with their tales of love, requited and unrequited, betrayal, elopement, relentless passion, and stolen moments of ecstasy.

"What shall we have for lunch?" he said.

"You're always thinking of food."

"I'm not getting fat."

"Always thinking about work keeps your weight down."

"You just said I was always thinking of food."

"When you're not thinking about work."

"Suppose I take a promotion and retire?"

"Would you? I'd love it."

"I might have to. Especially if I thought they might fire me if I didn't."

"That's an odd situation."

"Petropoulos wants to get rid of me, and he doesn't care if it's by promotion or by disgrace."

"But Antonidis likes you, and he's the brother-in-law of the prime minister."

"Brothers-in-law don't always have the greatest influence."

"All right, you win. What shall we have for lunch?"

"*Barbounia.*" Red mullet. "And I was just joking about retirement. I'll retire when I'm old and not before."

"With potatoes and garlic sauce and a village salad?"

"Who's hungry now?"

One of his neighbors passed by carrying a wicker-covered empty demijohn. "Hey, Spyro, down at Mihali's they opened a new barrel of wine, and it's the best of the year. Better get some before it's gone."

"*Efharisto.*" Thanks. Turning to Victoria he said, "That's perfect. I'll go find a large empty bottle, and you go to the taverna and order the fish, potatoes, and rest."

"All right." She went in, got her purse, and came out again. Suddenly the expression of happy anticipation on her face changed. "The thought just came over me. I mean, Spyro, is there any chance that he...."

"He won't be here. Xynos can't have any idea where you are. He wouldn't even know I have a place here. You're in no danger, dearest. I wouldn't leave you for a moment if I thought you were."

She walked off, and he was glad he had convinced her. She couldn't live her whole life fearing to take a step without him. His work dictated so much of his own life that it was impossible to protect her around the clock every day of the week. They had to play the odds and decide which occasions required protection and which did not. And yet, if he thought something was safe and then it turned out it wasn't...if anything happened to her, he'd die.

He went to Mihali's and sampled the new barrel. His neighbor was right—it was delicious. He brought back his filled demijohn, and a moment later Victoria returned with their lunch ready to eat.

"This is great," he said, after another taste of the wine. "This is wine that you only see once in five, maybe ten, years."

"She drank a sip, followed by a larger amount. She tossed it around in her mouth, let it rest on the back of her tongue, then swallowed with a click of her tongue and the attitude of a connoisseur. "It's good, to be sure. But Spyro, really, do you think you and the others can tell the minute difference between the barrels?"

"But of course we can."

"It's the same wine in all the barrels during the season. It might differ from year to year, but all the barrels there now come from the same harvest, the same foot pressings, the same fermenting and storing—it's all the same wine."

"Nevertheless, Victoria, there's a significant difference from barrel to barrel. And you can't be sure it's all made exactly the same."

"But I can. You've taken me to Koropi where they grow the grapes. I've seen them harvest the grapes. I've taken off my shoes and stockings and helped press the grapes. I've seen them put the juice in the fermentation tanks, and I've seen them storing the wine in the barrels."

He laughed. "Ah, to see your dainty little feet pressing those grapes. It sometimes seems as if the grapes might win." He drank more wine and he felt good. Anything to get her mind off that beast.

She drank her wine, and they finished their meal and rested. After a couple of hours they decided on a swim. Then they returned to the house, took a shower, and made love. It was past seven o'clock in the evening when they got back to her apartment carrying two smaller bottles of the same wine with them.

"It's been a good day, darling," she said.

"It's been lovely."

"Such a rest."

And then a loud ring interrupted them.

"Not that hated messenger of bad news," she said.

"*Empros.*" Go ahead, he said, speaking into the mouthpiece.

It was Pano. "You'd better come over quickly. That swindler we arrested last night. He's dead. There's trouble."

"Nick Savvas? Dead? What happened?"

"I'm not sure. I'm still questioning the guards. But it looks like big trouble."

*   *   *   *

Also on Sunday while his father and Victoria were enjoying themselves at Kavouri, after lunch Dimitri Roussos called on Marilyn Pickering at the American ambassador's residence to show her around as he had promised. The Athertons were not pleased at the thought, preferring that she let Bob Jensen do all the showing around that was necessary. But she was of age, and they could not really point to anything wrong about her being with Dimitri.

In the car Dimitri explained to her that he had an errand to do first, but this would give her a chance to see one of Athens's most beautiful northern suburbs, Kifisia, some ten miles further out.

Marilyn asked, "Isn't that where one of my kidnappers, Yorgo, lived?"

"His father Nestor has a house there, but Yorgo had an apartment in the city."

By now Marilyn had fully recovered physically from the ordeal of being kidnapped, but she still felt somehow damaged by her captivity. After they drove in near silence for some ten minutes, she said, "I'm sorry I'm not good company, but I can't completely forget about those men. You know, the ones in the black sweaters who so inhumanly killed all the kidnappers. And the way Yorgo died, I can't get it out of my memory."

"I understand, but you realize that the kidnappers knew what they were getting into. They could have expected some form of harsh retribution when they seized you."

"But who were these men, these commandos? They weren't any kind of official Greek force, were they?"

"I don't think so. Many nations have secret military or paramilitary organizations, but I don't see how the government could operate if they had kept something like that a secret even from DSI. Consider this: My father's group was on the verge of rescuing you, and if they had arrived a little earlier, they would have encountered the commandos. Then what would have happened? My father's group would have attacked the commandos, who would have fired back. There could have been many killed on both sides. No government can be so invidious as to allow two armed government agencies to kill each other out of ignorance. If the commandos had been a government group designated to rescue you, my father would have had to have known."

"Who were they then?"

"We don't know yet. There is a complication in this whole case involving your kidnappers. If they are a group of army revolutionaries, then army security has some jurisdiction over it. On the other hand, DSI is charged with investigating anything that appears to threaten the stability of the country, and a revolutionary group certainly fits into my father's jurisdiction as well. But it's always messy when we're dealing with split jurisdictions. My father is trying to get the matter clarified, but he is overloaded with assignments these days. You can't imagine all the work we have to do. I'm lucky just to get today off."

They drove a while more, and Dimitri pointed out various interesting places along the way. On their right was the entrance to the riding club to which he belonged. A little later on their left was Maroussi, famous for its large, ornately decorated garden ceramics. Dimitri drove slowly past the outdoor stands so she could see better. Some pots were as large as those encountered by Ali Baba, and these were brightly painted or covered with glass tesserae that brilliantly reflected the sunlight.

"They're lovely," said Marilyn.

"Would you like to stop to get one?"

"I guess not. I don't know how I'd get it home, and in Washington our only garden is a microscopic one on the balcony of our condominium apartment."

"Something else of possible interest about Maroussi, or Amaroussion, its formal name, is that Henry Miller used it in the title of his book *The Colossus of Maroussi*."

"I've heard of Miller, of course, but I've never read anything by him. I associate him more with Paris than Greece."

"He spent some time here. He was a great friend of another writer, Lawrence Durrell, whom perhaps you've read."

"Oh, yes, I enjoyed his books about Cyprus, Rhodes, and Corfu, and also the *Alexandria Quartet*."

"Durrell perhaps captures the Greek soul more than any other foreigner could. But he still misses the sensitivity that you find, for example, in Kazantzakis, although he was a Communist and I should not be recommending his books."

"Why not? Can't a Communist be a good writer?"

"Ah, yes, but you are not familiar with our background. After World War II, there were several guerilla forces in Greece, including some that were Communist. We then fought a most bloody war against the Communists. Only the aid given us by your President Truman prevented them from taking over the government. Most families in Greece, including mine, still have memories of the savageries that took place in that war. My great grandfather fought in it, and my father has told me many stories about the butcheries. It's as vivid in our minds today as your own Civil War might have been in your country a generation after it was over."

He had turned serious as if his mind had suddenly become troubled. Marilyn got an impression that the thoughts triggered by his words about Greece's civil war had progressed to other matters, matters that he was not going to speak about.

"Later," he said, "if we have time, I will tell you about Captain Ari, the bloodiest of them all until his own head was cut off and displayed on a stake."

He followed these words with an addendum that didn't quite seem to fit, saying, "Those who live by shedding the blood of their brothers must be willing to pay the price."

"It sounds terrifying," she said. She made a mental note to start reading more on modern Greece. She was surprised that she knew so little other than what she had gleaned from reading Durrell.

They reached Kifisia and Dimitri parked the car close to an outdoor ice cream stand that had a few tables and chairs in front. "Would you care for a dish of ice cream?" he said.

"I'd love it. What kind are you having?"

"Pistachio. It's especially good here."

"I'll have the same."

They sat at one of the tables and watched a large number of people casually walking by. Marilyn noticed there was water running down the side of both the street they were on and the street that made the nearest intersection. She said, "It seems much fresher here than in Athens. And I see so much water, which my uncle told me was very scarce in Athens in the summer."

"That's why Kifisia is so popular. It's on the slope of Mount Penteli, where the marble comes from, and there are many springs that send water down the sides."

"What business do you have to do here?"

"I've already done it. I had to deliver a message to the owner of the ice cream stand. He has a confidential position with us, but that's off the record. Please don't mention it."

"Oh, I won't say a word."

They drove back along the same main road toward Athens, and again Dimitri pointed out places of interest. "On your right," he said, "you can see in the distance some of the new buildings built for the 1996 Olympics, but the committee selected Atlanta instead. We couldn't understand it, since the first modern Olympics were in Greece in 1896, exactly 100 years earlier. Of course, they will still be used now for the 2004 Olympics."

Although she sympathized with him for the 1996 disappointment, again Marilyn kept her thoughts to herself, lest she say something she shouldn't. She knew now that there were certain topics to be avoided in any discussion with a Greek, and she also knew that her views as a foreigner and a woman would not be regarded highly. She thought of Dimitri's fellow police officer, Eleni, whom she had met on Skyros. Dimitri's father seemed to think highly of her, but Marilyn wondered how much influence she really had as a woman. Was she the token woman superintendent on the force?

After a little more driving, Dimitri took a sharp right turn to enter the suburb of Filothei. He said, "This is the one I like." He was in good humor again now. "I'd like to buy a house here someday. It's modern, clean, and more open than some other close-in areas, and not as expensive as next-door Psychiko. Many foreigners, including Americans, live here."

What impressed Marilyn, as it had during the entire ride, was the lack of grass and greenery. The houses looked modern and attractive. Many were one-story with flat roofs, and almost all were surrounded by verandas, balconies, and patios. But the yards were mostly of gravel, uniformly crushed stone sometimes painted green to resemble grass from a distance. She commented on this phenomenon.

"Ah, the lack of grass. Well, you have already seen the effect of the lack of water in the summer, except in places like Kifisia. Sometimes you will see small raised geometric plots of grass cultivated almost like precious plants and flowers in the middle of the gravel. Water is so expensive."

"It never rains here in the summer?"

"Well, as they say in Gilbert and Sullivan, 'hardly ever.' I remember one summer when it rained once in July, but that was long ago."

"Dimitri, you speak excellent English. And you are obviously highly educated. Where did you go to school?"

"I am just about to show you."

The car was moving along a slight incline toward the top of a ridge. "This hill is the dividing line between Filothei and Psychiko, the really posh suburb. And you see that building on the ridge? It's called Psychiko College, or sometimes the American School, although it is actually Greek. It's a pre-university school where the rich people send their children. I was very fortunate that my father used much of his savings to send me there. Students in that school learn English from an early age."

"Did you go to a university?"

"I have a university degree, but it is the pre-university school that develops the boy into a man. You must forgive me for being so proud that I was able to go to the American School."

They had crossed the ridge and were now descending into what looked to Marilyn like a small but broad valley with geometrically designed streets and more trees than any of the other areas she had seen since leaving Kifisia.

Driving around in Psychiko, Dimitri pointed out the various types of architecture of the houses. Marilyn noted the many balconies and patios. "Greeks must like the open air. Your houses are so oriented to the outside."

"We Greeks would suffocate if we couldn't live in the outdoors. Houses are for sleeping, and preparing food, and storing books, but it is in the open air that we are alive. I've had many meals on a veranda at the back of that house," he said, pointing to a house they were passing. "An American friend of my father lives there. Greeks eat outside as much as we can. And surely you remember that the schools of ancient Greece were all outdoors. The word 'academy' itself comes from an olive grove in Athens where Plato held an outdoor school."

They left Psychiko and turned again into the main road heading toward Athens, soon passing the American Embassy on Vasilissis Sofias. As they drove up to the base of Mount Lykavittos, Dimitri explained how difficult it had become to drive in Athens. There were so many cars in the streets, increasing every year, that Athens had become one of the most polluted cities in the world, and sometimes it could be faster to travel in central Athens by foot. As for parking in central Athens, it was almost impossible. The number of places available was so limited that people had been killed in disputes over parking spaces.

"First," Dimitri said, "we will see the most spectacular overview of Athens that you can imagine. I think I can find a parking place not far from the funicular, even if I have to get an illegal one. When we leave here and go to the other places

I want to show you, I will have to park at DSI headquarters and we can continue by foot or taxi."

Dimitri led Marilyn to where they could approach the funicular. "You will not mind walking a little up a steep hill?"

"How little and how steep?" she said, glad that she had decided to wear flats for her sightseeing.

They continued a short distance and then came to the bottom of the cog railway. She followed Dimitri to the diagonally perched car. The funicular rose slowly, and gradually the city came into view, more panoramic with each second as they ascended. There were a small, whitewashed church and a restaurant on top. Outside the restaurant were a large flat terrace and a belvedere filled with café tables. Dimitri chose a table close to the protective wall.

Marilyn was enchanted. The most magnificent view of a city she had ever seen spread out before her eyes. There was the Acropolis looking small yet elegant from where they were viewing it. The day was crystal clear and a purity was imposed on everything by the brightness of the sun. So clear, so bright, that she had to shield her eyes. It was almost too much to behold. Colors melded into their solid hues under so intense a light; the buildings looked stark white or gray, the sea sapphire blue, and the trees a jade green.

Dimitri described what could be seen. "Now you can see how close, or how far, Athens is from the sea. That is Piraeus to the right. You can make out two of its three harbors. To the left is Tsitsifies—I shall have to take you there sometime to visit its bouzouki taverns at night. You will find them unique. And there, further over to the left, you can make out the airplanes on the runways at Ellinikon Airport.

"Again, way over on the right where the land meets the sea beyond Piraeus, you see the island of Salamis—from here you cannot distinguish that it is an island because it seems to blend in with the mainland. In ancient Greece, the Battle of Salamis saved Athens and all of Greece from Persian domination. Xerxes had killed the valiant 300 Spartans at Thermopylae Pass and overcome everything in his way until he took and burned Athens. The Greeks under Thermistocles retreated to Piraeus and other seacoast areas, and then the tide turned. The Greeks were able to watch the defeat of the great Persian fleet by the much smaller but more maneuverable Athenian ships. Only one of the Persian allies did well, the ships of Queen Seramis. That was when Xerxes, sitting on a throne on top a hill to watch, declared, 'My men fight like women and my women fight like men.' He had no choice but to retreat back to Persia."

"I remember some of this from my ancient history course in school. How thrilling to be able to see where it all happened."

"When the Greeks returned to Athens, they built the Parthenon so that the city was more beautiful than ever." He went on to tell her stories about a number of other sights, some of them amusing, and they laughed.

Marilyn opened her lips widely when she laughed, making the dimples in her cheeks much more pronounced.

"You have beautiful teeth," he said. "In fact, you have beautiful everything. You are a very lovely woman."

Marilyn was surprised because in the United States most people don't discuss teeth in casual conversations. But she recalled that her uncle had mentioned the great curiosity and openness of Greeks. She sat back in her chair and said, "With orthodontal treatment, anyone can have beautiful teeth." She noticed again that he too had lovely teeth and a most attractive smile.

"If they can afford it. In Greece it is very expensive."

"Dimitri, you said your family was not rich."

"It's not. But I have a very self-sacrificing father. He has done everything for me, and has even endangered the comfort of his retirement days so that I could develop the way he wanted."

"You must love him very much."

His voice changed to an emotional whisper. "I do."

Marilyn was silent, content just to look at this man with the face and figure of a Greek god. She knew she was supposed to be admiring the view over Athens, but, as lovely as the city was, she found the view across the table more fascinating.

"Do you have any brothers or sisters?" she asked.

"None."

"Isn't that unusual?"

"Not at all. We Greeks are a very proud people, and we usually don't have more children than we can comfortably provide for. Most Greek men marry around age thirty and then have an average of only two children. My father was an exception because he married much younger than usual. Doctors then told my mother that she could only have one child if lucky, none if not. So I'm an only child, with all that that implies."

"Is that why he gave you all his affection and attention?"

"I don't really know the reason. All I know is that my father has been as kind and understanding with me as any father ever could be. He'd give his life for me—not that I'd let him."

Although Dimitri didn't speak the words, Marilyn sensed that he did not plan to marry until he was higher in rank. He would certainly want only the best for his wife and two children. She felt the woman who married him would be fortunate indeed.

Dimitri called the waiter and they ordered French coffee and croissants. There was a delightful breeze, and Marilyn was engulfed in a most comfortable feeling, sending a frisson of excitement through her.

Dimitri said, "We are more than 300 meters above the Athenian plain, so it is always airy and refreshing here. But I must be truthful and tell you that there is more of a breeze today than usual, and it has cleared much of the smog away. Days like these are becoming rarer in Athens. We have made much progress, but I'm afraid we are a victim of our own success."

While they enjoyed their snack, Dimitri pointed out the Parliament Building on one side of Syntagma Square. "For years that was where all the grand hotels were, until the Hilton was built far to the southeast."

He looked into her eyes as if he were becoming as smitten with her as she with him. The pause became embarrassing, until he coughed and said, "Drink your coffee, little one. It's getting cold."

"What did you call me?"

"I am sorry. I think of you in my mind as *moraki*, which can be translated as 'little one,' but with an inexpressible difference. In Greek among other meanings it can be a way of addressing a child, or a close friend, or a woman for whom one has a special feeling."

She was amused. "And which am I?"

"None of these. I mean, you are a friend, perhaps a special friend, but I should not have used the term. I shall just call you Marilyn."

They finished their coffee and for a few minutes again just stared at each other, this time without any sign of embarrassment. Being with Dimitri made it such a pleasant day and Marilyn was completely relaxed. She was glad now she had come to Greece. And Dimitri made up for much of the bad memories she would always have of being kidnapped. She had an indescribably light feeling of comfort and contentment she had never known before. She stretched back, crossed her legs, folded her arms, and breathed a sigh. Was this the ecstasy of love? she asked herself.

It was getting late in the afternoon and the breeze was dying down. She wondered what Dimitri would take her to see next when a jarring ring interrupted her thoughts. It took her only a moment to realize it was a cell phone, something it seemed as if she had not heard in weeks, although in reality it had been just days.

Dimitri had his cell phone up to his ear and he was expressing agreement to someone. "*Malista, amesos. Nai, katalavaino. Nai, isos media ora. Den boreis na mou pis perisotero? Entaxi.*" Of course, immediately. Yes, I understand. Yes, perhaps a half-hour. Can't you tell me more? All right.

"That sounded horribly official," Marilyn said.

"My office. Chief Superintendent Maniatis tells me something bad has happened, and my father wants me at the DSI building. Come on, I'll take you home first."

✳   ✳   ✳   ✳

That same Sunday afternoon Eleni was in bed with General Omiros Zavalas, who was now asleep. Having seen his dossier, she knew he was seventy-three years old. For a man of his age, he had been a surprisingly virile partner. She was proud of him and felt herself satisfied.

At the beginning of the Colonels' Revolt in 1967, Zavalas had been a major in the Greek Army. He had written a book suggesting new army tactics for the defense of the Greek peninsula, and had thus established a reputation as a brilliant military theorist. The colonels expected him to join in with them and were surprised when he didn't. They still treated him with respect, promoted him to lieutenant colonel, and gave him an important non-political post in the Greek Pentagon.

Toward the middle of the Colonels' Regime, he surprised everyone by changing his mind and accepting a political position in the Ministry of Propaganda. When the Colonels were overthrown in 1973 and a democratically elected civilian government took over, Zavalas was a problem. He was well liked among the younger army officers, and the new government decided to give him a reprimand, but allowed him to remain in the army. Ultimately he was promoted to major general. He retired in the 1980s, but his name was linked to various abortive army plots, and he was tried in court for treason. However, there was not enough evidence against him, and he was found not guilty. Shortly after, he went into voluntary exile in Paris.

Light was streaming in from the windows as Eleni propped herself up on a pillow and looked at the peacefully sleeping figure beside her. She thought how strong he must be. She had given him a potent sleeping liquid in his last glass of wine just before they went to bed, and she was surprised that it had not taken effect until after his performance. It was just as well, for she had had a new experience as a by-product. But immediately after their gambol, he had turned over and fallen fast asleep. That was the important thing.

Checking once more to satisfy herself that he was out, Eleni, still naked, slid out of bed and walked around to the other side. There on a nightstand beside the sleeping general was a small key on a chain. Quietly picking up the key, she knelt to look under the bed. The box appeared to be on the other side, so she tiptoed around and knelt again to take another look. She reached to grab the handle and slide it out.

Placing the box on the seat of an upholstered chair a few feet from the bed, she inserted the key in the lock and turned it. Success—she felt the inner lock slide and she was able to open the top. There were just a few letters inside, plus a passport and some money. She placed the box on the floor, sat down in the chair, and started scanning the letters.

There were four of them. They were all dated in the early 1970s, and two were signed by military officers. The other two were written in the same handwriting, but bore no signature. These two were on stationery from the Greek Parliament. They had to be the ones that Petropoulos was interested in because she knew Antoni Antonidis had been a younger member of parliament at that time.

The first-dated letter was a plea to Zavalas to use his influence with Colonel Papadopoulos, the head of the colonels' government, to find an important position in the government for the writer. Apparently the writer came from the same country area, *patrida*, as Zavalas, and their families knew each other. The writer swore eternal allegiance to Zavalas, and he promised to report secretly to him anything and everything the writer's political party was doing which might be to the detriment of the colonels' regime. In return, he hoped to be given a high-ranking position in the colonels' government. At the bottom in another handwriting was a notation with Zavalas's initials reading "Not trustworthy. Ignore."

The second letter was even more pleading. It denounced the head of the writer's party in parliament, the Christian Socialists, who, he said, were plotting with several high-ranking army officers to overthrow Papadopoulos and his government of colonels. It named the disloyal army officers and some other Christian Socialist leaders and suggested that they should all be shot for treason. At the bottom of the letter was another, one-word notation over the initials of Zavalas. The one word in Greek was "*Skatopaido!*" Shitboy!

"I thought that was what you were after," said a voice from the other side of the bed. Zavalas, equally naked, had risen to his feet and was now rapidly walking toward her. Her surprise was such that he was able to grab the letters from her hand before she fully realized what was happening.

She found herself temporarily incapable of speech. For some reason she was ashamed of her nakedness now, and she recovered her clothes from another chair where she had left them. She quickly dressed.

The general, still naked and looking in good physical shape for one of his age, was glancing at his papers. "I guess these are the two you were after," he said, holding two single pages in his hand, "the ones from Petropoulos."

"From Petropoulos?" She had found her voice, and the extreme shock in it betrayed her lack of knowledge of the true facts. She recalled that it was Petropoulos who had told Roussos the letters were written by Antonidis.

"If not Petropoulos, who did you think they were from?"

"Minister Petropoulos wrote you those letters?" she repeated.

"Of course he wasn't a minister at the time. But he was from my *patrida* and he had just been elected a member of parliament. He was always an ambitious, though unscrupulous, man."

Standing on the other side of the room from Eleni, Zavalas put on some clothes and stuffed the papers in his pants pockets. "Who did you think they were from?" He opened the nightstand drawer.

Eleni thought that she might have the most to gain from being honest about the situation. She might yet be able to convince Zavalas to give her the incriminating letters, and they were far more valuable now that she had learned they were written by Petropoulos. She said, "Minister Petropoulos ordered Police Director Roussos to get the letters from you, saying that they were from Minister Antonidis and implying that he wanted to save Antonidis."

"Save him? Hah! Are you unaware that Antonidis is Petropoulos's biggest rival to become the next prime minister? Petropoulos just wanted to save his own skin?"

"You don't seem to think much of Petropoulos."

"He's the worse specimen of a human being that I've known."

"Then you wouldn't want him to become prime minister, would you?"

"I don't give a damn what he becomes."

"But you'd want to save Greece from him."

"Save Greece? Why? What has Greece done for me? I've been frustrated at every turn of my life. And now, just when I'd have the best chance ever to take charge and give the country what it really needs, I'm too old. Not to mention dying."

"Dying?" Eleni felt she was playing twenty questions.

"I have cancer, my dear. It's spread from my colon to my liver. I'll be dead before the year ends."

Eleni was again surprised at this new revelation, and she genuinely felt sorry for the man. There was something in him, she sensed, of the tragic Greek heroes of old. But it was her duty to get those papers, and she was determined to do just that regardless of the cost. She said, "I…I don't know what to say. I admire you, your courage, your manliness, and I'm really sorry to hear that you're dying. But surely you don't want to do Petropoulos any favors. Give me his letters and I promise you that I'll put them to the best possible use. Petropoulos will never become prime minister."

Zavalas walked over to his nightstand, put the folded letters into a large ashtray, flicked a cigarette lighter, and set a flame to the letters, all four of them. From the open drawer of the nightstand he took a revolver and pointed it at Eleni, who had run toward him to try to save the papers. Zavalas held her back with the gun until the letters were reduced in size and gradually burned down to nothing. Now he put the gun back in the drawer and closed it. Eleni had been powerless to stop the destruction of the all-important evidence.

"Why?" she said, "but why?"

"Because they belong to the past just as I belong to the past. All you police people are following my every move, breaking into my house, seducing my maid—yes, I knew about that—all so convinced that I'm a menace to you. Really, all I wanted was to return to the land of my birth and die in peace. I seek revenge against no one. I don't want to save anything. I'm not a crusader. I don't believe in life after death, and I don't care what happens to anything or anyone after I'm gone. I just want you to go back to your chief and tell him that I want to die in peace. I want to go to the coffee shops and sit peacefully and quietly with the few of my old friends who are left, sit out in the sunshine, and drink my *ouzo* and eat my *tyropites* as long as I can until it's time for me to take that journey across the Styx, which won't be long."

Eleni felt she needed more of an explanation. "I can appreciate your desires now under the circumstances. But I can't understand why you don't want to help stop Petropoulos."

He laughed. "Do you know why I joined the colonels in 1970, when others were starting to flee from them? I was still idealistic then, and after seeing the colonels in operation for several years, I began to realize that they were doing good for Greece. They were using strong measures, and I didn't approve of all of them, but Greece needed something drastic. The colonels were getting rid of corruption, stopping foreign influence from ruining the country, and eliminating the grasping amoral opportunists like Petropoulos. When the colonels were overthrown, I wanted to continue the good parts of their program without the excesses, but I was frustrated at every turn.

"I'll try to improve government no more. You can go now, Eleni. Thanks for that extra treat in bed. I hadn't expected it, but it was a fitting climax. The letters you want are gone. You can save time for your department by having your fellow officers leave me alone. I'm no use to anyone. I'm no danger to anyone. Go!"

She left with many regrets. She had failed in her mission. She was afraid of Petropoulos's growing power. And she felt diminished by having gained an understanding of Zavalas just when it was too late to do either of them any good.

As Eleni left Zavalas's place, she turned her cell phone on again. No sooner had she done so than it immediately started ringing. It was Pano Maniatis. She was needed at Headquarters. Something horrible had happened.

CHAPTER 14

▼

The first person Roussos saw when he got to his office late Sunday afternoon was Police Underdirector Jason Thanos. Thanos was standing in the corridor outside Roussos outer office, leaning back against the wall and nonchalantly maneuvering a toothpick against his teeth. He grinned as if he was proud of some accomplishment.

"Back from Paris I see," said Roussos. "I hope you've got some good information on Zavalas."

"No, there was nothing in Paris. Nothing on Zavalas." Another grin. "For me personally it was amusing, but I'm glad to be back at work."

"You no doubt know that we arrested Nick Savvas and that something happened to him."

"Oh yes, I've heard." He stood up straight enough to shrug his shoulders. "Well, at least that's one crook who won't be bothering us any more."

"I understand he's dead."

Pano entered the room. "Murdered is the word."

"Dead, yes," said Thanos, appearing startled, "but hardly murdered." His eyes widened and his face turned paler. "Who said he was murdered?"

Pano grabbed Roussos by the arm. "Am I glad to see you, Chief. Come here and I'll show you."

Thanos said, "I'll go with you to explain."

Pano quickly glanced at Roussos and squinted his eyes in a silent signal. Roussos understood immediately and said to Thanos. "No, you stay here until I get back."

"But I should be with you to explain."

"That's an order, Thanos. You stay in your office until I call for you. Lead on, Pano."

Savvas had been locked in one of the single-person cells. Although there had been other prisoners in nearby cells, they had been taken elsewhere so there was no one in this block now except the quite dead body of Savvas.

No one could have believed Savvas to be anything but dead. The walls and floor were splattered with blood. His clothes were torn and his face and body were blood streaked. His head had been bashed in as if someone had used a heavy club to beat him senseless. Pieces of bloodied flesh from his body were littering the floor. An arm was twisted backwards and broken so he looked like a collapsed and irreparable marionette. Roussos had to wonder if there was a bone in his body left unbroken.

Pano called a policeman and said, "You can get the photographer now." To Roussos he explained, "They phoned me about two hours ago. This is what I found. I wanted to get the body photographed immediately, but Thanos pulled rank on me and prevented it. The two guards for this block told me privately that they tried to prevent the murder, but again Thanos was their superior officer."

"So Thanos did it?"

"Yes. You've got as witnesses Superintendent Vlahos, the two guards, and the two prisoners who were in these adjoining cells before I moved them. Both prisoners were still trembling, thinking that Thanos might come after them next."

"My God, how did it happen?"

"Thanos came back from Paris and immediately checked with the office to catch up on any news. Hearing that Savvas had been arrested, he went to his office and made a telephone call. When he returned, he insisted on seeing Savvas, and this is the result."

"Do you know who Thanos telephoned?"

"Not exactly, but I'd guess it was Minister Petropoulos."

"Why Petropoulos?"

"You'd better let Vlahos tell you so you get it straight."

"Vlahos was in charge at the time?"

"Yes. He said he tried to stop Thanos, but Thanos had the rank."

"Why didn't he call someone?"

"He said he was afraid of Thanos, and he had no idea that it was going to be like this. Thanos said that Savvas had given him some wise guy answers, and he was going to teach him to respect the police. By the time Vlahos realized how serious it had become, it was too late. And besides, Vlahos is 54 years old and getting close to retirement, and he's afraid to take chances. He was sure that Savvas was dead, but Thanos just kept beating and kicking the body anyway. He used a metal-weighted truncheon. Vlahos telephoned me and I rushed over immediately."

"I should have known," said Roussos. "I should have given an order that Thanos was not to be left alone with any prisoner."

"Don't blame yourself, Spyro," said Pano. "You didn't even know he was back, did you? None of us could have guessed that this would happen. And how could anyone prevent the second highest-ranking man in DSI from visiting a prisoner if he wanted to?"

"God damn to hell that bastard Petropoulos! I should have refused to accept Thanos."

"And you would have been removed and Thanos would have been made acting chief. And that would have been worse because then he could cover up. But he won't be able to cover up now."

"I swear to Jesus Christ he won't!" Roussos hollered to Superintendent Vlahos, who was standing at the other end of the cellblock. "Vlahos, I'll talk to you later about this. Right now I want you to arrest Police Underdirector Thanos. Strip him of his clothing and anything else he has and put him in the completely isolated cell with audio and turn the recorder on."

"Arrest the underdirector?"

"You understand Greek, don't you? Do it!"

Vlahos left to carry out his orders. Roussos said to Pano, "It will be good if we can get him to incriminate himself before Petropoulos hears about this."

Pano smiled. "Do you think Thanos knows that every word he says will be taped?"

"Perhaps not. They don't have those kinds of cells in the usual police stations that he's accustomed to, and he hasn't been around here long enough to learn everything about the way we operate. Now I want to speak to the witnesses in my office. First the guards for this cell block, and later all the prisoners who saw and heard what was happening. Wake them up if you have to, and call in as many people as necessary. I want complete photographs tonight. I want an autopsy. I want people to take down sworn statements from anyone who has any knowledge of this. And that includes Thanos. And call Eleni and Dimitri to help you."

As Pano started to leave, Roussos said one more thing to him, "I'm giving you a heavy load, old friend, but I need one more favor."

Pano said, "This load is a pleasure, Chief, and your favor's as good as done."

"I have no idea when I'll be getting home, if at all. Call your wife and see if it's all right for Victoria to stay overnight with her. You know, because of Xynos. I'll explain to Victoria and have one of the guards accompany her in a taxi to your house."

Roussos went back to his office. The time was almost ten p.m., and he had much to do. He was owed favors by a number of police officers in the higher ranks, so he started phoning them in spite of the time. Thanos was not well liked among his fellow officers, and he would find out now how important it was to not to make enemies among the people one worked with.

By the time Roussos had talked to the witnesses, some of the personnel called by Pano had arrived. Roussos gave them all instructions, then he and Pano visited Thanos in his isolated cell.

At first Thanos was indignant. "How dare you do this to a fellow police officer? I demand that you release me at once."

Then Thanos went into explanations. "I was only trying to help you, Mr. Director. I was afraid that he'd weasel out of the charge somehow, and I was only trying to get a confession."

"Your usual way, of course?" said Roussos.

"Of course, how else do you get a confession? But I wasn't trying to kill him. I just wanted to muss him up a little."

"Like you've mussed up others in the past who have gone from you to the graveyard."

Thanos grinned to show he was proud of his accomplishments. "You can't make rabbit stew without hurting the rabbit a little." He then reverted to defensive pleading. "But Savvas was insulting. He called me a stupid swine. He said you were a stupid swine. And when I heard him talk about you like that, I got mad."

Then he went into a second level of excuses. "I was only doing my duty like we all do. Haven't you ever beat up a prisoner? Is there a policeman alive who's never beat up a prisoner? I was only doing what we all do all the time."

Roussos shouted back at him with indignation. "Such as making prisoners lie on their belly on ice with a broomstick up their ass? Such as making them into a cocoon with heavy rope twined around them so you can beat them without marks showing? Such as using the bastinado on bare feet? Such as the telephone dial wired to their testicles with each higher number dialed giving a greater shock? Are these the approved ways to get confessions?"

"Of course I've used those methods. That's normal police work, isn't it?"

"If that's normal, then why have you got a reputation with your fellow officers for being a sadist? Why is it that you're one of the most hated men on the force?"

Thanos managed a grin, but shyer this time. "They're jealous of me because I get results."

Next he tried pleading. "I'm naked and cold. At least let me have my clothes."

"You are a prisoner charged with murder," said Roussos. "How do you treat prisoners charged with murder?"

Now came threats. "Wait till Minister Petropoulos hears about this outrage. You'll be the sorry one then. You'll be pleading with me then. Petropoulos will get your ass."

"For my treatment of you? Forget it. When Petropoulos sees the evidence I have against you, he'll think twice."

"You think so, hey? Let me tell you, I've got enough dirt on Petropoulos to send him to prison for the rest of his life. What do you think about that?"

"Sure. Well, you can talk to the public prosecutor about it, and he might reduce the charge to a lesser offence." Turning to Pano, Roussos said, "Give him some prisoner clothes to cover himself with. If we keep him like this, I'll have to charge him with indecent exposure also."

The police director started walking back to his office. As he left the cell area, Inspector Vlahos said he'd like to talk to him privately. They went into Roussos's office.

"All right, what have you to say, Vlahos? You were in charge. It doesn't look good for you."

Vlahos was a dark-complexioned man from northern Greece whose service record was mixed. He had made some good arrests and obtained a large number of convictions. But he had had disciplinary actions taken against him for negligence, cowardice, and stealing money from a prisoner. On one occasion he had been demoted, but quickly regained his rank when he solved another important crime.

"Sir," he began, "there is something you should know. Before Underdirector Thanos arrived, Nick Savvas talked to me. He said he had heard that Thanos was now with DSI, and he begged me to keep Thanos away from him."

"Why?"

"He was trying to tell me something without further incriminating himself. Although he didn't say it explicitly, I gathered that he, Minister Petropoulos, and Thanos had been working together. Petropoulos was giving Savvas protection, and Savvas was giving Petropoulos a large share of the money he obtained from his swindles. Apparently Thanos often acted as their go-between."

Roussos said, "Then why should Savvas have been afraid of Thanos?"

"Savvas said that Petropoulos had told him to keep away from high-ranking government officials. He was supposed to confine his swindles to non-influential businessmen. He disobeyed Petropoulos when he took money from Nina Papazoglou, who was both the daughter of Minister Antonidis and the niece of the prime minister. After we put him in a cell, he began thinking that this could become a highly publicized case, and Petropoulos would be very angry."

"And do what?" Roussos was already ahead of Vlahos, and he could now understand why Thanos had beaten him to death, but he wanted to hear it from this man who could be the key witness in a trial against Thanos."

"He was afraid that Petropoulos would want him killed. And knowing Thanos's reputation, he was afraid that Thanos would come after him. He begged me to protect him."

"Well, why didn't you?"

"I'm only a superintendent, sir. Underdirector Thanos was my superior, and I could hardly tell him that he wasn't allowed to be in a cell with a prisoner."

"Didn't you see that Thanos was carrying a truncheon?"

Vlahos hesitated, then said, "Er, no, sir. I didn't see anything."

"But you certainly saw it when Thanos was using it on Savvas."

"I was outside the cell, sir. There were two guards closer than I was. When we realized that Thanos was beating Savvas to death, we yelled to him to stop, but he wouldn't."

"Superintendent Vlahos, must I remind you that beating a man to death is against the law, seriously against the law, even if it's being done by a policeman. It was your duty to enter that cell and stop Thanos."

"It was impossible, sir. Thanos was like a madman. We would have had to shoot him to make him stop, and I couldn't give the order to shoot my superior officer. I was in a horrible position, sir. Please understand." He was almost in tears and acting as if he knew he was pleading for his career and retirement.

"We'll talk about any possible disciplinary action later. Right now I want you to write a report containing everything Savvas told you and everything you saw and heard in connection with this crime. And when Thanos comes to trial, I will expect you to testify against him."

Vlahos's eyes lit up. "Yes, sir. I'll testify against him. I'll tell the whole story to the court."

"And what's this about Thanos making a telephone call before going into Savvas's cell?"

"Well, he went to his office in a hurry and left the door open. I saw him on the phone and heard just a few words, but it appeared that he was talking to Minister Petropoulos."

"I want that written report no later than tomorrow noon. Mention the telephone call, but if you don't know for a fact that he was talking to Minister Petropoulos, leave his name out. When you get to the part about Savvas telling you of his fear of Thanos, write it up exactly as you heard it, no guesswork on your part, just what he actually told you."

When Vlahos had gone, Roussos called Pano Maniatis in and told him what Vlahos had said.

Pano said, "That should cinch the case against Thanos. But can you use the information about the part of Petropoulos?"

"It's based on hearsay, and would be highly political. I honestly don't know, Pano, but first things first. We'll get a formal charge against Thanos and see what Petropoulos's reaction will be. At the very least, we're onto Petropoulos now, and we can use this to start building a case against him."

"They are both very tricky men."

"I know, my friend. We will see. In the meantime, Pano, you still have your contacts with certain reliable newspaper reporters?"

"I don't consider any newspaper reporter completely reliable, sir, but I have some good contacts."

"I want you to pick out some of the most appropriate photographs of Savvas's dead body with all the bruises and everything. Use them judiciously, but I think it would help our case, and perhaps hold Petropoulos a little in check, if some of the photographs appeared in a few newspapers without specific attribution."

CHAPTER 15

▼

Monday morning Roussos went to his office early. He still had telephone calls to make to call in favors. He would have to work fast because once Petropoulos found out about the arrest of Thanos, there would be trouble. He didn't know how or when it would come, but he was certain that Petropoulos would cause him strife.

He checked on Thanos and found that his situation had not changed. He was still in his cell and yelling threats at everyone he saw. The body of Savvas had been taken to the police morgue for further examination.

But other business had to go on also. When Eleni wanted to see him with her latest report on General Zavalas, he readily had her come in. When he heard what she had to say, his emotions were divided. On the one hand, he was pleased to see that his instincts had been right: Zavalas was not plotting any revolt or apparently anything else. He could mark "Closed" to the Zavalas file.

On the other hand, he felt sorry for the general. They had differed politically, but he had always considered Zavalas an honorable man. Eleni's report on the letters was another disappointment. Such letters could greatly have diminished Petropoulos's standing in the eyes of his fellow Christian Socialists, but their destruction rendered them useless. Eleni's unsupported word as to the contents of the unsigned letters, as well as to the general's naming the author, would not be of the slightest help. The issue was closed. As far as Zavalas was concerned, Roussos would let him die in peace.

Just a little before ten o'clock, Roussos got a telephone call from Petropoulos's office. An aide said, "The minister wants to see you in his office immediately."

Roussos thought to himself, so he has finally heard. He joked to his secretary as he left that he should be wearing fireproof armor for this particular visit. He reported to Petropoulos's outer office at five minutes past ten. He was told to take a seat and the minister would be pleased to see him shortly. He waited. The minutes passed, then an hour. Some of the ministry employees were getting ready to leave for an early lunch and siesta, and Roussos was still waiting. The minister's secretary told him how insistent Petropoulos was that Roussos not leave. "He said it was his direct order for you to wait." Little suspicions began dancing in Roussos's mind.

Just before noon Antoni Antonidis stuck his head in the door and said to the secretary, "Isn't Minister Petropoulos back yet? The minute he comes back, tell him I have to see him urgently." Then Antonidis turned to Roussos. "What are you doing here, Spyro?"

Roussos explained.

Antonidis said, "But Petropoulos is at your office. He's been there all morning."

Roussos looked at the secretary and shook his head. Taking Antonidis by the arm, he guided him out to the corridor, saying, "I have something highly confidential to tell you." He proceeded to describe all the events of the previous day concerning Savvas and Thanos.

"But why did Petropoulos call you here when he knew he was going to your office?"

Roussos gave him an ironic smile. "Apparently Petropoulos wanted me out of the way this morning so he could free Thanos and intimidate my people." He and Antonidis parted, and Roussos walked calmly back to his office in the certain knowledge that his case against Thanos was in the process of being destroyed.

*   *   *   *

Roussos was not surprised when he entered his outer office and his secretary made unusual grimaces at him. She stood up and whispered in his ear, "Minister Petropoulos and others are in there. I'm supposed to tell them when you come in."

"Then tell them." He gave her a few seconds to pick up the phone, then entered his office.

Petropoulos was seated on Roussos's chair behind his desk. The four guest chairs were occupied by Thanos, Superintendent Vlahos, and the two cell guards who had been present when Thanos was in Savvas's cell beating him to death.

These four turned so they could also be looking at Roussos. In the center of the room was something new, a small chair from one of the interrogation rooms.

Petropoulos told him, "Sit!"

"Since my own seat is occupied, I prefer to stand."

"Sit! That's an official order."

Roussos stood looking at him for a short while, nodded gravely, and sat in the chair.

Petropoulos rose to his feet. "How dare you! You stupid, arrogant, god-damned idiot, how dare you! How do you dare arrest your own deputy, the man that I personally selected to assist you in doing your job? Who do you think you are?"

"Mr. Minister, if you are going to call me names, I think we had better tape this interview for the record."

"The devil take you," Petropoulos shouted. Pausing, he half closed his eyelids, then said, "But it's not a bad idea to have something on record. I suppose you already have a recording device here, just turn on the switch. Where is it?"

Before Roussos had a chance to answer, Superintendent Vlahos rose and walked to where Petropoulos was standing. "The switch is here, sir, underneath the desk on the inside right pedestal." Seeing assent from the minister, he reached down and activated the recorder.

From Petropoulos's next words, it was obvious to all that the tone of the meeting had changed. With the recorder on, he became more formal and less vituperative. Nonetheless, he was still relentless in his accusations. He said, "Police Director Spyridon Roussos, I am Minister of Public Security Achilles Petropoulos, and I am in your office to preside over a meeting to look into charges of serious dereliction of duty and malfeasance on your part. Today is Monday, July 9th, and the time is 1:20 p.m. With me are Underdirector Jason Thanos, Superintendent Ioannis Vlahos,"—he stopped to look around on his desk. Thanos quickly took a piece of paper from his pocket and gave it to the minister, who looked at it, then continued, "Senior Sergeant Athanasios Venardis, and Sergeant Mihail Kostopoulos."

The minister sat down, then spoke again, "Do you have anything to say?"

Roussos responded, "Specifically what am I accused of?"

Petropoulos said, "On Sunday, July 8th, you caused your own deputy, Police Underdirector Jason Thanos, an experienced and highly commended officer with sixteen years of service, to be arrested, stripped bare of all his clothing, and imprisoned in a high security cell. You then taunted Underdirector Thanos with ridiculous and untrue accusations of his past conduct, and you threatened to have him tortured into making a false confession in regard to the death of a notorious criminal, Nikolaos Savvas. You further attempted to subvert some of the officers under your command to make false statements of accusation against Underdirector Thanos."

"All that?" Roussos looked in turn into the faces of Vlahos and the two sergeants. Vlahos appeared especially contrite. Roussos had forgiven him a lot in view of the good side of his record, and Vlahos knew he was under special obligation to him. The two sergeants had not been with Roussos long, and although neither had been known to get in trouble, Roussos did not know them well enough to have any sound view on their dependability.

The three men turned away as he scrutinized their faces one by one. They would be witnesses to support Thanos.

As if to confirm Roussos's impression, Petropoulos asked questions of each of the three, and they put on the record that Savvas had made much noise in his cell and was insulting to every police officer. Thanos had entered the cell to talk him into being more quiet, when Savvas viciously attacked him. Thanos defended himself, and Savvas tripped so that his face hit the bars, causing the injuries leading to his death. Roussos had come to his office with liquor on his breath and began swearing at Thanos, ordering him stripped of his clothing and locked in a high security cell. Thanos had tried to explain the situation, but Roussos wouldn't listen to him. Instead he called him names and threatened to have him tortured.

As they each recited the story, almost word for word in agreement with each other, the three men seemed downhearted, even ashamed. Too late Roussos realized the extent of Petropoulos's insidious power. No wonder he had such influence over his associates in parliament. Even those who might be expected to despise him were too fearful of him to oppose his will.

Roussos asked if he might put some questions to his subordinates.

Petropoulos said in a sympathetic tone, "Of course, Director Roussos. I am only trying to get to the truth of this matter. I want you to have every opportunity to clear yourself of these gravely serious charges."

Roussos said to Vlahos, "You claim I threatened to torture Underdirector Thanos. What did I say that implied torture?"

Vlahos answered, "Among other things, you threatened to put him naked on a cake of ice and shove a broomstick up his...up his...his *kolos*. You had us take all his clothes off to prepare him for this treatment."

Well, thought Roussos, *so this is what I'm going to have to put up with.* He tried again. "Last night after you arrested Thanos on my order and put him in a cell, I asked you to turn on the audio so that all our remarks could be recorded. Did you do that?"

Vlahos said, "Yes, sir."

"Where is the tape?"

"There is no tape, sir. Either the machine was empty, or someone took the tape. I looked all over this morning and could not find it."

"I see. Very well, Superintendent Vlahos, did you ask to speak to me privately last night?"

"Yes, sir."

"What did you tell me?"

"I told you that I did not think it right for you to be treating Underdirector Thanos like a common criminal. I told you that it was all Savvas's fault. He had been causing trouble all afternoon, and I had been tempted to administer him punishment myself."

"Interesting," said Roussos. "In view of these grossly false answers, I have no more questions." His eyes burning into Vlahos, he said in an admonishing tone of voice, "I hope, Superintendent Vlahos, that if this matter comes to trial, you will not continue to perjure yourself."

Turning to look at Petropoulos, Roussos said, "Right now, however, since there seems to be some problem of knowing whether a recording device has tape at the time it is turned on, I want to ask Superintendent Vlahos to check and verify that there is tape for the recording that we are now making of this interview."

"Not interview," said Petropoulos. "This is an investigation."

Vlahos looked to the minister, who nodded. The superintendent then went to a cupboard in the wall and checked the recording machine. He turned to the room and said, "There is tape in the machine and it is now running."

Roussos asked, "Is there a numbering meter on the tape recorder?"

"Yes, sir."

"What number is it at this moment?"

"It is 1,712—no, 1,713 now."

"Let us all remember that number in case of future need," said Roussos, "1,713 and the time according to the wall clock is ten minutes after one o'clock in the afternoon."

"I don't know what all this number recording is about," said Petropoulos, "but you may be assured, Director Roussos, that I will personally take charge of that tape and see that it's integrity is maintained."

"Of course," said Roussos. "I would expect you to take charge of it."

"Are you being sarcastic?"

"I have not intended any sarcasm."

"I don't think you realize how serious this matter is," said the minister. "But you will. Police Director Spyridon Roussos, I am hereby relieving you of your position as the head of the Department of Sensitive Investigations pending a formal inquiry and possible trial for your actions. You are suspended from duty with full pay pending further notice. Police Underdirector Jason Thanos will be the acting head of DSI in the meantime. Are there any questions?" The thick smile on his countenance had been growing, and now it seemed to ooze throughout his entire lower face like foam running down a glass of beer.

At that moment, the telephone rang. Petropoulos picked it up and yelled into the receiver, "I thought I told you we were not to be disturbed. Oh. Oh, of course, put him on immediately."

His smile had disappeared, and he looked deadly serious as he listened to the voice at the other end. "Yes, prime minister, of course, sir. No, sir, I didn't do that. I intended to take care of all the formal details later. Yes, sir, I have relieved him of all duties, but on full pay pending a further inquiry. Underdirector Thanos. No, sir, there are just six of us in the room, myself, Roussos, Thanos, and three junior officers. Yes, sir, immediately, sir. I didn't understand. Perhaps I should have checked the procedures more thoroughly first. I'm sorry, sir."

As he hung up, he glared at Roussos. "How the devil did you get word of this to that senile bastard, the prime minister?"

Thanos tugged at his sleeve and pointed to the cupboard holding the recorder.

Petropoulos yelled at Vlahos. "Shut that goddamned thing off and bring me the tape." When he had the cassette in his hands, he crushed it and painstakingly removed all the tape. Turning a metal wastepaper basket upside down to empty it, he then turned it upright again and burned the tape in it.

Roussos said, "I expect every person in this room to remember what that tape represented and what the minister just did with it."

With a snarl, Petropoulos said, "You can go to the devil with your tape. This meeting is hereby wiped off the record. There was no meeting. Director Roussos is still in charge of DSI. However, in view of what has transpired between him and you men, I am hereby effecting a temporary transfer of Underdirector Thanos and the other three of you to my office to staff a special inquiry detail. I'm going back to my office, and you four can get your personal possessions and report to me in one hour. Two hours, I must have lunch."

As he was leaving, Petropoulos paused in the doorway. "Don't think this is over, Roussos. I intend to make official criminal charges against you and see you stripped of your rank and sent to prison."

✳   ✳   ✳   ✳

"So much has happened, Chief, that my poor mind can't keep track of it," said Pano Maniatis, who was seated with Dimitri Roussos and Eleni Karolou in front the director.

"But how did Minister Antonidis hear of this even while it was happening?" asked Eleni.

"Petropoulos fired you and then reinstated you?" Dimitri said.

Roussos spoke. "His last words were that the meeting never took place, so officially I was never fired and didn't have to be reinstated."

Pano said, "But how can a meeting that happened suddenly never happen?"

"Ah, Pano, when you get to be a minister, you'll see that ministers can do amazing things. What saved me was that by chance I ran into Minister Antonidis when I was wasting my time in Petropoulos's office. I gave him a quick summary of how Petropoulos had tricked me. He added up the known facts and realized what was going on. Remember, the prime minister is his brother-in-law, and he got in touch with him immediately."

"Yes," said Eleni, "but Petropoulos has the support of many Christian Socialist deputies. Would the prime minister want to risk a party revolt just to protect a police director?"

"I think the question rather is would Petropoulos want to initiate a showdown with the prime minister at this time and over this cause? He's shrewd, and he'll want to pick the time and place of any battles of that size."

Pano said, "So for the moment we're protected, but how long will it last?"

"I'm afraid, my dear associates, that I've unwillingly involved us in politics. I'm not a politician and there's not much I can do at this time, other than carry on business as usual. But I'm not forgetting about Thanos. That's a criminal matter, and I intend to pursue it to the utmost of my ability. Now, what have we remaining of the special cases?"

Eleni said, "It seems that we no sooner finish a case than another case is generated by it, and the work load never goes down."

"How true," said Dimitri.

Eleni continued. "The Savvas case is finished, but now we have the Savvas murder case, or perhaps we should call it the Thanos case. The case of General Zavalas is finished, but it leaves the question of what I told you earlier, the strong probability of Minister Petropoulos having written the politically damaging letters—I'm not sure what we should do about that."

"You've done excellent work, Eleni," said Roussos, "but under the circumstances it would appear that case is finished."

"As you know," said Pano, "the Xynos case has generated nothing new. If it weren't for the fact that he confronted Miss Renfrew in her apartment and then viciously murdered one of our men, poor Sotiri, I'd swear Xynos wasn't even in Greece. If he's here to do some dirty work, why isn't he trying to do it?"

Roussos said, "Because he's clever, Pano. He wants to wear us down. But don't relax your vigilance. You're still in charge of this case, Pano, and it's still our most important one."

Eleni said "But another case that ended successfully, the matter of the kidnapped niece of the American ambassador, has forced a new case on us that might be even more serious than the Xynos case."

"Right," said Roussos. "Although seven of Miss Pickering's kidnappers are dead, according to her statement there must be more than a dozen still in circulation. She thought she could remember about twenty distinct kidnappers having been on Skyros at one time or another during her captivity. Who were they? What did they really want? And what are we doing about it?"

Dimitri said, "We have now identified all seven of the kidnappers and we find they had several things in common. They were all about the same age, and each had been a graduate of the *Scholi Evelpidon*." The School of Hopefuls was the Greek equivalent of West Point. "Each became an army officer, although several resigned after a varying number of years. One became an executive in an insurance company. Another was a manager of the national radio and television service. And another was in the transoceanic shipping business."

"Yes, thank you, Dimitri," Roussos said. "I have your report. Since they were around your age, do you remember any of them from the School of Hopefuls when you were there?"

"One, Haralambo Evyenitis, was the top student in my class and a friend of mine. You might remember I brought him over to our house once. He stayed on in the army and became a major, the highest ranking of the seven dead ones."

"And the others?"

"I was acquainted with three of them, but not well. One, Karlo Fomidis, was the radio-TV manager, and reports show that he had still maintained much contact with activist army officers."

"What do you mean activist?" asked Pano.

"The ones who had been in contact with survivors of the Colonels' Regime."

Roussos asked, "Had any been in contact with Zavalas?"

"Not that I know of."

"Do you think they were trying to restore the objectives of the Colonel's Regime?"

"Remember," said Dimitri, "there have been rumors of various military take-overs ever since the colonels were thrown out. But that's all they've been, just rumors. No actual attempts. And it doesn't seem logical that there would be any attempt now."

"Why?" asked Eleni.

"For the very fact that the Colonels' Revolt was so thoroughly discredited. Another army attempt to take over the government might succeed initially, but it couldn't possibly be sustained. They would need popular support, and there would be none. Can anyone here see a sizeable number of Greeks backing another revolt by younger army officers? Or older ones, for that matter?"

"No," said Eleni, "the people wouldn't stand for it."

"Let us tentatively consider them disaffected army officers whose exact purpose is to be determined," said Director Roussos. "But what about those commandos?"

"Well," said Pano, "they don't seem to be working for the same objective. Is there any chance that the government has some paramilitary group so secret that even you don't know about them, Chief?"

"I just can't see it," said Roussos. "Under the colonels, for example, some such group might have flourished unknown to any of the other services. But for a democratic government? It would have to be a conspiracy between the two major political parties. And there would always be the possibility that one of the men in black sweaters might become disenchanted and talk about it. It's unimaginable."

"Could they be some rival army group with the same goals, but wanting control of the government for themselves?" asked Pano.

"Doubtful," said Dimitri, "but I suppose it's possible. Keep in mind that we don't have monolithic ideology in the army. There are some officers who still admire the ideals of the overthrown colonels. Others are fanatic royalists and want to bring King Konstantino back from exile. And there are even crypto-Communists."

"And perhaps," said Pano, "a few who believe in democratic government?"

Dimitri laughed. "Of course. There are many who believe in and will fight for democracy. But I haven't even begun to tell you of all the opposing ideologies in the army today."

Eleni, looking deep in thought, suddenly spoke up. "Is there any possibility that the commandos are a non-government paramilitary group formed by and under the instructions of Minister Petropoulos? Could he be plotting some over-throw of the democratically elected government?"

"Anything is possible," said the director, "but do you have even the slightest evidence of such a thing?"

"No, not really. But you recall I summarized the letters he wrote. Even as a young man he was ready to do anything, including betraying anyone, to get what he wanted. Do you think it would be beneath him to be plotting against the gov-ernment in a non-military coup d'état?"

"I think we can agree," said Dimitri, "that nothing would be beneath Petropoulos."

No one else answered, but all looked as if they were seriously considering the thought.

"All right, Dimitri," said the director, "this is your assignment. Keep to it. Do you still maintain contact with your former *Evelpidon* school chums?"

"Oh, yes. Some of them are good friends."

"See what you can elicit from them. One thing we Greeks know is that you can't keep a secret in Greece for long. If a large number of army officers are involved in a plot—or in two separate plots—it's almost certain that there will be some other army officers not directly involved, but knowledgeable of what's going on in general terms." He looked each of his subordinates in the face, noting their reactions. "Undoubtedly each of us here has heard one or more rumors of a coup being plotted. The difficulty is separating idle rumors from real facts."

Recalling to himself how Superintendent Vlahos and the two sergeants had gone against him, he momentarily wondered about the complete loyalty of the members of his Special Team. But he could not imagine any of the three people now sitting in front of him going over to the other side, even if Petropoulos tried to force them. He considered himself supremely blessed for having three such loyal team members.

Pano said, "It is true. I hear of impending coups all the time. But when I ask for names, places, dates, witnesses, I get nothing. The coffee shop regulars love to impress their listeners with their great knowledge, but they never have anything specific."

Roussos decided to close the meeting. He said, "Dimitri, you're still assigned to the case of the kidnappers and commandos. Eleni, I hate to do this to you, but you are assigned to the Thanos case. Discretion is the word here, and the object is to get enough information on the Savvas murder so that even Petropoulos can't reverse it. In that connection, I'll give you some names of high-ranking police officers who can tell you more about Thanos's past. They're not ready to testify in court yet, but I think they'll cooperate with you on a confidential basis."

"I don't have to sleep with Thanos, do I?"

"No, you don't have to sleep with him."

Pano said, "That would be an assignment worse than death."

"One other thing, Eleni," said Roussos, "I'm not ordering an investigation of the minister, but you mentioned in connection with the letters Zavalas burned that they probably were written by Petropoulos. If you come up with any further information on the minister, see me right away. All of you should keep this is mind: Petropoulos wants to see some vast changes in DSI, which you would not like any more than I. But Petropoulos is the only person with the power to effect those changes. By himself neither Thanos nor anyone else can threaten us. Petropoulos, because of the political power he commands, is the principal; all others are simply agents."

"I have a feeling," said Pano, "that Xynos will strike when we least expect him to."

"I have the same feeling," said Eleni, "that Petropoulos will do likewise."

CHAPTER 16

▼

It was while Victoria was showing Marilyn Pickering the central shopping center of Athens that the incident occurred. Victoria had called Marilyn and apologized for not getting in touch earlier, pleading the demands made on her by the *Tosca* rehearsals. They met at Victoria's apartment and walked across Kanari Street to wend their way toward Stadiou.

"Why did you want to escape your bodyguard?" asked Marilyn.

"I don't think I'll need him if I'm with you. I want to get away from everything today. It'll be so much fun shopping with you."

Victoria explained the layout between Syntagma Square and Omonia Square, the two centers of downtown Athens. Obliquely from two corners of Syntagma ran the parallel Panepistimiou and Stadiou Streets until they entered Omonia Square. Directly opposite the Tomb of the Unknown Soldier and straight down from Syntagma ran Ermou Street. On these streets and the short cross streets running off from them were found the large fashionable stores, small specialty shops, and trendy avant-garde boutiques.

"There are two things to remember about shopping in Athens," said Victoria. "First, it's not Paris, but second, it's not Podunk Junction either. The dress designers are first rate, and the milliners are tops, too. You can find fashionable lingerie, shoes, handbags, costume jewelry, and all the other accessories you might want. The silversmith and goldsmith shops are very reasonable in price, and you can also find bargains in fur coats and goatskin rugs, the famous Flokati rugs."

"And for souvenirs?"

"Tell me what you want, and I'll tell you where to go. There are a lot of tourist mementos for sale, but I don't think you'd like them."

"No," said Marilyn, "but I would like to bring some high quality articles home as gifts. My father's a coin collector, and my mother likes oil paintings. And I'd like to get something special for a special friend—oh, I forgot, you know him, Jake Sommers."

"We could go to Diamantis, the big department store on Ermou. Or we might go to the flea market, a little out of the way, but not too far. We can stop at Diamantis going or coming back. We should be able to find some ancient coins in the flea market on Ifaistou or Pandrossou Streets, a little off Ermou in the Monastiraki area."

They spent several hours looking and buying in various stores. Marilyn got a painting of the Acropolis for her mother, which Victoria arranged to have delivered to the American Embassy. For her father she bought a thick silver tetradrachma from the time of Alexander the Great's successors, and she found some eighteen-carat gold cuff links for Jake.

Victoria said, "Eighteen-carat gold is much more popular in Greece than the fourteen-carat that we see more often in the States. This shop charges a little more than some others, but I know the owner and I can assure you that you're getting genuine gold here. It's easy to get cheated when you go for the lowest price."

They walked back and had a late lunch at a sidewalk table at Flokas on Korai Street, not far from Syntagma. Victoria told Marilyn that she and Spyro wanted to invite her for dinner at their apartment on Friday night. "For a fourth, who would you like to have? We can invite Spyro's son, Dimitri, or perhaps there is someone at the American Embassy you'd prefer."

"Oh, no," Marilyn hurried to say. "Dimitri will be fine. I'd enjoy that." After a moment, she said, "I don't know your Spyro very well. Are he and his son alike?"

Victoria smiled. "In a way, I suppose. Dimitri takes after his father, but also somewhat from his mother. I understand she was very open, not as serious as Spyro. Dimitri has both his serious side and his lighter side."

"But you're very much in love with Spyro?"

"I've finally gotten in life what I want. I'm fabulously happy with Spyro. Oh, I'd like to be better known in the operatic world than I am. But if I never sang on stage again, as long as I had Spyro I'd be happy. But I'm so fortunate to have both. Like Tosca, I live for my singing and I live for love. Of the two, however, love is the more important."

"I wish I could feel that way. I don't know my own mind from one day to the next. It must be wonderfully satisfying to know what you want."

"It is, but you're still young. You really do know what you want, but you just haven't sorted it out yet. If you keep your mind on the important things, you'll know what it is and you'll get it."

It was then that Victoria saw him.

"What's the matter?" said Marilyn. "You've turned absolutely white. Is something wrong?"

Victoria said, "As I get up to walk inside to the ladies' room, turn your head slowly in the other direction and take a good, but discreet look at that man sitting by himself at the furthest of the outside tables. He's wearing a suit and tie and looks like a businessman. Make a mental note and see if you can describe him later. I want to use my cell telephone, but inside where he can't see me."

When Victoria returned, the man was gone. "Did you see where he went?" she asked Marilyn.

"Down the street and through that park. The second your back was turned, he threw some money on the table and almost ran down the street."

Victoria kept rubbing her hands together in a fretting movement. "If they don't arrive soon, he'll get himself lost in that maze of streets on the other side of Stadiou. He could be going to the Plaka or toward the Keramikos, God knows where."

"Who is he? What's wrong, Victoria? Who are you waiting for?"

Two police cars drove up sounding the European high-and-low-pitched ooh-ooh alarm equivalent of an American siren, and several men got out of each. Spyro Roussos in mufti led the way, while the other uniformed officers started looking in all directions.

Victoria ran to meet Roussos and said, "That way through Klafthmonos Square, about five minutes ago."

"Are you positive it was Xynos?"

"Absolutely. He wore a thick moustache and he had dyed his hair gray so he looked older, but it was Pavlo Xynos, I swear it. I had Marilyn take a good look at him. Later you can show her some photos and she can tell you if she thinks he's the same man."

Roussos spoke to his men and they rushed off.

"This is important," said Roussos. "Do you have any idea whether he was here by pure chance or because he was following you?"

"I don't know. I felt eyes drilling a hole through me. I looked up and there he was. He turned his head when I looked. Marilyn said he ran away as soon as I went inside."

"So he knows you recognized him?"

"I think so. Spyro, what can I do? He'll never stop until he gets me."

"He'll probably hole up for a while now that he's provoked us. What happened to the man I assigned to keep close to you?"

"It's not his fault," said Victoria. She explained how she deliberately got away from her bodyguard. "Please don't be angry with him." After a moment, she added, "Or with me either."

As Roussos started walking to one of the police cars, Marilyn reached to touch Victoria's arm. "Before he goes, can you tell him something for me?"

Victoria called him back. As Marilyn spoke, Victoria translated.

"You were so concerned about that mysterious man that I haven't had a chance to say this before. I think I saw one of my kidnappers."

"Where?" said Roussos. "When?"

"When Victoria went inside. Two men came out talking to each other with great animation. They walked past me, but I'm sure they didn't notice me. I think one of them was one of the kidnappers who left before the commandos killed those who stayed."

"Describe him. How was he dressed?"

"They both wore uniforms, Greek army I think."

"What rank?"

"Oh, I wouldn't know. They were probably officers because they had metal squares on their shoulder straps. They were young, both around thirty. They both had moustaches, but I guess it's the custom here for all men to wear moustaches."

Roussos, conscious of his own moustache, smiled and said, "Not all, but probably most."

"He was of about average height and weight, strong looking as if he was into weight lifting. He had a very pronounced nose."

Again Roussos laughed. "So far a typical Greek."

"No, I mean a really big nose with a sort of bend in it near the top, like the beak of a bird of prey. But he wasn't bad looking in all other respects."

"Anything else? Unusually light or dark? Eyes? Color of hair? Any scars? Anything unusual about his hands or his walk?"

"No, no, I didn't see anything else unusual. They had military hats on so I couldn't see the hair color. I think the eyes were dark, but nothing else. Oh, well, this can't mean much, but he had very straight posture, and he had what I'd call a proud look on his face. Domineering, but perhaps that's just normal for some military officers."

"Could you identify him if you saw him in a photograph?"

"Perhaps. I'd have to see. Do you think there could be a connection between the man you're looking for, Xynos—is that his name?—and the kidnappers?"

Roussos looked as if he were again about to leave. Over his shoulder he said, "Most likely none at all. Just pure coincidence. But I want to see if you can identify Xynos as well as the army officers from photos. I'd like to have Victoria bring you to my office later if you're available."

"I'll be there."

When Roussos had driven off, a strange smile came over Marilyn's face, and she said to Victoria, "You probably know where I can get a good wig. Would you take me there? I have a sudden desire to buy a wig with a different color and hairstyle from my own."

Victoria said, "I know just the place. I'd be happy to take you. But you're not planning to do anything that your uncle wouldn't approve of, are you?"

"Of course not. How could you think such a thing? Doing something different is just a good way for me to calm down after something disturbing has happened."

She found a wig she liked, and they took a taxi to Roussos's office, which was almost deserted at this time in the afternoon. Although Marilyn looked at several hundred photographs, she failed to recognize any of her kidnappers. Shown several photos of Xynos, she thought she recognized him as the man at the outdoor table indicated by Victoria, but she couldn't be certain.

*   *   *   *

The next morning Marilyn had breakfast with her uncle and aunt, both of whom were going to attend the opening of a flower show. Declining their invitation to accompany them, she rushed to her room as soon as they left and tried on her new wig. It was dark brown and longer than her own hair, which she tucked underneath. She used different make-up to fit in with the hair, and she thought she could probably pass for a young Greek woman, at least if she could avoid having to speak. The maid called a taxi for her and arranged to pay the fare in advance, so Marilyn could avoid any language difficulty later.

She walked around the downtown area until noon, then repaired to Flokas on Korai Street. Carefully selecting a table just inside the door where she could keep her eye on many of the inside tables and most of those outside, she picked up a menu and put it in front of her face. Anyone coming in or out would have to pass in front of her, but she sat at an angle so that she could see the passing people easier than they could see her.

This was her first time out by herself, and she tried to repeat the words she had heard others use. She told the waiter, "*Sas parakalo, Amerikaniko kafé.*" She almost said *Por favor* at the end, being tempted to use her only foreign language, Spanish, but *Sas parakalo* already meant "Please."

The waiter said in English, "You wish to have some Nescafé?"

Disappointed, she reverted to English. "No, American coffee."

"In Greece we call American coffee Nescafé."

"No, well, I want the half cup of strong coffee with a small pitcher of hot milk."

"Oh, I understand. You want French coffee."

"Please," she said, adding under her breath, "if it won't trouble you too much."

About half an hour later she realized that she and the waiter were not going to get along. She had been nursing her coffee as if it were as precious as water in an Athenian garden, and the waiter kept coming up and asking if she was finished and wanted the check. She knew that taking up a table at lunchtime was making him miss out on prospective tips.

Finally she decided to enlist him in her aid, a technique she knew was almost certain to convert anyone from an enemy to a friend. "Could you please help me order some lunch? I'm not well acquainted with Greek food. I'm not too hungry, but I want more than a snack. Oh, and I don't eat meat."

At this the waiter's scowl turned to a flattered smile. "But of course, madam, I would be happy to help you. May I suggest a bean and pasta soup, *pastafasolia*—delicious!—perhaps with an eggplant salad? We serve a special salad called *imam bayaldi*, and there is a story that when a Turkish imam visited a house, the woman had nothing to feed him except an eggplant, an onion and a tomato, with some herbs and spices. But it was so good that after one taste, the imam fainted with delight, and that's the way it got its name, the imam fainted."

"That sounds perfect," she agreed with a grateful smile. "And perhaps a roll and butter, too."

He refilled her water glass and went away quite happy.

Now she felt that she had a right to hold onto her table, and she could concentrate more freely on her main task. All kinds of people passed in front of her or sat at the outside tables: two obvious American tourists with tee-shirts proclaiming "I rode the Trojan horse," whatever that meant; a Catholic priest in black cassock and round black hat; some turbaned people from India; Arabs; blacks; two very fair-skinned couples who were probably Scandinavian; Greek civilians; and even Greek army officers, but not the right ones.

She stayed there until three o'clock, even having a light dessert, some rice pudding, *rizogalo*, and another cup of coffee. The waiter she had converted to friendliness was beginning to stare at her again as if she were something peculiar. When she left, she was fairly certain that the man she wanted had not eaten at Flokas during the hours she was there.

The next day her aunt suggested that they go to a women's club meeting together, but Marilyn said she wasn't feeling well. The minute her aunt was gone, she put on her wig again and had the maid call a taxi. She arrived downtown at ten-forty and walked around to kill time. She felt she was beginning to learn some of the streets now. Just before twelve she again went to Flokas. The table she had yesterday was occupied, but she was able to get one almost as good across the aisle. Only a few of the outside tables remained beyond her vision, but the man she was after had sat inside.

She had the same waiter, who greeted her pleasantly. "Perhaps some soup and a salad or sandwich, madam."

"No, thank you, just a cup of French coffee and a croissant, please."

She was able to make the coffee and croissant last forty-five minutes, much to the increasing unhappiness of the waiter. Finally she said to him, "Perhaps I'll have a little to eat, after all. Could I have a cheese sandwich, and what do you recommend for soup? Vegetarian, remember?"

He suggested a lentil soup and seemed somewhat happier.

Again, she did not see the man she wanted. Again she stretched out her time and finally ordered "one of those things with custard between layers of pastry" and another cup of "*Galliko* coffee." As time passed, again the waiter grew increasingly impatient. And again it was a little after three o'clock when she left, her disappointment showing on her face.

Like hope being reborn every day in Puccini's *Turandot*, the next day she escaped from her aunt again and took her wig and taxi downtown. Entering Flokas, she was pleased not to see her regular waiter; it was probably his day off. She took the table she had the first day and waited for one of the waiters to come to her.

This time she had a sour-faced old man who took his time in arriving. She ordered a cup of French coffee, which lasted over half an hour. She was able to spend the next half hour alone with her empty cup, her waiter not seeming to care, or perhaps he had forgotten she was there. That wasn't so good because now she was getting hungry. The waiter walked past her four times before she caught his eye, and then he casually came to her table to inquire what on earth she could want.

"I'd like a bowl of bean and pasta soup, please, and an eggplant salad."

The waiter cupped his ear, and when she repeated it, he said, "*Sygnomi. Nein sprechen Deutsche.*"

He finally called another waiter over to translate, and Marilyn hoped that all these difficulties with waiters hadn't caused her to miss her man. No, it hadn't. He came in immediately after she ordered and sat in the back at one of the ground floor tables. He was accompanied by an older army officer who had a red band above the visor of his cap and who looked very important.

When her soup and salad were served, she insisted on paying the waiter in advance, leaving him a generous tip on the table even though she knew service was included and only a small extra was expected. She ate her meal slowly, frequently stopping to pat her lips with her napkin and looking at the rear of the restaurant. Her position at the table was awkward for seeing that one area unless she made herself stand out with her head turned. Very inconspicuously, she rose and changed to the chair on her left, reassembling her plates and glass in front of her. Now she could see the two officers in animated conversation, and she was positive they had not paid any attention to her.

When the two officers left, Marilyn followed them. The older one turned right on Akadimias while the one she was after continued straight to the next parallel street above before turning right, then up another block and left, as he zigzagged uphill. She could not read the street names, and she realized she was in completely unknown territory. The area they were now in had much older buildings than the ones where they had started. The higher they went, the more decrepit some of the buildings looked. What was worse, the streets had become less and less populated, and she was beginning to feel conspicuous even though she had by now allowed the man she was following to get ahead by almost a full block.

She began having regrets. She was a social worker, not a detective. She was also not very athletic, and the constant hill climbing was beginning to tire her. The army officer ahead continued at the same pace, uphill or flat seeming to make no difference to him. She couldn't imagine that he was going back to work because there didn't appear to be any suitable workplace for him in the area where she now found herself. She was glad that her side of the narrow street had a continuous line of cars parked on it, partially in the street and partially on the sidewalk, thus giving her a feeling of some shelter.

The distance between Marilyn and her target kept increasing. However, for a change the officer stopped his zigzagging and continued on the same street for several blocks, but on the other side of the street. Thus Marilyn could still see him over the tops of the parked cars even though he was almost two blocks away. Suddenly he stopped. He seemed to be looking at his watch. Marilyn crouched so that she was almost hidden by a parked car in front of her. As she stared through the car window and windshield, she saw him entering a building. She tried her best to mark that building in her mind, but she knew she could only approximate which one it was. She continued walking, picked a building on the other side of the street as the most likely one, and walked on past it.

She went two blocks beyond the target house, then crossed over and slowly started walking back. She was more in the open now and didn't like it. If he came out of that building at this moment, he could not help but see her for she was almost alone on the street. Occasionally a car or a boy on a bicycle drove past in either direction. Then there appeared from around a corner a group of people coming toward her. They must have been together by chance because they weren't associating with each other. Soon they were past her, but others appeared spottily on the street coming toward her from both directions. As she finished the first of the two blocks between her and the house, she decided to cross the street to hide behind the cover of the parked cars again.

At that moment, an army officer turned the corner of the cross street just before the block where the house of interest was. The very fact that he was in uniform made him suspicious in her mind. He proceeded to the house next door to the one she thought was the right one, and he entered it. She was close enough on the opposite side to see that there was no knocking, no bell ringing, and no need for a key. He just turned the door handle and entered.

She also saw that the open door led to a long carpeted corridor. There were several closed doors on one side of the corridor. Then the outside door closed again.

She thought she recognized that second man as another one of her captors on Skyros. Her first man had probably gone in the same house. Two of her captors whom the black-clothed commandos had missed were here. And there could be even more inside. This was something big. In fact, it was too big for her alone. She should try to fix in her mind something that would help her identify the house later and then get out of the area as quickly as she could before she was noticed.

She reached the corner and turned around to walk back just before a third man in army officer uniform turned a corner from the other direction, approached the house, and entered by merely turning the door handle. She was almost directly opposite him and could see the inside wall on the other side of the corridor. It too had several closed doors.

She didn't think any of the three men had noticed her, yet she couldn't swear that all three might not have. Suppose they all came out and came after her? She was beginning to get frightened at her own temerity. But she continued past the house and walked to the next intersection. There she stopped to think, and slowly turned to walk back to pass by the house again.

There were windows in front, but they looked heavily curtained. If any of those people were looking out a window, they'd surely get suspicious on seeing the same woman pass up and down in front of them. Still, if that were the case, it probably would have already provoked them to come after her. They had done nothing, so she was probably safe. At least for the moment.

She walked up to the next corner, crossed the street, and came down again on the same side as the house. A number of minutes had passed, and no one else had come to enter the house. Could all that were going to be there already be inside? Did she dare to enter the house?

She thought it out. The chances were that they were all in some room behind a closed door. She could go in very quietly to see. But what did she expect to learn? Even if she heard them speaking, she wouldn't be able to understand the language. Yet some strange force seemed to be drawing her toward that house. She felt as if she had to enter if only to prove something to herself.

This was the day when Victoria had invited Marilyn to dinner and she didn't want to be late. Already she was taking a chance that she wouldn't have time to go home to change clothes. All right, if necessary she'd call Victoria as soon as she could find a phone, and if she wasn't able to get back to her uncle's for a change of clothes, they'd understand. But in the meantime…?

She came even with the doorway and mentally flipped a coin. Heads, so she would enter. She walked to the door and put her ear up against it. She heard nothing from inside. Slowly she opened the door. Still no one to be seen or heard. She entered and closed the door quietly behind her.

Now she heard muffled voices. She put her ear against each door in turn until she found the right one. She opened it just a crack so she could first hear, and then, opening it a little more, see. There was a single lighted bulb hanging over a down stairway. She could hear the muffled voices a little better now and oriented herself toward their source. They seemed to be coming from some room leading off another corridor. She crept down the stairs.

It was obvious now which room they were in. Their voices were not only getting louder, but more animated as if they were having arguments. Suddenly she heard footsteps on the floor above her. Someone else had come in the house after her.

At first she was paralyzed with fear. Where could she run to? The man above was making no effort to be quiet. She heard him opening the door to the stairway. He took the first step downward.

Moved to action, she tried a door opposite the one from where the voices came. In the dim light from the overhanging bulb she could just barely make out some kind of closet. Whatever it was, it was safer than being out in the corridor. She hoped the approaching man hadn't seen her. Softly she closed the door behind her. Inside the closet, she trembled as she heard the steps coming closer. She hoped that he would just go into the opposite room and not give any alarm to those already there.

*   *   *   *

Victoria had prepared a meat-less *mousaka* for Friday night's dinner, but she also had some veal cutlets for the non-vegetarians. At one time she had casually thought of becoming a vegetarian herself, but her career was too demanding and she needed protein nourishment to replace that lost during a performance. Now she was glad for another reason that she hadn't taken that step as she realized how awkward was the gulf between vegetarians and meat-eaters, especially when invited out to dinner.

Spyro had selected two Greek wines, a white *Kambas* for the salad course and a full red *Naoussa* to accompany the main course. Dimitri arrived very early bearing a bottle of American chardonnay as a gift, then left to pick up Marilyn at her uncle's house.

The ambassador and his wife were surprised to see him. Mrs. Atherton said, "Why, she's not here. She left for some shopping this morning and hasn't returned." She looked to her husband.

"Is something wrong?" the ambassador asked Dimitri.

"I don't know," he said. "Several days ago we agreed that I'd pick her up here and take her to Victoria's place for dinner."

"Marilyn told us that," said the aunt. Again turning to her husband, she said, "Could she have been late and decided to go to the police director's apartment without coming home first?"

"Let me call," said Dimitri. He telephoned and then, keeping the phone line open, with dismayed expression informed the Athertons that neither his father nor Victoria had heard from Marilyn.

The ambassador took the phone and, not speaking Greek, talked to Victoria. As he put the phone down, he told Dimitri, "I'll go back with you to your father's place. Let's take your car. I'd never find parking there." To his wife, he said, "You stay here in case Marilyn comes home or telephones." He asked Dimitri to write down the number for his wife.

At the Kolonaki apartment there were deeply concerned discussions. The foremost question was whether Marilyn had been kidnapped again, or was she just lost? The ambassador had a photograph of Marilyn in his wallet, which he gave to Roussos. Atherton then telephoned the embassy to send a car for him. The director called to alert his people and get a search organized, and Dimitri, who already had a photograph of her in his office, went to have it reproduced and distributed again to all police stations in the downtown and embassy areas.

Now alone, Roussos and Victoria drew into themselves and were silent. Roussos sat beside the telephone with his elbow on the table and his head resting on his open palm. His entire body resembled a tightly wound spring, motionless but ready to expand into explosive animation if the need came for action. Victoria sat across the room from him, watching for the slightest change in his expression or the least audible sound from his pressed lips.

*   *   *   *

Marilyn waited in the closet. There she stayed for hours, afraid to come out even after she heard people leave for fear that some of them might have stayed behind. At some point she noticed that the hanging light bulb over the stairs must have been turned off because the sliver of light coming under the closet door had disappeared. Then she cautiously opened the door and found herself still in complete darkness.

Looking in the direction of the room across the hall, she could see there was no light coming from under the door there either. Thinking the way safe now, she moved very slowly with short steps in the direction of where she thought the stairs were. Finding them, she made her way to the upper floor and waited at the top to listen for any sign of people on the other side of the door. There was no noise, so she opened the door.

Very faint light came in from under the shade of a window in a room with the door open. The light allowed her to make her way to the front door, which she found locked. However, she felt a protruding metal lock above the doorknob that seemed as if it could be opened from the inside without a key. After leaving she would not be able to re-lock the door, but she wasn't going to worry about that.

When she was outside she found herself alone on a dark, deserted street with no lighting other than a lone bulb hanging from a telephone pole at a street corner. The parked cars of the day were mostly gone. Walking down the street, she tripped and lost the heel of one shoe so that she had to hobble along. She was tired, hungry, cold, and afraid. A group of three men approached from the other side of the street, and when they saw Marilyn, they started whistling and yelling at her. She was scared witless, but walked straight ahead as if nothing was happening. The men continued on their way without stopping.

She came to realize how stupid she had been in following that army officer. She had put herself in grave danger and still wasn't in the clear. As she crossed an intersection, she tripped again, and this time her other shoe came off and rolled down the hill of the cross street. It was too awkward to continue walking with a shoe with a broken heel, so she cast the other shoe off and walked in her stocking feet. That was also painful because of the roughness of the crudely paved road, but she persevered.

She decided to walk downhill since that was the way she had come up. She could see a better-lighted area in the distance and she slowly made her way toward it. At the next intersection she saw lights coming from a building on the corner, and she wondered if she could get help there. But as she came closer, it appeared that the building was a crude tavern, and she was afraid to enter. A man came stumbling out, stopped, and glared at her. His face held a cruel leer as he made some remarks to her. She tried to walk on, but he came up and threw his arms around her and started feeling her body with his hands. She screamed and ran in the cross street to get away from him. Over her shoulder as she ran she could hear voices of people coming out of the tavern, but she wouldn't go back for fear that they were more of the same type.

She turned again into a downhill street and walked toward the lights in the distance. Suddenly another man appeared in her path. She turned around, but didn't have the energy to run uphill. The man approached her and said something. As he moved to get within her vision, she saw to her relief that he wore a police uniform. He started asking her questions, and all she could do was to tell him in English that she was the niece of the American ambassador and she was lost.

He didn't seem to understand, but realizing that she was a foreigner he tried to make her see that he wasn't going to hurt her. "I help," he said. "You I help." He took her gently by the arm and led her across another street until they approached a building he pointed to. "Help here," he said. It was a police station.

She wanted to identify herself, but suddenly realized that she didn't have her handbag. She must have left it in that closet. Now if the kidnappers looked in the closet, they would know for sure that she had been there.

One of the policemen on duty could speak sufficient English so he understood who she was, and he telephoned first the American Embassy and then the ambassador's residence.

$$* \quad * \quad * \quad *$$

Dimitri telephoned his father about an hour after he had left the apartment. "She's been found. She's at a station near Ippokratou and Fanarioton Streets. I'm going to pick her up."

Roussos said to Victoria, "She's been found on the far side of Lykavittos near the football stadium. Dimitri is getting her and will be here shortly."

At Roussos's suggestion, Victoria called Ambassador Atherton and explained the latest development.

A short while later Dimitri returned to the apartment with Marilyn. She was minus her wig and her shoes and looked as if she had been in a hurricane. Victoria gave her some slippers and a glass of wine, and they sat in the living room to talk.

"Be easy with her," said Victoria. "She's obviously been through a lot. Let her tell it her own way."

Except for sore feet, Marilyn appeared to be all right. "I'll take another glass of wine, please," said Marilyn to Victoria with a smile as she finished telling her story. "Don't worry about me drinking too much on an empty stomach. The way I feel, I don't think I could possibly get drunk. And I'd feel so much better if I could wash up, too."

Victoria gave her a new pair of pantyhose, her own being completely worn bare on the bottom.

When she came out of the bathroom, they sat down to dinner. In between lively conversation they ate a little food, but no one was really hungry, not even

Marilyn. At Director Roussos's request, she went into more detail about the military men and the house.

"Could you recognize the house again if you saw it?" he asked via Dimitri.

"I don't know. I was concentrating so much on going in without being seen, and then later when I came out it was so dark. I tried to remember how the front door looked, but it was so similar to a lot of other front doors. I might recognize the area," she said, quickly adding, "if all the areas around there are not alike."

Roussos spoke to Dimitri, who in turn said to Marilyn, "If you are rested enough by next week, my father wants me to drive you around the areas on the northwest slopes of Lykavittos. But don't decide now. I'll call you tomorrow morning to see how you feel."

CHAPTER 17

▼

Monday morning Police Director Roussos was summoned again to the office of Minister of Public Security Achilles Petropoulos. He waited only fifteen minutes this time, then was admitted to the presence of the minister. Seated in front of the minister were Police Underdirector Jason Thanos and a man Roussos recognized as a public prosecutor. Petropoulos signaled to the two men that he wanted them to leave, and they rose and left. Neither said a word to Roussos or otherwise acknowledged his presence.

Petropoulos's eyes were focused on his desk. Suddenly he looked up, appearing almost surprised to see Roussos standing in front of him. "You, Roussos," he said, "what do you have to say for yourself?"

"I beg your pardon, sir?"

"What have you to say? That's simple enough for you to understand, isn't it? It was over three weeks ago that I gave you some special assignments. What have you done about them?"

Roussos, prepared to discuss his charges against Thanos, quickly switched his thinking. "Well, you know about the Savvas case. We had the evidence that he was swindling the daughter of Minister Antonidis, and we arrested him. Before he could be formally charged, he was brutally beaten to death by Thanos. It would appear that that part of the Savvas case is finished."

"What, what? What part isn't finished?"

Although he was hesitant to say more, Roussos knew he had to. "I am still conducting an investigation into the death of Savvas."

"The devil with your investigation. Police Underdirector Thanos was questioning him and he tried to escape, injuring himself mortally when he fell against the jail bars. It's a finished case. Do you understand?"

"I understand what you're saying, sir."

"And you don't agree? You refuse to obey my orders?"

"Pardon me, sir, but I'm not quite sure I heard an order."

"I just ordered you to conclude any investigation of Savvas's death and get on with other more important matters. Will you do as I order, or do you insist on being insubordinate?"

"Of course I'll obey your orders, sir."

"Good, now what about General Zavalas?"

Roussos said, "General Zavalas has terminal cancer and has not much time left. There is no evidence of any plotting by him, and he could not play any effective part in a plot anyway."

"And the letters?"

"I am convinced there are no letters. I sent you a report to that effect."

"Did you? Perhaps. I vaguely recall seeing something from you, but I must have given it to Thanos. But you didn't mention the letters that I wanted."

"I said I was satisfied there are no letters."

"How can you say that? How do you know?"

"Well, sir, the opportunity for a clandestine search presented itself to us, and we were able to see the contents of both a safe and a locked metal box that he kept under his bed. This is not the way I like to do business without having more to go on than in this case, but it is done, and General Zavalas will not be making any complaint."

"Again, how do you know?"

Roussos found the questioning more and more distasteful, but he could not lie to the minister. "Our agent went to bed with him and she searched his room when he was asleep. He woke up and became aware of it. But she can testify that there are no letters now and Zavalas will not make any complaint against her."

"She searched the safe and the metal box? What did she find?"

"Some money, some bonds and other securities, and some minor small items."

"Such as? Tell me, man. Do I have to drag everything out of you?"

"She found some letters, which he grabbed and burned. They were utterly destroyed."

"You said there were no letters."

"I said there are no letters. They were destroyed."

"How dare you play word games with me as if you were a Jesuit priest. That's grounds for dismissal from the police service in itself."

"I neither lied to you nor disobeyed you, sir."

"But the letters were absolutely destroyed? Did you, or she, actually see those letters?"

"She just had a chance for a quick glimpse of them. They were old letters, and there was no signature."

"No signature? Ah, yes, of course, you're right. No signature. Good. And they're destroyed?"

"Yes, sir. So that case, too, seems to be finished."

"Yes, of course, the case is finished. No more letters and he's dying. Why didn't you tell me this before?"

"I told you I sent you a summary report. I didn't know how much detail you might want."

"So you gave me none."

"I understood you to be a very busy man, sir, and I did not want to waste your time needlessly."

The minister glared at him. "You're clever, Roussos, too damn clever. All right, now how about the terrorist, Pavlo Xynos?"

"We have had two sightings in Athens, one last week. We are actively pursuing the case."

"You are, are you? He's been seen twice, but nothing more. No arrest. That doesn't speak highly for your much-advertised thoroughness. Very well, I'm considering taking the case out of your hands and assigning it to my own special investigative team, headed up by Police Underdirector Thanos. Be prepared to give him the dossier and let him question any of your people. Understood?"

"I object, Mr. Minister. We are doing everything we can on the case, and it is well within our charter."

"I can overrule you on that and you know it. You will do as I say."

"And if I refuse?"

Petropoulos presented him with his now well-known smile-grin, showing yellow rotting teeth and looking like some harpy from ancient mythology. "Let's be frank with each other, Roussos, shall we for once? You know I would love to have you refuse to obey my direct order. Go ahead, get it over with now. Refuse me. I've talked to the prime minister about you, and you don't know what a thin thread you're hanging by."

"I have not refused, sir."

"Not exactly, but you were close to it. I'm going to get you, Roussos. My special team with Police Underdirector Thanos is making a thorough investigation into all your activities, and I expect to bring formal charges against you soon. I'm going to get your ass drummed out of the police service. You'll be lucky just to escape a prison term."

"Is that all, sir?"

"No, don't go yet. What about the kidnappers of the American ambassador's niece? She saw more men than the seven who were killed—have you identified any of the others?"

"We are close on their trail. We're looking for some young army officers who may be plotting a coup."

"What, another coup? We seem to have rumors of one or two every year. But I'll give you another warning, Roussos. We all know that no coup is going to be successful. The Colonel's Revolt put an end to that because the populace just won't support a coup. But if one even starts, if a handful of officers so much as marches down the street singing revolutionary songs and gets arrested, it will just be one more charge against you. I'll have your ass served to me on a silver platter for gross incompetence, too. One way or the other, I'm going to get you, Roussos. Malfeasance, insubordination, or incompetence, or all three."

Petropoulos suddenly picked up the telephone. "How hot it is today," he murmured unexpectedly to Roussos. To the telephone, he ordered two lemonades to be brought in. Putting the phone down, and switching to a more pleasant tone of voice, he said, "Sit down, Mr. Roussos. Closer to me so we don't have to talk too loud."

With some reluctance Roussos moved a chair closer to the desk and sat.

"You've got one chance to save your skin and your pension. Write me out your resignation immediately, right now, and I'll see that you can leave with all honor. I'll even see that you get the pre-retirement promotion we talked about so you can have a larger pension. How does that sound?"

"With all respect, sir, I am not ready to retire yet."

An aide knocked on the door and brought in two cold glasses of lemonade. The minister took one and offered the other to Roussos.

"Why do you insist on sticking to a lost cause? I should think you'd at least want to keep your reputation from being ruined. What is it that you expect to accomplish?"

"With due respect, sir, I intend to build a case against Thanos and see him punished in the courts for the murder of Savvas."

Petropoulos looked surprised, but then smiled in apparent satisfaction. "Is that all? You want to see Thanos punished? Your perseverance is almost admirable, *Kyrie Astynomike Diefthynti.*" Resting his glass on the desk, he lifted the little finger of his left hand and started polishing the long nail with the thumb of his right hand.

Roussos waited for the expected eruption from the minister.

"Understand, Mr. Roussos, that I'm not a sadist or a vindictive man," Petropoulos said in a quiet voice. "I am pragmatic. I know what I want and I will let nothing, nothing, interfere with me getting it. I do not hate you nor do I love Thanos. To me you both are equally promotable or expendable. So if it's Thanos that you want...."

Somewhat taken back, Roussos responded, "Let me understand. You are offering to see Thanos charged with murder?"

The minister was still playing with his fingers, now pressing the tips of those of one hand against the corresponding members of the other. "I am willing to see Thanos punished if you will agree to ask for honorable retirement."

"I don't understand. What can be your purpose in getting rid of Thanos if you do not have a Thanos to replace me?"

"Thanos is not the only Thanos in the Greek Police. There are a number of others who would serve me well and not bring a Pandora's box with them. Thanos was an utter fool to have killed Savvas. I like a little more finesse in my operations. In fact, I would love to keep you in your position, perhaps with a promotion as well, if I could only be certain that you would be loyal to me."

Roussos waited.

"Well, what is your answer?"

"Answer, sir, to what?"

"Will you join me or not? I'm offering you the opportunity of being the second most powerful man in Greece, the chief lieutenant to the future autocrat of all Greece."

"You can be certain only that I will do the best I can for my country, and that precludes my joining you."

Petropoulos folded his fingers, those of his right hand making a tight fist. Putting his head down, almost as if in prayer, he slowly raised it and his eyes pierced Roussos. "I am not surprised. Then we are back to where we were before."

"Do you need me for anything further, sir?"

"No, go, go. I am finished with you."

As Roussos walked to the door and started opening it, he heard the minister speak again from behind him.

"Oh, Roussos, there is one more matter." The voice was soft and Roussos had to strain to hear him. "I have been looking into the matter of your son." The words dripped like honey off his lips. "I know what he's been doing. I am probably the only man in Greece who can save him. Think that over before you make a decision from which you cannot return."

"I beg your pardon…."

"Go, Roussos, go. You heard me. There's no need to repeat or amplify what I said. My offer is still open. At least for a short while. Think it over."

Roussos turned to face him again, his eyes blazing. "I want to hear what you have to say about my son."

"I said go, get out. Do I have to call the guards to eject you? Get out!"

Not intimidated in the slightest, but realizing now that he was not going to get anything further out of Petropoulos, Roussos left. Walking along Merlin Street again, Roussos reflected that he thought he had seen everything. The civil servant getting in bad with a political appointee and forced to leave his position. The high-ranking politician ambitious beyond belief. But this was different. This minister apparently believed he could make himself dictator of Greece. How? Could he be behind a group of army officers plotting another coup? Or could he be the brains behind the mysterious Black Sweaters? Or did he represent a third threat, a political coup based on his ability to blackmail members of parliament and other important people?

And why had Petropoulos exposed so much of his ultimate plans to Roussos? Obviously he would have liked to have Roussos join him, but he should have known that was impossible. Of course Roussos was now in a position where he could expose Petropoulos's ambitions and his willingness to desert Thanos to others, but would that do any good? Given the known animosity between Petropoulos and himself, would anything he could say against Petropoulos be believed?

More puzzling yet, what did Petropoulos mean by saying that he knew what Dimitri was doing? What did he mean by claiming that he was the only person who could save Dimitri? He wanted to believe that this was merely an idle parting shot from Petropoulos, but somehow he didn't think the minister was a bluffer. By God, he'd have to speak to Dimitri about this. Was Dimitri involved in something unknown to his father?

✱   ✱   ✱   ✱

Monday afternoon there was a full dress rehearsal prior to the opening of *Tosca* the next day. In her dressing room Victoria prepared for her entrance in the church in Act One. "Mario, Mario, Mario," she sang, knowing how important it was to get off on the right note with those three introductory words. She wore a fashionably high-waisted, long white linen dress decorated with a narrow gold ruffle around the top of the bodice and bands of ruffled gold forming a double hem. Her hair was swept up in neo-classical style held together with pins and gold ribbons.

A knock on her door was followed by someone saying, "Miss Renfrew, time for your appearance."

The opera was already in progress. In Rome in 1800 the conservative forces in control prepared for battle with Napoleon's invading troops, Napoleon at the time representing freedom from oppression. Mario Cavaradossi was in a church painting a portrait, and he would sing the famous aria *Recondita Armonia*, telling of his love for the singer Floria Tosca. He would help an escaping political prisoner hide. Tosca would enter, calling Mario's name, and on finding him and the portrait, become jealous of the woman he was painting. Mario would convince her not to worry, and she would leave.

Baron Scarpia, chief of the secret police, would then come in with some men to search for the escaped prisoner. When Tosca returned, Scarpia would try to foster her jealousy. She would leave again just before a cardinal and a large entourage entered to the accompaniment of a brilliantly orchestrated *Te Deum*. Aside, Scarpia would sing his own counterpoint to the *Te Deum* and tell of the satisfaction he would receive when he could punish Mario and take out his lust on Tosca. The act would end on this note.

Getting the cue for her entrance, Victoria went on stage and began singing "Mario, Mario, Mario." She continued with satisfaction, feeling that she had made a proper start so she could now relax and let her automatic reflexes take over. When her part in Act One was over, she left the stage, passing the assembled cardinal's entourage that was waiting in the wing to go on as soon as the conductor began the *Te Deum*.

Horror of horrors! There he was, in the middle of the entourage dressed as an acolyte holding a colorful labarum. She felt like screaming. Pavlo Xynos was only six feet away from her.

When the entourage started moving to enter the stage, the man she supposed was Xynos moved along with it. As he somberly passed her, she realized that it was not Xynos after all. He didn't even resemble Xynos. She had had another hallucination.

How could she go on singing under these conditions? She rushed to her room and took a tranquilizer, and in a few minutes felt better. She realized she had to change her costume and be ready for Act Two. Would the pill do the trick? Would it hold? Even so, would she have to depend on pills from now on, as some of the other singers she knew? What was expected of her next? Oh, yes, Act Two. In less than the blink of an eye, the entire next act suddenly unfolded within her mind.

Baron Scarpia, dining alone and telling in an aria how he preferred to take women by force rather than persuasion, would have Mario brought to him for questioning. Tosca would come in and Scarpia would have Mario taken to another room to be tortured. Unable to bear hearing Mario's screams, Tosca would tell Scarpia where to find the escaped prisoner. Scarpia would offer to spare Mario in return for Tosca's body. She would sing the most famous soprano aria of the opera, *Vissi d'arte, vissi d'amore*, I have lived for art, I have lived for love. Although Tosca might think that she had saved Mario's life, Scarpia would give a trick order to his lieutenant, outwardly telling him to let Mario escape, but secretly ordering Mario's execution. Alone with Tosca, Scarpia would now claim his reward. But Tosca would have other ideas. After getting a safe conduct pass for herself and Mario, she would use a knife to kill Scarpia, saying disdainfully, as he lay on the floor, "And before him trembled all Rome."

Suddenly the idea thrust itself on her. A knife. Xynos would certainly find some way of being alone with her again. Could she have a knife somewhere in her apartment? Perhaps another one in her dressing room? She knew there were folding knives—switchblades they were called—could she have one on her person at all times?

There was a knock on her door. "Miss Renfrew, Act Two."

She quickly finished adjusting her changed costume, patted her face in the mirror, straightened her hair, and left the room.

By sheer determination, she got through Act Two. Then Act Three. Victoria waited in the wings as Mario, under guard on the prison roof, sang his great aria, *E lucevan le stelle*, a poignant plea that he did not want to die. She entered and told him the good news that the firing squad had been given instructions to use blanks. Scarpia was dead and she had a safe conduct pass for the two of them. Mario was led to a wall and the firing squad went through the motions of executing him. Tosca did not know that the bullets were real. When the soldiers left, she rushed to the fallen Mario and told him it was over. Only gradually did it occur to her that it really was over. Mario was dead. The soldiers were coming back, now alerted to the fact that Tosca had murdered Scarpia. As they came running after her, she jumped over the side of the tower to her death, and thus the opera ended.

How she got through it, she didn't know. The director rushed over to congratulate her and make a small suggestion about the way she accomplished her jump. "Scarpia," now in street clothes, was waiting in the wings smiling at her. Everyone seemed to be smiling. She tried her best to smile, too, and hoped she was successful.

Back in her dressing room, she felt faint. She sat on a chair and quivered. Now the continuation of her previous thoughts came to her. Yes, that was it, could she kill Xynos just as Tosca killed Scarpia? It would be self defense, wouldn't it?

God, what was she thinking! Of course not. She couldn't kill anyone. It was beyond her. To think of her plunging a knife into the living body of another person. Impossible! She'd rather die first.

But she was feeling a little better now. Perhaps having conjectured the murder of her oppressor and then dismissed it had served as a palliative for her.

The telephone rang. It was Spyro calling from his office. "Yes," she told him, "I'm all right. The rehearsal went well, at least the director told me so when I finished." Just hearing Spyro's voice gave her new strength. "I hope you won't have to stay late at the office. Good. I'll be home in about a half hour. Yes, one of your men is in the theater waiting for me."

*   *   *   *

Victoria and Spyro sat up late that evening. She did not tell him about her most recent hallucination regarding Xynos. He had brought his own problems from work with him, and she wanted to spare him further concern.

She hoped she wouldn't hallucinate on opening night. She knew Spyro planned to have extra security coverage for her as well as for all the dignitaries who would be present. If Xynos showed up on opening night, he was almost certain to be caught.

However, listening to Spyro recount the events of his day, she wondered how much longer he'd be in a position to protect her. "This sounds serious, catastrophic," she said. "I guess I always thought there would be some give and take, but it sounds like Petropoulos's final offers, quit or join him, and you turned both down."

"Would you have me be his hatchet man?"

"Of course not, but you could take honorable retirement."

"To me, under those conditions it wouldn't be honorable. No, that's out."

"That's what I mean, catastrophic. You're determined to stay on until he gets you thrown out in disgrace and possibly put in prison. Isn't there any other way, Spyro?"

In the distance the Parthenon was brightly lit, appearing with a mystical aura about it. So much beauty, thought Victoria, amid so much trouble. She had never seen Spyro so lost.

"None."

She said, "Corfu is so lovely. That one time you took me there and we visited your mother on her farm, I really liked it."

"You're saying resign and you'll go to Corfu with me."

"Yes. Is that so bad. Voluntary exile, if you like. You know how much your mother wants you to take over the farm."

"Exile, voluntary or forced, seems to be a Greek trait. Our kings and statesmen and generals do it all the time." He gave her a smile of futility.

"Honestly, Spyro, do you think that by staying on you're saving Greece from some kind of horrible dictator? If Petropoulos is as powerful as you say, you're not going to be able to stop him either way." She turned to face him fully, clutching her fingers tightly into his sleeves and tugging on him, as if moving him physically would shake his stubbornness.

"No, I'm not trying to save Greece from anything." He disengaged her and spread his hands out palms up. "What am I to Hecuba or she to me?" he quoted with exasperation in his voice.

"I hate to say it, but do you realize you're putting me more in the position of Hecuba?"

"I'm truly sorry, my love, but I can't act against my conscience."

"So we just wait for the axe to fall. What does Dimitri think about all this?"

"I haven't seen Dimitri for a while."

"Will Petropoulos force him out, too? Or for that matter, all the officers who have been loyal to you, Pano, Eleni?"

"Possibly, but I hope not. I must talk to Dimitri about something else. He hasn't said anything to you that might indicate he's in trouble or anything, has he?"

"Come to think of it, I haven't seen him for a while either. What kind of trouble?"

"I don't know, but Petropoulos is acting as if he has some kind of ammunition against Dimitri that I'm unaware of."

"Spyro, please, won't you consider retiring now and spare us all this?"

"I'm sorry."

"So you'd keep your pride and lose everything else."

"If that's my fate, then it's my fate. *I moira mou.*"

She looked disappointed. "Oh, Spyro, why must you be so unyielding?"

"You think I'm wrong, my dear?"

"Well, it's not my way of doing things. I'd rather bend with the wind. I've had a hard life, and I don't want to fight any more. I want us to be comfortable and enjoy life together as we grow older."

"I'm sorry, Victoria. Perhaps I'm not the right man for you after all."

"Don't say that. Forget what I said. I'm getting so depressed because of Xynos that I can't even think. I don't know what I think or what I want to do. Or what I think you should do."

He reached to put his arm around her and they embraced, remaining tightly together for a long time. He said, "You'd better get some sleep. Tomorrow's a big night for you. I'll be there at the opera house, and if Pavlo Xynos dares to show his face, I'll take Petropoulos's original advice and shoot him on sight."

CHAPTER 18

▼

It was mid-morning when Dimitri arrived at Ambassador Atherton's residence and knocked on the door. Mrs. Atherton engaged him in polite conversation as he waited for Marilyn to get ready. Then he and Marilyn drove to the streets on the slopes of Mount Lykavittos.

He asked her if she remembered catching sight of the funicular at any time when she was following the army officer. When she said no, he explained his reason. From the meandering route that the army officer had taken, two things were indicated. First, it might seem as if her quarry was taking anti-surveillance measures. Could she be sure that he hadn't noticed her?

She didn't think so, but more importantly, if he had noticed her, why was she not captured when she ducked into their closet? And he did not look behind him during the walk, nor take other measures that she had gleaned from movies were standard anti-surveillance maneuvers, such as stopping to use store windows as mirrors.

Dimitri pointed out secondly and perhaps more pertinently that the officer's path could have covered a substantial part of the lower slopes of Lykavittos. The more they could narrow down their quest, the easier it would be for them. If she had not caught sight of the funicular, it could seem likely that she and her quarry had not covered the southeastern slopes.

"Let's start where you did," said Dimitri. "You saw him at Flocas and followed him up Korai Street. After another block you come to the university, so you had to turn left or right. Which?"

"Left."

"All right, and when you left the kidnappers' house you ended up near the football stadium. Since you didn't see any sign of the funicular, you must have been walking in a northeasterly direction on the northwest slope of Lykavittos. You didn't get as far south as the funicular."

"If you say so. I'm not very good with directions."

He smiled. "You have many other attractive features to commend you. All right, so you turned left, then what?"

"I'm almost sure I turned right at the next intersection. We were generally going uphill."

"Do you think your next turn was to the right or left?"

"Oh, lord, I don't know if I can remember. Let me see. I think left. Maybe."

"Okay, let's start that way. We'll drive up Ippokratous Street and look to the left. See if anything looks familiar. When we get as high as the roads go, we'll turn left and left again and go down Mavromihali Street, again looking left all the way down hoping to see something familiar."

The trouble was that too much looked familiar. They went up Ippokratous and as soon as the cross streets became narrower, Marilyn had Dimitri make a turn. On Valtetsiou Street, Marilyn identified three houses. On Arahovis, she saw two more that looked familiar enough to be the house in question. On Dervenak-ion she saw two more, and on Eressou three more. Dimitri decided to try the other side of Ippokratous, and again Marilyn saw too many houses that could be the right one, but in view of all her identifications, she was now not able to swear to any of them.

"Oh, Dimitri, it's a mess. The truth is that I didn't pay that much attention to how the house looked from the outside. Between the time that the army officer went inside and the time I went inside, all my attention was on whether anyone could see me. And even before, I wasn't paying any attention to the streets, only to keeping my distance without losing track of him. When I left the house, it was night and there were almost no lights, so I couldn't really see any details."

They decided there was no sense in continuing if Marilyn couldn't be sure about any given house.

"I hate to quit," she said, "but what can we do? Anyway, it's late. Past lunch time."

With an unhappy grimace he said, "I'm sorry, I can't ask you to lunch. I have another case I have to pursue as soon as I take you back home. I'll be in Pireaus all afternoon. I'd like to invite you out to dinner tonight, but I'm going to open-ing night at the opera."

"I am, too. Victoria sent me two tickets."

"Who are you going with, or am I being too blunt?"

"No, not at all. I'm going with Bob Jensen from my uncle's office."

"Oh."

Lowering her eyelids, she said, "Who are you going with?"

"My father. Victoria gave us two tickets, too."

"Victoria's nice. I guess she's almost in the position of being your stepmother, isn't she?"

"I naturally love my real mother, but I love Victoria, also. I wish my father would get a divorce so he could marry her. Perhaps some day."

"And perhaps we could go out some other time."

"Good. Such as tomorrow night? How about my taking you to dinner? We'll go to a taverna and I can show you some Greek night life."

"Wonderful. It's a date."

✳   ✳   ✳   ✳

Opening night for *Tosca* was a huge success. The President of Greece sat in the presidential box with the prime minister and his wife. The American ambassador and his party had box seats further over to one side; Bob Jensen and Marilyn Pickering had box seats to the other side; but Spyro Roussos sat in the middle of the orchestra by himself.

At intermission, Bob took Marilyn to the lounge, where she had a glass of sherry and he a whisky and soda.

"It was nice of you to share your tickets with me," said Bob.

She smiled. "I can't think of anyone my aunt and uncle would rather have me go with."

"I'm not that bad, am I?"

"I'm not sure. My aunt gives me such a two-sided impression of you."

"Oh," he said, with an exaggerated frown. "How?"

"On the one hand, she speaks as if you're the clumsiest dunce she's ever seen, but the next minute she suggests that I should see more of you. She says that no one would make a better escort to take me around Athens."

"Hmm, I take it that her feelings toward Dimitri come into this somewhere."

"That's what I sort of figured."

"Well, it's nice to feel so highly recommended, and really, Marilyn, I do enjoy being with you. If it would please your aunt, I'd be happy to see more of you. May I take you out to dinner tomorrow night?"

"I'm sorry, Bob." She was beginning to find him rather charming, but still not as charming as Dimitri. "I'm going to a taverna with Dimitri tomorrow."

"Oh." He looked at the floor. "Care for another drink? No? Well, mind if I have another?"

She shook her head and smiled. It was the first time she had seen him without his usual sense of humor. He seemed so downcast that she couldn't help but feel sorry for him. Gently holding his arm, she said, "Look, Bob, I'm beginning to understand you, and I do like you. You're nice and pleasant and sweet to be with. But there's someone else. Perhaps if things were different...."

He smiled again. "I'll tell your aunt you're rejecting me in favor of Dimitri."

"You wouldn't? But more seriously, tell me, how come some beautiful, charming woman hasn't grabbed you for a husband already?"

"That's the way to get me serious, all right," he began. "I don't usually mention this, but my wife died in a car accident. We'd been married for less than a year."

"Oh, I'm sorry, I'm terribly sorry." She wondered if that accounted for the flippancy that seemed to characterize him. "Oh, look, there's Police Director Roussos. I want to talk to him; will you interpret for me?"

Roussos smiled politely when Marilyn and Bob approached. Through Bob, she said, "Dimitri told me he'd be here tonight with you, but I saw you sitting alone."

Roussos shrugged his shoulders. "I have not seen much of Dimitri lately. He seems to be engaged in some time-consuming personal activity."

Marilyn tried to continue the conversation, but it was obvious that Roussos was not interested in saying much more. She noted how sad he looked, and she realized that he, too, was an individual, not just an institution, and he had his own problems.

Bob said, "The lights are blinking. Let's get back to our seats."

Victoria was never in better voice, and for a few moments Spyro Roussos felt cheered with pride for her. At the end of Act Three the company took a dozen curtain calls. The seven-year-old great granddaughter of the Greek President presented a large bouquet of flowers to Victoria. The prima donna looked to the audience, genuflected gratefully, acknowledged the presence of the President with a smile and a wave, and blew a kiss to Spyro.

Bob said to Marilyn, "I wouldn't be surprised if every other person in the audience is a secret service agent. Victoria Renfrew is apparently being pursued by some crazy man. Of course, it doesn't hurt to be the girlfriend of the chief of Greece's super security agency."

Marilyn said, "I hope she's well protected. She's one of the nicest people I know."

Bob said, "I might have exaggerated a bit, but the theater is certainly packed with dozens of plainclothes people guarding both Victoria and the presidential party. They're in every entrance and passageway."

After the theater cleared out and Victoria changed to street clothes, Spyro walked her home. Both were overjoyed at the success of the evening. Both were equally grateful that nothing untoward had happened. Pavlo Xynos had sat this one out.

*   *   *   *

Wednesday night Dimitri and Marilyn drove to the Plaka district, the back slopes of the Acropolis. They weren't able to park any closer than near the small ancient church called Monastiraki. "We'll walk from here. It's uphill, but not too much and not too far."

As they walked Dimitri explained that the Athens of classical times was clustered around the slopes of the Acropolis. "This was the north slope. The ancient government buildings and other public places and markets were at the bottom of the northwestern slope." He pointed to a large fenced off area comprising many stone ruins, some in various states of repair.

"There's still enough light," he said "so you can see the ruins and restorations on your right. That long building is the Stoa of Attalos, completely restored by the American School of Archeology. Most of the houses we're passing date from around the liberation of Athens from the Turks in 1833. The Plaka is the district where most of the tavernas are found, scattered between the old houses. They become more touristy all the time, but you can still find some good food in some of them and see a good floorshow."

They walked up crooked narrow streets with abrupt turns. People were outdoors in front of the small houses, which mostly touched each other, and they were talking, laughing, eating, resting, and enjoying themselves. The tavernas were on many streets and could be recognized easily by their signs, their lights, and their outdoor tables. Sometimes a doorman from one of them tried to entice them inside, and occasionally one of the touts would get a bit aggressive about it, but after a few sharp words from Dimitri, the overzealous employee, or sometimes owner, would quickly back off.

Dimitri chose the *Palaio Kastro*, the Old Castle, where he seemed to be well known. "It has a good floorshow, which is now also a Greek word, *flortso*, and flexible prices. They'll give us the non-tourist price."

It being a rather cool and windy summer night with intermittent sprinkling of rain, unusual for the season, there were few people at the outdoor tables. When Dimitri took her inside, Marilyn was surprised to see how spacious it was. At the far end of the large room was a stage with a mural of the Greek countryside at the rear. The stage itself was in the design of a grape arbor with wicker covered wine bottles hanging from vines attached to the mural.

The headwaiter ushered Dimitri and Marilyn to a table that was situated at an angle from the stage so that it and all the other tables could have a good view of the floorshow. Marilyn was fascinated by the tiers of shelves on one wall laden with pieces of intricately painted pottery. Attached at angles on another wall were ancient looking swords, a few shields, several helmets, spears, and some old-looking musical instruments. There were also shepherds' crooks, colorful embroidered pieces of traditional Greek clothing, and strings of ancient looking gold coins caught in large fishing nets.

"It looks like fun," Marilyn said. "Are these things on the wall authentic?"

"Some of the clothing and maybe a few other items might be a hundred years old, but most of them come from a factory that specializes in atmosphere. Notice the overall effect of being outdoors. When we can't be in the outdoors, we bring the outdoors inside with us. We'll have an early dinner here, and then I'll take you to a bouzouki place by the sea. The contrast will give you an idea of what you can expect in local entertainment."

They ordered a cheese-and-artichoke soufflé and French wine. "One good thing now that Greece is a part of the European Union is that we can buy French wine at decent prices. But I doubt that it will ever be cheap enough to drive the local vintners out of business."

Marilyn asked how the police investigation on her kidnapping was coming. Dimitri replied that they were checking out the known friends of each of the seven dead kidnappers, but nothing of any real interest had been discovered yet.

He said, "Police work is mainly dull plodding along. We have to check out a hundred leads just to get one productive one."

"What about those vicious commandos? Do you have any leads on them?"

"Not really. They came out of nowhere and went back into nowhere. You're the only living person we know who has seen them. And you can describe them only as shadows. We're checking out the 9mm bullets that they fired, but they could be from a number of automatic firearms. We're working on a theory that the kidnappers were plotting a revolution and the commandos were a rival group. Perhaps they wanted it to be their revolution."

"But the kidnappers would probably have some idea of the purpose of the commandos, wouldn't they? Maybe even their identities. If you could just get one living kidnapper, you could probably find out a lot."

"You make it sound so easy, Marilyn. Perhaps we should conscript you for the police force."

"You're laughing at me now."

"I didn't mean to. Ever since the Colonels' Revolt in 1967 showed how easy it was, the government has felt uneasy about the possibility of another coup. It gets very political, and Greeks take their politics seriously. For example, every member of parliament is convinced in his or her heart that there is only one person in all Greece capable of leading the country, and every member thinks that he or she is that leader."

"I'm not sure that's any different from the Republicans and Democrats in my own country."

"Well, as I say, we just keep plodding along."

As the hour got later, more people were arriving all the time so that fifteen minutes before the floorshow was scheduled to begin, the taverna was more than half full. Suddenly at the last minute droves of people came in to take up all the remaining tables. Dimitri said, "The latecomers arrive just in time for the floorshow, order a glass of wine, are entertained, and then go on to some other taverna for a new floorshow. Of course, they pay a healthy cover charge for that privilege."

The floorshow was entertaining, although not especially novel. A comedian told fast jokes in Greek, and Dimitri translated as much as he could so Marilyn could get the meaning. She laughed, although she had heard some of them ten years ago. A singer presented the audience with some of the currently popular Greek and European songs, and again Marilyn found Greek music hauntingly beautiful. A solo electric bouzouki player showed his virtuosity with the stringed instrument, and Marilyn liked it immensely. Even with, or perhaps especially with, the unusual half-tone notes, it was lively, catching, and mood-enhancing.

And then Bobbi and Jenni danced. They did some slow dances reminiscent of Fred Astaire and Ginger Rogers. For the first number they held a mask on a stick so their facial features couldn't be seen, which made it all the better to appreciate their figures and footwork. Some of the foot movements resembled the Argentine tango and others the French apache dance. They were good, really good, but the big surprise to Marilyn was the girl, Jenni's, figure. It was magnificent, and, wearing a dress with split sides in the skirt, she had the most beautiful legs Marilyn had ever seen, perfectly curved and proportioned. *I'd kill to have a figure like that,* Marilyn thought.

As the music concluded, Bobbi and Jenni took down their masks, and Marilyn couldn't stifle a deep "Oh!" of astonishment.

Dimitri looked at her, smiled, and said, "Yes, amazing, isn't it, how old they are?"

Bobbi's deep-lined wrinkled face featured a 1930s-style pencil moustache, and he looked old enough to have begun his career in that era. So, too, Jenni, the contrast between her heavily made-up face and her figure was like that of a prune and a plum.

Dimitri said, "I've heard people swear that they're in their nineties. I don't believe they're a day over seventy, but they're amazing, aren't they? You can see why they wear the masks in the beginning. Otherwise you wouldn't believe what you're seeing."

As the dancing couple concluded with several more numbers, Bobbi and Jenni received a thunderous applause from the audience with Marilyn as one of the most enthusiastic. "It's worth everything just to see them," she said.

The floorshow over, many people left, while others started dancing. Marilyn and Dimitri preferred to have coffee and talk.

She looked at him and for a moment wondered if he was the most handsome man she had ever seen, the most handsome man on earth. He was certainly kind and attentive with high intelligence and a great store of knowledge.

She asked, "Dimitri, you're a most unusual man. You're a Greek, but you speak highly fluent English. You seem to know about everything. You're so cosmopolitan. How did you get this way?"

"I took a pill, maybe?"

"I don't think so. Tell me, have you traveled abroad much?"

"Oh, yes, many times. I have taken holidays in the United States. I liked it there very much, and I have seen almost all of Europe, as well as most of the other countries bordering on the Mediterranean. I love the Mediterranean, the center of the earth."

"And you lived abroad?"

"Once, for eighteen months when I was assigned to the Greek Embassy in London."

"You lived in London? How interesting. Were you assigned there as a police liaison?"

"No, as the lowest ranking assistant military attaché."

"Military attaché? Oh, I forget, you were an army officer before you joined the police. Why did you become an army officer?"

"After I graduated from the American School, my father sent me on a trip to see Europe, which he felt was a part of my education. Then he expected me to go to the university and on graduation join the police, as he had done. But I was young, stubborn, and determined to do things my way. So I applied for entrance to the *Scholi Evelpidon*."

"What's the *Scholi Evelpidon*?"

"Strictly speaking, it means School of Hopefuls, but actually it is our officer military academy, the equivalent of your West Point."

Marilyn appeared deep in thought, then she spoke, pausing between her words as if she wasn't quite sure how to express what she wanted to say. "Did you know any of those men who kidnapped me?"

"My father asked me the same thing. Yes, I knew one of them quite well and some others as casual acquaintances."

"Why did you change your mind and join the police?"

"I guess I grew up. Don't misunderstand, I liked the army. But as I said, I was young, stubborn, and selfish. My father had done everything for me, and he had looked forward to my joining the police. After a while, I realized how much I had disappointed him, so, as we say, *Kallitera arga para pote*, Better late than never."

"That's fascinating."

"So are you, little one. You fascinate me. You are a lovely woman, so lovely that I am almost afraid of you."

"Of me? Why should you be afraid of me?"

"Because you tempt me to forget myself. My first responsibility is to my career, and right now it is my only responsibility. I only want to do my duty, and do it well. But you tempt me to think of you all the time."

The lights had dimmed again for dancing, and Marilyn and Dimitri leaned toward each other as they talked. Now their heads were just a few inches away from each other, and slowly Dimitri bent even closer. She met him halfway, and they kissed. It was a light kiss, just a brushing of the lips together, but it was a meaningful one for both of them. Marilyn thought she could completely lose herself with Dimitri.

They left the *Palaio Kastro* and walked hand in hand to the car. They talked little, but every now and then they would squeeze each other's hand in wordless communication.

They drove down Syngrou Avenue until they reached the sea. "If we turn left here," he said, "it would take us to Ellinikon Airport. However, we will turn right instead toward Piraeus, but not all the way. The best bouzouki places are in Tsitsifies, and they are just opening for the summer season, so they will not be crowded yet. Truthfully, they're at their best in winter, but we can't have everything. Anyway, you will see that it is a different kind of tavern."

It was different. Bare walls, scratched wooden floors, worn tables and chairs, and a different type of clientele. Marilyn could spot no one who looked like a tourist. The customers seemed to be more working class, mostly in open shirts with sleeves rolled up and sometimes wearing an unbuttoned vest. Only two others besides Dimitri had jackets. Dimitri took his jacket off and draped it on the back of his chair.

"Here we will have Greek wine and *mezedes*, various little appetizers, even though we no longer have an appetite. Perhaps a little cheese, olives, and, if you like, small pieces of fried octopus."

"Greek wine? Good, I'll have *retsina*. But I'll skip the octopus, *merci beaucoup*."

"You may not like *retsina* at first."

"My uncle introduced me to it. I'm getting used to the pine tar flavor."

"Very well, and we'll each have an apple."

"Why?"

"We Greeks always eat something when we take alcoholic drinks. Very few Greeks—only low life—drink a lot. Even though we're having *mezedes*, I always like a few apple pieces with my wine."

The bandstand was empty when they arrived, but soon a group of entertainers made a procession from behind a curtain to sit in two rows of chairs perched on the stand. First came a violinist and guitar player followed by the clarinet and trumpet players with the drummer behind them. All these sat in the rear row. Two women and a man not carrying instruments came out and sat in the front row of the stand. After a short interval, two more men came out carrying electric bouzoukis. The bouzouki players made their way to the front row and sat beside the previous three.

The music started, a fast piece with a beat of its own, featuring many half notes that Marilyn could almost feel in her blood. It was a kind of music that enslaved the body and dazzled the mind, the rhythm rising to a pitch that put one in ecstasy. It was primitive, exciting, invigorating, and uninhibiting.

She was getting the strangest feeling, as if she suddenly wanted to stand up, dance furiously, and take off all her clothes. Was that what half-tone music did to one? Stifling the feeling, she quickly assumed a prim pose and hoped that Dimitri had not gleaned any clue as to her momentary lapse. She concentrated now on the entertainers instead of the music itself. Every now and then one of the women or the man without instruments stood up, reached for the microphone, and started singing as if spontaneously.

Marilyn sipped on her *retsina*, and following Dimitri's lead, cut off a piece of apple to eat. The waiter served them the *mezedes*, including some small triangular cheese tarts called *tyropitakia*. As she ate, her movements were automatic. She swayed with the music, silently humming along with it. Suddenly she had to catch herself again from unthinkingly surrendering to the beat. This music is dangerous, she thought.

The bouzouki players had been sitting as they played, just two more players with the band. Now they took turns in standing up in front of the microphone and performed hot rhythmic solos while the band played in accompaniment. Again this was frenzied, half oriental music, heating the blood and making it wild. When they were finished, there was a moment of silence, then the customers applauded with tremendous animation. Marilyn, caught up in the exaltation, felt herself alive.

When the band commenced again, it was with similar music, but played much more slowly, more solemnly. It vaguely reminded her of a Scottish bagpiper playing a lamentful *pibroch*. Suddenly one of the male customers stood up, as if some spirit had just incited him, and began a slow turning in time with the music. The other customers started yelling, slowly and softly at first, "*Opa!*" Gradually as the dancer went through more elaborate variations of his steps, the chorus sped up with their own "*Opa! opa! opa!*" This kind of dancing Marilyn recognized from having seen movies on Greece. She was not surprised when the dancer picked up a chair and maneuvered it as an inanimate partner.

Later, groups of male customers arose and spontaneously performed group dances, which Dimitri named with words such as *hasapiko* and *syrtaki*.

"Do the women ever dance?"

Dimitri looked embarrassed, then said, "Of course, at times. Especially out in the villages, but not so much in tavernas."

"If I were moved to get up and strut around, would it be all right?"

"As a foreigner, a very lovely foreigner, you would be much appreciated. We Greeks have a keen sense of hospitality. It's all part of our concept of filotimo."

"*Filotimo?* What's that?"

"It's a concept of honor, but one that is probably unique to us Greeks. It takes on several aspects. One is to be courteous and hospitable to strangers. There are some darker aspects, too."

"Such as?"

"A lot of murders take place in Greece in the name of honor. The people of Crete are especially noted for their strong adherence to *filotimo*. Along with the strong sense of honor, there's an equally fierce concept of avenging dishonor."

"It sounds primitive."

"I'd never thought of it that way, but you're probably right."

"Tell me more about this *filotimo*."

"Some other time, little one. It's getting late. I wouldn't want to offend your aunt's concept of honor by keeping you out too long. There's no guessing what she might do to me."

She laughed. "Oh, Dimitri, it's so much fun being with you. Now tell me, I haven't seen anyone break any plates yet."

"They are waiting for someone to start it. Perhaps you."

"Could I?"

Dimitri called the waiter and ordered ten plates. "Go ahead," he said to her.

"Oh, no, I wouldn't know how. You smash the first one."

For an answer, as the music continued and the dance floor was empty, Dimitri rose and started his own version of a terpsichorean solo, clicking his fingers loudly as he did so. When he was close to his own table again, he reached for his half-filled wineglass and drank it down in one gulp. The crowd yelled "*Opa!*" Dimitri responded with an impassioned yell, "*Thelo na ta spaso!*" "I want to smash them!" With frenzied energy he flung the first plate to the floor, where it broke into myriad pieces.

Marilyn stood up, drank the remainder of her drink, yelled something approximating "*Thelo na ta spaso!*" and threw down another plate to join Dimitri's in fragments. Dimitri, still standing, smashed a third, and Marilyn quickly followed with a fourth. And then other tables joined in. What a feast of plate smashing followed with tireless energy.

When their ten plates were gone, Marilyn sank in her chair, now finally exhausted. Dimitri, too, collapsed, and they laughed as if they couldn't stop, and they held hands. The crowd was with them. Marilyn couldn't possibly understand what remarks were directed their way, but she needed no translation. They were roars of approbation.

"They like you," Dimitri said.

"I like them. And I like you, Dimitri."

She didn't want to leave, but Dimitri said he really should take her home. "I don't want to break the spell, but I also don't want you to dislike me in the morning when you wake up late with an aching head."

They drove up Syngrou and veered to continue on Vasilissis Sofias. Marilyn, head nestled next to Dimitri's shoulder, said, "I don't want to go home."

"I don't want to take you home."

"Then don't?"

"Where shall we go?"

"To your place. You must live somewhere."

"Surprisingly, my small apartment is on Vasilissis Sofias just before we get to the American Embassy, but on the other side of the street."

"Let's go there."

He slowed the car and glanced at her. "Marilyn, I like you so very much, but I don't want to take advantage of you."

She laughed. "Think of it as me taking advantage of you."

Now he laughed. "Then my place it is."

✳   ✳   ✳   ✳

"Ned," said Louise Atherton, as they sat down to breakfast.

"Yes," he replied. He had already found his newspaper.

"Your niece telephoned early this morning while we were still sleeping and left a message with the maid."

"Why would she do that? Anything she has to tell us, she can say when she comes down."

"That's it. She won't be coming down. She said she spent the night with a friend."

"Too bad she wasn't speaking Greek, which I think has a male form and a female form for every noun."

"You don't have to guess very hard to know that friend was probably male."

"The Greek police officer?"

"Who else?"

"There's the American opera singer. Perhaps Marilyn stayed there."

"Sometimes I wonder if you're too dense to be an ambassador."

"She couldn't be safer than with a police officer?"

"There are different kinds of safety. I know times have changed, but it just doesn't sit right with me. Imagine what the tabloids would say if that girl gets herself pregnant while a guest of the American ambassador. How much longer does she have to be here?"

"Hmm, let's see. We said a month, and she's been in Greece more than two weeks. Of course, I'm not going to say to her on a given day, 'Well, your month is up. Go home now.'"

"No, of course not. But perhaps you could tactfully sound her out and get her to thinking about making departure reservations."

"I guess you're right. Ordinarily I wouldn't be in any hurry to get rid of her, but she does have a knack for getting into trouble, doesn't she? Perhaps I should have sent her home right after she was rescued from being kidnapped. I'll ask her what her plans are."

CHAPTER 19

▼

Ambassador Atherton was pacing the floor of his office. Bob Jensen was trying to keep up with him, but Atherton told him to sit down. He sat. He felt uncomfortable sitting while the ambassador was on his feet, but Atherton had a way of making him feel uncomfortable most of the time anyway.

Atherton said, "The spooks down the hall finally got around to telling me that they're convinced the people who kidnapped Marilyn were Greek army officers involved in a conspiracy to effect a coup. Apparently their plan was to use Marilyn as a hostage to get me to recommend a hands-off policy to Washington once the coup started."

"We usually do have a hands-off policy until we've had time to assess the significance of any coup."

"There's more to it than usual policy. These officers are plotting something unusual. They're convinced they can take over the government, but they're even more concerned about holding onto their control after."

"As damn well they should be," said Bob. "Every person I've talked to is convinced that a coup might be successful, but couldn't be sustained. There's no popular support for it. The country is prosperous, and the almost even division between the two main political parties keeps them both from riding roughshod over democracy. Successful revolutionaries would be in power less than a week."

"Why would they be so concerned about what I might report to Washington then? In any case, I wouldn't hide facts even if they were holding my niece. They should know that."

"Then it would seem they'd want you to do something where you might have some discretionary power."

The ambassador said, "Yes, discretionary, that sounds possible. But such as?"

"I don't know. Your resignation? Your acting as intermediary between them and Washington? You're using your good offices between them and a third party?"

"In other words, neither one of us has any real idea."

Bob said, "How about these commandos in black? Do the spooks have any idea on them at all?"

"If they have, they're keeping it close to their chest. I said I'd like to know more about the so-called commandos, and they said, 'So would we.'"

Apparently tired of walking up and down, the ambassador took his seat behind the desk. Bob immediately stood up and approached the desk.

"But," said the ambassador, "I didn't call you in to discuss what these people might want. It's moot anyway because Marilyn is here safe with us. What I want is to talk about your extreme carelessness in protecting my niece. And you'd better hope that nothing further happens to her before she goes home. You foul up one more time and you'll go home before she does."

∗   ∗   ∗   ∗

Bob was shaken as he backed out of the ambassador's office, but he didn't want to show it. Closing the door, he turned his frown into a smile as he faced the secretary and started to walk past her.

She asked, "How was it?"

He was about to reply with a wisecrack, changed his mind, and said, "There's nothing in my job description that says I have to be a nanny for the ambassador's niece."

"There's nothing in my job description that says I have to kiss his ass, but I do a lot of puckering up every day."

Bob smiled. "You should go on strike."

"What did he say?"

"He acted as if I should know where she is at all times and keep her out of trouble. I'm not a babysitter."

"But you are the security officer, and wouldn't that come under the heading of security?"

"Yeah, yeah, I guess, especially considering that she's already been kidnapped once."

He went to his own office and telephoned the ambassador's residence. When the maid answered, he asked in Greek if Marilyn Pickering was still home."

The maid replied, "She came home two hours ago. I think she's getting ready to go out again."

"Where did she go so early in the morning?"

"Mr. Jensen, sir, I don't think she came home last night at all."

Uh-oh, Bob thought. *There's the trouble.* To the maid he said, "If she wants to go out again, give me a call immediately and tell me everything you know about it. I'm speaking for the ambassador. If she asks you to phone for a taxi, use this number," and he gave her a telephone number.

There was a small taxi company up the street, and Bob kept on good terms with the owner as a practical business matter. Usually he wanted to keep track of some visitor to the embassy, but a taxi company could be handy in this case, too. Bob telephoned and made arrangements, if the maid called, to have one taxi go to the residence and another come for him at the embassy.

It wasn't much later when the maid called saying that Miss Marilyn wanted her to call a taxi. Bob left immediately and waited for the second cab to pick him up. Via radio communication, the second cab was soon in pursuit of the first as it drove toward downtown Athens.

Seemingly oblivious of being followed, Marilyn had her cab stop in front of the Diamantis Department Store. Bob had his cab let him off a bit further on and he watched her enter the store. Now he guessed, she was probably just on a routine shopping trip, and he was afraid he was wasting his time. Still, he cautiously continued after her. She was in the wig section and he watched her try on a number of different wigs before she purchased one. Then she went in the ladies' room. When she came out, she was wearing her new wig. What on earth was she up to?

Leaving the store, Marilyn walked the few blocks to Flokas and took a table just inside the door. There was a bookstore across the street and Bob entered and started browsing. He could see her table and the lower part of her body, but not her face. At least he could tell that she was alone. He pretended to be looking at a book while taking frequent glances at her. An hour passed and she'd made contact with no one. When she was still there a half hour later with no one yet joining her, he made his decision. He left the bookstore and walked to the corner of the next street up, Panepistimiou. Crossing the street he came down the side Marilyn was on and casually entered Flokas.

"Well, well, well," he said, as he started to pass Marilyn's table, "if it isn't my favorite ambassador's niece. What in the world are you doing here all by yourself?"

"Oh, er, I was just about to order some lunch."

"You look charming with your new hair style."

"Oh, well, you know, it's only a wig. I wear one every now and then."

"It makes you look so, er, so unrecognizable."

"You apparently didn't have any trouble recognizing me."

"Are you expecting anyone?"

"No, no, I'm just by myself. I may do some shopping later. Victoria showed me the shopping area."

"That's nice. I've got to get some lunch myself. Would you mind if I joined you?"

"Well, no, not really. No, actually it would be pleasant to have some company."

They ordered lunch and made small conversation. Bob noticed that Marilyn kept glancing at every newcomer who entered, but in a surreptitious way, raising her eyes slightly instead of moving her whole head upwards. She was also keeping track of the people sitting outside. Obviously she was looking for someone, but was it a friend or someone she didn't want to recognize her?

"I guess you'll be going home soon," he said to her.

She turned to look at him. "I suppose so. I don't know that I really want to go back. But I think my uncle and aunt are looking forward to having me leave."

"I wouldn't say that."

"Of course you wouldn't. You'd only think it. I imagine you'll also be happy to see me go. I've been a lot of trouble to you, haven't I? Ever since getting myself kidnapped in the beginning."

"Well, no, not exactly. It wasn't your fault that you were kidnapped. But after an experience like that, I'd think you'd want to get back to somewhere safe. And then with your most recent experience after following one of those army officers to a safe house…."

"Is that what you call it, safe house? Bob, what does the embassy—you and my uncle and the others—think about the kidnappers? Who were they? Why did they kidnap me? And who were those mysterious blacksweatered killers?"

"We don't know. Your uncle thinks the men who kidnapped you wanted to use you as a hold over him. But it's anyone's guess. Possibly the men who held you on Skyros were really kidnappers after all who hoped eventually to get a ransom for you. And possibly the commandos were terrorists."

"That doesn't make sense. When I was talking to Dimitri, he said the police think the kidnappers were revolutionaries who want to take over the government, but he doesn't have any idea who the commandos were. But in either case, what you say or what Dimitri says, why would terrorists want to kill revolutionaries or kidnappers?"

"Good question. If the police could just find one of the kidnappers who did not get killed, they could probably get the answer to everything."

"That's like something I said to Dimitri. If only I'd been able to find that safe house again. If they could just get their hands on the man I followed."

They lapsed into silence as they ate their food.

After a few minutes, Bob said, "Is that why you came here? Hoping to see that man again?"

She turned red. "Why, no, not at all. Oh, damn it, Bob, why lie? Of course that's why I came here, and you knew it all the time. And if we're going to be truthful, that's why you're here, isn't it? Sent by my uncle to spy on me?"

"'Spy on you' is not the way to put it. But, yes, Marilyn, I'm here to protect you. Is that so wrong?"

"No, but it almost seems as if we're working at cross-purposes."

"What would you have done if you saw your man today? Would you have followed him to the safe house again?"

"Only to identify the place so I could show the police where it is. I don't know Greek, but I could write down the characters of a street name so it would be recognizable to the police."

"But even that could be dangerous to you. Suppose they found signs of your having been in their house. Might they not want to bait and trap you?"

"No. If they thought that anyone had found their house, they would obviously have abandoned it. They wouldn't know what I had been able to tell the police."

"So you think they're ignorant of the fact that you got in their house?"

"Yes." *At least I hope so*, she said to herself, thinking of the handbag she had left in the closet.

"And you want to spot this man and follow him again?"

"Yes, sort of."

"Marilyn, on behalf of your uncle, I forbid it. You know damn well he would be horrified if you did that again."

She looked as if she were pouting. "Well, we don't have to worry about it today, do we? There's no sign of him." As if tired of sitting so long, she stretched her arms in the air and took in a deep breath.

Bob said, "You look tired. Were you out late last night?"

"Yes. With Dimitri, if it's any of your business."

"Oh, it's none of my business. I'm just an unwanted and unwanting chaperon."

"I'm sorry. I don't mean to be rude, Bob. I guess I am tired. Not to change the subject, but I learned a new word from Dimitri last night, *filotimo*. Do you know it?"

He grinned in an amused sort of way. "It's just a word meaning 'love of honor.' Some Greeks take it more seriously than others. Especially the Cretans. Shall I tell you a little story?"

"Please do." With her elbows on the table, she leaned closer to hear him. "I want to learn more about Greece and the Greeks."

"It may be apocryphal—there's a good Greek word for you, it means revealed from having been kept hidden—but I know people who swear this is true. A stranger came to a home in a Cretan village where there was no hotel. Naturally one of the families there offered to let him spend the night in their house. A strong sense of hospitality, that's one form of *filotimo*. But the visitor abused the family's hospitality and seduced the daughter. He was caught in *flagrante delicto*—that's Latin, not Greek...."

"I bet you teach your grandmother how to suck eggs, too."

"Sorry, didn't mean to be patronizing. The truth is, Marilyn, I don't know what you know and what you don't. You expressed interest in learning."

"Greek, not Latin, which I had enough of at school."

"Anyway, the father killed the visitor with a butcher knife. That's another form of *filotimo*. Abuse of hospitality has to be avenged. The father would have lost much face if he had not. The father was tried in court and sentenced to three weeks in jail—but here's the point: not for murder, for such acts in hot blood are not considered murder, but," he started chuckling, "but for abusing Cretan hospitality. More *filotimo*."

She joined him in laughing and said, "I'll make sure I don't seduce anyone while enjoying their hospitality. But seriously, aren't you exaggerating a bit?"

"I tell you the story as I heard it. Here it's true enough to life so it's easy to believe. Even the women involved frequently avenge themselves. It you read the newspapers, you'll see that one of the most common things in Greece is for a woman who's been seduced under promise of marriage, but then abandoned, to confront her former lover and throw acid in his face, scarring and sometimes blinding him for life."

"More power to them."

He gave her a wink. "That's why I never abuse anyone's hospitality."

"You've never seduced a Greek girl?"

"Well, that's a different matter. But I make the family sign a waiver first."

"Just don't expect any waiver from me. Well, I guess I'd better get started on my shopping or something."

He paid both checks with a credit card and made a mental note not to forget to include it in his expense account.

"Do you really want to go shopping now?"

"No, that was just an excuse. Let's go back."

"Okay. We'll go down to the corner and get a taxi."

As they started to walk toward Stadiou, Marilyn grabbed Bob's arm and whispered to him. "Don't make it obvious, but I think that's him on the other side of the street."

Bob looked cautiously and saw a man in Greek army officer uniform on the other side of the street walking past the bookstore."

"Is that the one?"

"I'm sure of it. It's the same walk, same everything."

Bob said, "We'll follow him just briefly while I telephone my office and have them get in touch with the police, who can then take over. God damn it! Where's my cell phone? Hell, I left it in the office."

They had already changed direction and were now walking up Korai toward Panepistimiou.

"Look," said Bob. "I'll keep following him and you get to a phone and call the embassy. Ask for Bradford Brewster, my assistant, and tell him to get the police on this."

"No, I'm going with you. By the time the police could get here, you'd be in a maze of streets and they'd never find you. With two of us, we can keep better track of them, and one can always act as messenger later."

"No, I tell you, no. Your uncle would have my scalp."

"Are we going to let him go?"

"No, damn it, I'll follow him."

"And I'm crossing the street so I can follow from the other side. By splitting up we won't look so conspicuous."

"No, Marilyn, no!"

She had crossed the street and was now on the same side as their target. More than anything Bob needed a telephone, but if he stopped at a kiosk to use a public phone, both Marilyn and the target officer would be gone. He had to keep following just to keep track of her.

The officer continued with the path he took the previous time, zigzagging his streets, but always climbing higher on the slopes of Mount Lykavittos. They left the wide streets behind them as they approached streets of middle size. The officer stopped at a kiosk and apparently bought a package of cigarettes. Bob ducked around the nearest corner and wrote down on a pad the names of the streets taken so far. As the man walked on, Marilyn continued after him while Bob stopped at the same kiosk and bought a newspaper that he could use to hide his face if the officer turned around. There was no time to telephone. He had to walk fast to catch up. He wished he wasn't wearing a suit. They were getting into streets where a dressed up look was becoming more out of the ordinary. He was also concerned because Marilyn was closing the gap between her and the target.

As their man turned a corner, Bob moved ahead of Marilyn on the other side and signaled to catch her attention. Patting the air with his hand, he tried to get her to understand that she was getting too close. She caught on and let a few seconds pass before she turned the corner. Now Bob was in the lead, and had to check himself from walking too fast. Too close and they'd be discovered. Too far away and they'd lose him.

As the uphill streets became steeper, the man himself was slowing down. He took a corner to another side street, and suddenly Marilyn crossed the street and approached Bob on his side.

Catching up to him, she said, "I think I recognize this area now. See how the cars are all parked on this side only and halfway on the sidewalk as well. This side is better for both of us so we won't be seen."

Bob couldn't disagree, so he took the outside position and put his arm around Marilyn. She at first winced, then realized what he was doing, and she put her arm around him also so they would appear to be lovers. Lovers perhaps under unusual circumstances, but it might be a little less conspicuous. As Marilyn had done before, Bob tried to use the parked cars to partially hide them.

The streets were thinning out. Once or twice someone passed them on this street, but it was now the most deserted of all the ones they had covered. The cars were still good cover, but they also tended to hide their target from them. They suddenly saw that the officer was gone.

"That's the house," said Marilyn. "I think that's it."

The houses all touched each other, and most of them had a graying white-washed look. Very few of them had numbers, including the one Marilyn had pointed to. Bob noted that several houses away was one that bore the number "583," and he jotted that down on his pad. He knew that some of the more recent streets they had covered didn't even have visible names anywhere. However, the number alone would eliminate many of the streets in the area, and then he and Marilyn shouldn't have difficulty recognizing the exact one.

He said to Marilyn, "Our job is done. Let's go. It's a police matter now."

She said, "Wait, they're obviously here for a meeting. Let's stay and see if we can recognize some more of them. They may leave before we can get the police here."

"And they may come back some other time. We don't know but what the police might want to put a stake-out in one of these buildings and make it possible to catch even more than are here now."

Marilyn said, "Why don't you go find a telephone and call the police. I'll go inside and hide in that closet where I was before."

"Look, you crazy little fool, this isn't a game. It's deadly, and you're risking your life."

"It's mine to risk, isn't it?"

"Not as long as I'm employed by your uncle, it isn't. For the last time, let's go."

It was too late. They both saw that in a flash.

Coming up from the far corner were three big men, two of them in army uniform. From the near corner and bearing down on them with a fast walk were three other men, one in uniform. The door of the house they were looking at opened, and three more men, all in uniform, came out and started crossing the street just feet away from them.

"Run! Grab my hand." Bob began running to the near corner, holding a hand behind him for her. He thought if they could run down the closest three men, they might knock them over like bowling pins and make their escape. Looking over his shoulder, however, he saw that Marilyn had already been captured by the three men from the house, who were now taking her back across the street. He stopped running, knowing that he couldn't desert her.

He turned and yelled back at her. "Marilyn."

She saw him and hollered, "Save yourself!"

"Not without you."

It would have been useless to continue running anyway. The three men from the near corner were immediately in front of him, and the three from the other corner were right behind him. All six at once grabbed him and virtually carried him across the street like a stretcher case to the house. Along with Marilyn he was taken into a front room, where they were tied up back to back on the wooden floor with a heavy metal pipe running from the floor to the ceiling between them. The room was getting crowded as more men kept pouring in to take a look at them. Marilyn recognized three of the men who had visited Skyros while she was a prisoner.

Then through the open door came another man whom both Marilyn and Bob recognized: Dimitri!

"You just couldn't stay away," he said, a savage expression on his face. "I tried my best to save you."

"No!" cried Marilyn. "This can't be true. No, Dimitri, not you. Please tell me you're not one of them. You can't be." She started sobbing.

One of the men who had tied them said in Greek to Dimitri, "*Ti tha kaname m'aftous?*"

Dimitri said, "*Tha perimenome os apopsi,*" and he continued with a long answer.

They left the room and Bob and Marilyn were alone.

"Why did it have to be Dimitri?" asked Marilyn. "I can't believe it? Not Dimitri."

"It sure looked like Dimitri to me."

"What did he say?" asked Marilyn.

"One of them asked what to do with us, and Dimitri said they would wait until tonight. Apparently tonight is the big night they've been waiting for. A lot of people will be meeting here and then they'll put certain plans in effect. He said something about perhaps still being able to use you for their original plan." Bob was silent for a minute, then continued. "His last words were that they had no need for me and after their meeting tonight they would kill me."

CHAPTER 20

▼

"Spyro, Spyro, Spyro!" sang Victoria as Director Roussos entered their apartment.

"Shouldn't that be 'Mario, Mario, Mario?'" he asked with a playful smile.

"Look, darling, a letter from London. From the Royal Opera. They want me to fly to London to discuss playing Rosina in this coming December's production of *The Barber of Seville*. They even enclosed a voucher for a round-trip ticket."

Getting more serious, he said, "Isn't that a mezzo-soprano part?"

"It can be either. They must want a soprano for this production. *Il Barbiere* was one of Callas's best known roles." She grabbed Roussos by both hands and twirled him around in a waltz. "To think, I'm following in the footsteps of Callas. One of the Royal Opera's artistic directors saw me play *Tosca*, and he liked it."

The sun streaming in from the open window illuminated the crest of her hair, making it look like a tiara. Roussos thought he had never seen her looking more regal. *My princess, my queen*, he thought. He said, "This could be the great opportunity you've always wanted."

"Yes, wouldn't that be wonderful?"

"Yes," he said with some hesitation, "I guess it would." The words came out of his mouth increasingly sadder as he said them. "If they liked you and wanted you as a regular performer, it could mean you'd probably live in London. But that's speculation at this time. More importantly, do the dates conflict with anything you have scheduled here?" There was ever so slight a hopeful note in his last words.

"That's the sad part. It's the same time as my commitment here for the lead role in *Lucia di Lammermoor*, and I've always wanted to sing her."

"You must choose between the two."

"It's exactly what you tried to pin me down on before, keeping my commitment here or getting a chance to make it big. Only when it comes to real life, it's not so easy to make a decision."

"You mean you can't turn down a possible chance to achieve your lifetime dream." To himself he thought, *You really mean it's not so easy to tell me you're leaving.*

"If you retired, instead of going to Corfu we could live in London instead."

"You'd take me with you?"

She rushed over and patted his cheek lightly in a pretended rage. "Stop it. You know I'm going to be with you whatever happens. If you don't come with me, I'll just tell them I won't go."

"I never thought about living anywhere but Greece."

Her mouth opened but no words came out. It was as if she was realizing for the first time the full ramifications of this new development. She moved out of the light and away from him, hiding her face in the shadows. "It's not the same as asking you to leave your career. Your career is leaving you, and this is fate summoning us on to something new."

"Fate plays strange tricks on men. Oedipus. Agamemnon. Theseus."

"Stop it, Spyro. This is not a tragedy. If you don't want me to go, I won't."

"How soon do you have to answer?"

"The letter says they would like to hear by next week. If I telephone, I can wait until most of the performances of *Tosca* are over. We'll have a chance to talk about it more. But I hope you'll think it over before we talk again. I hope you'll see the wisdom of retiring so you can come with me."

He wondered if she realized how much her words showed her mind was already made up. He wondered also if she understood that retirement might no longer be available even if he were willing to consider it. His situation was daily getting more precarious. His friend, Minister Antoni Antonidis, was phoning him constantly to let him know the progress that Minister Petropoulos was making with the prime minister. Thanks to Antonidis, the prime minister was resisting, but Petropoulos was putting more pressure on every day to get agreement for an indictment and trial on the charge of gross malfeasance in office.

"What are you thinking about, Spyro?" asked Victoria.

"You want the truth? I'm thinking that it's probably too late to retire. Petropoulos will no longer be satisfied with that. He's vindictive. Now he wants to humble me, to imprison me if he can. He won't settle for anything less than a trial and conviction. Not that I care. Even a trial would be preferable to dishonoring myself with a forced retirement."

"You're not serious?"

"I'm deadly serious. I think a court would be reluctant to sentence me to prison, but I could be found guilty, given probation, fined more than I can pay, and left free in permanent disgrace. Nonetheless, I could live with disgrace easier than I could live with dishonor."

"I don't see the difference."

"Disgrace is what other people think of you. Dishonor is what you think of yourself."

She was silent for a while as she looked out the window and gazed upward to the heavens. "But, but that's silly, Spyro. Think of it this way. If you were disgraced, you wouldn't want to live here. And people in London would care less. Either way, my darling, resignation and dishonor or trial and disgrace, living in London would seem to be the answer."

"Would you want to live with an older man without power and without money who couldn't even stand living with himself? Could I tolerate a position as lap dog to a famous opera diva?"

"You're not old and I would always love and cherish you. You're my life."

"Perhaps London would be best for you. That is, if you get anything more than just this one opera. But you'll do well, my dear, and you'll finally get the recognition due you."

"But you'll come with me? I'll accept and you'll agree to come with me."

"Certainly I want you to accept."

"But you'll come with me?"

He hesitated and then, before he had any further chance to answer, the telephone rang. It was Antoni Antonidis for Roussos. When he hung up, Roussos said to Victoria, "Antonidis says the prime minister wants me in his office as soon as I can get there."

"In the Parliament Building?"

"Yes."

"Shall I drive you?"

"No, it shouldn't take more than ten minutes to walk."

"Spyro?"

"Yes."

"If I accept the Royal Opera, you'll come with me?"

"Let's wait and see what happens."

He left, and Victoria went to the bedroom, tossed off her shoes, and lay on her stomach on the bed. Why, she wondered, was he being so difficult? Slowly the idea came over her that it was London he objected to. Away from the Mediterranean, so far from Greece, he had built up his defenses against it. He would have accepted Milan, if only Milan were willing to accept her. Milan might even be preferable to him over Corfu.

At that moment the telephone rang. It was a man speaking English with a foreign accent who introduced himself as Giancarlo Panini, an assistant artistic director of La Scala. He was at Ellinikon Airport, and wondered if it would be convenient for Victoria to come to the airport to discuss a role they had in mind for her.

She couldn't believe her good fortune. She had just been thinking about La Scala, and here it was in the person of a Giancarlo Panini wanting to see her at the airport. Would she come? She spoke her assurance into the phone instrument that, yes, she could make it, how long would he be there?

"We will not discuss fees or terms. I just want to talk to you about some of the artistic challenges. You would be interested in playing Susanna in *Figaro*, perhaps? My plane leaves in two hours."

"It could take me the best part of an hour to go to Ellinikon."

"Then we will have an hour to talk. It will be worthwhile, I assure you."

As if walking on air, she went out the back way to get the car. The DSI plainclothesman guarding the alley saluted her and asked if she was going some place. She told him she had to go to the airport unexpectedly. The policeman suggested he should go with her.

"Oh, that won't be necessary."

"It's my duty, and I'm under orders."

Victoria knew she had been foolish when she and Marilyn eluded her guard. She didn't want to get this one in trouble, and it was probably a good idea anyway. As long as Pavlo Xynos was loose, she needed the protection.

She did the driving, and her bodyguard sat beside her. She asked him about his family and if guarding her had caused them inconveniences. He assured her no and said that it was an honor to protect her. Then in a cautious tone, he wondered if it would be proper for him to ask a favor. She said certainly.

"I hate to ask, but if sometime it looks as if all the seats for one of your performances are not taken, would it be possible for you to get passes for my wife and me?"

Victoria laughed. "I'd be pleased to. I'll make sure tomorrow that I get you two passes for next week. Are you free in the evening?"

"We work evening hours, too. But I have a day off on Wednesday."

"Then Wednesday it shall be."

They continued in silence. The Royal Opera. La Scala. Perhaps even the Met. It almost seemed now as if her opportunities would be unlimited.

But would it mean leaving Spyro behind? She feared he might adamantly refuse to go to either London or Milan. Yet she felt she couldn't stay in Athens. Not with Xynos on the loose. Of what use would she be to Spyro if Xynos caused her to lose her mind. Spyro already had a wife who was crazy, would he want a loony mistress, too? She would almost be doing him a favor to get out of his life. No, that wasn't true. She didn't know what she meant. Her thoughts were too mixed up. But didn't it come down to a double need for moving on: her ambition and her sanity? Why was Spyro so bull-headed?

She parked at Ellinikon, and they went inside. She was to meet Giancarlo Panini in front of the Alitalia ticket counter. First, the guard asked, would it be all right if he went to the men's room? She agreed to wait outside the W.C. in plain sight of all the people in the busy airport.

After a long while she grew a little impatient. She only had so much time to meet Signore Panini. Then an older looking man came out of the W.C. and approached her. He prodded something in her back and said, "I have a knife, and I will kill you if you make a sound."

She recognized the voice as that of Pavlo Xynos and almost fainted. But she thought of the guard and asked where he was.

"Don't worry about him. He will be all right. Walk in that direction until I give you further orders. We're going out to the car park. Can you feel my knife? It is right under your heart."

Now it came to her that his voice over the telephone had been disguised as Giancarlo Panini. How could she have failed to realize it at the time? It was her own fault. It was wishful thinking that clouded her mind to keep logic out.

He directed her to proceed to his car. After ascertaining that no one was watching them, he opened the trunk and forced her to crouch down inside. "You will be all right. We are to take a short drive so we can be alone and talk. That's all I want now, just for us to talk. I won't hurt you, my dear Victoria."

Her sense of direction and the sounds she heard gave her to believe that Xynos had crossed over to the Olympic side of the terminal. But then they turned left. They were heading on the seacoast road away from Athens.

Too late, she realized that she should have put up resistance in the airport where they were surrounded by many people, including the police and armed guards. Now she was horrified and getting more frightened as they drove away from Athens. She was completely in his power.

*   *   *   *

Unlike his long waits in Petropoulos's outer office, Roussos was kept waiting no more than two minutes after he arrived at the prime minister's office. Antoni Antonidis ushered him it. The three of them sat by an unlit fireplace.

Roussos had seen the prime minister only once since his party had won the election, and that was at a distance during the swearing in ceremony. His lion's mane of white hair and his tall spare figure gave him the appearance of a younger man, but the worried look in his face told the story of the stress he was under. Coffee was served, and the prime minister stated his purpose.

"I know you by reputation, and my brother-in-law, Minister Antonidis, has told me so much more about you. I have heard what wonders you have done with DSI and what a reputation you have for efficiency and honesty. It is sad that this misfortune has come to you."

Antonidis said, "Spyro, we just want you to know that the *Prothypourgos* sees your side and wants to help as much as he can. Petropoulos is the most hated and most feared man in parliament, but he has a sizeable bloc of members of our party who feel they have to support him. Whether they follow him out of fear or for hope of reward, is not material. The fact is that he has been acquiring more real power than any other politician in Greece."

The prime minister said, "He has power even over me. If he resigns from my government and his followers join in a vote of no confidence, I am finished. We waited three years to get the government back from the Radical Republican Party, and now after just a month we could be thrown out. And Petropoulos would become the new party leader and increase his power even further."

"Yes Sokrati, and it's perhaps even worse," Antonidis said to the prime minister. "Think of what will probably happen if Police Director Roussos is sacrificed. Petropoulos will put his own creature, Thanos, in as head of DSI. That will give him control over dossiers that may contain incriminating or embarrassing information on virtually all members of parliament. After all, politics is a dirty business, and most of us have something in our background that we would hate to have publicized. I'm afraid that could put Petropoulos in a position to blackmail enough other members of parliament, besides his own bloc, to get himself voted in as your successor."

The prime minister stretched out his arms with palms facing up. "You are just saying that we are damned no matter what we do."

"You would lose the prime ministry no matter which course you take. But might it not be better to let the opposition go back to governing a while once again rather than hand over our own party to Petropoulos? He is the greater evil. In just this short while as a minister, he has already made himself the most powerful man in government."

"You know, Antoni, that I cannot take action that will provoke Petropoulos to strike. If I can just keep him quiet for a little while longer perhaps I can build enough support to stop him from getting any more power than he has."

Roussos spoke. "Excuse me, sir, but when you say keep him quiet, you mean me. If I am out of the equation, you may have the time you need to change some political alliances in your favor. Is that right? Well, it's simple then. I'll just retire and he will probably be satisfied."

"No," said the prime minister.

"No," said Antonidis, "it is no longer possible. Petropoulos has given the prime minister an ultimatum. Either he will allow the charges to be brought up against you, or Petropoulos will provoke a crisis of government. He no longer will be satisfied by your retirement. He'll settle for no less than to have you drummed out of the police service. He even wants you to go to prison. Of course, that would be up to the court."

Roussos said, "He can't possibly have the kind of evidence that would convict me."

"Ah, my friend, remember that with charges against you, you would have to be suspended. It would be on full pay, but you would be out of DSI. Petropoulos would make Thanos the head of DSI, and then stall your trial long enough for Thanos to research the files and get him enough information to blackmail even members of the court."

The prime minister said to Antonidis, "Then what can we do?"

"I'm afraid, Sokrati, that there is only one answer. Stall, and be prepared at worse to turn the government over to the RRP rather than let Petropoulos win."

The prime minister turned to Roussos and said, "I called you over because Antoni thought it would be the decent thing to do. I'd like to take his advice, but I have no choice. You will have to be charged. Between the indictment and the trial, you will have to be suspended from office. Petropoulos has given me one week to act as he insists."

"So I have one more week before I'm out of office," said Roussos.

Antonidis said, "I guess that's it, Spyro. I'm sorry."

"Thank you both. You've been most decent, *Kyrie Prothypourge*, and I appreciate it. I will carry on my functions until there is an indictment, but if in the meantime there is anything you wish me to do—resign or anything else—please let me know." Turning to Antonidis, Roussos said, "Sir, I'm aware that your defense of me may hurt you politically. You have behaved with great honor, but, please, now feel free to stop defending me and start protecting yourself. There is no need to stay with a sinking ship."

He left and walked back to his apartment. Retiring to help the prime minister could have been an acceptable option, letting him at least keep his honor because he would have been serving a greater cause. Now, if he were convicted but not imprisoned, he might go to Corfu, but—and he hoped Victoria would understand—he could not leave his country no matter what.

His thoughts turned to Dimitri. He had much that he had to talk over with his son, but he hadn't seen him for several days, in fact had no idea where he was. Of course he wanted to advise Dimitri of how his situation was coming to a head, but perhaps more importantly he had to ask him about the strange remarks made by Petropoulos. What was Dimitri doing?

Entering the apartment and calling for Victoria, Roussos was surprised when she failed to answer. He looked throughout the place for her. Then he went downstairs and talked to one of the plainclothesmen in front. The man told him that she had pulled up to him in her car and the bodyguard beside her said that they were going to Ellinikon Airport.

Spyro called his office for a car and rushed to the airport.

*   *   *   *

When released from the trunk, Victoria, in a daze, found the glaring daylight too much for her, and she closed her eyes quickly. Slowly reopening them, she let them get adjusted to the brilliant sunlight, then looked on in disbelief. There in front of her was the path across to the small market she and Spyro used. To her right was another familiar path down to the beach. Through the trees and across the water she could make out the beach at Vouliagmeni. The large, luxurious hotels that had invaded Kavouri were all around her, their high-rise stories appearing above the trees.

She was aware that Pavlo Xynos was with her, but somehow she thought he was under restraint. Her Spyro had captured him and rescued her. But where was Spyro? And why were they at Kavouri? And they were parked at some unknown summer place, not Spyro's beach house. Was she fully awake?

Xynos led her gently by the arm. Unlocking the door of the summer house, he directed her in, then closed and locked the door. The shades were down, but thin streaks of light from the sides admitted sufficient light for her to see that she was in a sparsely furnished room. Xynos maneuvered her into one of two beach chairs, and took the other for himself. The only other furniture was a collapsible camp table and two upright chairs near a door to the kitchen and an old single bed against a wall. Getting up again, he opened the shade of one window, exposing a view toward the beach.

"Clever, isn't it?"

She looked at him without comprehension.

"I mean where better to hide than in a rented house just a few meters away from the beach house of the police director who is looking for me?"

Gradually her ability to understand was coming back to her. Now she realized her situation, and her fear grew again. She shivered.

"Do not be frightened, my love," he said. "Think of yourself as my guest, not my prisoner."

"Am I free to leave when I want?"

He laughed loudly and said, "Guests are not supposed to be rude to their host. It would be rude to leave too early. No, my dear one, we will rest, relax, and talk for a while. And then I have business to do. The only question I have is what to do with you as my business here comes to an end. Shall I free you, take you abroad with me, or what? You are a problem to me, you know."

"I don't understand what you're talking about." She looked around more and found the room in a mess. There were dirty dishes and glasses and an empty wine bottle on the table. On the floor under the front window was a radio with cobwebs between it and the wall. The curtains on that window were torn and hanging down lopsidedly. There were more bottles in a corner, some looking unopened and others empty. The floor looked as if it hadn't been swept for a year.

"I assure you that I am not going to hurt you. You must stop fearing me. It is not good for you to have this much fear."

"How can I help but be afraid? You impose yourself on me. You kidnap me. At times you have been violent with me. You refuse to leave me alone. Why can't you leave me alone?"

Xynos stared at her dreamingly. Turning his head toward the window with the open shade, he said, "You can see Roussos's house just over that little hill. See your veranda poking out from the trees. Several times now I have sat here watching you and him on that veranda. Once I saw the two of you going to the market and coming back with groceries and wine. And once I saw the light go off in your bedroom and I tried to visualize what you must have been doing. You, taking off your clothes and lying down. He, moving his hands all over your delicate body. In my mind I acted with him in knowing you. When I leave here I will have such sweet memories."

Again Victoria shuddered. The memories of the happy occasions she had spent with Spyro in that house became clouded over as her mind wanted to deny what Xynos was saying. How could she have enjoyed making love with Spyro under the very proximity of the one man on earth who most tormented her? Some of her most precious moments were being sullied by this man who defied all understanding.

Who was he? What was he? How could he be so obsessed?

And then thoughts of Spyro came into her mind again, the trouble he was in, the disgrace that he faced. The decision she must make regarding London. Could their lives ever be the same, hers because of Xynos, Spyro's because of Petropoulos?

Yes, the decision was over London, not La Scala. La Scala didn't want her after all. It had been a miserable trick by this horrible man.

Xynos was looking as if he wanted her to talk, but she remained silent. "I love you," he said.

I hate you, she thought, but still said nothing.

"To possess you for one hour in bed, to make love to you, to have my naked body next to yours, to be united with you in sexual ecstasy, I would give anything in the world."

"Would you really?" she asked.

"Would you consider it?"

"No, never. Never, never, never." She knew he could take her anytime he wanted. He could have on other occasions, too, but didn't. Now she was completely his prisoner, and if he so desired he could keep her here indefinitely. Spyro would never think of looking in his own back yard for this animal.

Another thought came into her mind. If he was so obsessed with her, why didn't he take her? Was he really afraid of hurting her? She didn't think so. Why was her willingness so much a part of his motivation? She wondered, could it all be an excuse? Could he be physically unable to perform the sexual act? Could his insistence on her willingness be pretense so he could continue to think of himself as manly? Briefly, ever so briefly, she toyed with the idea of giving in to him just to see what he would do. But no, never. She was afraid she might be wrong. And anyway, even just the attempt would be as gruesome to her as the real act.

"Say the word, my dear, tell me you'll have me, and I will be your slave."

"Never, never, never."

"Then go to hell," he snarled, standing up and smashing a glass on the floor. "Do you know what I'm going to do? Next week I'm going to assassinate your Minister of Scientific Development, Antoni Antonidis. And do you know what else I might do because of you? I might also kill your precious Police Director Roussos. No more will you lie in his bed across the way. No more will I watch the two of you going down to the beach."

The volume of his voice lessened as he paced the room in front of her. "Ah, watching you go down to the beach in your swimming suit with a towel wrapped around as a skirt. How I delighted in following the two of you, and I'd lie on a sandy incline and watch you from so close as you took off the towel before going into the water. Oh, what a magnificent body you have. Ah, if only I could possess it."

She wanted to get him off the subject of herself and her body. By now she was realizing that not only was he dangerous because of his volatility, but he was also easily led from one thought to another. If only she could use that fact to manipulate him a little. She thought it was worth trying.

"How long do you intend to keep me here?"

"As long as it pleases me. Or, until I have other business to do. Would you care for something to eat, my dear?" He was speaking more rapidly than before. "Of course, it must have been hours and hours since you've eaten. What would you like? I don't have much. Bread, butter, some cans of tuna fish, some canned beans, cheese, there's half a watermelon, olives, and caviar. Would you like some caviar? I have money and can afford anything. How do you think I can afford to rent this place? My leaders have given me much money for my assignment."

"No caviar, thank you. Bread and cheese and watermelon would be fine."

"And some wine. Sometimes I buy my retsina from the same place where you and your lover get yours. But I don't want to go there too often, so I buy in the big grocery stores also. Would you like a glass of retsina?"

"A small one, please, but I'd really like some water. Could I have some water as well as wine?"

"You can have anything you want, my darling. You can have anything in the world. Now you will have to come into the kitchen with me because I can't let you out of my sight."

He gave her a glass of water. Victoria helped clean the kitchen by washing the dirty plates, glasses, and utensils while he sliced some bread and cheese. She eyed the knife in his hand. Perhaps when he put it down.... He cut the watermelon and started to leave the knife on the counter. With a shake of his head, he put the knife in a cabinet, locked the door, and put the key in his pocket.

They returned to the main room and sat at the camp table. Xynos poured some wine into two of the glasses she had just cleaned, ceremoniously handing one to her and toasting her with his own glass.

She took a sip to appease him. They ate slowly. As she chewed her food, she tried to think of what else she could do to help get herself out of this predicament. At a very minimum, she thought it desirable to keep him talking, but on innocuous topics.

"You used to be a student at the university."

"Yes, I was a good student. I love learning. I love history. I know Greek history and European history. Would you like to ask me questions about history?"

"I'd like to, but I wouldn't know what to ask."

"Let me tell you about Greek royalty. Did you know that the kings of the Hellenes have not had any Greek blood in them?"

"I vaguely recall. Remember, I'm an American and I know American history better than Greek."

"Wonderful. Then I can teach you. Listen. When Greece got its independence from the Turks, it needed a king, but no Greek had royal blood. So the leaders invited Prince Otto of Bavaria to be their king. Otto was the brother of mad Ludwig, Bavaria's king. Have you heard of mad Ludwig?"

"Oh, yes, he was a great patron of Wagner."

"Yes, yes, that's the one. I love the music of Wagner. Mad Ludwig built that beautiful castle, Neuschwanstein. Anyway, King Otto was a tyrant and in 1862 the Greek people booted him out. But they still wanted a king, so they invited Prince Georgio of Denmark to come in as King Georgio I. But the people would not let him be the King of Greece, like Otto, so he became the King of the Hellenes––King of the Greeks—it was more democratic, you see. But still he was not a good king, and he was assassinated in 1913. You see, assassination does not necessarily have to be bad."

"But it's always bad for the individual to take the law in his own hands."

"No, you don't understand!" He jumped to his feet and scowled to show his anger. After a few seconds, he slowly sat down again. "But you will, my love, you will. Georgio I was succeeded by his oldest son, King Konstantino I. He was pro-German in World War I and he was forced to resign the kingship, leaving the throne to his son, King Alexandro, in 1917. Alexandro married a commoner and had to have a morganatic marriage. Do you know what a morganatic marriage is?"

"Their children would not have the right to succeed the father because the mother was not considered a real queen."

"Yes, that's it. You are smart as well as beautiful. You're doing well, my sweetheart. You see we're getting along. King Alexandro died in 1920 and King Konstantino I came back, but he abdicated in 1922. His son became King Georgio II. I won't tell you now about all the things that happened to him, but he had many troubles. He died in 1947, and his brother succeeded him as King Pavlo. I was named after King Pavlo, you know."

"But you must have been born after he died?"

"Ah, you know something about him. Yes, he died in 1964. My father was one of his secretaries. He was a good king, although his wife Queen Frederika was very haughty. In 1964 their son, the young King Konstantino, took over, but he was too inexperienced, and when the Colonels' Revolt succeeded in 1967, he fought with the military junta and had to flee the country. He is still living, but in exile."

He began laughing almost uncontrollably. "It's so funny. Alexandro was the only king to marry a Greek woman, but because it was a morganatic marriage, their children couldn't succeed him. So no king of the Hellenes ever had Greek blood. Greece is now a republic, and we have a president, who is not supposed to be political. The government is led by a prime minister, who is very political. Can you understand all that?"

"Well, more or less, but I certainly learned a lot from you. You would have made an excellent teacher, perhaps a professor at the university."

He scowled again. "Oh, that! I could never be that now, you know. I killed my professor at the university. It was all for you, Victoria, all for you. I told him of my love for you, and how much I adored you and had to have you. He was cross with me. He said I was unreasonable and I should give up pursuing you. We argued and he hit me. I killed him but it was self-defense. He hit me first. That is why I had to leave Greece and join the terrorists."

"Do you believe in terrorism?"

"No, it means nothing to me, but they pay well, and they gave me good training."

"But they kill so many innocent people, Pavlo."

"That's the first time you've called me by my name. Say it again, please."

"All right. Pavlo."

"It sounds so nice when it comes from you. Now that I've taught you history, what can you teach me? I know, will you sing for me? Please."

"I don't have any accompaniment."

"But it will still sound beautiful. It can be short, but do a little."

"All right. Is there anything you would especially like?"

"I know. Sing that 'Ave Maria' from *Otello*, you know, the one just before Otello kills Desdemona because she betrayed him."

"But she didn't betray him. He only thought so because of the treacherous words of Iago."

"Sing it anyway."

Victoria was about to start, but somehow felt apprehensive about why he picked that particular opera. She lied to him, "Anyway, it's not in my repertoire. I can't sing it."

"Okay. Sing something from *Carmen*. I like that one because of Don Jose getting revenge by killing her."

"I don't have the voice for *Carmen*." She did not like the trend this was taking.

"You must know something. You're a famous opera star. All right, how about something that Nedda sings from *Pagliacci*. You know, the opera where Canio kills Nedda for betraying him with another man."

"No, I can't sing that one either."

A look of fury appeared on his face. "You won't do anything I say. You won't do anything I want. You're making me mad. I want you to sing from *Pagliacci*."

"No! I can't sing that. I don't feel like singing today anyway. I can't sing when I don't feel like it. I can't sing when I'm so terrified that I think I'm going to die. Why are you trying to make me sing all these operas where the prima donna gets killed for infidelity?"

"I'm sorry. I didn't mean any harm. It was just by chance. I won't make you sing, dearest, if you don't feel like it. You wanted to teach me something. Why don't you do that?"

She was on the verge of crying, but with his last words she picked up hope. "Pavlo, something you said made me think of dictators. You don't like dictators, do you?"

"I don't like them. But I'll work for them if they pay me well."

Victoria felt frustrated, but she kept on trying. "Do you know what is happening in Greece?"

"Yes, there's a manhunt out for me. They want to kill me on sight."

"I don't know about that. But I mean in Greek politics. Why do you want so much to kill Minister Antoni Antonidis?"

"Because I have orders and because he was the Minister of Public Security when they tried me for murder. It was self-defense."

"It may have been. I don't know because I didn't see it."

"Can't you believe me when I tell you?"

"Yes, of course, you wouldn't lie to me. But I don't want to talk about Antonidis. I want to talk about someone else, a very bad man."

"Who? Who is worse than Antonidis?"

"It's the present Minister of Public Security, Achilles Petropoulos. Let me tell you about him."

"I have heard much about Petropoulos. He is a dirty man. I don't like him."

"He is trying to put his own man in charge of the Department of Sensitive Investigations, a man called Thanos."

Xynos laughed ironically. "Ha, I know about Thanos. He is a killer masquerading as a policeman. I saw the newspaper photos of what he did to Nick Savvas."

"Police Director Roussos brought charges against him for that and wanted to bring him to trial. But Petropoulos set him free and uses him in his own office now until he can put him in charge of DSI. Then Thanos will have access to information that Petropoulos can use to blackmail members of parliament, other government ministers, court officials, and media people, and everyone. He plans to make himself absolute dictator."

"I never heard that before. I don't think it's true."

"Won't you believe me when I tell you?"

"Well, of course, my darling, I believe you. If you say it is true, then you must believe it. But you might have wrong information. At any rate, nothing will stop me from killing Antonidis."

"You said something about also killing Police Director Roussos. You wouldn't really do that, would you?"

"No, I was just showing I was mad at you. I hold nothing against Roussos. He was only doing his duty. And in a way he is my friend. We share something important together."

Her voice grew lower, and she said in almost a whisper, "Let me ask you, would it be just as easy for you to assassinate Petropoulos instead of Antonidis?"

"The people who pay me wouldn't like that. They want me to kill Antonidis. They say he is too pro-American. I don't know. I'm a soldier and I just obey orders."

"You think about it, Pavlo."

They talked the rest of the morning and into the afternoon. Then Xynos said, "I'll tell you what I'm willing to do. If you sleep with me, if you give yourself to me without any reservation whatsoever, I will do anything you ask. Within reason, of course."

"I couldn't do that Pavlo. I don't know why, I just couldn't. I can't resist you if you force yourself on me, but I cannot give in willingly to you."

Why, she asked herself, was she hesitating when it concerned someone other than her Spyro? She knew she'd do anything Xynos wanted if it were necessary to save Roussos.

Xynos said, "Suppose I kill your Roussos, too. What would you do to save him? Sleep on that, little one. I have so many things to think about. When you awake, we will talk about how you can save the life of your lover."

Although Xynos indicated that she should lie in the bed, she preferred moving over to one of the beach chairs, but it was impossible for her to sleep. She watched as Xynos continued sitting at the table and poured himself a glass of wine. From the way his lips were half moving, she thought he must have been talking to himself. Several times he glanced at her, but dreamily, as if he were in some other world. Once he laughed to himself, and once he pounded his fist on the table, making the bottle, the glasses, and the plates jump up without breaking.

She wondered what was going on in his mind. Apparently he had decided to force her to have sex with him. So she was wrong about him being impotent. With Spyro's life in danger, she knew she would have no choice, even though the thought of Xynos being intimate with her was almost unbearable. Could she direct the conversation again to get his mind on something else?

Several hours passed. Victoria tried to withdraw from Xynos's sight as if by being quiet and unmoving she might become invisible to him. She did not want to fall asleep, however, but in spite of her efforts to stay awake, she found her eyelids drooping. The lack of motion and the increasing darkness outside were soporifics.

Suddenly she found herself being touched, then lifted. Xynos was carrying her over to the bed. Gently he laid her down. This was it, but she didn't know if she should resist, or for Spyro's sake give in to him. She opened her eyes still undecided. Looking up, she saw him staring at her with lust in his eyes. He nodded his head slightly as if confirming to her that now was the time. Reaching for his belt buckle, he opened it and let his pants slide down.

She expected him to get in the bed with her, but there was no further movement. All he did was to look down at himself. He was much more concerned with himself than with her. And she saw the reason. She had been right. He wasn't going to be able to do a thing. He was impotent. Even his eyes would have told her that. She had never seen such sadness in a man's eyes. He looked as if he were about to cry.

The two of them remained unmoving, untalking for a while. Then Xynos put his pants back on. "Go to sleep," he said. "We'll do it in the morning. We're both tired now."

He sat again at the small table and poured himself another glass of wine. He drank it in two swallows and poured another. He was staring straight ahead toward the bed where she lay, but he seemed to be looking more through than at her. Suddenly his eyes focused on hers, and in an angry yet mournful voice he said, "It's all your fault, damn you."

The fear came back to her and she froze. Had his eyes been laser beams, they would have cut her in two. She didn't know what fault she had, but she was in no doubt that at that moment he hated her. Just one wrong word might have prompted him to kill her.

He drank some more from his glass and slobbered his words. Now she heard him say, "I thought...I hoped...that with you it would be different. You're just like all the rest."

Involuntarily she gave a shudder, and she commanded herself to be perfectly still. She prayed that he would take no notice of her.

As he emptied his glass and poured still another, Victoria felt the first glimmer of hope. She prayed that he would continue to be more interested in his glass than in her. Fear slowly oozed from her body. Not only was she apparently safe from him for the night, but he was going to drink himself into oblivion to destroy the thought of his inability to perform. He wasn't even thinking of her now. She didn't think he'd confine her in any way. The most he seemed capable of was to fill his glass, seize it with both hands, and tremblingly lift it to his lips. She was free to think up a way of escaping him.

She had no idea of how much wine he could take before disabling himself, but he wasn't a superman and if he finished that second bottle he would probably be finishing himself for some hours. She mustn't give herself away, mustn't call any attention to herself. Just let him sulk in his own self-pity.

How much time had passed, she didn't know. She was aware that she had slept a bit, but that was probably good. It should have allayed any suspicions on his part that she was planning to make a move. Now cautiously she peeked toward the table. The dim light was still on, and there was a third wine bottle on the table. Xynos was slouched in his chair with his arms loosely hanging toward the floor. Groggily lifting his head, he took still another large swallow from his half-filled glass, then slumped down again. Yes, she thought, she couldn't have planned it better.

She waited. If he could still lift a glass, it was too soon. But she didn't dare fall asleep again. She was conscious of her breathing. If she hadn't paid any attention, it would have been all right, but just trying to keep her breath from making any sound seemed to her like too loud a noise in itself. Suddenly she heard movement from the table. Peeking through half-closed eyes, she saw Xynos getting to his feet. He started walking toward her. Her heart was beating loudly. She thought he must know that she was wide-awake. Now he was standing beside her.

He bent down, and she waited for his body to join her in bed. But nothing happened. He wasn't standing beside her any more, but he wasn't in bed with her either. He had disappeared. She looked down. He was there on the floor collapsed on his back in a spread-eagle position, and she realized he had finally passed out. Her chance had come.

Looking around, she wondered if there was anything she could use to restrain him in case he awoke. Perhaps she could rip and tie some of the bedclothes together, but it would be chancy. Better just to quietly get out.

From the pre-dawn light faintly showing through the window, she guessed it might be four o'clock. She had earlier thought over several plans for escape. She was afraid to search for the key to her car. She could run down to the beach and swim over to Vouliagmeni, but she was just a fair swimmer and he might be better. Not that she thought it likely he would be coming after her, but she didn't want to take the slightest unnecessary chance. There were some big resort hotels on the peninsula, and she should be able to get to one and hope there would be someone on duty at this hour.

The front door had a sliding lock. She eased herself silently off the bed on the side opposite Xynos. Her shoes were by the chair she'd been sitting in, but they were high heels and she didn't want to be handicapped by them. She reached the door and slowly slid the lock back. It made a slight clinking noise, and she froze. She stopped breathing, but now there was another noise in the room. Xynos was stirring. She saw him rise from the floor. Should she just open the door and run anyway, hoping that she had the advantage over a man who must almost certainly be incapacitated by alcohol?

No need for that, she realized, as she saw the outline of Xynos's body clumsily throw itself on the bed. He was only making himself more comfortable. She opened the door just wide enough for her body to pass through, then closed it from the outside. She was free.

✳   ✳   ✳   ✳

It was morning when Victoria arrived at her apartment by taxi. The moment she got out, the two plainclothesmen rushed over.

"*Despoinis* Renfrew, where have you been?" said the first to reach her. "The Police Director is frantic. He has been searching everywhere for you."

The second said that he would phone DSI headquarters and tell Roussos.

She just barely walked into her apartment when Roussos burst in.

"Where have you been, my darling? What happened to you? I was afraid that Xynos was hurting you. He killed my plainclothesman in the airport W.C., you know."

"Oh, no, I was so afraid that he might have. Let's have a drink and talk, Spyro. Something strong. Brandy."

They sat on the balcony and she told him how Xynos had tricked her and taken her to his hiding place in Kavouri, of all places. She told him what they had talked about and any observations she was able to make. She finished by saying, "I must visit the poor widow of that plainclothesman." She started crying. "I promised him free tickets to the opera."

"She will at least get his pension."

"I was Xynos's prisoner for hours and hours."

"Did you," began Roussos, "did you…, er, did you sleep with him?"

"No, I swear it."

He said in a soft, almost tearful, voice, "You realize that if it had been a matter of saving your life, I would have understood?"

She smiled. "That's because you're from Corfu, my love, instead of Crete. But I would not have slept with him in order to save my life, believe me. Yes, I would have to save yours, but it wasn't necessary. He tried but he's impotent. We talked and argued for hours, and he is determined that he is going to kill Minister Antonidis, as he is sworn to do."

"How did you get free?"

She told him all that had happened until she got outside. "I went to two hotels, but their doors were locked and I couldn't get anyone to answer the bell. Having started, I had no choice but to walk out to the highway. After a few cars passed me by, a truck driver stopped and took me to Glyfada, where I found a taxi."

"You could have telephoned me from Glyfada."

"I wasn't thinking clearly, Spyro. All I wanted to do was to get back into your arms."

Roussos reached for the telephone. "So he's still there in the beach house?"

"He should be. With that much wine, he should have slept for hours."

Roussos order his office to contact the police station in Glyfada and arrest Xynos immediately. Then he turned to Victoria again. "My poor angel. Let me help you to the bedroom. You need rest."

"Of course, you're always right, my darling. But before I sleep I want you to know something. I'm not going to accept any London offer. After that last ordeal with Xynos, I know all I really want is to hold onto what I already have. Yes, I live for my art, but even more for my love, and my love is you."

"But the London audition is only a one-time possibility."

"That conflicts with my obligation to the Greek National Opera. They gave me my first chance and I don't want to let them down. More importantly, my darling, I'd be afraid that it might lead to a permanent offer, and I can't do that to you. You couldn't be happy anywhere except in Greece, and I couldn't be happy unless you're happy."

Roussos said, "Without my permission, Minister Antonidis told Petropoulos yesterday that he would persuade me to retire. Petropoulos said that if I wanted to avoid a trial the best he would accept now was my resignation, perhaps with a reduced pension. He is determined that I have to pay something for the trouble he says I've caused him."

"What did you tell Antonidis?"

"Nothing yet. He told me to think it over for a day or two."

She took a shower and covered herself in bed. Spyro watched over her. Just before she went to sleep, she said, "I guess I'm lucky there are no performances at this time. I'll get a good rest this weekend and be ready to sing again Monday night."

As he watched her flutteringly close her eyes and yield her consciousness and body to Morpheus, Spyro thought, *Good night, dear lady, you and Dimitri are all I have.*

When the telephone rang, he ran to pick it up before it could sound a second time so as not to awake her. It was his office. The police had gone to Xynos's beach house, but the place was empty. Xynos had disappeared.

CHAPTER 21

▼

Marilyn's hands had long since gone numb, and her body was in pain all over. She was surprised that the kidnappers hadn't gagged her, but she had a feeling she could yell all she wanted and no one would hear except the kidnappers themselves.

"How much time has passed, Bob?" she asked.

"I'm not exactly in a good position to look at my watch," he said. "Maybe several hours."

"What are you thinking?"

"I guess my knell is rung. Several hours closer to oblivion."

"He couldn't have meant it, Bob. They can't kill you."

"You're preaching to the converted. Please inform them of this little fly in their ointment."

"Oh, Bob, sometimes you're adorable, but this isn't one of them. Can't you ever be serious?"

"Sure. If I could think of some practical way to escape, I'd be serious enough."

"It's my fault, isn't it? If I had just done as you said, if I hadn't insisted on staying here, we'd be all right now."

"And if I had been born thirty years later, I'd be too young to be in this mess." After a while, he said, "I think your aunt was right. Dimitri's not the man for you."

"I thought he was. Oh, I thought so much that he was. Tell me, Bob, what's going on?"

"Well, as close as I can figure it, Dimitri is part of a group of revolutionaries that want to take over Greece, just like the colonels did in 1967. Only this time it looks more like a bunch of captains and majors. Dimitri seems to be one of their leaders. They all went to the *Evelpidon* military school. Then some of them left the army to go into other careers. Or it looked as if they were going into other careers. It's obvious now that they were infiltrating key parts of the economy so as to have complete control when the time came, and the time is apparently now. They're in communications, transportation, energy, the police—that's where your Dimitri comes in. He'll probably end up as chief of all the police if the revolution is a success."

"Can it be successful?"

"Unequivocally no! They might be able to take over power by surprise and hold it for a day or too. But don't they see, they could retain it only with the good will of the populace? After the colonels, the people have had enough. There's no way they'll support the revolution. They'll drag their heels, hold demonstrations, commit sabotage, and give a revolutionary junta so much trouble that the junta will wish it had stayed in bed."

"How about Dimitri's father? Do you think he's in on it?"

"I seriously doubt it. He's too smart and experienced for something like that. He would know there'd be no popular support. You'd have to be wet behind the ears to try something this crazy."

"It's Director Roussos's job to prevent something like this, isn't it?"

"Yes, and it won't look good for him if he doesn't, all the more so with his own son involved."

"If it fails, what will happen to Dimitri?"

"No one can tell now. If the revolution is not too bloody, he might go to prison for life, like Papadopoulos, the head of the Colonels' Revolt. But if a lot of lives are lost, there could be a demand for his execution."

"I hope not."

"That a girl. Here I haven't done anything and he's just sentenced me to death, but you're hoping that he won't have to suffer any penalty. Remind me not to send you a Christmas card this year."

They could hear more people coming in from outside, and every now and then someone would open the door to take a look at them. From the failing light creeping in from behind the shades, they could tell that it was close to dusk.

Marilyn said, "What's this about holding me as control over my uncle?"

"I don't understand that part. Your uncle thinks that was the reason they kidnapped you in the first place. But your uncle's not going to have anything to say about things. The United States Government will sit on the sidelines and watch, just as it did last time. If the revolution should be successful and appears to be able to sustain itself, and if it promises to honor all the obligations of the over-thrown government, the U.S. will recognize it. If not, the U.S. won't have anything to do with it. There's no room for the U.S. to be influenced sufficiently by your uncle. What the U.S. does in a situation like this is so automatic that it could be decided by a computer algorithm."

"If that's true, then they might kill me, too."

"We can die in each other's arms."

"I don't want either one of us to die."

Three men came into the room. One held a gun on them, while the other two untied their hands.

"You will please go downstairs," said the one with a gun.

"Haven't I seen you at American Embassy receptions?" said Bob to the gunman.

The man smiled pleasantly. "It's possible. I've been invited to a few because of my position in the Foreign Ministry."

"You're not in the army any more then?"

"No, I resigned."

"But you were a graduate of the *Scholi Evelpidon*?"

Now the man's smile grew huge and he was obviously well pleased. "Oh, yes, I'm a graduate."

Marilyn said, "How can you be so damned decent when you're holding us prisoners and you're planning to kill one of us, if not both?"

The man with the gun said, "I was brought up to have good manners. We do what we have to do. There's no need to be nasty about it."

Marilyn said, "Not if you're the one holding the gun. Just give me that gun and I'll show you what good manners I can have."

"You've got spirit, little one. I like you."

He motioned to them with his gun to move out of the room.

"Where did you learn such excellent English?" asked Bob.

"I went to the American School, and later I spent a year studying in Washington, D.C."

Marilyn said, "Do you really have to kill Bob?" With her hands free, she was now rubbing her wrists vigorously to regain full circulation.

"If it were my decision, Miss Pickering, no. But, as I say, we do what we have to do."

Bob said, "Here lies Robert Jensen, executed in cold blood by really decent killers."

"If it comes to that, we will make it as painless as possible."

"A bullet dipped in anesthesia perhaps?" said Bob.

The last door on the other side of the hallway led to the basement, and the five of them went downstairs, Marilyn and Bob first. They were in another hallway, and with a slight motion of her head, Marilyn whispered to Bob, "That was my closet."

They could hear voices coming from behind a door on the other side of the hallway. After being marched in, they found themselves in a large room where there was a meeting in progress with some thirty or more people present. These were sitting on folding metal chairs on two sides of the room with an aisle between them. Three men were on a low platform facing the audience, the one in front standing near a flipchart easel. The voices hushed as Marilyn and Bob were led in.

The man who had ordered them downstairs had the other two bring Marilyn and Bob to another metal pipe extending from floor to ceiling. Each of the two men had a pair of handcuffs, which one used to handcuff Marilyn's left arm to Bob's right, while the other handcuffed Bob's left arm to the pipe. The prisoners now had some limited freedom of action, and Marilyn continued to rub her wrists and hands.

"You must be absolutely silent," said the gun-holding man, "or we will have to put a gag on you."

In spite of that injunction, when the man with the flipchart continued speaking, Bob gave Marilyn a brief whispered translation. Standing slightly behind the man giving the flipchart presentation was Dimitri. The speaker turned the meeting over to Dimitri, saying, "Now it's Jimmy's turn." Dimitri stepped up to the easel.

Bob translated.

Marilyn said, "Jimmy? Dimitri is the mysterious Jimmy who the kidnappers were waiting for on Skyros?"

Bob whispered, "Jimmy is a popular nickname here for Dimitri. I could have thought of that before except that it's so much in common usage. There are a lot of Greek men named Dimitri and not a few of them are called Jimmy as a nickname, especially by those who know some English."

"What's he telling them?"

"Keep your voices down," said the man closest to them.

The man who had been in charge of bringing them into this room walked down the aisle and mounted the platform.

As the leaders on the platform continued to describe the overall plan, Bob continued to give Marilyn a summary translation. He said, "Although a few of these men are in key civilian positions, most of them are military—captains, majors, and a few colonels. The four on the platform are the top leaders. The rest of them are the heads of various cells. This is apparently the first time all of them have been together. Many of the cells have been unknown to each other for security purposes. Each man here has responsibility for some important operation when the coup starts. Dimitri will take control of the entire police organization. The man closest to him will be in charge of all communications in the country. Another one on the platform will give the signal to seize all tank commanders throughout Greece who are not part of the coup. Then the tanks will roll into the big cities and take control over important military and civilian installations. Generals commanding large army units will be given the choice of being with them or put under arrest. They also have a list of high-ranking officers who will be purged one way or another."

Dimitri used a pointer to indicate his place on the flipchart. He was talking in an excited voice, and they were all giving him their rapt attention.

"What's Dimitri saying now?"

"They've been planning this for years and it will start tomorrow. He says that he will have all suspected troublemakers rounded up and either jailed or executed. He has not mentioned yet how his father will fit into all this."

The audience was quaking with excitement, and Dimitri's words were greeted with frequent applause and shouts of approbation.

"Is Dimitri the leader?"

"All four up there seem equal, probably an executive committee. If successful, they will probably be the new junta."

"So it's just another coup."

"There may be more to it. For one thing, they seem to think that they will easily have the support of the entire country. Apparently taking over the government is just Step One. They've alluded to a Step Two taking place immediately after Step One, but they haven't mentioned what it is. Uh-oh, this may be it."

As he finished, Dimitri was given a standing ovation. Another man took his place to the sound of heavy applause.

"What's he saying?"

"He's explaining Step Two. They will immediately launch a campaign to "liberate" Istanbul. Several army corps will attack by land, and the air force will start bombing strategic points in and around Istanbul."

"What will happen?"

"I think we're witnessing the beginning of World War III. The first thing, of course, is that the conspirators think if they can capture Istanbul, or Constantinople as they call it, they will have the overwhelming support of the Greek populace. That is how they expect to keep power once they achieve it. But then they expect to go on and take over Macedonia. If you've been reading lately about what a powder keg Macedonia is, you'll know what I mean. They seem to think the seizure of Constantinople would involve only a localized war between Greece and Turkey, but it would be virtually impossible to keep it "localized." And certainly the annexation of Macedonia by Greece would explode the whole world."

Marilyn said, "The funny thing is that Dimitri once warned me that the Greeks would eventually retake Constantinople after losing it centuries ago. He was almost in an ecstatic trance when he told me. But I didn't think they meant this soon. Can they really conquer it?"

"With some element of surprise, they might be able to initially."

"Then what happens?"

"As I said, World War III. The Turks will fight back of course. Russia, whose Orthodox religion is very close to the Greek Orthodox religion, along with some Balkan countries will support their Greek co-religionists. Most of the rest of Europe would side with the Turks, since the Greeks would be the aggressors. And for all we know, either the Greeks or the Turks or both may have access to atomic missiles."

"Do you really think it will be World War III?"

"I haven't the slightest doubt. Once the Greek army occupies Istanbul and Macedonia, the fat will really be in the fire. Just the Greek attempt to take over Istanbul would make World War III inevitable. Remember, World War I started in the Balkans, and the rest of Europe joined in."

"What can we do?"

"Unfortunately, we may not be around. At least I might not." He paused, then said, "You know what is beginning to bother me? The people in the Embassy whose business it is to know about this kind of thing don't seem to be concerned. World War III is about to begin, and our people don't seem to give a damn."

"What does that mean?"

"It may mean that they know something that we don't know, and I'm beginning to get an idea of where the commandos fit in. But I think it's too late for us, or for me. I'm not sure."

"I'll speak to Dimitri. I know he had some feeling for me. I'll plead with him."

"Keep in mind, Marilyn, that he's probably not rational. The stupidity of this whole plan shows that it's been concocted by completely irrational people."

Dimitri stepped forward on the platform and said something first to one of his co-leaders and then to the audience.

"He's telling the one called Hari to take over while he disposes of the prisoners. He says he won't be gone long."

Dimitri was rapidly approaching them. He unlocked the handcuffs that held Bob to the pipe, and he kept the other one on that held Bob and Marilyn together. Now with a gun in his hand, he ordered them to move out of the room and up the stairs.

"What are you going to do with us?" demanded Marilyn.

Dimitri ordered them out through a door that led to a back veranda. It was now inky black outside. Having them stop on the veranda, where there was still a sliver of light showing through the curtains, he tied a nylon cord to their handcuffs. He also had a flashlight, which he held together with the other end of the cord in his left hand. The gun was still in his right hand.

Marilyn said, "Dimitri, if I ever meant anything at all to you, please, you don't have to kill Bob. You can keep us locked up somewhere until it's over. We can't interfere with your plans."

From behind them, Dimitri ordered, "Go down those steps into that field."

There was no street lighting in this neighborhood, and they stumbled in the dark. Only forms could be distinguished. Dimitri said, "Keep to the right."

Marilyn remembered that the houses on this street touched each other, so they would be walking toward some adjoining house, or the field behind it. There seemed to be no light in the building next door, and only a thin ray of light could be seen in the house they just left. Everything seemed desolate. A perfect place for an execution. Two bodies full of bullets found on the slopes of Mount Lykavittos. With the coup scheduled for tomorrow, what difference would newspaper headlines like this mean? Dimitri and his cohorts would control everything.

Bob whispered to Marilyn. "There's one consolation. They have to fail. Even with support, the ensuing world war will destroy them. The only trouble is that they'll destroy us first."

Dimitri said, "Keep quiet. No talking."

Marilyn asked, "What will you do if we keep talking? Kill us?"

Dimitri directed them with the motion of his flashlight to the house next door. They walked in front, and Dimitri held the cord that served as a constant locator. Even if they were momentarily out of his sight, he would know exactly where they were. Being handcuffed together, they wouldn't even have the opportunity of separating to try to escape or overcome their captor.

The house next door was similar to the one where the revolutionaries were holding their meeting. Marilyn and Bob stumbled onto some kind of concrete platform or patio that was next to a veranda. Dimitri had them open the door, which led to an inside corridor. As they entered the house, Dimitri pushed them toward steps leading to the basement. Marilyn and Bob tripping and trying to maintain their balance cautiously descended the stairs. The basement corridor was lit by two bare light bulbs dangling from the ceiling and producing a faint illumination.

Dimitri said to Bob, "Knock on that door slowly but loudly three times. Then come back here with me." He had put the flashlight in his pocket, but still held the gun.

A man opened the door and came out. He had an automatic rifle, and his ferocious eyes seemed full of hatred. He spoke to Dimitri in French.

Suddenly Marilyn gasped. The man was dressed completely in black, sweater and all.

CHAPTER 22

▼

Marilyn said, "Why are they speaking French?"

Whispering in her ear, Bob answered, "It's probably their only common language." He translated for her. "Dimitri is telling that fellow that all the revolutionary leaders are in the basement and suspect nothing, and that it's the first time all the main coup leaders have been in one place. The man was curious about us. Dimitri said he'd dispose of us. The man said he recognized you, and he is concerned because now you have seen his face. Dimitri assured him he has nothing to worry about."

The blacksweatered man opened the door to the room he had just come from and called inside in some kind of language that Marilyn could tell was neither Greek nor French. A file of men dressed completely in black and wearing balaclavas, trooped out in a long line going up the stairs. Each carried an automatic rifle. The leader put on his own balaclava so that only his fierce eyes showed as he followed his men upstairs. Just before he got to the upper door, he turned to look down at Dimitri, gave him a salute, and was gone.

"He didn't have to do that," said an enraged Dimitri, more to himself than anyone else.

"That final salute?" said Bob.

"Taunting me with this horror. God, when will it end?" He threw his hands up to cover his face, then stopped and quickly lowered the one holding the gun. Wiping tears from his eyes with his other hand, he said, "We might as well go in the other room and sit it out. It shouldn't be long."

He seemed exhausted, and Bob momentarily wondered if he could make a play for Dimitri's gun, but still being handcuffed to Marilyn made it unlikely that he could succeed. The three of them sat on small wooden armless chairs, Bob and Marilyn side by side, and Dimitri about ten feet in front of and facing them.

Bob asked in English. "Turks?"

"Yes."

"They're going to slaughter your friends?"

"Can you understand why?"

Instead of answering the question, Bob said, "You were the one who told the commandos that Marilyn's kidnappers were holding her on Skyros."

"Yes."

Marilyn said, "But why, Dimitri? Why did you betray your friends?"

"It had to be."

"And Yorgo was one of them."

"Yorgo was one of my best friends."

"You didn't mention him when I asked if you knew any of the kidnappers."

"I didn't think it wise at the time."

"Were you in Washington with him when I boarded the plane?"

"Yes, we had planned that I would come, too. But suddenly I saw Victoria Renfrew at the Olympic counter, and I couldn't let her see me, so I left. I took the next flight out, but I kept away from Skyros so I could make arrangements for the Turkish commandos to go there. Knowing the details of my father's plan to rescue you, I made certain that the commandos would do their work and be gone before the rescuers could arrive."

He looked at Marilyn and added, "I told them they were not to harm you under any circumstance."

"You don't think being pistol-whipped hurts?"

"They were wrong, but they must have interpreted my instructions as meaning only not to kill you. You'll recall, they did take you out of the burning building."

Bob said, "Do you think you're giving them instructions? Don't they really just select whatever part of your words suits their purpose and ignore the rest?"

Dimitri tightened his lips.

Marilyn continued. "You told me you had the same objective as the men who were slaughtered. You gave me to believe that the recapture of Constantinople was your most sacred dream."

"It was and is. It is the dream of all patriotic Greeks. But we are divided on timing. Those poor fools next door have no chance. Did they not think that they would be discovered by the police, by the army itself, by the Turkish, American, Russian, British, French, and other embassies? You can't keep a secret like that in

Greece year after year. All they could do would be to embarrass our county, or worse, destroy it. If they started, they'd immediately be killed, but would it end then? God only knows where it would end."

Bob said, "I just found out that my Embassy knew something about it."

"You yourself might not have known about it earlier, but there are other compartments within your embassy."

"You mean the spooks?"

"I don't know what you call your most secret part, but my counter revolutionary friends made sure that the United States would not be caught off guard. Apparently your secret element was able to keep the information secure, which was one of the conditions of revealing it to them. Of course, we didn't tell them everything."

"Even the ambassador just found out?"

"He would have been informed only if both we and Washington wanted him to be informed."

"What did you expect from Americans?"

"That they would support Greece against Turkey."

"Never as the aggressor."

"I know, but my army friends didn't understand that."

"Even your father didn't know what you were doing? How could you keep it from him?"

"Every report that concerned the army came to me. I destroyed or altered anything that could have alerted my father. For his own good."

"So everyone was playing double-dealing games, and your army friends lost, thanks in good part to you."

"It's our inheritance from Byzantium."

Marilyn said, "But, Dimitri, the Turks are your traditional enemies. How could you inform the Turks against your own kind? How can you sit here idly waiting for your friends to be butchered?"

"It is their fate,"

Marilyn had heard the words before, but never with such powerful emphasis.

Dimitri continued, "They must be sacrificed for the greater good."

"But why this way?"

"No patriotic Greek should execute other patriotic Greeks. We're letting our enemies do our dirty work for us. The Turks can't afford a war any more than we can."

She was silent for a while, then asked, "What happens to us?"

"We must wait until we are sure that it is done, then you will be free to go."

Marilyn looked both relieved and perplexed at the same time. "You're not afraid that we might make the whole story public?"

Bob said, "Dimitri knows that we will check with the American Embassy before we do anything else. And I think we can guess what the embassy will tell us."

Dimitri opened his lips in a sardonic laugh. "Everyone will know and no one will say anything. That's the way it's done. Everyone except the people. Our secret will be locked away in the safes of a dozen countries."

Marilyn asked, "You're sure your father doesn't suspect anything?"

"As far as I know, he's in the dark. But in this business no one really ever knows for sure. In any case, if my father knew what I've been doing, I am sure he'd approve in his heart. It's my fate that I was the one designated to be the liaison with the hated Turks."

"Who are the people doing the designating?" said Bob.

"You know I can't tell you that. There are some people in high-up places who are determined not to allow this drastically premature plan to take effect—because I was my father's son, they knew I'd behave in the honorable way. There's no organization as such, just some statesmen who occasionally meet to exchange views. It's very informal. And there'll be no need for even these informal meetings to continue now."

Marilyn asked, "Will you tell your father what you have done?"

"I'll never see him again. But when you see him, Mr. Jensen, please tell him that I am eternally grateful to have had such a father. And tell him it is my wish that he divorce my mother and marry Victoria."

Suddenly they heard faint noises coming from the adjoining basement, sounding like string after string of small Chinese firecrackers on the Fourth of July.

Dimitri crossed himself, Orthodox style from right to left. He said, "Wait a few more minutes so they can get out of the area, then it will be safe for you to leave."

"You're staying here?" asked Marilyn. She knew he would not be leaving alive, but her mind did not want to accept it.

"In a short while there'll be a special detail to pick up the bodies. They'll be taken on a boat and the boat will be sunk in the deepest water. Their relatives will be told that they died as heroes during a training exercise."

"But you?"

"I'll be among the bodies."

"No, Dimitri, no!" yelled Marilyn. "You can't do that to yourself. There's no need."

His answer was a grim smile.   .

"But why, Dimitri, why?"

"It is my fate."

He unlocked them from the handcuffs and motioned for them to leave. "Take this flashlight," he said to Bob. "You'll need it."

Marilyn clung to Dimitri's arm, tears in her eyes.

"Marilyn, if you should ever go to the City—*eis tin poli*—think of me."

Bob gently led her away. They walked out of the room and toward the stairs. As they started ascending, they heard a single shot from the room behind them.

CHAPTER 23

▼

Dimitri was gone. They had had so many things to talk about, but they never had the chance. Roussos still could not stop the tears from flowing. He wondered if Dimitri's death had anything to do with Petropoulos. No, he dismissed the idea, probably not. But what had Petropoulos meant with his cryptic references to Dimitri? Probably just an insinuation that he would try to get Roussos on a charge of nepotism, as well as all the others.

At least Dimitri was a hero, like his great grandfather. The police director had no idea what Dimitri had been involved in, but he respected the need of government to have secrets. The important thing was that Dimitri died as a hero.

What would Dimitri have thought of his father? That had been one of the things Roussos wanted to talk to him about. He could have used Dimitri's advice now for any insight into what decision to make?

Between Scylla and Charybdis. He could resign, probably with a reduced pension, and be a coward, a traitor to the memory of both his grandfather and his son. Or he could let them put him on trial and be cashiered out in disgrace. Neither of his two heroes would have wanted that either. But what other choice did he have?

But also he owed an obligation to the living. That is, to Victoria. She had given him everything. And what had he given her in return? He couldn't even offer her marriage. But that was not an impossible obstacle, was it? He could, he should, divorce his wife and marry Victoria. He should have done it long ago. Whatever decision he made, he should consider Victoria foremost.

Well, that was easy, wasn't it? Victoria wanted him to resign. That was the practical choice. If he resigned, only he would know that it was not because it was the easy way out. But no matter, let them think whatever they wanted. He and Victoria could have a life together. A happy life, perhaps, if only he could live with himself. If he let his grandfather and son down, whatever he did, he couldn't let Victoria down.

Well, that was the answer, wasn't it? He had no choice but to make a decision, and that decision had to be the one most respectful to his love. He had to resign.

With paper ready and pen in hand, he addressed Minister Petropoulos and wrote, "For personal reasons, I herewith submit my resignation from the Greek Police. Respectfully, Spyridon Roussos, Police Director."

When Victoria entered the room, she found him for the first time since she had known him with tears in his eyes.

CHAPTER 24

▼

On Monday morning Police Director Spyro Roussos had what he called his final meeting with his Special Team. Only Pano Maniatis and Eleni Karolou were in the room with him. Neither knew what to say. They had awkwardly offered their condolences for the loss of Dimitri, and now were silent.

All Roussos said was, "I didn't even have a chance to talk to him."

They were all quiet for a few minutes. Finally Eleni spoke up. "Excuse me, chief, but will this horrible tragedy of the boat sinking delay Petropoulos's actions against you?"

Pano said, "I don't understand what Dimitri was doing on a secret training exercise with the army and navy in the first place."

Roussos, wearing a black armband over his tunic, said, "That's because it was secret. Secret exercises are not meant to be known by everyone."

"Not even you?"

"Not even me. Well, I'll be leaving DSI."

He did not tell them that on his way to the office he had put his resignation in the mail. It should arrive at the Ministry of Public Security the next day.

"My career is finished," he told Pano and Eleni. "I'll go back to my native Corfu." He looked first to one, then the other. "Pano, you have enough years to put in for retirement if working for Thanos becomes too much an ordeal. You, Eleni, may wish to put in for a transfer. I'll give you the highest recommendation; that is, if you think a letter from me would do any good under the circumstances."

"I wish I could retire, too," said Eleni.

"You've got a brilliant career ahead of you once you're free of Thanos. Well, I guess. I'll be clearing out my personal material. Tomorrow I'll go around and say farewell to everyone here. I can't tell you how much I appreciate their expressions of support."

Pano said, "It's not just in DSI. Some of the highest-ranking officers in other departments have been telling me how much they'll miss you. You were an inspiration to all of them."

"Thanks. Yes, I've heard from some, too. Well, we all have to leave one way or another. If only Dimitri…."

A buzz on the phone from his secretary led to her telling Roussos that Minister Antonidis wished to speak to him.

Antonidis had already talked to Roussos about the death of Dimitri, and he repeated his sincere condolences. He said, "Even Petropoulos offered his sympathy this morning, although I can't be sure how sincere it was."

"I have nothing to say to him."

Antonidis continued, "Spyro, I know you need time to grieve, but the future is coming on us so fast that I have to ask you something. I've reserved the presidential box at the opera tonight, and I've invited Petropoulos to attend with me. I'd like you to be there, too. I think introducing him to Victoria after her performance could do you some good. The four of us could go out for dinner afterwards and see if we could come to some sensible arrangement."

"Thank you, Mr. Minister, you're right, I need time to grieve privately. Nothing would be accomplished by my seeing Petropoulos. You know, of course, that I'm not willing to compromise myself."

"You wouldn't have to grovel. You could live honorably and comfortably. It's better than the only alternative. And I'm sure it's what Dimitri would have wanted for you under the circumstances."

"It's too late."

"Spyro, I wish you'd be reasonable and come to the opera and at least talk to Petropoulos."

"I'll be at my office tonight not far away because Xynos is still loose. We know he intends to take some action against you, and Victoria says he told her it would be this week. I'd have some guards there anyway for Victoria's protection, and I'll double the number now that I know you'll be there."

"You haven't given me an answer yet on Petropoulos's last offer to compromise."

"I put a letter to him in the mail this morning."

"You've offered to do the reasonable thing?"

"I suppose you would call it reasonable. I'm resigning."

"I'm sorry it turned out this way." There was a pause, then in a hopeful voice, "Getting back to tonight, you wouldn't object if I introduced Petropoulos to Victoria?"

"I have nothing to say about that. Victoria, of course, will speak and act for herself."

"Goodbye my friend," said Antonidis.

"I can't tell you enough how much I appreciate your friendship. And do take care of yourself. Xynos is much more dangerous than you seem to think."

*   *   *   *

Bob Jensen entered the ambassador's office with trepidation. He had failed again to protect the ambassador's niece. He confessed to himself that it was his own fault; he just didn't know how to handle a strong-minded woman who was determined to do as she pleased. He should not have let Marilyn continue up the slopes of Lykavittos following that officer to the safehouse. They should have found a telephone and called DSI. So now he was in the soup again.

"Jensen" said the ambassador, "I've got to make a powerful decision. I've either got to send my niece home because she always gets in trouble, thanks in part to your asshole ineptitude, or to send you home because you seem to be incapable of keeping her out of harm's way. Which do you think I should do?"

"Why don't you keep us both here; let her be security officer; and let me be the one who always gets in trouble."

Atherton stared at him with his mouth open. Suddenly he burst out laughing. "Only you, Jensen, would have the temerity to say something like that. All right, she's going back home. She wants to. She apparently is all broken up about that son of Director Roussos, and she has to get away. My wife, incidentally, holds you responsible for her falling in love with him. You should have made yourself more attractive to her."

"Then you might have had me for a nephew, sir. But I guess you can't make a silk purse out of a sow's ear."

"For once I agree with you—wholeheartedly. Anyway, you surprised me by doing some good reporting on this whole thing. You've even got important items down there that the spooks missed. That will make us look good at the Department."

"Thank you, sir." He was wondering what he had reported that was so good.

"I mean those commandos. I have a feeling that Washington wouldn't have rested until they found out who the commandos were. Did you see the TV news this morning?"

"Sorry, sir, I overslept. You said it was all right in view of the circumstances."

"Of course I did. I'm not criticizing you."

"Turning over a new leaf, sir?"

"Don't push your luck, Jensen." Atherton looked at his face to make sure he understood. "It appears there were two boats sunk last night in different parts of the Aegean Sea. One, of course, was the boat full of the Greek 'heroes.' It was in deep water, and the Greek government made the decision not to try to recover the bodies. There's a hint these men were experimenting with a new type of weapon that exploded and left no trace of their bodies anyway. They were all past or present army and navy officers, and they will get full military honors."

"As you know, I was aware that was going to happen."

Atherton continued, "The other boat was even more mysterious. It had no markings, and a Greek patrol boat ordered it to halt and be boarded. Instead, the unmarked boat fired on them with machine guns. The Greek boat fired back, and the mysterious boat was blown to smithereens. A few bodies were recovered, however."

"Don't tell me they were wearing black sweaters."

"Yes, exactly. They seemed to be Turks, but the Turkish government disclaimed all knowledge of them and said they were probably drug smugglers, although no trace of drugs was found. There couldn't have been any survivors. The Greek boat pounded the daylights out of the other boat. Thanks to you, your report lets us answer two questions: We can identify the people on that mysterious boat as the Turkish commandos, and now we know what happened to the Blacksweaters. The one answers the other."

"Glad to do something right, sir."

"All right, you can go," said the ambassador, but something in his attitude suggested to Bob that he still had more to say.

Bob hesitated in his walk toward the door. "There was something else, sir?"

The ambassador leaned forward over his desk, pushing his palms on the desktop as if he were getting ready to do pushups, but he didn't say anything.

Uh-oh, thought Bob, here it comes.

Still the mission chief was silent. Then, coughing to clear his throat, he said in quiet words slowly spoken, "I guess today's as good a time to discuss it as tomorrow. Well, you know how Washington is. I wouldn't have had to send you home.

In fact, I want you to know I had nothing to do with this. They think it might be time for you to serve a tour at the Department."

"In Washington?" Bob said with a choke. To himself he thought, *The old boy's really getting rid of me.*

"It's not mandatory, I say. I told them I doubted that you'd want to leave Greece at this time, and I thought you were doing a great job here."

"You did, sir?"

Still clearing his throat with a loud guffaw, Atherton said, "In fact, I'd like to have you here with me for another tour, if you think we can stand each other that much longer. Well, what I mean is, all this give and take aside, I think you've done an excellent job and I'm writing that up for your performance rating. The Department and I decided that we'd leave it to you." He was glancing at the desktop as he finished his words.

"You mean you really want me to stay?"

"Well, it's sort of six of one, half a dozen of the other. Your decision."

"Thank you, sir. You were right, I doubt that I'd be interested in a Washington desk job at this time."

"You know, you've got to serve another tour in Washington sooner or later for the good of your career."

"I know, sir, but not necessarily at this time. Could I have a day to think it over?"

"Why not? Sure. Let me know tomorrow."

As Bob left the ambassador's office, the secretary asked him how it went.

He replied, "Like a charm. The ambassador liked the way that I took care of his niece so much that he wants me to stay on for another tour. I might accept, if he'll promise me he doesn't have any more nieces coming over."

Back behind his own desk he started reading some reports. After an hour, he found he wasn't concentrating well, so he threw down the papers and leaned back with his hands clasped behind his head. Unbidden thoughts came into his head, and he found himself thinking about Marilyn Pickering.

As if his very thoughts had summoned her, Marilyn herself came through the doorway. "Thank you," she said, "for everything you've done for me. My uncle has explained why I must be quiet about Dimitri and the whole affair, and I assure you I'll not say anything. Secrets are locked not only in safes."

Bob suddenly felt shy. He stood up and walked toward her, awkwardly stretching out his hand.

She accepted his handshake, but asked, "Is there something wrong?"

"No, I guess not. But I realize you're leaving in, what?—a little more than a week? And I know you loved Dimitri, but I was wondering if you'd care to have me show you around Athens before you leave."

"Thanks, but I'm leaving tomorrow. I told my uncle and aunt that I couldn't enjoy myself under the circumstances, so I'm going home. And I think they're just as glad."

"I understand." He suddenly felt like a teenager trying to gather enough courage to ask the prettiest girl in class to the spring prom. "I suppose I never stood a chance, did I?"

"You want the truth? No. Well, I mean I guess not. But you're better off this way. I guess I'll go back to my old boyfriend, Jake. He's known me and all my faults for years, and he's willing to take me with the good and the bad. You've only seen my good side. Anyway, I know I don't love him, but I'll probably marry him anyway just to satisfy my mother."

Bob choked. "Your good side?"

"I've been on my best behavior during this trip. At home I'm a regular brat."

"And to think, I was falling in love with you."

She rewarded him with a faint smile. As if she were thinking aloud, she said in a distracted manner, "Do we really know what love is? I thought I was in love with Dimitri, but it was just the infatuation of the moment. Love is like an opera, beautiful but sad. I don't want that. I realize now that I don't want the ecstasy followed by the misery. I don't want to get slapped around. I don't want to be yelled at. I don't want a husband who from minute to minute might get his head blown off. I want someone who can love me, cherish me, treat me tenderly, care about my feelings, and stay around for a long time."

"That describes me perfectly."

"I want someone who would even be willing to convert to vegetarianism for me."

"I've been eating less meat over the years."

She was about to say more, but stopped. She looked around the room slowly, then turned to Bob with a puzzled expression on her face. "And I want someone amusing, someone who'll make me laugh."

He smiled bashfully and said, "I guess I don't qualify on that score. I'm far from being a comedian."

As if coming out of a trance, she let the words rush out of her mouth, "You liar! You're a laugh a minute. I could do worse. But anyway, I'm leaving right away, so we won't have a chance to see each other again."

"I don't suppose you're interested, but your uncle said I could transfer to the Department in Washington if I wanted."

"Really? Foggy Bottom's not far from the high-rise condo I live in."

"If you think it might help to know each other better, I could look for an apartment in the same place."

"You wouldn't!"

"Try me. Seriously, I would for you. If you'd give me your address."

She stepped closer to him until they were face to face. Looking up to his eyes, she made that extra effort to place her lips in front of his.

They kissed, lightly first, then they threw their arms around each other and did it again with more meaning.

"Let's try that one more time," she suggested.

As they unclenched for the second time, Marilyn said, "Here, let me write down my address for you."

*   *   *   *

"Mario, Mario, Mario," sang Victoria, and from the beginning she knew she would do her best this night. She was well rested, and her voice was in fine condition. Moreover, having made her decision to stay in Greece with Spyro no matter what, she had relieved her mind of a disturbing problem. And with all the guards inside and outside the opera house, she felt secure. Only the absence of Spyro from the audience was a disappointment. He had been adamant that he wouldn't be there.

When she had a chance, she looked up straight ahead to see who was using the presidential box. As expected, Minister Antonidis was sitting beside Minister Petropoulos.

It should have been Spyro sitting with Antonidis instead of Petropoulos. She was beginning to regret that she had agreed with Antonidis to have dinner with him and his fellow minister. But she mustn't let anything interfere with her singing. She already could feel that she was going to have a great evening ahead of her.

The opera proceeded smoothly. The tenor had received heartening applause after singing "*Recondita armonia*" in the first act, and Victoria was rewarded with a standing ovation in the second when she finished "*Vissi d'arte.*"

She didn't like the part in Act Two where the evil Scarpia was to force her into the bargain of giving him her body in return for a false agreement to release her lover. It reminded her too much of Xynos, but she continued and outwardly did not betray her true feelings. When Scarpia embraced her, she took the knife from the table and stabbed him to death. Then she arranged the candles on the floor by his body, leaving the room while saying, "And before him trembled all Rome."

In the third act the tenor again received tremendous applause after singing "*E lucevan le stelle.*" Now the two of them looked forward to freedom. The firing squad went through with the supposedly fake execution. Mario fell, the soldiers left, and Tosca approached her lover. With a horrifying scream she realized he was dead. The soldiers returned to arrest her, and she jumped over the wall to her death far below. The curtain came down.

She felt it was the best performance of her life, and the audience seemed to think the same. She and the company took curtain call after curtain call. The audience couldn't get enough, and the cast took turns in varying combinations to come out again and again to acknowledge the homage of the viewers.

Even Minister Achilles Petropoulos in the presidential box rose to his feet to join Antonidis in sustained applause.

"She was great," said Petropoulos. "I like that woman. She is attractive, too."

"I told you she would be good."

"So this is Roussos's lover," said Petropoulos. "She looks so much younger. And so lovely. You know, Antoni, it's a shame that she will be separated from him when he goes to prison. I could see that she might appreciate the—the, er, protection, shall we say?—that a powerful man might give her."

Antonidis was finding his self-appointed task of trying to heal the rift between Petropoulos and Roussos getting more distasteful, but he continued, "Why don't we go meet Victoria? She'll be pleased, and you'll find her personality is equal to her voice. She's expecting us in her room."

"I look forward to meeting her. And will we still have dinner together—the three of us—even though Roussos spitefully refused to come? It will be more pleasant without him anyway. This way she can concentrate on me. We may be seeing much more of each other with Roussos out of the way."

"We'll have to see if Victoria will still want to come with us if Roussos isn't there."

Petropoulos said, "As long as she doesn't expect me to excuse Roussos for his crimes."

Police guards were blocking access to the area of the dressing rooms, but when they saw Petropoulos, they stood aside and saluted. Petropoulos smiled and said to Antonidis, "I guess you were used to this kind of deference once. I must admit that I like it."

There was a long corridor that they had to pass through to get to Victoria's room. Stagehands were still around moving things, and a lone cleaner was sweeping the floor where the corridor intersected with a hallway leading to an exit.

Victoria was expecting the ministers, and she had promised herself that she would be especially pleasant to the man who had the power to save or ruin her lover. She waited outside her door, a forced lovely smile on her face, as she saw the two important men approach.

Suddenly everyone saw something at the same time, but no one seemed to see the same thing. The man sweeping the floor had reached into a large basket of used costumes to pull out a gun. Pandemonium reigned.

Victoria yelled, "It's Xynos!"

"Stop him!" shouted someone else.

"Get him!"

"Shoot! Kill him!"

"Get out of the way!"

One guard kept his senses and threw his body in front of Antonidis. Petropoulos went down to his knees and tried to hide behind the used costume basket. Guards came running down the corridors from both ends. Victoria stood by her door with her hands raised to her head. She looked on in horror.

Xynos tried to maneuver so he could get around the policeman who was guarding Antonidis with his body. He tried to aim the gun so as to hit Antonidis in the side or back, but the police were almost on him.

From the far end of the corridor, Spyro Roussos came running. He slowed down as he reached Victoria's side, saying, "I couldn't stay away. I was in the back of the auditorium."

Petropoulos from his awkward kneeling position was crying, "Don't let him kill me. Please don't let him kill me."

Antonidis took out a gun and said, "He's not after you, you fool. He wants to kill me." Antonidis was now effectively protected by two police guards between him and Xynos.

Xynos fired at one of the guards, but the bullet ricocheted off the man's gun. The policeman knelt to recover his weapon. His movement left an opening between Xynos and Antonidis. Xynos was ready to fire again, but Antonidis dashed around the corner, then presented only his head and the hand that held his gun as he peered out to fire back at Xynos.

Xynos tried to re-position his gun for an accurate shot at his now much smaller target, but the human forces coming upon him were too many and too close. He couldn't fire, and he turned and ran into the hall leading to the exit door. The police from both parts of the corridor came after him. Roussos turned and ran down the end of the corridor from which he had come, yelling, "Some of you come with me. We can surround him." Pano Maniatis rushed to the hall through which Xynos was fleeing and followed the others who were in hot pursuit.

Antonidis, gun in hand, ran behind the police. The few civilians present sensed that Xynos was a cornered rat and followed at a distance to be in on the kill. The corridor, which had just been full of so many people and noises, was now quiet, almost deserted. Only two people remained. Victoria walked slowly from her dressing room door to approach the kneeling Petropoulos.

He said, "Help me up. Give me a hand."

Only Victoria had noticed that as Xynos ran out, he dropped his gun, and it slid to rest by a side of the costume basket near Petropoulos, but not close enough for him to reach. He too now saw the gun and yelled to her, "Help me up. And get that gun. It's evidence."

She was oblivious to the noise from outside, the shouting and the shooting. She heard only Petropoulos telling her to get that gun. She slowly walked over to the revolver, stooped to pick it up, looked at it, saw the remaining bullets staring out at her, gazed at the gun unbelievingly, and then noticed Petropoulos again.

"Help me up." He didn't seem to have muscles strong enough to recover from the position into which he had fallen.

Victoria pointed the gun and fired a single shot into the area of his heart. Tossing the gun in the costume basket, she rushed back to her room.

There she removed her gloves, put them in a drawer with other clothes, washed and dried her hands, and put on a new pair of gloves similar to the ones she'd been wearing before. She walked out of her room just as Roussos, Antonidis, and a number of policemen were returning, all looking amazed at the sight of Petropoulos lying on his back with blood oozing out from his wound.

One of the policemen said, "Look, Xynos killed the minister."

Another person said, "No, it must have been someone else. The minister was alive when Xynos ran out."

Still another person yelled, "No, Xynos shot him. I saw him shoot at him just before he exited."

Antonidis said, "He must have had an accomplice. Which way did he go?"

Pano yelled, "I thought Xynos shot him just before he fled."

Others were asking, "What happened?"

There was no one to tell. Only Victoria and Petropoulos had not taken one of the two avenues of pursuit to follow Xynos, and Victoria said she had gone to her dressing room.

Roussos said to her, "Was Petropoulos alive when you left?"

Victoria put her hand to her forehead and closed her eyes. She seemed faint. "I don't think so. Oh, I don't know. I saw him fall. Was that when he was shot?"

"Don't worry about it. At least, Xynos won't bother you any more. He's dead with a hundred bullets in him. Now let's get his accomplice."

Pano said, "If there was an accomplice."

Someone else was shouting, "Xynos killed Petropoulos."

"The accomplice must have gone out to the orchestra," said Antonidis. "Everyone was chasing Xynos. We'll never find him if he gets mixed with all those people leaving the theater."

"Are you all right now, darling?" Roussos asked Victoria.

"I think so. I'm still a little shaken. You say Xynos will never menace us again? I've been living under fear of him so long that it's hard to believe."

Most of the police were rushing toward the orchestra to look for a possible accomplice. Roussos said to Pano, "Search for Xynos's gun. That should tell us if he or an accomplice killed Petropoulos."

Antonidis stayed back with Roussos, Victoria, and Pano. He said, "Petropoulos won't be making charges against anyone now, Spyro. Your job's safe." After a pause, he added, "But I wouldn't say as much for Thanos. You're free to make your own charges against him now."

Roussos jolted as his eyes widened. "But, but, I mailed in my resignation this morning. The Ministry will receive it early tomorrow."

"I forgot. But anyway, at Public Security they'll all know that I'm the most likely one to replace Petropoulos. I'll get over there tomorrow morning and make certain that no deputy or assistant minister accepts it. Don't worry."

As Antonidis walked away with Pano, Roussos put his arm around Victoria's waist and guided her back toward her dressing room. Reaching her door, she turned to take one last look at Petropoulos's body.

A police photographer was already taking photographs of the dead minister. He was lying on his back, belly high, white shirt streaked with clotting blood, eyes glaringly open as if in rage, left leg bent unnaturally under his right ankle, and his left arm curled protectively at his side as if he were trying to prevent his little finger's long nail from being broken.

Victoria gazed at the grotesque corpse a moment, then said under her breath as she reached for the hand of her lover, "To think, before him trembled all Athens."

Spyro said, "What was that, my darling?"

"Oh, nothing. I was just thinking about the performance tonight."

"Your singing was beautiful, my love. It was a great performance."

"Yes," she said. "All I had to do was think of how much you mean to me."

END

About the Author

Gene Stratton, a former CIA case officer, has lived all over. He resided seven years in Greece and speaks the language fluently. He has had two fiction and two non-fiction books published. His *Plymouth Colony*, now in its sixth printing, has been in continuous print for sixteen years.

0-595-65850-4